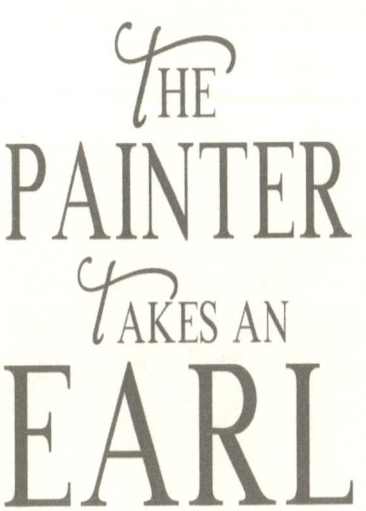

THE PAINTER TAKES AN EARL

MISTY URBAN

OLIVERHEBERBOOKS

Cover art by Dar Albert at Wicked Smart Designs

Published by Oliver-Heber Books

0 9 8 7 6 5 4 3 2 1

CHAPTER ONE

SOMERSETSHIRE, 1765

Harriette Smythe was the first girl Renwick met who could make a boy cry.

The new earl was accustomed to shedding tears, most of them resulting from the harsh discipline of his tutor or the thundering disapproval of his father, the late earl, when his tutor's relentless corrections failed to remedy his heir's many inadequacies. Tears were familiar friends, brought on by humiliation, frustration, rage. Ren dreamed of a time—perhaps one entire day, or long stretches of days—when he might be free of tears entirely.

Being a soft-hearted boy and not prone to violence, Renwick didn't wish for the death of his tutor, just as he hadn't wished for the death of his father. Instead he dreamed of ways his faults could disappear, as happened so often in fairy tales. Frogs kissed by a princess turned back into a handsome prince. The werewolf who terrified everyone became a regular man when the enchantments upon him were removed. The misshapen child of the unbelieving sultan turned into a beautiful prince when baptized in the water of faith. His father would look upon his remade heir with admiration, approval, love.

Then the earl died, taking with him any chance Ren had of redemption. He cried then, too.

His mother, the countess, did not cry. She had endured many trials in her marriage and disappointment in both her children, and with no hope now of a new and better heir coming along, she might as well enjoy her life as a widow. She sent her daughter to the family seat in the north, took up residence in the London townhouse, and sent her son to the small town where her grandfather had made the fortune that caught the eye of aristocrats and where the new Earl of Renwick could be out of her sight and no further cause for worry. That is, until he reached his majority and took control of the estate, whereupon she would be obliged to remind him of his duty to support her in the style she preferred.

So it was that at an age when he ought to be training to take his high place in the world, the grieving and essentially orphaned Renwick was sent south to rusticate in Shepton Mallet and found he had merely exchanged one set of tormentors for another.

He also found Harriette Smythe.

It was a spring day, one of the first with real warmth in the sunshine, and Ren discharged his lessons as soon as he could so he might go to The Meadows, the grassy embankment in the north part of town. Here the River Sheppey flowed restful and quiet, unlike the east end of town where the mills crowded the waterway, scooping its current to power their looms. In The Meadows, soft bowls carved the sides of the hills, offering spots to lie and daydream in the shade. The mounds had been forts for Roman soldiers and the peoples they came to subdue, and Ren imagined he could hear the old Roman legions, marching the Fosse Way to their forts in Ilchester and Bath. Straight and strong and determined those soldiers must have been, hardened by years of training and weathered by their posting in the north.

A weak, malformed boy like Ren would have been abandoned in Roman times, left by a market cross or on a hill to perish of exposure. The late earl being cast in the same iron mold, Ren lay in the soft grass and wondered why his father had not done the same: set him outside to die like a runt lamb, or drowned him like a useless kitten.

The Shepton Mallet boys were all the things Renwick was not: large, well-formed, strong from lives of rigorous labor, and toughened by cruel treatment. Their hands were rough from work while Renwick's were pale and soft. Their clothes were sturdy leather and woolens in browns and drabs that didn't show dirt the way Renwick's pale yellow breeches and silk waistcoat did. Renwick had already torn his white stockings. These boys wore no stockings at all, nor shoes, tramping barefoot like those old Romans down the Wells Road, calling insults to each other and laughing, bold and brash and unafraid. Ren heard them coming long before they came into sight.

He shrank into the steep wooded slope, praying they would not see him. They gathered with their fishing rods at a pool where the river surfaced from its underground run through town and occupied themselves with arguing over which of the shady spots was likely to hold the most fish. Ren held still and quiet as a baby deer, fearing even to breathe.

Fishing. Now that was one normal boy's occupation he could engage in. He would ask his tutor where one was to find a fishing rod. His tutor would be likely to use this desire as a cudgel with which to beat Renwick at every turn, or he might use the pole itself when he felt a caning was called for. Mr. Mortmickle had been set by the countess to the task of making Renwick normal. So far, his attempts to beat any faults or delicacy out of the young earl had been unsuccessful, which caused poor Mr. Mortmickle to exert himself in ever more varied and strenuous ways.

Ren was safe, though, as long as the boys didn't see him. And they didn't until a tiny patter of falling rock rolled past him down the slope and plopped, with slow and deliberate tiny crashes, into the water.

All three boys looked directly at him, and Renwick froze. He had not moved or caused that rockfall. What cursed luck had made him known to them?

The ironmonger's son's face split in a wide, evil grin. "Oy, boys," he said loudly. "Lookoo it is. The Duke o' Limbs. What's 'ee doing lurking about?"

"The footy fellow's spyin' on us. Out to steal our fish," said the wainwright's son.

"Nay, 'ee's a molly, this'un," said the ropemaker's son. "'Ee's watching and dreaming of buggering us all."

Ren flushed in an agony of humiliation. He didn't know what buggering was. He knew he was sheltered, with a tutor instructed to rarely let him out of the house, his guests and his books restricted to those of which his mother approved. He would know what it meant if he were allowed to run about like these boys, but the free way they used the word marked the difference between them as clearly as their tanned skin against his paleness.

The ironmonger's boy grinned and put down his pole, a flash of wickedness in his eyes. "A backgammon player, is 'ee? Maybe we ought to show Lord Queer Pins that fine waggish lads like us don't care for his peeping and prying."

"Aye." The wainwright's son rolled the loose sleeves of his stained shirt. "Old Hopping Giles. We'll teach you to tag after us."

"We'll hoop your barrel good and sound this time." The ropemaker's son started climbing the hill toward Ren's perch. "Give ya a right basting, we will."

Ren looked about for escape. Thus far his tormentors had

satisfied themselves with insults and hectoring, shoves and cruel laughter, but he couldn't guess how long his name would protect him. There was a thicket to his left and what looked like a cave opening on his right, a notch in the limestone bluff. He'd let them thrash him senseless before he'd climb in a wet, dark cave.

He turned to scramble up the slope as best he could, knowing with his foot he wouldn't be able to escape them. He wondered how far he'd get before they reached him, and how badly they'd hurt him before they were done. Break his bones and throw his body in the river? Or leave him able to crawl home, quivering and bleeding? He knew well the cruelty of men to those deemed weak and inferior. The lesson had been left on his body early in life, and he had the scars to remind him in case he ever grew careless and thought he might go about like sure-footed folk. That had been his error today, and he might very well pay for it with his life.

His hands scrabbled against a rockfall. He braced his bum foot in a small depression and tried to lever himself up, but his leg, the curse of his life, betrayed him. His knee buckled and he fell, scraping his arm against a bare outcropping of rock.

"We got ya now, ya puny pup," one of them crowed, and Ren imagined the harsh hands upon him, the blows and taunts, and nothing nearby to protect him.

Then a shrub before him rustled and from it rose a small, avenging goddess with a halo of muddy red hair and a drawn slingshot, pointed at Ren.

"Stand down, ya bull calf, or I'll draw your cork, I will."

Ren froze, and a flash of rage joined the heat of humiliation coursing over him. That he would be beaten and turned over to his tormentors by a mere slip of a girl!

A shout of answering rage came from behind him. "Skip off, ya ragamuffin! Our rumpus is with the Earl of Runtwick 'ere."

"I know what you're about, Abel Cain," the girl shouted. "I

heard your sparking blows. The whole of Shepton Mallet heard 'em, great, braying donkey that ye are. Now leave his lordship alone, or I'll flatten your nose."

Ren grinned against his will. The imp with the wild hair and spatter of freckles across her nose was taking his side.

"Rantipole!" the wainwright's son shouted. "Rag-tag tatter-demalion!"

The slingshot swerved to a point beyond Ren's shoulder. "Want a blinker, Bram Wright? I'll give ye two," she threatened. "Love to hear you explain yer blackened peepers to your mum."

"Spoilsport," chimed the ropemaker's boy. "Mar all. Addle plot. We're just 'avin a bit o' fun."

The rustle behind him told Ren that his attackers drew close. He didn't dare turn for fear his foot would unbalance him and he'd go tumbling down the slope.

"You lay a hand on 'im and I'll squeak to the whole town that you thrashed 'im, you three! That'll addle your plot well and good," the little fury shrieked.

Ren revised his assessment. This girl was no avenging angel but something closer to a hellion. The white lace tucker at her bodice was askew, her bodice was stained with berry juice, and her apron boasted a long tear. As she stepped around the bush, the stone in her slingshot still aimed at the boys, Ren detected that she was barefoot. But why was she protecting him?

"Saucebox," the ironmonger's son, Abel, roared. "Time you learned your place!"

Ren braced himself as the scrape of stone and brush of leaves told him the larger boy had launched himself toward them. The hellion curled her lip and released the stone in her slingshot without hesitation. A thump and a resounding howl told Ren the stone hit its mark. He glanced over his shoulder to see Abel clutching his shoulder. Indignation filled the boy's expression, but also a grudging respect.

"Now tail down and pike off, all of ya, like the jolter heads ye are," his avenging fury called.

The wainwright's son lunged up the slope. Quicker than Ren could follow, a stone appeared from a hidden apron pocket and flew at the attacker's leg. Bram yelped and grabbed his thigh, hopping about in pain.

The slingshot swerved to its third target. "You're too white-livered to touch a girl, Gil Roper," she taunted. "I've got bigger ballocks than you do."

Ren held on to a branch for balance and turned to watch his three adversaries retreat down the slope. Grabbing their fishing poles from the bank, they scrabbled down to the road along the river and set off upon it, the ropemaker's son blubbering and wailing, and the wainwright's son limping worse than Ren did.

He turned to face his deliverer. Her hair waved free in the wind, no cap to restrain it, and she pocketed the slingshot in her apron with casual ease. Then she wiped a hand across her cheek, leaving a smear of dirt.

"I w-w-wish I could say I didn't need a g-gul to potect me," Ren said. "But it seems I d-do."

She grinned at him, a wide, gamine grin, and Ren's humiliation ebbed. Her eyes took in everything, the way he clung to the branch for balance, his oddly shaped shoe. She'd heard his speech, but her face didn't cloud with scorn the way so many faces in the village did. She merely looked him in the face, bold, direct.

"Give you a hand down, shall I?" she said briskly. "Afore we both go arsey varsey."

Ren normally went stiff-backed at any offer of assistance. It was generally offered with pity, or with sly condescension. It was not the way of the world he lived in that an earl should be a malformed weakling. But this girl simply stuck out her arm, bent at the elbow, and Ren felt no shame in taking it. Her arm was thin and strong as the rest of her.

"You certain—" He concentrated. "Certainly have a way with you." He was astonished to hear all his words emerge correctly. For some reason he didn't panic with this girl, the words tumbling out half-formed or confused, or worse yet, not coming altogether. She had a steady way about her that calmed him. He could take a breath and that extra half-second to think about how the sounds should feel in his mouth.

"Oh, I'm every bit the ragamuffin they say," she said cheerfully. "But I've run into those boys before. They like to bully everyone. Used to be me. Watch, your lordship, that's a snake hole! Don't you put a foot wrong there."

"I am well accustomed to putting a foot *wrong*," Ren said.

He delivered the line perfectly, without one stammer or halt of his twisted tongue, the first true joke of his life. She tipped back her head and gave a riotous shout of laughter, and Ren could have died with joy right there on the hill above the gentle River Sheppey.

He didn't know her name yet, but she was his friend for life.

Once they had safely descended the hill and gained the road, she pointed at his shoe. "What's it, then?"

"Clubfoot," he said, clenching his teeth.

The late earl had been incandescent with rage at his son's deformity, insisting the midwife had twisted the boy at birth, marring his precious heir. The delivery of his sister a few years later with her own abnormalities had rather suggested there must be some stain upon the Earl of Renwick, the sins of the father marked on his progeny, just like the medieval legends. The countess withdrew into opium and cards, not one to put her own happiness on the line to protect her children from their father.

"Rotten luck," his new friend said, and that was the end of

the discussion. She matched her gait to his as the river dove back into its underground outlets and buildings sprouted along the lanes to town, growing steadily bigger and older.

"You're the new Earl of Renwick, then? Living in the old Manor House on Leg Square?" She grinned. "Lucky you, with the Blinder Wall."

The large house was hard to miss, and its location near the churchyard and the center of town meant Ren felt under watch all the time. He had some protection in the infamous Blinder Wall, a hideous fence of bricks that his ancestor built to keep neighbors from spying on him. It was rumored the source of Ren's grandfather's wealth was not lucrative woolen mills but something darker in character.

"And you?" Ren asked shyly. Etiquette said they required an introduction, but she already felt familiar to him. It must be her direct, forthright manner that put him at ease, as if they had a long history. Aside from his secret fondness for fairy tales, he was not a boy given to fancy, or Ren would have thought about kindred spirits, past lives, old souls finding each other in new clothes.

"Harriette Smythe," she said. "Of Ivy Cottage, over by the cattle market. It's not ours. The Demants took kindly to me mum and now she's companion to Missus Demant. I was just a babe when Mum brought us to England, and she was knitting stockings to support us when Missus Demant found her and knew she was too genteel for her unfortunate circumstances." She said this as if rehearsing a story she'd heard many times. "She's the soul of kindness, the missus, to take in me mum and a hoyden such as I am, and to feed me from her table and put clothes on my back."

A hard tone entered her voice at the last utterance, and she assumed a defiant air, as if daring someone to challenge her. Ren guessed that Madame Demant's Christian mercy was grudging at best. From his own mother's example he knew there were ladies who preferred not to be bothered with children, which perhaps explained why the sprite next to him was roaming the hills, linens torn, dress stained, feet bare. Ren was watched with too much care and fretful oversight, and Harriette Smythe had none.

"Nice to meet you, Haow—Haow—" He gulped and stumbled, ashamed that she should see his weakness.

She watched his eyes, his mouth, his eyes again. Her gaze was clear and steady and thoughtful, her eyes a lovely mix of brown and gold and green.

"Call me Rhette," she suggested.

"And you may call me Ren," he said, the words for once flowing easily.

"Ren and Rhette." Her mouth curved in that impish smile that struck him to the core. Every wild, joyful impulse of youth that had been so long stifled stirred and came alive in his chest. "What a pair of odd fellows we are, don'cha think?"

And that was their beginning. The start of a summer of freedom and adventure the like of which the earl's son had never known, and a friendship that would survive wind and cold and the long ravages of time. The Earl of Renwick would follow Harriette Smythe into hell if she led him there, and he had no doubt that she would as readily lay down her life and limb if it spared him anything. Though he hoped the sacrifice would never be demanded, as he wanted her in his life, his steadfast support, his single unending source of joy, to the end of his God-given days, if he were allowed the choice.

Which of course, since he was an earl, he wasn't.

CHAPTER TWO

Young earls, even if they are tongue-tied cripples, are not allowed to consort at liberty with nameless orphans, no matter how amusing a guide or how skilled at wilderness craft she might be. They had one summer, the most precious and brilliant summer of Ren's life, filled with endless stretches of blue-grey days and fleecy clouds, green fields dotted with slow-moving sheep, when Harriette Smythe led him through every trail and well, hill and byway that Shepton Mallet could offer. He lost his fear of caves when Harriette took him exploring the small shafts and holes the locals called a swallet, and he laughed as she held the guttering candle beneath her chin and spun chilling myths of giants and robbers, or told wild tales from her Silesian homeland.

They explored Ham Woods and climbed Beacon Hill, where she pointed out the spire of Glastonbury Tor rising from a hollow of mist. They dug holes around Maesbury Ring, looking for iron weapons, then threw the trinkets they found into St. Aldhelm's Well as wishes. When Mr. Mortmickle forbade the housekeeper to open the door to her, Harriette climbed the tree leaning against the Blinder Wall and pitched pebbles at Ren's window to lure him away to adventure. If he fell asleep at his lessons the next morning because he had spent the day rambling about the countryside, he considered the extra beatings from his tutor a fair price to pay.

One night, Harriette drew him out at dusk and dared him to walk with her over the ancient burial grounds on Barrow Down, telling him stories of barrow wights guarding buried treasure and other unsightly apparitions. They spent hours and days inside St. Peter and Paul, while Ren read a book and Harriette sketched the old Saxon stonework, including the runes etched on the baptismal font. Ren preferred the town's more recent history, especially the heroic and tragic tale of the Duke of Monmouth, who passed through Shepton Mallet leading his men in a short-lived scheme to overthrow James II, for which a dozen of the duke's supporters were hanged and quartered before the Buckland Cross in Market Square.

But Harriette liked the old tales, the older the better, and in their rambles she was forever stopping to dig for Roman coins or brooches. The smallest broken potsherds delighted her, leading her into speculations about the lives of the people who had lived there before. Ren loved her imagination; her people were always daring, living dramatic lives of danger and passion, not lives of disappointment and shame and ridicule.

One day, as they traveled the Fosse Way, reliving the battles of the Roman legions against the wild stubbornness of the native tribes, Harriette found a small, circular bronze amulet with a symbol he recognized from church, an X overlying a P. She stared at the object as if it were pure gold.

"The chi-ro symbol," she told him. "From the Greek letters *chi* and *ro*, which spell Christos in Greek."

He already knew this, but wondered how she did. He hadn't mastered Greek yet, despite daily toils with his tutor, but Harriette, who taught herself by poking about Mr. Demant's library, was full of odd and useless bits of knowledge.

"This was the sign Constantine put on his standard, the one that came to him in a dream—*in this sign shall ye conquer*." She traced the bronze circle, her eyes lighting so that the gold in them overshadowed the brown. "Some early Christian carried this, praying for protection and guidance. Where's my sketchbook?" She groped about the pockets of her apron for the small pad and the porte crayon she always carried.

"It's not rare," Ren snapped. "There must have been Christians about since the beginning of Roman times. Since Joseph of Arimathea planted the thorn tree at Glastonbury."

They'd been to Glastonbury once or twice, walking through pastures and swallets to the storied town and its great ruined abbey, climbing the tor to the stone tower that commanded a view of all Somerset. It delighted Ren to see the place like a regular pilgrim, without any of the attention he'd attract as an earl. And he'd never let Harriette see how the walk had made the calluses on his clubfoot blister and bleed.

"I like it." Harriette's eyes narrowed. When she was angry or annoyed, the green emerged. "And I mean to sketch it."

"Fine." Ren threw himself to the ground with a surly growl. Or rather, he wished he could throw himself to the ground. He lowered himself into an awkward crouch among the tall, rough grasses lining the road. "I'll stay here and be bored out of my skull while you putter about with your crayons, shall I?"

"What's eating you?" she demanded. "Is your foot hurting? We've walked a long way."

"I'm not an invalid, and not everything is about my foot," he snapped.

"Nay, some things are about the arse you carry about atop your neck!"

She stomped off a short ways, something she did to let off

steam when she came to a full boil. He admired how she knew to find a valve for her strong feelings. He just nursed his until they festered.

"Come back," he called, struggling to his feet to follow. "I'm blue-deviled today and taking it out on you, as usual."

He was surly because he'd gained an extra beating that morning for not finishing his porridge before it grew cold. He'd been remembering how Harriette had taken him fishing the day before, and how, when his three old bullies had come nosing about, all she'd needed to do was take her slingshot from her pocket to send them slinking away, spitting insults.

His tutor had also delivered rather unexpected news.

She came back immediately, another thing he liked about Harriette. She never held a grudge. She plopped down on a tuft of grass beside him and the skirt of her petticoat, much tattered and mended over the course of their summer romps, spilled over his leg. The casual encroachment on his space was another habit of hers he'd grown fond of. She never recoiled from him, not when he was in pain or raging or sullen. She never let him remain cross for long, and she never withdrew from him, not when he stammered so much in front of other people that he strangled for breath, not when she'd seen his foot unbound.

Not even when she'd found him, many times, in the kitchen of the Manor House, sucking back tears and gritting his teeth against the welts and bruises his tutor had raised on him with the cane. Being Harriette, she merely began carrying witch hazel in her pocket, and soaked cotton cloths in it that she then pressed to his wounds, all without saying a word.

"Why are you blue-deviled?" She flipped open her sketch-book, laid the amulet beside her, and picked up the small metal cylinder that held her black chalk. She had a swift, steady hand and a remarkably good eye. Ren had put many of her sketches up in his room, though not the ones she did of him.

He wondered how she would receive his news. Harriette, he'd been surprised to learn, was only ten years old. She acted older. He was fourteen, and the years between them, at their age, ought to have meant a gap of worlds, one a child's and one of a boy verging on manhood. But Harriette was more canny and matter-of-fact about the world than Ren was, and in many ways, he felt his sheltered life had kept him a child. That was why he longed for a change, and was terrified of it.

"My mother is coming to visit," he said. "And I suspect that means she's decided to send me to school at last."

"You said you asked to be sent to school," Harriette reminded him, her hand moving quick and sure.

"And my father always denied me, since he didn't want his shame known. That his heir was a cripple."

"You are not a cripple," Harriette said. "So why did the countess send you here when he died, instead of off to school? To give you time to mourn?"

"To remove me from her sight, I think. My tutor told her I wouldn't do well in school. That the boys would be cruel and hurt me, and the canings there when I am slow or stupid or disobedient would be worse than the ones he gives me."

Harriette paused and considered him. "And because Mr. Mortmickle, the great ogre, would lose his salary were you sent away." She snorted. "Someday, Renwick, I wish you would use the cane on him, so he can see how it feels."

She only called him Renwick when she was feeling peevish or stern.

"You'll miss me, will you, lass?" he said. Adopting the southern Somerset accent, its round smooth vowels, made the question feel less heavy.

"Of course. No one here is half as quick in his wits as you. Who shall I chum with then, Abel Cain and his gang?" She scoffed.

Something tightened in Ren's chest as he watched her. It was a typical cloudy day, warm but breezy, and her hair frizzed about her face in its usual fashion. Her cheeks held yet the round softness of the child, but Ren thought he saw, for an instant, the outline of the woman she would become: strong, beautiful, confident.

"You'll grow up and forget all about me," he said.

She shrugged. "Like as not. And you'll forget me the moment you set foot in Harrow or Eton or wherever her ladyship chooses to send you."

"I won't," he vowed, and the force of his own words surprised him.

She was a half-orphaned girl of no family, and he was destined to take his seat in the House of Lords. It was fated that they would part and have no more to do with each other. He wanted to go to school, no matter how much he expected he would be teased and humiliated and beaten further. He longed for it.

But he would miss these days of freedom, of roaming through the countryside following every whim. He would miss the sense of discovery he had with her, the sense that the world was not hostile and disapproving but rather wondrous and remarkable, shot through with surprise and beauty.

He would miss her.

"Come find me," he said suddenly.

"Hmm?" She finished her sketch, several copies of the amulet with various shadings, and closed her book. The crayon and the notebook disappeared into a pocket, but she held the amulet, regarding it curiously.

"Come find me. When I'm back. Or whenever you need—a friend."

It sounded so feeble when he said it, he wished he'd kept his mouth shut. But her eyes when she raised them to meet his gaze said that she understood.

"You'll marry," she said. "Have a countess of your own. Raise all sorts of little lords and ladies."

For the first time, he hoped that would be true. He could imagine a family and children in his future, and not just to perpetuate the line. He wanted someone in his life who loved and accepted him, like Harriette did. He wanted the joys of companionship, someone to share his thoughts with, to vent his feelings to. Someone who touched him as easily as Harriette did, without flinching.

"And you?" That sharp twist came again in his chest. After this summer of constant companionship, she would grow up into the strange separate world of women and he would never know her this way again.

He might never know anyone this way again.

She shrugged and pushed away a lock of hair waving before her eye. "I don't know. Mum says we'll have to go back to Silesia sometime. That's where she's from, you know. She says my grandfather will want me, that he's someone important, though I suspect we're nothing but peasants and she made that up to please Missus Demant. She's making me practice the language, and she says as soon as they send word that it's safe, we'll go back."

The twisting thing tore then, deep and hard, and Ren felt as if he were bleeding inwardly. She wouldn't be in a separate world. She'd be in a separate country.

"Write to me?" His voice sounded hoarse. Harriette was his lifeline, the one person who understood him. If that connection were severed, the one person he relied on gone, he might truly descend into madness or despair.

"If I can. Here."

She slipped a thin cord through the hole in the amulet to create a necklace, then handed it to him.

"What if it is valuable?" he said in surprise.

He'd seen how she lived. Her mother depended on the Demants for everything, her food, her shelter, her clothing. Mrs. Demant got to boast that she was sheltering a refugee from another country, a highborn woman in desperate straits who'd been forced to flee her homeland leaving behind her husband, her wealth, her very name. Mrs. Smythe might enjoy sitting about in stricken poses, playing the role of wilting outcast, but Ren couldn't see Harriette spending her future dependent on anybody.

"Did you know the early Christians thought madness was sacred?" Harriette stood and scanned the sky, her curls lifting in the wind. "Divine inspiration. In the Dark Ages, the simple or touched in the head were called innocents. And those who were marked or had deformities, they were sacred, too. It was the sign of God's will, of his chosen. Their extra suffering would purify them."

Ren clenched the amulet in his hand, anger taking him by surprise. His suffering hadn't purified him.

"You're not like the others, Renwick, and you're not meant to be. Keep this as your reminder." She covered her hand with his. "It's all right if you're different."

A strange warmth bloomed around his hand where she touched him. It was like the warmth of a spell, or a holy prayer.

"In this sign I will conquer?" He'd meant to be glib, but the words came out low and urgent, more like a promise. Or a prophecy.

"Yes," she whispered. "If you stay who you are."

He didn't know what she meant, not then. He wanted to be anyone other than who he was. He'd give up being an earl's son to be strong and whole and golden-tongued. He'd give up his lands and his inheritance if he could marry someone like Harriette Smythe and have a warm, quick, loving companion to the end of his days.

They wandered back to town, Harriette only stopping to sketch a mere half dozen things along the way, and Renwick earned an extra beating that evening for fumbling as he rehearsed the bow he would have to deliver the countess. She arrived the next day in splendor, with a coach-and-four, a lady's maid and two footmen, panniers that were wider than the doorways of the Manor House, and a powdered wig towering atop her proud, noble head.

The next time Harriette scaled the Blinder Wall, she found the house shut up and empty. Ren was gone.

He wrote her, long letters that crossed lines and crossed them again to fit in all his thoughts, but they never reached her, for he never sent them. Unmarried girls were not supposed to receive letters from unwed gentlemen, and he would have died with shame if anyone but Harriette read his inmost thoughts.

He moved on to the world of an earl's son, the world of school and country houses and a long grand tour across the courts and ruins of the Continent, and he never knew what became of Harriette Smythe. But she remained in his heart, a ghost and a gift, in the chi-ro amulet that the Earl of Renwick wore about his neck and never parted with. He gave up much to be accepted in his new world, and he would give up more, but not that. It was his sign, his promise that he would eventually conquer, and he needed that hope more than anything.

CHAPTER THREE

LONDON, 1776

"This is a terrible idea, Harriette, *Liebelein*," said Princess in her heavy accent.

Jock squinted at the big, gracious house with its neoclassical pillars and high windows gorgeously lit by hanging lamps and tall braziers. "A swell's ken," he announced. "No place for your scampers, Miz H."

Though his position was properly that of groom, and he wore the striped coat of his station, Jock rode atop the big Yorkshire coach horse that pulled the luxurious cabriolet. Out of instinct, he shifted his weight to calm the animal as a string of carriages rolled noisily by, disgorging their brightly plumed passengers before the expansive edifice fronting Grosvenor Square.

"The countess'll have you on the carpet for it," rumbled Beater, the big man with the squashed face standing on the groom's platform at the rear of the carriage.

"Which countess?" Harriette retorted. "My own dear aunt, or the Countess of Renwick, who has no reason to love me and will not condone my sneaking into her house?"

Princess rolled her eyes at Harriette's insouciant tone, but Beater pondered the question. "Both," he decided.

"I daresay it was mere oversight that Lady Renwick did not respond to my card," Harriette said. "She must know that I, too, want to welcome her son home from abroad. After all, we were good chums the summer he lived in Shepton Mallet."

"That was more than ten years ago, *Liebelein*." Princess shook her head. "He's a young man and has had many adventures since then. How can you depend on him to remember?"

Harriette bit her lip. She considered herself even-tempered and sunny, but her emotions had been in a roil ever since she heard the news that the Earl of Renwick was returning to London. She'd grown and changed a great deal, and he would have seen much in his years at school and then abroad on the Continent. What if, indeed, he had forgotten all about her?

She needed him to remember. She needed his help. They all did.

"I'm not easy to forget," Harriette said with the devil-may-care tone that would not fool Princess, but might at least reassure the men that she knew what she was doing. "Now let me off at this corner, and I'll sneak in behind the Duchess of Devonshire. No one will notice me when she is about, and I'll contrive to make my way inside."

"You'll be caught," Princess warned. "And what a fine *contretemps* that will make if you are! We're trying to blaze our way into the *beau monde*, not scandalize it."

"Nay, our Miz H is sly enough to go upon the sneak," Jock argued. "And see here, not a pair of peeps in the place! A clever tradesman could crack the crib in a jiffy."

"Could 'ee?" Beater asked with interest. "But 'ow'd ye cart it all off?"

A glare from Princess silenced him. "There will be no talk of robbing the house while Lady Renwick is throwing a party," she said sternly. "Beater and Jock will return to wait for you in the mews, Hari, and I expect a full accounting in the morning."

Harriette regarded her friend. Princess was wearing a splendid plum silk robe that showed every swell of her figure, and her tall, powdered wig was adorned with purple morning glories that fluttered with each movement.

"You expect your assignation to last the night, then?" Harriette teased.

Princess raised her darkened eyebrows, which stood out against her pale face and rouged cheeks. "Will yours?"

"A few minutes, half an hour at most," Harriette replied. "I am not invited to the party, mind you."

She needed enough time to ensure the Earl of Renwick was still the soft-hearted boy she remembered. If so, she would plead her case and no doubt win his support. Ren had never been able to deny her anything.

Though if the rumors that had floated home ahead of him bore any truth, Renwick was much changed from the sweet, stammering boy she remembered. He was now a man of the world, a British peer, conscious of what he could command with his name and station. He was a man of experience, if reports were true of the expensive courtesans he'd kept at various ports of call.

Harriette suppressed a flutter of fear. This had to work. He was the only one she could think of to ask.

"If he does want to touch you up, set a fair price first," Princess whispered as the cabriolet merged into the line of carriages inching along the square. The bright glare of a lantern set into the fence along the garden wall matched the flare of embarrassment that ran through Harriette at those words.

"Mum, you!" she said crossly. "We are artists, not bawds."

Princess shook her head, and the jeweled pins set into her

wig glittered in the passing light. "All the same to this set, and you know it, *Liebelein*."

She did know it, and it was one of the reasons Harriette had resolved to storm his family's townhouse and demand to see Renwick. She needed a champion. Her aunt had given her a roof over her head and clothes upon her back, but Harriette needed more if she were to make a name for herself as a painter. She needed a powerful patron, and the Countess of Calenberg was considered too eccentric to be embraced among more exclusive circles—the kind of circles that paid the best commissions.

Those were the circles in which Renwick moved. But he would have been besieged by hopeful toadies the moment he set foot in town. Crowds of supplicants would turn up hoping he would use his station and influence on their behalf. How could she be so crass as to attempt to use him the same way?

She reminded herself she had something to offer him in return. A fair trade, not a favor.

Beater helped her descend, ensuring her skirts did not catch on the tall wheels of the carriage, and Harriette looked up at the high wall that enclosed the garden that ran alongside and behind the house. The lanterns clustered in front of the house lit the way for distinguished guests, leaving shadows lining the garden wall that continued down the side street. But in surveying the house earlier that day—snilching, as Jock called it—she had noted a tree in the side garden that conveniently grew alongside the balconies lining the first and second floors.

She shivered, and not only because she'd left off a shawl and the late June evening held a damp chill she felt along all the bare skin exposed by the deep neckline of her gown. Doubtless one room above would have the sash lifted, perhaps that designated as the card room or the retiring room for female guests. It had been a long time since she'd climbed a tree, and never wearing a full set of skirts and petticoats. But the goal was simple: slip inside, find Ren, speak with him, and have the matter settled within moments.

"You could come with me tonight." Princess gathered up the ribbons. "Perhaps my—er, patron could commission a portrait. If he declines, we'll simply go along as we have been."

A house full of outcasts living on my aunt's charity, Harriette almost said, but caught herself in time.

"I need to contribute to our keep," she said instead. "My aunt has already done much for me. And I don't want to be known for my roués and courtesans, the painter of the *demi-mondaine*. If I am to exhibit in respectable places, I need a respectable clientele."

"Good luck finding that here." Princess withdrew beneath the hood of the small vehicle. "Very well, *Liebelein. Guten Abend.*"

She flicked the whip lightly and the horse trotted away before Harriette realized her insult. The Princess was the closest friend Harriette had made among the eccentric circle of orphans and refugees collected around the banished Countess of Calenberg, and she'd sat for Harriette more than anyone. There'd be some groveling to do come morning.

Or worse than groveling, if this evening didn't go as planned.

The key to the garden gate was exactly where the gardener she'd spied on earlier that day had left it when his work was done. She wouldn't have asked someone to prop the door open for her. London's all-too-active criminal element wouldn't refrain from attempting to rob a house with dozens of people in it. The city's thieves were wildly inventive, according to Jock. Men slid into houses during the day and then hid to let their cronies inside at night. Boys were pushed through windows to open an inside door, or lamplighters enjoined to leave ladders against the sides of houses. How Jock knew all of this, she couldn't guess, since his former profession had been respectable.

She could, of course, have chosen the simpler but more unreliable approach of milling around Grosvenor Square waiting for Renwick to step outside his house. She could still try to stroll inside with the other guests and ask the butler to announce her.

And what would he say? "Miss Harriette Smythe of Shepton Mallet, presumed bastard daughter of a refugee foreigner posing as a noblewoman. Would-be painter." No wonder Lady Renwick had not called back when Harriette left her card.

Ren had not called, either.

The tree was not a strong one, and Harriette scrabbled with hands and feet to haul herself onto the lowest branch. It bent dangerously under her weight, and for a moment her heart stopped. Going in through the front door was a much better idea after all. A shadow moved across a second-floor window, tall and threatening against the glass, and her heart shrank and quivered.

She risked her life continuing upward if someone thought she was a housebreaker indeed, but she couldn't see a way down. She would be stuck in this tree until dawn came or she cried for someone to get her. Oh, *why* had she assumed seeing Ren would be as easy as scaling the old Blinder Wall at the Manor House in Shepton Mallet?

The shadow moved again, and her heart thumped. *Ren.* She had to see him. Harriette clenched her teeth and pulled herself up through the foliage, feeling her skirts catch in a hundred places, hoping the fabric proved heavier than the clutching branches. She crept along an upper branch and finally threw a leg over the decorative railing that lined the upper floor. It held her weight, thankfully, and she swung both legs over, then inched along the tiny platform until she came to the window where the shadow moved.

Her heart slammed her chest with the force of her excitement, nervousness, and fear. Before her mind could cast up the many reasons this was all a terrible, terrible idea, she forced her way over the threshold of the window and into the room.

The man stood at the far side, his back to her. Her heart stopped beating. He was tall and intimidating and his stride was firm and long. He wore a small white wig, and the black ribbon tied back a small queue that hung down a back that was broad and very firm-looking under a tight expanse of dark blue silk. The tails of his coat brushed a rear that was equally firm and well-shaped, and the blue silk breeches and white stockings fitted legs that were muscled and straight.

This couldn't be her Ren, but perhaps he knew where Ren was, and whoever he might be, he was a well-formed fellow. Harriette held her breath waiting for him to turn around. She'd risk being thrown out on her ear, or into the watchhouse, just to see what kind of face went with such a splendid, well-proportioned body.

He appeared to be pacing the room, a large dressing room, probably his, and when he reached the end of it he wheeled around. Harriette's breath stopped altogether.

His face was a gift from the gods, strong-featured, clean-lined, with the kind of elegant symmetry perfected in ancient Greek sculpture. Strong jaw, straight nose, and a noble, thoughtful brow that drew into an immediate scowl when he spotted her. He froze, and they stared at one another while the rest of the world melted away. The blue of his suit made his eyes searing, brilliant. They burned into her, scattering thought.

"Well, that's luck," Harriette breathed. "I got the right room. Hello, Ren."

He'd grown into a man, but she knew those eyes. She flung

herself across the room at him, wondering if he'd feel as good as he looked. She lifted her hands to slip them around his neck, thoughtless in her relief and surprise and something else, something unnamable and unknown, that shook her powerfully at the sight of him.

Faster than her eye could follow, his hand moved. He caught her wrists and held them away from him, hauling her up short. His eyes were the blue of deep ice and his frown forbidding.

"You presume much, miss, when we do not know each other."

Her mouth fell open. The cool, distant expression on his face doused her like a cold rain, freezing her veins. In every scenario she'd run through in her head, never had she thought of this one.

She tried to tug her hands free. He was much, much stronger than she was, holding her wrists in his powerful grip. She stared into his stony face with astonishment and despair.

"I know you," she whispered. "You're Renwick. How can it be you have forgotten your Harriette?"

THE VISION IN RED SILK, up close, was a bigger shock than she had been across the room. His senses reeled under the onslaught. Her enormous eyes were an earthy brown color with golden flecks that seemed to shift and sparkle. She was quick and lithe, the hands he held warm to the touch. Her skin shone with a healthy rosy hue that looked warm and soft all over, including the tops of her breasts, pushed up toward his eyes by the tight bodice of her gown. Her hair was dressed in enormous puffs but was the dusty-red color he remembered, sunset behind a veil of smoke.

Once she had dared him to eat the mushrooms they'd found,

the small yellow-brown discs that she swore gave one magical visions. Instead the mushrooms had made him feel wobbly and off balance, foolishly excited over the smallest things, and that was exactly how he felt now as her eyes, her skin, her hair, her scent overwhelmed him. Somehow she always smelled like fresh wind and new-mown hay, and he wanted to close his eyes and revel in the giddy tide that threatened to drown him.

Harriette.

Harriette? This exquisite creature in taunting red, with the mouth-watering curves of a woman full formed, bore no resemblance to the scruffy, frizzy imp who had led him on tramps through the meads and woodlands of Shepton Mallet that golden summer. He stared into her face, searching for anything he recognized. Her lashes were thick enough to get lost in, making the golden flecks in her eyes stand out brightly. Her red mouth had an enchanting pucker to the corners, as if she were smiling at some inner delight. Her neck was smooth and long and it led down, down, to that beckoning shadow between her perfect breasts that made a man want to burrow in and discover what lay beneath.

He knew her. He knew the moment he touched her. He knew, actually, the moment she landed in his room. Who else but Harriette Smythe would dare?

But beautiful women did not throw themselves at the Earl of Renwick. Even now, he couldn't afford to let down his guard.

"Rhette?" His voice rasped in his suddenly dry throat.

Impossible. In his memory, in his dreams, she had simply been a taller version of herself, with the sprinkle of freckles across that nose that turned up at the tip, that same tendency to set her jaw when she was annoyed or angry, that same long stride, and the ability to face life head on, usually with colorful language. Never had he imagined she would become—delicious.

The pucker at the corners of her delectable mouth deepened into an impish smile. "Of course it's me. Aren't you going to kiss me hello?"

He stared stupidly at her luscious lips, feeling lost. Harriette, here. She'd found him after all. She'd come for him.

Eleven years disappeared, erasing the composure he'd acquired and the persona of the polished gentleman that he'd constructed with much effort and help. The wisdom, the guard, the studied distance he'd learned to assume around others—all of it vanished and he was the tongue-tied, stammering, ill-gaited Earl of Renwick that the village boys laughed and threw stones at.

And unlike before, this new, crimson-clad, dangerously alluring Harriette didn't offer escape or rescue or refuge. She was danger and temptation and sin. If he kissed Harriette Smythe, he knew with utter certainty, he would tumble down some well deeper than the caves that laced Shepton Mallet, and there would be no retrieving him.

If he kissed Harriette Smythe, he would cross some threshold, enter some new knowledge, and be lost to this world completely. He wasn't ready to disappear like that.

"You're as bold a baggage as I remember, Harriette Smythe," he said, lowering her wrists and releasing her. He took a step backwards and a bracing breath of air. "All right, let's have it out then. What is it you want from me?"

CHAPTER FOUR

H e'd been right: she was after something. The flicker that chased through her expressive eyes told him he'd guessed true. She wasn't the same open book he'd known, with every thought written on her gamine face. She was a woman now, with a woman's ploys and secrets.

But she was still Harriette. She crossed her arms over her chest and scowled. He tore his eyes from the inviting swell of décolletage and the cleft between her collarbone that dared him to press his lips there, and fastened his gaze to her face.

"How did you know I wanted something?"

Her candor made him smile as it always had.

"I am the Earl of Renwick. I'm wealthy and unmarried. I'm of age and in full control of my fortune, and when Parliament opens in the fall, I'll take my seat in the House of Lords. Everyone wants something from me," he ended bitterly.

She leaned a hip on a heavy wooden chair and shrugged, completely at ease, and the move disarmed him. It was so much like she'd been that golden, lost summer. Her eyes traveled slowly down his form, tracing the wide lapels of his tailed coat, the fall of his neckcloth, the embroidery on his waistcoat, and the march of silver buttons down his chest and belly. She studied the line of his thigh showing through the blue breeches, down the white stockings to his buckled slippers, and she looked thoughtful, as if she could see the clever construction of the shoe that helped turn his misshapen foot to its intended form.

He was still reeling from the sensuousness in her bold, thoughtful assessment when her eyes slid back up, and the path of her gaze left a print as hot as if she'd swept her hand along him. He shifted to ease the sudden reaction of his body.

Harriette Smythe walked into his chamber—back into his life—and every fantasy he'd harbored about her in eleven long years roared to the surface. The reality of her didn't cast all his memories and fancies into dust, as it ought to have. She was the face and body of his unspoken longings, as if his deepest urges had taken shape before his eyes, fed by his need for her to be real.

The devil always came to offer a deal, offering the thing his victim most wanted. He knew the old stories. The devil went straight to one's weakness, and he always exacted a painful price.

"I want to paint you," she said.

Her breathless tone caught him first, and his eyes snagged on those carmine lips, slightly parted and moist. Lips begging to be kissed, just as the rest of her begged for him to draw her into his arms and—

"Paint me," he echoed. He ought to have been surprised, but he'd spent long months in the company of Harriette Smythe. He knew anything was possible with her. He still *knew* her, after all this time, despite how much she'd changed, and that awareness burned him more deeply than her leisurely study had done.

She nodded. "I'm a painter. I require commissions. You're the exciting Earl of Renwick, fresh and new on the London scene, and nobody's done your portrait yet." She frowned. "Have they?"

She straightened and turned suddenly, her skirts flaring about her, and despite the elaborate shaping of the gown Ren saw that beneath all the layers of fabric she was still slender and strong, the Harriette who could tramp from dawn to dusk over the Somerset hills sketching everything that captured her interest.

A painter, was she? How she would have loved what he'd seen in his years abroad, the exquisite Dutch masters and the Italian Renaissance greats, the limpid Botticellis and the riveting portraits of Velazquez, the royal art collection at the Louvre palace and the Borgia Apartments of the Vatican. He wondered if she was any good, then pushed the thought away as disloyal.

"You've been all over Italy." She began to pace the room as he had been doing moments before. "Greece, too. And there are some very fine artists in France—I suppose you've sat for dozens of sketches. Had a portrait done in every country, by every sort of hand." She turned on him accusingly. "Have you?"

She looked like an outraged mistress who guessed he had trifled with another on the side. Ren tamped down a smile. He'd let her paint him if she did nothing more than slop some gobs of color on a canvas and call it a likeness.

It wasn't fair, that. All Harriette Smythe had to do was stroll back into his life and he was willing to grant her anything.

"Did you climb the tree?" he asked, wondering how she had appeared in his dressing room so suddenly, and before the window to the balcony, of all things.

She waved a hand in the air. "You'll want to see to that, I imagine," she said. "It's very easy to access a window, and house-breakers could—never mind. You haven't answered my question. Can I paint you?"

His Harriette to the core, but in this delectable shape and with the face of a fallen angel. He was lost. Ren spread his arms wide, reveling for the moment in his good fortune. After all he'd experienced, all he'd endured, wasn't it right that he would suddenly be granted this most magnificent and unexpected gift?

"My dear Rhette," he said, "you may do anything you like with me."

She snorted, which was precisely what the Harriette of old would have done. So this new Harriette, with this dangerously shapely body and distractingly soft skin and mind-blankingly lissome manner, was still his Harriette after all. The knowledge gave him a thrill of delight.

Then her eyes narrowed, the outraged mistress again. "How many other artists have painted you?"

He pretended to consider this and began counting on his fingers. "In total? None."

Her eyes widened with disbelief. The green lines in her eyes, usually dormant, were starting to stand out. Something was moving her deeply. "Impossible."

"I'm to sit for hours with some stranger staring at me, scrutinizing my every flaw? No, thank you."

She stepped close, her eyes investigating every line of his face. His skin felt tight and hot.

"You must have been asked," she said, and her voice dropped to a lower tone that made the hair on the back of his neck lift in arousal.

"Why do you say that?"

"Ren. Look at you." She drew a hand through the air, shaping his outlines. "You've turned out splendid."

"D'you think so?" His voice, too, dropped an octave. His chest rumbled as she stepped closer still. Lifted her hand as if she meant to touch him. He held his breath.

"Ren*wick*!"

The high, acidic voice from the other side of the door broke the spell between them. Harriette reared back, startled.

"You can't stay in there forever," the voice called. "Come down and greet your guests."

"C-c-c-coming, M-m-m-mother," Ren answered. "I need a m-m-moment of p-p-peace."

He closed his eyes so he wouldn't see Harriette's face change. She'd called him splendid. She'd looked at him with interest. She hadn't remarked on the special shaping of his shoe that made his leg and foot look like any other man's. His stutter never seemed to come out around her, not since their first meeting. But she'd heard it now. She'd know he hadn't changed, not really. He was still the same afflicted, misshapen, pitiful boy she'd rescued back in Shepton Mallet.

There was nothing she could admire about that.

Suddenly a warm, soft, scented form burrowed into him, nearly knocking him off balance. Ren's eyes flew open. Harriette pressed herself against his chest as if she meant to hide behind him. When his eyes widened, questioning, she laid her gloved hands on his upper arms and shook him. Her face was full of panic, but not revulsion.

She was touching him again.

"Is that your mother? She can't find me here!" she hissed. "Ren, you must hide me. Quickly!"

RENWICK HAD NEVER BETRAYED HER, not in all their time together. Not when they were found in a scrape or caught committing a mischief, or merely seen traipsing across a farmer's field or pasture, swatting the sheep. Not when he was blamed for lobbing stones at the village boys while Harriette stood next to him with the slingshot in her hand.

But he betrayed her now. Instead of shoving her into a

wardrobe or behind a curtain, which would have been the logical move, he slid an arm about her and turned toward the door.

"On the con-contrary, I think it's high time for my mother to ma-meet you," he said, and then raised his voice. "Come in."

Harriette's heart paused, then leapt erratically. The whole purpose in leaving her card with the butler had been to let Ren know she was in town. She had never met his mother, and never wished to.

The door flew open, and Harriette got her first look at the Countess of Renwick.

She was tiny and terrifying. An open robe of shimmering coral silk was pinned to a stomacher glittering with gems, matched by the enormous coral necklace spanning her chest. A petticoat cascading with ivory ruffles peeked through the skirts heaped over panniers broader than the doorway. The powered wig towered at least a foot above her head, with some confection perched upon it that Harriette didn't have time to study. Disapproval filled her face from the frown on her white brow to the pinched line of her lips.

Harriette had chosen her best gown for the task of seducing Ren, but the experienced eye would see that the crimson silk had faded and a line of pinpricks showed where it had been converted to the popular nightgown style. Harriette's hair powder was a dull grey that failed to disguise her natural muddy red color, and she wore no jewelry but a thin gold chain her mother had given her when she left Shepton Mallet for school.

She may have matured into a woman since Ren had seen her last, evidenced by the bosom pushed up by the low bodice of her gown and the tiny waist enhanced by her corset, but to the Countess of Renwick she would never be more than a brawling, nameless country orphan who could not afford to patch her shoes. Including her current ones, which, having been borrowed from Princess, who had larger feet, were clinging to Harriette's only through a combination of will and luck.

And she had been found in Ren's dressing room, alone with him. Were she of higher birth, or of known virtue, it was obvious what the consequences would be.

"Renwick," the countess said with a cold glare, "if you're going to smuggle harlots into this house, have the taste to choose from a better class."

Harriette drew back her lips in a feral grin. What had she expected—that the countess would recognize and welcome her? Of course not.

Ren stiffened. "Rhette," he said, quite against protocol, "may I introduce the Countess of W-W-Renwick. Mother, this is my v-very good friend—" He paused to concentrate, and Harriette squeezed his arm lightly. "Miss Harriette Smythe."

His mother's eyes narrowed. Ren had not endeared Harriette to her by choosing to introduce the woman of higher rank to the lower. "A name not, to my recollection, among the invitations I sent out," the countess said.

"An oversight I have c-c-c-orrected," Ren said. "I shall be de—" He paused and took a breath. "I shall be delighted to introduce Harriette to your guests."

If possible, his mother's countenance grew even more contemptuous. "*Your* guests, Renwick," the countess hissed through her teeth, "are quality. Among them are several marriageable young ladies of rank and station. You will not make me notorious by bringing this—this trollop into my house."

Harriette's heart dropped into her too-large slippers. So the countess *had* heard of her, even if Ren hadn't yet gleaned the gossip. This had been a terrible idea after all. Princess was right.

"Now, send her off through the back door and come down to the party, Renwick," the countess said.

She glanced around the room as if Ren might be hiding

other women among the hangings and heavy chairs. It was a dark room with outmoded furnishings, not at all to Ren's style, and Harriette suspected it had belonged to the previous earl. Of course, much about the Countess of Calenberg's house was also outmoded, so Harriette was in no position to scoff. But this new Ren, with his quiet dignity and understated elegance, suited this room as well as a bear at tea. Harriette wondered what other molds his mother was attempting to force Ren into, despite his inclination.

"I wish Harriette to stay, M-m-mother. You did tell me I m-might invite who I wi-liked," Ren said.

His mother's eyes widened with shock, and Harriette gathered that Ren did not often gainsay her. She saw the countess gathering her forces to flatten him, and indignation reared up, warring with her wiser instinct to flee.

"Perhaps I can help Ren meet a marriageable young lady," Harriette suggested.

Milady's penciled brows rose ludicrously high. "Ren*wick*," she said, enunciating each syllable, "could not possibly benefit from any information *you* could offer."

"I b-beg to differ, Mother," Ren said, shifting his weight to lean toward her. "Haow—Rhette has been in town much longer than I have. She knows the young way-ladies well."

It was fortunate Harriette had nothing in her mouth or she would have spit it across the room at this outrageous bouncer. The countess gritted her teeth as Ren turned and presented Harriette his arm. "Shall we?"

She knew to go with him would be utter folly, and she knew with equal surety that she could deny him nothing. His eyes held appeal and wariness and doubt and resignation, as if he fully expected her to reject him.

But there was something else in his gaze as well, a deep flare of interest that made some sleepy, heavy serpent in her stomach stir and lift its head. Harriette would fit among the wealthy, well-bred acquaintances downstairs about as well as Ren fit his father's dark house, furniture, and legacy. But she also knew she would accompany this Ren to the edge of the wilderness if he wanted her to.

She shouldn't. She'd let a man lure her into folly before and regretted it ever after. But this was Ren. He needed her.

She slid her hand around his arm, enjoying the luscious slide of silk beneath her glove and the press of warm, firm muscle beneath. A giddy sensation bubbled through her belly. She was on the arm of an earl. Her Ren, still, but so different. She wanted to learn him all over again.

She gave him a smile full of impish glee. "By all means, Ren*wick*," she cooed as his mother hissed again and flounced from the room. "Let us find you a bride, and then you can commission me to do a portrait of you both."

CHAPTER FIVE

"So, your duty," Harriette murmured as she floated down the curving staircase of Renwick House from the chambers on the second floor to the large, formal staterooms on the first. "Is that why you've returned to England?"

"In part," he said briefly. He watched the stairs, not her. She glanced at the portraits and landscapes lining the plastered walls, an odd mixture of oils and watercolors, all of them conventional, none of them terribly good. "My mother's been attempting to summon me home for years. I felt it was time."

"Do you want to marry?"

"I must. There's no one else. The title reverts to the Crown if I end the line."

He halted as she paused at the curve, and she studied him. The blue of the suit brought out the deep tones of his eyes, the sky of an endless summer. He smelled like a cake of fresh soap, a blend of citrus and spice. His skin had turned bronze by exposure to sun, and she would wager the brown of his natural hair had acquired golden highlights as well. The mature lines of his face were a painter's composition, every feature symmetrical and in proportion, but they came together in a compelling, animated way.

And he was an earl, with estates all over Britain. Every woman alive would want him.

But of course, being Ren, he wouldn't know that. The old tenderness pinched at her heart. Eleven years abroad and he'd become an intriguing man, but the eyes looking at her were the same old Ren—guarded, hopeless. In all those years, no one had made him see his own strength or beauty.

She would. She would produce a portrait that showed him true, the depths of his mind, the integrity of his character, the playful side and the serious side and his most secret, hidden dreams. She would bring him so alive on the canvas that every viewer would see his worth; she had that power. She'd spent the past eleven years studying her craft and while she had much to learn, she was better than any other artist she'd seen hung on these walls so far.

She hugged his arm, relieved that she could do something for him. She wasn't using him to gain a foothold among society painters. Well, she was, but he would benefit, too.

And she would make sure the bride he chose was worthy of him. She would find him someone beautiful and kind and also wealthy. Someone who could offer him everything Harriette did not have to give.

"Your limp is much improved," she noted as they proceeded down the broad marble staircase. He held with one hand to the elaborate bronze balustrade, and she held to him, supporting him, though he didn't need her to. He didn't hobble as he had as a youth, but instead he put his good foot on each step, then brought his lame foot to meet it, like a child learning to descend stairs. But he did it with such cool deliberation that one had to know him to know he was compensating for something.

"I met a doctor in Italy who is developing new cures for

clubfeet," he said. "A young professor named Scarpa. He put me through a series of exercises and manipulations, and then he tried a surgical correction."

A smile quirked up half his mouth. "I nearly lost my foot to sepsis, but after I pulled through, the good doctor designed me a special shoe." He held it out to show her. "I had a cobbler here cover it in leather and make me a matched set, and if I ever break it or wear it out, I shall have to return to Italy to find Dottore Scarpa again."

"Does it hurt?"

"Always." His smile faded as they reached the bottom of the flight and paused in the small marble hall. "In the Scandinavian folktales, when the waterborne creatures like selkies or undines come ashore and take their land form, their feet feel as if they are walking upon hot coals or knives. It is the price one pays to appear human."

"Oh, Ren." Brave, noble, determined Ren. She knew a bit about sacrificing to appear like others, but she didn't walk on knives as a consequence.

The countess had already swept into one of the two formal drawing rooms from whence the sounds of conversation and amusement drifted. Harriette stood still, taking one last moment to have Ren all to herself before she had to turn him over. Was there a woman in these rooms who deserved this man?

"And your speech," she said, searching his eyes. Where was his confidence, his assurance? There weren't a hundred men in all of Britain who held precedence before him. He owned this house and the land it stood upon, and many other lands besides. He acted like all this was a suit he might lay aside at any moment, when he could never escape his position or what it demanded of him.

That fine lip twisted with bitterness. "There's no remedy for that, I'm afraid. I'm going to look a fool in front of all these people, but I think that's what my mother wants. She shows the world that her son is a simpleton and a cripple, so she might be pitied and petted for bearing up so nobly under such affliction. Then, if I marry a girl like her, she will have someone to complain to of the burdens she's been given to bear."

"You are not a simpleton and you are not a cripple," Harriette said sharply. "I haven't heard you stammer once with me."

"Because you don't terrify me nearly as much as my mother," Ren said. "Ready to throw yourself to the lions?"

Her smile mirrored his, more of a smirk. If only he knew how closely that thought echoed her own. But she was not the pure, noble Christian being thrown into the ring by a cruel Roman emperor to suffer torments that would lead to her sainthood. She was the furthest thing possible from a saint.

The countess had recognized her name. Most of the people in these overly ornamented drawing rooms would also.

And in all too short a time, Ren would know it, too—what she'd done to get where she was. He'd risen above his circumstances, and she had fallen.

She pressed his arm to her breast, needing his strength, his solid warmth. If she could overcome his deep dislike of exposure long enough to paint him, she would make a portrait so beautiful it could go a long way toward redeeming herself. Not enough to be worthy of him—she'd never be that. The thought plunged a knife through her heart.

He gave her a quizzical look, but she wasn't ten anymore, with no secrets and not a single thought for her future. She saw now, all too well, how wide a chasm gaped between her and her childhood friend.

But he offered, for the moment, a place beside him, and she was weak enough to take advantage while she could.

. . .

THE FORMAL DRAWING room of Renwick House occupied the front part of the first floor, positioned to best catch the light from the tall, narrow windows that faced the square. The last time Renwick had seen it, the room had been a heavy tomb of dark paneling and massive Jacobean furniture, reflecting the era when Renwick power and influence had been at its peak. His mother had redecorated in the neoclassical style, but without any sense of the restraint or harmonies that made that style work. Everything was heavily curved and a bold red or green or gold, and being currently thronged with people all dressed in outrageously bright costumes of varying colors, the room assaulted the eye as well as the nose.

Beside him, Harriette stiffened, and he wondered if she regretted her decision to come to his rescue yet again. He laid his free hand over the slim fingers curled about his arm, holding her in place.

"No bolting now," he murmured. He steeled himself to endure the usual reactions of strangers with the discipline honed by the many new experiences of his tour. He would not show his aversion to notice and curious stares. He would pretend not to see the revulsion on the faces of the delicate. He would hide his annoyance at their pity and his irritation at those who would attempt to become too familiar because of that pity, or because he was the Earl of Renwick despite everything.

Normally, facing a room full of the cultured and elegant and well-born and rich, he felt suffused with dread at a long night of guarding his tongue, saying as little as possible so his stammer did not strangle him. Were he a common man, in a common trade, his disabilities would scarcely be a matter of note, when so many of the population were marked by injuries or illness or scars.

But in the nobility, among those born to power and rule, such afflictions were a curse. His father had taught him none of the things other men learned from their fathers—how to hunt, how to shoot, how to gamble, how to make a fine leg—but the old Earl of Renwick had ferociously impressed upon his son all that his title and station demanded, and all the ways he failed.

The minute he'd lighted on English soil, his mother reminded Ren of his responsibility to bear an heir and perpetuate the line. His father had bragged that the earls of Renwick won their title and lands by helping Henry Tudor keep his throne, then looked around at his heir and complained that a line of strong, fierce warriors for cause and king had degenerated to weaklings. Didn't his mother equally fear what madness and deformity might await further in the line? Ren did.

Yet the fear receded with Harriette at his side. Along with the alarm and desire her dress and exposed skin and delicious scent aroused in him, he felt the old, steadying calm in her presence, as if the world had fallen into perspective. He'd dreamed of this, in deepest night: of entering fancy parties armed with a gorgeously dressed Harriette who would whisper in his ear and make him feel the absurdity of it all, not the pain of inadequacy or fear of humiliation. His mother could throw fits later about his squiring Harriette about, but tonight, for now, she was here.

She glanced up at him, and the gold lights in her eyes warned of impending mischief. Her red lips curved in a smile that brought out tiny grooves at the corners of her mouth. She'd had that impish pucker as a girl, but on her woman's face, it was a powerful enchantment.

"Who's bolting?" She straightened him with a quick, light touch, smoothing his coat over his shoulders, flicking at his neckcloth to adjust the folds, and rubbing her thumb over a silver button to erase a smudge. Then she brushed her hand over his temple, tucking a lock of hair under his wig.

He stood struck to stone by her attention, every nerve ending fired alive at her touch. These were the simple attentions a woman paid a man she cared about, but he had never known them. He had never had a woman at his side who cared about anything more than the price she would be paid for a night of companionship.

He met Harriette's eyes and felt trapped in the lift of her dark lashes, the steady inquiry of her gaze. If it were true that the eyes revealed the soul, then he saw all of Harriette Smythe, the girl she had been and the woman she'd become, and all that lay in between. His heart slammed against the silver button she'd just touched, as if trying to throw itself into her hands. The surge of blood in his head blocked out all the voices of the room, everything but her.

Harriette.

His pulse beat out a knowledge that dizzied him with its sudden surety. He felt unsteady, and he felt as if he'd just arrived at the fundamental truth of his life.

Harriette, at his side. That was all he needed. That was everything.

He stared at her lips, fighting back the blood pounding in his ear so he could hear her. "—future countess is here somewhere, Renwick. We'll find her."

She looked away, and the ground beneath him shifted. The rock of truth he stood on was his alone.

She didn't want him.

She felt the old tenderness for him, that was clear, but she didn't *want* him the way a woman longed for a man.

Well, whoever had wanted him? Ren thought, sliding down the black hole toward the despair that was his oldest and most familiar companion. He followed like a block of wood as Harriette stepped forward, and because he wasn't thinking about his foot, the cursed thing dragged along with him. Behind him he heard the butler announcing them, and every eye turned just in time to watch him lurch into the drawing room.

Harriette stopped at once, beaming a polite smile around the crowd, waiting to let him steady himself against her. But the damage was done. Everyone had seen his weakness. He had only to open his mouth to seal his doom.

He froze in humiliation, the terrified boy he'd always been, but Harriette gently tugged him forward. "Charlotte Stanhope," she murmured. "Grand-niece to the late Lord Chesterfield. You've read his *Letters to his Son,* I'm sure?"

"I heard they are full of im-im-immorality," Ren stammered as the small knot of fashionably dressed women stared at their approach. This was an agony past bearing. He watched the youngest sweep her eyes down his form and fasten on the foot he dragged forward to meet the other. His moment of paralysis had stripped away every trick he'd mastered, every guise he'd learned to affect.

The young lady's eyes darted back to his face with a look of horror, and Ren gritted his teeth. What did he care if every woman here scorned him? Harriette was trying to give him away to another. She didn't want him herself. No other knowledge was able to enter his head around that.

The young lady gave him a brief curtsey as Harriette made introductions. In a pretty silk robe the color of milky tea, with demure rosettes marching down lines of broad stripes, the Stanhope girl looked like a plain little wren next to Harriette's exotic scarlet finch. Her chaperone made some polite noises, and the ladies with them acknowledged Ren with the courtesy due an earl and their host. None of them turned to chat with Harriette, which struck him as odd, if they were acquainted.

The chaperone asked whether he had visited Sir William and Lady Catherine Hamilton in Naples.

Ren gulped. This was what he most hated about such gatherings: the questions that required answers. He could avoid dancing, but not the direct address.

"I sss-stayed some time with them at the Villa Angelica in Pu-Portici."

Oh, miserable, miserable; he sounded like a stuttering fool. He focused on Harriette, who was watching him with rapt attention, so he did not have to see the distaste on the faces of the others. "In fact I had the honor of accompanying Sir W—" He concentrated. Harriette didn't hurry him. "—Sir William on one of his visits to M-Mount Etna." *Ignore the others. Focus on Harriette.* "He is preparing his observations about volcanoes for publications, I believe." He faced the chaperone as if he had been speaking to her all along.

"How interesting," the chaperone murmured, sounding bored, though Ren had broken a sweat putting so many sentences together for strangers. She stared at his leg as if she doubted his ability to move anywhere, much less clamber across uneven surfaces, and he felt a wave of fury at her scorn. Couldn't she *see* how hard he was trying?

As if she sensed his emotion, Harriette lightly squeezed his arm. "I've studied the engravings Sir William has published of his substantial collection of antique vases." She smiled at Ren as if he were the most fascinating man in the room. "But I would particularly like to see his collection of paintings."

The other women met this effort with silence. It was not quite the cut direct; they simply pretended that she was not there.

This diverted Ren from his own agonies. Why would these ladies spurn Harriette? But she didn't seem affected; indeed she didn't seem to realize anything was wrong.

"I will take you to the Palazzo Sessa sometime," he promised her. "Sir William will be delighted to show you his collection. Wadies." He nodded at them, smarting at his final slip, and drew away. He let himself entertain for a moment, as consolation, the thought of travel abroad with Harriette. Harriette with artistic crumbling ruins behind her or the dramatic profile of a volcano. Harriette drenched in the golden sun of southern Italy.

Across the room, his mother paused in fawning upon the Duchess of Devonshire to give Ren a fulminating stare. He gripped Harriette tightly as she pulled him along to the next group. "Bess Hervey is the brunette," she whispered. "Young, but considered uncommonly handsome."

Handsome women made Ren's throat tighten and his tongue swell in his mouth. He concentrated on walking evenly as Harriette floated to another knot of gorgeously dressed women and made introductions. It was the same with the Hervey girl and her contingent. They met Ren with cautious courtesy and did not engage with his companion, though the Hervey girl watched Harriette out of the corner of her eye as if keeping an eye on a half-feral pet. The others clustered around Ren.

"Do you ride, your lordship?" asked one young thing, whose name he had forgotten immediately.

"A little," he said. In truth, he felt much at his ease on horse-back, where his clubfoot didn't matter.

"Renwick cuts an excellent figure atop a horse," said Harriette, who had never seen him ride. "Ren, you ought to take them riding sometime."

"I'd much prefer driving in the park." Another girl peeped at him above her fan. "I'm sure you have a very dashing vehicle?"

Ren's neck itched beneath his neckcloth. Was she flirting with him? Women did not flirt with him. These girls moved too much, all flutter and rustling and the waving of fans and curls and whatever they had pinned in their wigs. Beside him, Harriette stood completely still, like a steady column of flame, throwing a most distracting heat.

"I have a gig," Ren meant to say, but just then one girl bent to one of the others and whispered to her behind her fan, pointing her stare at Harriette. The second gaped, giggled, and then slapped a hand over her mouth. Harriette pretended not to hear, nor to see that she was the object of their gossip, but Ren felt all the air leave his body.

"I have a g-g-g-g-g—" He tried to gasp out the word and couldn't. Shame suffused him, but worse, when he turned to seek help from Harriette, he stepped on the train of Miss Hervey's gown. An irate glare swept over her face, swiftly mastered, but Ren botched the apology, too.

"M-m-m-miss Herv—I—b-b" His airway closed, his mouth proving as disobedient as his leg. Raw humiliation burned across his brow.

"Why, there is Lady Bessington!" Harriette trilled. "You'll excuse us, won't you? I've been hoping to make Renwick known to her. She is a great patron of the arts." She beamed at the group, extracting Ren from the scene of his shame.

"As if *you've* ever had a respectable patron," one of the girls remarked under her breath as they moved on. Ren, shocked, tried to look over his shoulder to find the source of this contemptuous remark, but Harriette pulled him away.

Instead of throwing him to the next stage of the gauntlet, though, she paused in a small space between the jostle of decorated, powdered, and perfumed bodies. Ren took a deep breath, dragging air into his lungs, and tried to focus on something calming. The glimmer of the candles in the chandeliers draped from the tall, plastered ceiling. The floating melodies of the string quartet positioned between a bay of soaring sashed windows. The tap of heeled slippers on the wooden floor as couples danced.

Harriette. Where other women smelled like hair powder and musty fabric and floral cologne doused over native odors, Harriette smelled of clean air, turpentine, and chalk.

"Fancy a reprieve?" she asked.

He searched her expression for signs of pity, contempt, or superiority, and found none. She watched him with a curious intensity, tracing each feature with her eyes as if she were thinking of light and lines and composition, painting him already in her head.

"I fancy leaving here altogether. Do you think we could? Run away?"

How he'd love to take her back to his dressing room, or better yet his bedchamber. Order his man to bring up food from the kitchens and a bottle or two of red wine, and pass the whole night talking with Harriette, hearing everything she had done with herself for eleven years.

Harriette near his bed was too much a temptation. Could he stand to be near her, burn like this, and know she was not moved in the same way?

Her lashes flickered, her expression growing veiled. "Your mother won't allow me to see you again."

"My mother can't keep you from me," he growled. He curled his fingers into fists to keep himself from reaching for her, as if he could hold her against him and not let anyone take her away.

That smile, that distracting pucker at the sides of her lips. He wanted to kiss each one.

"Why won't they talk with you?" Ren burst out. His tongue felt enormous. "The others. They pr-pretend not to see you. Is it me?"

"Of course not." She looked away, showing him a perfect profile. "It's me. I am, as your mother observed, not good *ton*."

"Why not?"

She was the most beautiful woman in these rooms, he could see that at a glance. She held her head high and moved with an assured grace that commanded admiration. When the movements of the other girls seemed affected, every gesture calculated for effect, Harriette was relaxed and at ease. Serene in her own skin. He'd always admired her calmness, when he was so easily troubled or overset.

"Mmm. Let's save that story for another time. Whom should you meet? Lady Derby is happily married, and from the style of her robe, expecting again." Her eyes scanned the glittering crowd. "The Duchess of Hunsdon is lately returned from the Continent, and she recently lost a court case over her late husband's estate. She'll be in search of a new protector, but far too cold-hearted to be a match for you, Ren."

She swiveled, spotting a row of rout chairs set against a wall near one of the doors. "I wonder who that girl is? She's been sitting alone ever since we came in."

Ren spotted her, too. The only person with dark skin in a room of powdered and painted paleness, she sat with quiet dignity, watching the dancers. Her plain dress, wool not silk, and the turban wrapping her hair suggested she was someone's dependent. Ren wondered at Harriette's interest.

"But I suppose we should—" Harriette faltered and her face grew slack with surprise. "Lady Bess. Bessington. Your ladyship." She dropped into a clumsy curtsey. He had never seen Harriette clumsy with anything. "What a most unexpected pleasure," she said, her words rushed and overeager.

The stately matron before them was the pinnacle of *ton* and style. Her wig, powdered a pale pink, glittered with rubies, and the rose silk of her gown peeked through cascades of elaborate embroidery and what might have been diamonds. At the tip of one rouged cheekbone perched a black silk beauty patch in the shape of a tear. Her reddened lips curved in a smile that was amused but not unkind.

"Miss Smythe. How pleasant to see you again. But where is your very interesting aunt? I do wish the Countess of Calenberg would show more of herself at these functions. I look forward to making her acquaintance."

"You wish to know my aunt?" Harriette looked dazzled. "But she is not here. Through some, er, remarkable oversight, Lady Renwick did not include my aunt in her invitation. Your ladyship, do you know the Earl of Renwick? Renwick, the Countess Bessington. She leads one of the more interesting salons in London, and her husband is one of the few Scottish peers in the House of Lords. You will be certain to encounter him when you take your seat."

"You may call me Lady Bess, if we are to be friends." Her ladyship acknowledged Ren's bow, which was no less awkward than Harriette's. His foot felt as stiff as if it bore an iron shackle, and he didn't trust his tongue. He wondered what about this glamorous lady intimidated Harriette, who, he guessed, was otherwise daunted by nothing.

Harriette pressed her hands together, giving her ladyship a look mingled with adoration and apprehension. "*Would* you be friends with me, Lady Bess? I seem to be *persona non gratis* here tonight."

Ren moved closer to her, his protective instincts stirred. Lady Bessington merely smiled.

"Your...connection with the recently departed Graf von Hardenburg seems to be much envied," Lady Bess said. "And much talked about, I'm afraid. He was considered quite dashing, and you did seem a particular favorite of his."

A hot bolt of jealousy shot through Ren. It was a sharper pain than the various manipulations the good Dottore Scarpa had performed on his foot. He felt a sudden urge to locate this foreign count and strangle him.

Harriette shook her head. A bit of powder wafted free from her hair, settling on her shoulders. "The Graf von Hardenburg was lately in London on a diplomatic mission from Prussia," she explained to Ren. "I met with him to try to find out more about my mother's family, since she has told me nothing.

"I think the count took an interest in every young lady who came into his purview," she remarked to Bess. "But I did a lovely pastel for him to take back to Prussia with him. For his wife."

Lady Bess chuckled and moved her fan lazily before her chin. "I think what excited talk, my dear Miss Smythe, were the very titillating sketches of the count that circulated through all the London bookshops."

"Ah." Harriette's eyes shifted guiltily over the room. "I suppose everyone here read that gossip paragraph in the *Morning Intelligencer* identifying me as the artist."

"Were you?" Ren blurted, shocked.

She met his eyes, a shadow moving through hers. But as always, she was forthright with him. "Yes, I drew them. I should have told you at once, Ren. Those sketches have made me notorious. I'm not at all the person to help find you a bride." She bit her lip, leaving a groove in the natural berry-red. He wanted to kiss it away. "Your mother was right," she said unhappily.

His mother was wrong. Anyone who wanted to keep him from Harriette was wrong. "How notorious?"

"Enough that anyone with the pennies to do so bought as many as they could." Lady Bess's black silk patch crinkled as she smiled broadly. "I myself own several. I don't doubt the fame will increase your commissions, Miss Smythe."

Harriette's mouth fell open at this and she stared at Lady Bessington, speechless, hopeful, and a tad undignified.

"Countess Bessington. How lovely to have you in my home." Ren's mother bore down on them, a buccaneer determined to board a stately galleon. "I take it you and Renwick have been introduced?"

"Welcome back, your lordship," Lady Bess said to Ren. "We are all very interested to hear what you think of us."

Ren answered this with an incline of his head. He didn't trust his mouth to speak. His mother neatly cut Harriette out of the group, and the butler stepped up beside her to block her from the rest of the room.

"Miss Smythe," Lady Renwick said, disdain lacing her voice, "perhaps you will come with Dunstan and identify the rather disturbing persons who are currently occupying our mews. I'm afraid I will have to call the watch on them if they don't depart soon."

Harriette's shoulders stiffened, her chin lifting. Ren recognized what his mother was doing: casting the unwelcome guest out on her ear.

Fight, he urged Harriette, wanting to see that small avenging goddess with her slingshot emerge. He wanted confirmation that beneath the gloss and sophistication she was still his Harriette, a tiny warrior who neglected to comb her hair.

"Those will be my friends," Harriette said. "Employees of the Countess of Calenberg. Men of impeccable character. They are waiting to take me home."

"They have informed me they are ready to take you now," Lady Renwick said, with nothing pleasant in her tone. Lady Bess floated away, looking above their heads to study the artwork as if she heard nothing of the exchange. "Dunstan?"

What was he doing? *He* was the one who had to fight for Harriette. "I w-w-w-wish for Rhette to st-stay, M-mother," Ren stammered.

"You'll never meet someone suitable with her hanging about your neck," Lady Renwick said sharply. "See to your guests, Renwick, and tell your friend goodbye."

"I'll see myself out," Harriette said defiantly.

"I'll take you." Ren slipped a hand about Harriette's arm. She was as slim and strong as he remembered. He limped beside her as Dunstan, without appearing to crowd her, steered Harriette toward one of the open double doors.

"You may go, Dunstan," Ren said once they were at the top of the broad marble stairs swirling down to the ground floor. "Attend your mistress."

It had not escaped him that the servants in Renwick House obeyed his mother, not him. In fact he suspected they ran all his orders by the countess for confirmation and approval.

"If you wish, your lordship." The butler gave Ren a stiff bow, ignoring Harriette altogether.

Ren sensed the burning fury in her, but she kept it bridled, matching her steps to his gait as they made their way down the stairs and through the long hallway that ran toward the back of the house and the mews. The garden was cloaked in darkness, and Ren led them out into the scented air, following the graveled path to the back gate and the stables. The streetlamp shone over the tall iron fence, turning Harriette's powdered hair to silver.

"You needn't leave because my mother wishes it," Ren said, thinking of his earlier plan to whisk her away to his room and spend the night with her. Ply her with wine. See behind that crisp, cool calm she projected to the rest of the world. Discover her secrets, and what her mature woman's body looked like beneath that gown. Didn't she want to spend time with him?

"I don't want to cause talk. You don't need that cloud about your head." She didn't stroll but walked briskly to the rear of the garden. Ren opened the gate, and she whistled to the man seated in the driver's perch of a small, fashionable cabriolet. She was truly leaving him.

"Where can I find you?" he asked desperately.

She paused to look into his face. Her scent drifted beneath his nose. "Did you get my card?"

"I didn't get anything."

She lifted a slender hand and traced the bones of his face, following the line of his brow, his cheekbone, his jaw. Curls of warmth spread from the path of her fingers, slightly callused.

"It's best I don't tar you with my brush, Ren. I would so like to paint you. You always were beautiful, but now—there's something about you that I would love to capture. I wonder if I could."

His throat closed as once more she gave him that searching, considering look. She thought him beautiful? No one had ever, in his life, used that word in association with him.

He couldn't let her walk away. "You told me before to give you a kiss, and I didn't," he said, his voice a low rumble.

"I'll take it now," she said without hesitation, and stepped into his arms.

He froze in astonishment and momentary panic. The women he'd kissed—the mere handful of them—had all, in his mind's eye, worn Harriette's face. The women he'd taken to bed in his fantasies had all, rather unimaginatively on his part, been different versions of Harriette Smythe. But the reality of her was so exquisite, so potent, that he barely trusted what his senses were telling him. It might be a fantasy Harriette slipping her ungloved hands around his neck and lifting her lips to his.

The softness, the heat, the delicious scent of her hit him with the force of a collision. For a moment he couldn't breathe. There was no place he would rather expire than in the arms of this woman, but he didn't want to miss a moment of finally, *finally* kissing Harriette Smythe, for real this time, not in his dreams.

Her lips were soft and moist and supple and moved against his like a dance. Her hair tickled his temple. Her skirts swallowed his legs. He dimly comprehended the breasts pressed against his chest as she leaned into him—oh God, the very thought of her breasts made him hard—and then her tongue slipped into his mouth to dab against his, and his cock sprang to attention with such a bolt of pleasure that he groaned.

Part of his mind was paralyzed with fear that he would do something wrong, or become so overwhelmed with sensation that he would spend right here in his breeches. Too eager, too fumbling, grabbing like an untried boy—that's what the Italian courtesan had said when he paid for a night of her company. What if he did something wrong with Harriette and turned her off him forever?

But she kissed him with ever deeper intensity, her tongue tangling with his, leading, teasing, probing, and she shifted slightly so that he pressed not into her skirts but against *her*, some part of her, he wasn't sure what because his head was a mass of stunned sensation, and he wouldn't be ashamed if he did climax simply from kissing Harriette Smythe, because her mouth on his, her body against his, the scent of her desire in his nostrils was the most intensely erotic thing he had ever experienced in his life.

With a small moan from the back of her throat—a moan that made a pulse go through his already enflamed body—she pulled away, disentangling tongue, hands, skirts and putting a cool, sobering space between them.

"Well," she said. "Someone taught *you* how to kiss proper, milord Renwick."

No one had taught him. The courtesan had laughed and said he slobbered. The prostitute in Paris hadn't let him kiss her at all. But Harriette didn't make him feel like a buffoon. She made him feel strong, confident, in charge, bold enough to press her against the fence and pull up those infernally enormous skirts and—

"If ye wanted a tup, liefer ye'd done it inside, where's we didna have to watch ye," grumbled a man's voice.

He had forgotten that her carriage stood in the mews just

beyond them. A hulking form leaned against the step and a smaller, bent shape perched atop the huge horse waiting patiently in its traces. Ren squinted through the shadows and was shocked to find the rider was not a boy but a man, his shoulders set at uneven angles, his legs hanging crookedly along the horse's sides. But his striped livery hugged a chest and arms covered with wiry muscle, and his expression was sharp and mocking as he regarded Ren.

Harriette's groom was a cripple like he was. Worse, actually. Ren stared, too many questions fogging his mind for him to voice just one. As he stuttered for breath, Harriette took the hand of the footman—a huge man, twice Ren's size, though something about the shadows on his face seemed wrong—and climbed into the smart vehicle. The groom picked up the ribbons.

She was going to leave just like that? Without a word?

"I want to see you again," Ren blurted, putting a hand on the side of the carriage.

She reached out gently, squeezed his fingers. He couldn't see her face in the shadows, but he heard the sadness in her whisper. "It's best if you don't. For your sake. Goodbye, Ren. Be well. Be—happy."

Her voice wavered on the last words. The groom tossed her the ribbons and the huge footman hauled himself onto the platform at the back. Harriette flicked the ribbons, and the vehicle rolled away.

Ren's hand fell to his side. She was leaving *him* this time, going away to worlds unknown, leaving him stranded in a place he didn't want to be.

The parting didn't feel like a sweet sorrow. It felt like a hammer to his chest.

CHAPTER SIX

"Only look, Hari, there's a gossip paragraph about you again in the *Morning Intelligencer*," the Countess of Calenberg announced to the group of women gathered around the breakfast table in the dining room of her Charles Street home. She adjusted the reading glasses attached to the bodice of her morning gown by a long chain and read in a self-important drawl.

"The Countess of R—'s evening to welcome her son home from his tour abroad boasted many fine ornaments, among them Lady B-ss-n, who seems to adorn all the approved places, and Her Grace the Duchess of H-d-n, of whom this paper faithfully brought you every detail of her recent defeat in a suit to reclaim the estate of her late husband—"

"We know this, *Engelein*," said Princess, kicking off her jeweled slippers and shoving them beneath the long mahogany dining table. "It was quite a transformation, *ja*? The Duchess of Hunsdon's bastard stepson miraculously produced marriage lines showing that he was the rightful duke, and now he is in possession of the estates, the wealth, and soon a wife. Unfortunate, since we might have pitched Hari at him otherwise." She scratched underneath her wig, dotted with tired flowers and fading powder.

Harriette topped off her cup of chocolate and blew gently on it. "I know his intended," she murmured. "She came to Miss Gregoire's Academy while I was there. I ought to call on her."

Speaking of transformation. Renwick had certainly changed from the thin, pale boy Harriette remembered. She'd put some color and muscle on him in their summer of racketing about Shepton Mallet, and she'd been certain he would hold his own at school, that his title would provide him some measure of protection along with the small defensive moves she had shown him, like where to kick a boy who was tormenting you, and how to aim a slingshot.

But the Ren who'd returned from his tour abroad was an astonishment. He'd acquired poise and polish as well as correcting his gait and, to some extent, his speech. He'd filled out to manly proportions—very nice manly proportions—and that angelic boyish face of his, with its strong lines and perfect symmetry, had become devastatingly beautiful in maturity.

Heavens, how she wished to paint him. To capture that indefinable glow that lurked in his eyes. And that expression on his face as he confronted a room full of strangers, as if he were looking past them to something very far away, some secret vista that brought him joy. What was it?

She wanted to know this Ren. Desire licked through her at the memory of that impossible, intoxicating kiss. She wanted to know him in a carnal fashion as well. There was no denying that. She lost herself in another sip of chocolate that was nearly as hot and delicious as the Earl of Renwick's mouth.

"—listening, Hari?" Her aunt shook the paper in Harriette's direction. "It's about you.

"'But the most surprising ornament was a fetching damsel in a crimson nightgown, capturing the Earl of R-nw-k's arm and the attention of the room. Your author knows this apparition to be Miss H-r-t Sm-th, the artist responsible for the salacious but highly entertaining sketches of the G- v- H-b-g which circulated recently among London's printers and booksellers. Your author has it on strictest authority that Miss Sm-th is an acolyte of the eccentric Lady C-l-b-g, the foreign countess who has a penchant for collecting unattached women of artistic bent in a salon known as the Catherine Club, which'—and more of the usual. They deign to recognize my humble self?" The countess laid a heavily ringed hand to her ruffled bosom. "I am in transports."

"Did we ever decide on the name the Catherine Club?" The demand came from Darci, who had, as a child, washed ashore in Ireland after a shipwreck and made her way into the Countess of Calenberg's household on the tide of London's poor and desperate. "I recall we discussed it, but never confirmed."

With her parentage unknown, no one was able to guess where Darci's dark curly hair, brown skin, and cinnamon eyes had come from, but frankly no one in the countess's household much cared about anyone's past. They lived in the present, day to day, pleasure to pleasure, and looked with dream-filled eyes toward the future.

"St. Catherine of Bologna is the patron saint of artists, among other things," said Melike, who was fascinated with Christianity and knew more about it than the rest of the household, most of whom were negligible churchgoers at best. Melike had been the embarrassing secret of an English gentlewoman who was kidnapped abroad and sold into an Ottoman harem. The lady's release was negotiated by the British government, but her return necessitated giving to the workhouse the daughter she'd borne to her captor, and Melike had made her way through various occupations around London until the Countess of Calenberg found her. She recalled enough of her early childhood to lend both a Turkish and

Muslim outlook on things, enhancing the supposedly exotic aura of the household.

"And we're all artists here," said Natalya, motioning for Harriette to pass her the chocolate. Natalya was their most recent addition. She had come to Britain as the mistress of a roving Russian prince and found herself abandoned when the prince found someone he liked better. As she was still mastering English, Natalya tended to state the obvious. "Darci is a sculptor, Melike paints jewelry, Harriette is our painter, and I—" Her soft, rounded face, usually complacent when not wreathed in sunny smiles, assumed an expression that was, for her, troubled. "What do I do again?"

"You're our model, oh beauteous one," Harriette said. She accepted the letter her aunt held out to her, a thick, creamy vellum bearing the Graf von Hardenburg's seal. Harriette sighed, wondering if her past follies were coming back to haunt her. She might have fit perfectly well among the Countess of Renwick's guests if not for the mischief created by whoever exposed her as the maker of those terribly indecent, but awfully lucrative sketches.

She didn't want to be famous for her caricatures. She wanted to be known, and sought after, for her magnificent portraits.

"What else does the paragraph say about us, Aunt?" She might as well know, though Lady Renwick needed no further reason to bar her son from associating with Harriette. The thought of not seeing Renwick again burned her throat worse than the chocolate.

His solid heat at her side, protecting her as they faced disapproving faces, had been such a welcome discovery. His wry, mischievous sense of humor hadn't changed a bit. And, what had always been her favorite thing about him, he still wore his heart on his sleeve.

He'd confessed that he stammered less around her. That admission lifted her heart and pierced her belly at one and the same time.

"Oh, they have no more than the customary complaints." The countess folded the sheet of newsprint and passed it along to Princess. "We are unattached women who live as we please, so we must be engaged in riotous or nefarious activities, or both. Dear me, these British are easily scandalized. They ought to see what takes place in courts abroad." She focused on Harriette. "How did you find Renwick?"

"Gorgeous," Harriette blurted. "Top of the trees." She turned her jasperware cup in nervous circles as the attention of the others settled on her. "And the night was a disaster. His mother chased me out of the house with the butler on my heels. I'll never have the chance to paint him and have a portrait that will gain me commissions from those of *ton*."

"We'll never be good *ton* anyway," said the countess. She had been much admired as a dashing and rich young widow when she first arrived in London, celebrated for her foreign beauty. But she proved too beautiful and dashing for the arbiters of taste and Polite Society, and as her list of lovers and scandals grew, the invitations to certain events and noble houses ceased. She was still celebrated in the circles known to be riotous, dissolute, and quite uncaring of social niceties, but those people tended to be frequently in debt, and the Catherine Club, or whatever they were to call themselves, lived on the same food that regular mortals did.

"Who says we need *ton*?" Their cook-housekeeper, Sorcha, trucked into the room with a fresh pot of coffee and thunked it on the table. "Never understood what that meant anyway."

She sank into the open chair beside Darci and poured herself a cup. Sorcha, their wild redhead, was the only one among them who could say she'd been born in the British Isles but not, as she reminded anyone who would listen, on British soil. She was Manx, and the Isle of Man was a self-governing territory, even if the British crown had purchased the right to call themselves Lords of Mann.

"*Ton* simply means style," Harriette said, reading the gossip paragraphs over the shoulder of the Princess. "Taste. Something like tone, but in French. It signifies quality. And those who have it possess the wealth, and the respectability, to keep us all in fine style for a good long while."

"Our style is fine enough, ain't it?" Sorcha crumbled sugar into her coffee and slurped the hot liquid. She'd been brought into the house as one of the countess's strays and had quickly appointed herself as housekeeper and caretaker of the others, a natural expression of her skills.

"And we are already quality, *dah?*" Natalya stretched her arms, pale and plump in the sheer fabric of her morning gown.

"I will agree wit dat." The butler, a tall, broad-shouldered man with a patch over one eye, strode into the room with a large silver tray laden with more breakfast items. He placed each woman's favorite before them, starting with the countess and working around the table, before unloading the rest of the tray among the other dishes on the sideboard.

"Good morning, Abassi," the countess greeted him. She tapped a fold of the paper beside her plate. "Can you countenance, there is another advertisement in the *Intelligencer* today looking for a runaway male slave. 'Black skin, missing one eye, of low, mean countenance, escaped from the *Zong* eleven months ago.' But that cannot be you, Abassi, as your countenance is in no way low or mean." She smirked at her butler as he refilled her chocolate, and he grinned back, showing a gold-capped tooth.

"My word, after eleven months you'd think Mr. Gregson

would accept defeat," Melike observed. "A Barbary pirate would have moved on long ago."

"This man, he must be very valuable," Abassi said in his soft Caribbean accent. "P'raps he was a pirate once too, eh? Or very strong." He flexed unnecessarily as he picked up the empty tray.

"You might join us, Abassi." The countess waved for him to pull up one of the extra chairs stationed against the wall. Quite against all usual protocol, and one of the many reasons her household was considered so outrageous, the Countess of Calenberg dined and conversed with her employees.

"*Non*, dis morning I teach Jock and Beater how to shoot." Abassi pretended to sight a gun with his good eye, pointing his finger toward a portrait of the long-dead Count of Calenberg that graced the wall above the fireplace mantel. "They need much practice."

"Well, go somewhere quite safe, and don't blow the wigs off any passersby." The countess handed Abassi the offending paper. "What's next for you now, Hari?" she asked, returning to what was apparently the morning's theme. "Netting Renwick was an unsafe bet from the beginning. Consider what you might do with your salacious sketches, however."

"The ones of the Graf von Hardenburg were very like," Darci agreed with a wide grin. "And very—instructive?"

"And vulgar, as our dear gossip called them." Harriette put her letter aside to read later. It had done wonders for the Graf von Hardenburg's popularity when sketches of him in *dishabille* proved the latest fad among London's print-hungry populace, but she hadn't thought her hand would be quite so easily exposed, or she would meet such censure for them.

Before last night, she would have agreed with Sorcha and Natalya that they rubbed along just fine without need of Polite Society. But she had seen the disdain of the ladies of fashion— all except Lady Bessington, bless her heart—and the indignation of being herded out of the Countess of Renwick's house cut deep. Harriette had never cared about her reputation until she realized that, in the eyes of many, it made her unfit to associate with the Earl of Renwick.

And then there were the practical concerns. "I can't make a fortune on pennies from sketches." Harriette pointed to the dark, yellowing image of the Count of Calenberg, her great-aunt's long dead and not-much-lamented husband. "A commission for an oil that size could fetch me hundreds of guineas. A little less for a pastel or gouache, but still a fine price."

"I'll p-p-ay it."

From the doorway came a deep voice that was not the butler's, though Abassi stood behind, examining the small white calling card the visitor had produced.

Every woman in the room straightened, even Sorcha, who, after losing a child and several years of her life, had sworn off both gin and men. Darci smoothed a hand over her plush curls. Melike touched her throat. Natalya thrust out her breasts, the most prominent of her many admirable features. Princess slipped her feet back into her slippers and adjusted the enormous amethyst collar that hung about her throat. Even the countess took a long moment to inspect the newcomer and appreciate the splendid figure he cut.

Harriette stared at him greedily. He was more striking in the light of day, his features sharply defined and animated by the warm intelligence in his eyes. He filled out a butter-yellow morning coat and breeches with a sleekness that hinted at the muscle of exertion, not the fat of indolence. Instead of a wig he wore his own hair, lightly powdered, and his neckcloth had fallen out of its elaborate twist.

She rose and moved toward him without conscious thought, her head filled with the memory of his arms about her, his mouth on hers, the evidence of his desire for her pressing against her hip. His dark blue eyes, riveted on her, held the same memory, and a languorous curl of desire woke and stretched in her belly. She might very well have walked straight into his arms and kissed him again, losing her head completely, if Abassi hadn't spoken.

"The Earl of Renwick, your ladyship."

Harriette pulled herself up short before she did something that even in her aunt's permissive household might be considered unorthodox. But the urge to touch him was too much to deny. She was not a creature to deny herself anyway, a trait her aunt had cultivated. She tidied his cravat, reshaping its stylish twist, and let her fingertips brush the warm skin above his collar. His eyelids flickered, and a small, wicked triumph joined the other emotions swirling in her lower regions. He was affected by her, as she was by him.

And he was here, when she thought she might never see him again. "You found us."

"The Countess of Calenberg is well known, it seems." He bowed to her aunt, who responded with a gracious incline of her head.

"Aunt, this is my Ren. Renwick, my great-aunt, the Countess of Calenberg." That slipped out; he wasn't 'her' anything. Having ceded to the impulse to touch him, now she could not seem to take her hand away, and let it linger on the embroidered lapel of his waistcoat. Heat. Strength. *Maleness*.

Goodness, she'd never been made giddy at the mere presence of a man before. She was acting like a wet goose. "Ren, these are my friends. Miss Darci Kilcannon, who sculpts. Miss Melike Yilmaz, who does exquisite miniatures. The High and Well-Born Natalya Dobraya, our model. And Miss Sorcha Cowley, who makes scones that will make you think you have died and gone to heaven. Oh, and I have saved the highest among us for last: Her Royal Highness Casimira, Princess of the

Kingdom of Galicia and Lodomeria. You may simply call her Princess, as we all do."

Ren regarded her with interest. Princess stared boldly back, an approving smile curling her lips as she studied him from wig to boots.

"I have not heard of your pr-pr—" Harriette caught the slight pause as he gathered himself. "–that principality, your Highness," he said politely.

"It is quite new," Princess responded. "Created by the Hapsburgs in the Partition of Poland. Fond as I am of the formidable Empress Maria Theresa, my family lost a great deal of their lands and dignity when the greater powers carved up my country, and so I decided to live abroad for a time."

Harriette spotted the letter she had left by her plate, and her insides twisted. Princess's plight mirrored her mother's own background, what little she knew of it. Displaced nobles were a common sight across a Europe being almost continuously reshaped by wars and alliance. Harriette had always suspected her mother had fled her homeland not because her noble name was in danger, but because she was hiding an illegitimate child.

Her aunt had never said anything more than what Harriette's mother told her, except to insist that their family was good enough for her to be accepted in the best circles, and good enough for Harriette to receive schooling at the very selective Miss Gregoire's Academy for Girls.

But her unknown birth was another strike against her. She was not the well-bred, mannerly type of society wife that Renwick required for his countess. She was neither an able housekeeper nor a proper hostess, and she hadn't the smallest streak of decorum in her bones. No matter how high her mother's rank, an illegitimate daughter would never be good enough for the Earl of Renwick. Not while Lady Renwick lived.

"Does your mother know you're here?" she asked Ren.

She loved how that wry smile quirked up one corner of his mouth. "My mother does not direct me, Rhette. I own the roof she lives under and I pay for the servants who attend her. We had a dis-discussion about it last night, after you left."

She knew by this that he must have had an out-and-out row with his mother, and she flattened her palm against his chest in a soothing gesture. That must have hurt him. The Ren she knew hated rows, and above all hated disappointing his parents.

"You've come to call?"

This smile lifted both sides of his mouth, and her lungs emptied at the beauty of him. "You asked to paint me. I consent."

CHAPTER SEVEN

F*inally.*

That was all Harriette said in response to his declaration—his full-scale and unhesitant capitulation to whatever she wanted, whatever she planned to do with him. Never mind he had left his mother weeping into her morning coffee when she heard him leaving to call on the Countess of Calenberg.

"You won't like what comes of associating with such people!" she'd cried when Ren made it clear he had no intention of cutting Harriette from his life and, if she was not welcome under his own roof, he would go to hers. "You'll regret this!"

So far Ren regretted nothing. Not the dirty water that had splashed on him by a wagon passing his horse in the street, soiling his specially designed riding boot. Not the excruciating scrutiny of the curious females in the countess's dining parlor, who doubtless detected all his flaws and deformities. Not whatever discomfort might ensue with having Harriette examine him closely, for an extended length of time.

Alone together.

He noticed little else but the sway of her skirts as she climbed the stairs ahead of him to the first floor. But as she pushed open the door to a large drawing room that looked in no way how a formal drawing room was supposed to look, he perceived he had committed himself to torture.

He would be alone with Harriette for an indefinite length of time, and with no foreign presence to restrain him, he would have to rely on his own gentlemanly restraint to keep his hands off her. That incendiary kiss had sent him arsey varsey, as the younger Harriette would have said. That kiss was the prime reason he had barreled out the door of Renwick House determined to find her. He was a green schoolboy again, on fire with physical sensations that drowned out the voice of sense. Being near Harriette made sense. Nothing else did.

She had told him they must say goodbye, told him not to seek her out, and he had immediately disregarded her wishes. The thought made him stumble into the room.

She had also given him a kiss that had left him aching all night, the memory of her lips and her scent and her delicious warm softness finding him on the edge of dreams. How could she kiss him like that and then abandon him?

He had come to find out if he could change her mind.

He had come, in truth, hoping he could kiss her again. And again and again and again, until she melted in his arms, until she wanted him, until she chose to stay with him forever, come what may.

The thought drenched him in a sudden hot sweat. *Forever.* How had his mind leapt ahead to that conclusion? He was far too given to fantasy, as his tutor had impressed on him time and again. He must guard against that.

"Welcome to our studio. Well, my and Darci's studio. Melike likes to work in the library, which is downstairs."

She held out her arms and turned about. The long room was papered in a lovely sky-blue silk, with patterned moldings and gilt-touched carvings on a high ceiling that turned the place into a graceful cavern. Tall windows let in light that shone on the waxed wooden floor. Instead of the customary seating arrangements, one end of the room held several clay sculptures in various stages of completion, a large block of polished marble, and a table full of tools he couldn't identify.

The rest of the room was a painter's haven, with large canvases lining the walls, some bare and many more painted upon, propped against others draped in fabric. One corner was arranged to look like an Oriental boudoir, with a long couch, a Turkish rug, a painted screen, and a lamp with dragon's feet stationed near it. Next to an easel standing atop a cloth arranged on the floor was a tall stool and a long table filled with brushes, jars and bottles of a dizzying array of colors, and bowls and other assorted implements. It was a peek into Harriette's mind and soul, and he moved toward the canvases, mesmerized.

One portrait held a finished central figure though the background was not yet complete. A mature woman stared back at him, the secrets and wisdom of her life written on her face, a gleam of mischief and sharp intelligence in her eyes.

"The Countess of Calenberg," he said. "It is her to the life, Rhette."

"Mmm, that one turned out well. She hasn't decided if she wants to be standing before the ruins of Pompeii or the sack of Rome, so I will finish the background once she has chosen."

There were smaller canvases of the one they called Princess in various seductive poses, all of them showing a great deal of skin that looked soft enough to touch. He wondered at the woman's age, though she was older than Harriette; the visage in the portrait held cleverness, mockery, and a hint of wistfulness.

"Her expression is so beguiling," he remarked. "These are very good."

"You sound surprised," she said with amusement, coming to stand beside him. He smelled again that blend of turpentine and chalk, her painterly preparations. Something more complex and earthy beneath that called to him. The scent of her body, warm and luscious. She wore a loose morning gown, a heap of wispy fabric that clung to her waist and those delicious, shapely breasts.

"I knew you liked to draw, but this—this takes a great deal of skill."

She walked with him along a line of pastel portraits of the Russian woman she had called Natalya, in a variety of poses and levels of light.

"The year you left Shepton Mallet, my aunt—my great-aunt, properly, that's the Countess of Calenberg—she contacted my mother and said she had found a girl's school that would board me, and she would pay for everything. My mother agreed, and so I went to Miss Gregoire's Academy in Bath. My drawing mistress introduced me to watercolors, and from there to oils and pastels, and I was in heaven. That's her, Miss Gregoire."

She moved aside some other portraits to show Ren a lovely, fine-boned woman with a cloud of blonde curls, a simple ruffled gown, and an expression that combined knowing, humor, sadness, and mystery. Ren stared, sensing he looked not just upon a likeness but the inner character of the woman, brought to life on the canvas.

"These are astonishing. These are good enough for exhibition, Rhette."

"Someday, I hope to." She nodded. "I take lessons from Angelica Kauffman, and she wants me to do a portrait I can exhibit at the Royal Academy of Fine Arts. She is one of only two female members, but she wants there to be more of us. I've been attempting my mother," Harriette went on, moving past two versions of a darkly lit, brooding figure Ren recognized as Mrs. Smythe. "But you, Ren." She tossed her arms into the air with a dramatic flourish. "You could be my masterpiece."

He snorted. "A tongue-tied cripple." He peeked at her table and saw papers scattered across it, all bearing a very familiar face. "I see you've already begun."

"Yes, I didn't sleep well last night, so I made some initial sketches. I'll do much better now that I have you in person. Give me a moment to prepare."

She went to the sitter's corner and with a few whisks and tugs she rolled up the Turkish carpet, draped a large linen sheet over the couch, and replaced the claw-footed ornament with a tall bronze stand with hanging lamps in antique style. She laid down a woven mat patterned with a geometrical mosaic and tossed a tasseled pillow upon the couch, and suddenly the corner was transformed into the boudoir of a Roman emperor.

"I'll decide later if I want you standing or sitting. For now, come here, and stop calling yourself a cripple." Her eyes moved down his body as he started toward her, and his blood heated. "You were wonderful last night. Very commanding."

When he thought hard about it, he could move easily, or with something passing for a measured gait. He'd been taken off guard last night. "I nearly fell on my face. And you heard me stammer. It was awful, Rhette, after you left. The looks of pity and all the stares—" His throat closed, his tongue swelling. "Don't leave me like that again."

"Did you talk to that very interesting girl in the corner? She was watching me as if she knew me. I want to find out who she is."

She guided him as he sat, studied his posture, and then her hands were on him again, pushing at a shoulder, pulling a thigh forward, rearranging his neckcloth. Heat coursed through him from every place her hands touched. He couldn't help but respond to her nearness, to the whisper of fabric, to the sight of her dusty-red curls falling against her sleek neck. She smoothed his hair, tightening the strip of fabric he'd used to tie it back, which brought her bosom directly before his face, close enough to kiss. Ren stifled a groan and hoped she wouldn't notice his cockstand.

He didn't want her pity, either. He was the sodding fool who wanted a woman who didn't want him back, not in that way. Her touch held nothing coy or loverlike, and her expression held the calculation of a professional as she went to the window and adjusted the curtain until the light fell exactly as she wanted. The light also outlined the shape of her through the white fabric of her gown, and she was more perfect than he'd imagined. Ren adjusted his seat slightly so the fabric of his breeches didn't pull quite so tightly across the straining volume in his crotch.

"Everyone wanted to know more about you," he said. "The ones who didn't talk to me out of sheer pity were quizzing me for information on you."

"There's little to know about me." She went to her table and sorted through the papers until she found her sketchbook. "Harriet Smythe, painter to the Earl of Renwick. I'll make you so appealing that young ladies will be forming a queue."

"I don't want a queue." The posture she'd put him in was, surprisingly, not uncomfortable. He sat erect, but his body was relaxed, the humiliations of recent memory fading in their sting. "My mother, of course, wants me to reach as high as possible. But none of those young ladies—" His throat tightened, steering him away from a confession he didn't want to pursue. "I see you still carry your porte crayon everywhere."

She held up the small brass cylinder she'd produced from a pocket. "The great Sir Joshua Reynolds says an artist should never be without her porte crayon." She sat on the stool, her skirts settling in a soft nest around her, and pushed up her wide sleeves. She flipped open the pad across her knees and pointed at one of the oils propped against the wall. "Look there, at

Mama, and wear the expression you had in the ballroom last night. That 'I don't want to be here but I will suffer these fools with patience' countenance."

He curbed a smile. He'd been suffering from something much different last night, mostly a wealth of confusion and dread at being exposed to strange eyes, mixed with debilitating desire over how luscious Harriet Smythe had become. "How is your mother?"

"Gracefully ailing and beset by nerves, as usual. She's grown increasingly ill and bitter in the past years. She spends hours complaining to Mrs. Demant and anyone who will listen how unpleasant it is to be dependent on a merchant's family, when she was raised in a castle with hundreds of servants, a whole realm at her feet, or so she says. Frankly it was a relief to leave her for school, and I'm afraid I'm not the dutiful daughter I ought to be. Mrs. Demant took her on fancying to have a forlorn princess under her roof, and Mrs. Demant can keep her. My aunt and I send money. That's enough."

"But if she is noble, Rhette, that would change things for you, wouldn't it?"

"Doubtful." She paused, debating her next words. "She might go back to Silesia, and in truth I don't know why she hasn't, if she had it so much better there. I think my aunt receives communications from the old country, but even if my mother does return there, I don't see why I should. Turn your chin a hair to the left—no, your left."

Ren studied the elegant oil of Harriette's mother, in which she had captured the air of lost nobility and softened the woman's habitual sour expression. Harriette's lack of loyalty to her mother didn't bother him. He felt no loyalty to his parents, either, only a sense of duty. But he sensed Harriette would walk on live coals for her aunt, and he understood that feeling.

"Amalie is coming to visit," he remarked, looking for ways to bring her into his life.

"Lady Amalie? Your sister?" Harriette lowered her crayon. "I've never met her. She's coming to see you?"

"I suppose that is her purpose. I meant to travel up to Bolton Abbey when I had things in order here, but she wants to visit London. She's never been."

"But she's coming at the end of the Season. Your mother won't be able to launch her until the fall."

"Oh, Amalie doesn't want to be launched, and my mother won't do it." At Harriette's surprised look, he attempted to explain, and found the words lacking. "Amalie is—like me. There are...imperfections."

Harriette shrugged. He didn't understand how she had never cared about his physical limitations, or anyone else's, when the rest of the world regarded these as outward signifiers of inward lack. "Surely not enough to prevent her from being introduced to Society."

"I don't think she wishes it, and Mother wants to spare herself the talk." And stares of pity. And speculation about what, exactly, the Countess of Renwick had done wrong to spawn not one monstrous child, but two.

"I want to meet her." Harriette went back to work with her porte crayon. "Is this why her ladyship wants you to marry well? Because she supposes your sister won't?"

"That, and I am the heir. I have to pass on the noble name and all its burdens," Ren said bitterly.

She paused and considered him from a new angle. "Don't you want children?"

"I do." The firmness of this declaration surprised him. He'd always known he was obliged to produce offspring. When Harriette asked him, he found he wanted to. But he still felt the old dread about what any child he sired might inherit.

"I find, though, I have a sentimental vein. I want to raise my heirs with a woman who adores me. I want my children to have an indulgent papa and a doting mama." Figures he had never had in his life, certainly. "You think that silly?" he asked when she raised her brows.

"A fantasy, rather," she murmured. She looked at him intently, drew a few lines on her pad, looked up at him, and used the side of her hand to rub out a line and try again. Her concentration, even though she was merely analyzing the shape of him and not peering inside his soul, made his breeches stir anew.

"What you'll find is a well-mannered and well-trained trained woman who marries you to secure her station in life," she said, her hand moving as she spoke. "She'll decorate your home and bear the requisite children. You will provide her pin money and hope she will be discreet about her affairs, and you will look elsewhere for passion and amusement."

Elsewhere. Did that mean her? His chest tightened at the thought. "Don't you want a husband who adores you?" he asked. "Children who think you the center of their world?"

"Bah," she answered. "I can think of nothing less conducive to my art. A doting husband and children shall be ever wanting my attention, when I could be drawing or painting. And they shall expect me to do things like make puddings and sew buttons, and take trips to the spa, and make a fuss over birthdays and Christmas. I should have no liberty to do as I pleased."

His throat ached at the thought of Harriette at the center of such a pleasant domestic scene. "What if you had a husband who let you do as you pleased?"

She paused, the porte crayon and its black chalk hovering above her paper. "Does such a creature exist?"

He would let her do as she pleased. He would allow her anything, in return for the gift of Harriette under his protection, under his roof. In his bed. If only he could marry *her*. "What about passion?"

"Fine for a night, or three. I've found infatuations fade quickly."

Her look was that of the trained artist, her gaze tracing his brow and examining his eyes. He wanted to take the pencil from her hand and lace his fingers with her slim, capable ones. He wanted to make her remember how she'd pressed shamelessly against him, her mouth open to his seeking tongue, the low moans of pleasure that had escaped her throat.

That memory was doing nothing to ease his cockstand, either. He couldn't be at attention the entire time she sketched him, which might be awhile, as she tore one page from her book, moved her stool a few inches to the other side, and began again.

"I find it di-difficult to believe any man's infatuation with you would fade."

"Oh, you darling. My first patron, my very first commission when I came to London, a corpulent old squire, I thought he was sincerely interested. But his attentions were not very— mmm, flattering, shall we say? And after I allowed it, because I wanted to understand what all the fuss was about, I found he expected I would reduce my fee because I had enjoyed his favors."

Ren was both fascinated and outraged at the thought of another man touching Harriette, gaining access to her delectable body. The thought of a fat, self-satisfied squire churning away atop her, taking the pleasure Ren wanted for himself, made his cock harder.

He was filthy and wrong. He'd often thought so.

"Have there been others?" he growled.

"There was a military man. He was going to a posting abroad and wanted to take me, but I didn't want to leave my aunt, and Mrs. Kauffman had just consented to tutor me. I would have gone to Paris, where I might meet Élisabeth Vigée Le Brun or Adelaide Labille-Guiard, who is portrait painter to the royal family. But he was going to Madrid, and I know of no female painters working in Madrid."

"And then?" Ren asked miserably. He didn't want to hear that other men had known Harriette Smythe, had the liberty to touch and pleasure her. And yet he wanted to hear every detail, because the torment of not knowing was worse than the torment of knowing.

She shrugged. "A German margrave—not the Graf von Hardenburg, I knew he was married when he arrived. But the margrave was a mistake, and I'm old enough to have learned my lesson."

Ren smothered a strangled sound. Harriette was all of one-and-twenty, four years younger than he. But as always, her knowledge of the world and her self-command made her seem older.

She ripped a page out of her pad and held it up, comparing the sketch to his face. "You look appalled. Surely you left a string of lovers scattered across several countries. The papers were keen to report on the beautiful courtesans you kept company with."

Courtesans, not lovers. He had to pay women to touch him, and the experience had been, collectively and individually, so awful that the very thought of attempting to make love to a woman gave him a cold sweat and shaking hands.

Any woman, that is, but Harriette Smythe. In her case, he could imagine making love to her all too vividly. It was causing him extreme discomfort.

"And your lover now?" he asked, assuming that was the reason she was not trembling and sighing and giving him looks of open longing, as he was her.

"No more mistakes. No more indulgences. I intend to focus on my art." She flipped to a fresh page in her sketchbook.

A biting jealousy reared up. He'd stopped by a bookseller on the short jaunt to Charles Street, intending to satisfy his curiosity, then wished he hadn't. "The way you focused on your sketches of the Graf von Hardenburg," he said.

Her crayon paused in mid-air. "You don't approve," she observed. "Neither does your mother, nor anyone else at her *soiree* last evening, except perhaps Lady Bess. I knew those sketches were going to cause me nothing but trouble."

"You made him—" He couldn't say it. The man staring out from those sketches had been insanely, almost unconscionably attractive. She'd made him look dashing and yet insolent at the same time, untouchable, yet inevitably a man whom scads of women, and some other men, would want to touch.

She lowered the crayon, regarding him with an expression that was suddenly not professional in the least. "I could do the same for you, Ren," she said.

His throat went dry. "What do you mean?"

"It worked for the count, and you're ten times finer looking than he is." She drew the outline of his head and shoulders in the air. "I'm still going to do your portrait. A beautiful pastel, with Roman ruins behind you. But you're already an object of interest, the mysterious young earl coming home from abroad. Prints of you would sell madly. And if you were the new fashion —think of it," she whispered, her eyes glimmering with green lights. "No more pity. No more stiff courtesy or barely veiled politeness. Women would fall over themselves for the chance to meet you. Start fights for the honor of a dance."

"I don't dance," Ren said in a hoarse voice. How could he, with his foot? "I don't think I want that kind of attention, Rhette."

"Not be the subject of admiration?" She rose from the stool

and moved toward him, holding out the latest sketch. Her breasts were at his eye level, the skin of her bosom flushing pink with excitement. "The object of fantasy? Look at you."

She held out the sketch, and he was amazed. She'd somehow managed to soften every flaw, the plain hair, the too-heavy brow and jaw, the cheekbones that belonged on a woman, the lips that were too straight and the forehead that was too high. She'd made him look... He swallowed.

"But that's illusion," he said. "Not me. They'd look at the real me and be disappointed."

"You underestimate yourself, Renwick," she whispered. "No one could look at you and be disappointed."

He held her gaze, and a hot wave rolled from his neck to his groin. Her eyes were wide, soft, full of mischief. Her lips were still that natural red that looked as if she'd been eating berries. She was magnificent, with her long lean limbs and unbelievable breasts, all graceful curves from neck to ankle. He wanted to pull her down atop him and never let her go.

"Besides, how can this possibly be comfortable?" She held out a hand at waist level, palm up, and he thought she was indicating his very obvious erection.

"Er." He shifted, trying to lessen the ache. "It's because you keep staring at me, I'm afraid."

"Most of my sitters can't hold a straight posture for so long. You've already proven more patient than Princess, that's certain. We shall take a pause and try something new." She placed her hands on his shoulders, pushing him gently backwards against the low back of the couch. The movement made the loose draw-string neck of her gown gape, and he stifled a groan of agony. "Let me try, Ren," she said in a sultry voice.

"Try—" Climbing into his lap, settling that lovely bottom against his groin, kissing him until they both forgot where and who they were? *Yes.* "Try what?"

"Prints. Aquatint or mezzotint, whatever works best. I'll get the finest printer in town to make etchings and sell them out of her shop. A head or three-quarters, or perhaps full body. We'll see how they sell and if you're a sensation, we'll make more."

"Not the foot," he said as she pulled gently at the thigh of his bad leg, urging him to place his boot across his other knee, a relaxed and negligent posture.

"Shush. No one cares about your foot as much as you do, and with the boot, you can't tell." She rested a hand on the gleaming black leather that had appeared cleaned and polished at his command to his valet that morning, though now spotted with soil from London's dirty streets. "I want to see what this marvelous doctor achieved."

"Not today." He had already bared enough of himself to her. And knowing she had sexual experience, that her comfort with touching him was not solely because it was him but because she was familiar with the terrain of the male body—all his self-doubts and self-hatred flared to the surface.

Her eyes moved upward from his boot, her gaze flickering over his cockstand, and the damn thing bobbed, as if waving at her. A smile quirked her lips, bringing out that enchanting pucker at each side. Her movements were slow and sensual as she lifted her hands to his neckcloth and started untying it. He nearly groaned as her warm fingers brushed his neck. He held his breath as she unbuttoned the top of his waistcoat, revealing his shirt and a bit of skin, and the amulet he wore on a small silver chain.

She touched the chi-ro symbol with a fingertip, her expression melting. "You still wear this?"

Her look made him want to fasten his arms around her. "My sign that I will conquer. Something. Someday."

"First we're going to conquer all the fools who don't see the real you."

She peeled his morning coat off his shoulders and laid it on the couch, then made him lean back with his elbows draped over the back of the couch, hands dangling at his sides. She set to arranging the sleeves of his shirt, the ends of the neckcloth, and the amulet just below his collarbone, daringly bare.

"The real me needs to be undressed?"

In truth he could sit like this all day, with Harriette hovering near him, touching him, seducing him with her lovely scent. He might expire from the agony of sustained arousal, but it would be worth it.

"You're too intimidating in full dress," she answered. "I want you in *dishabille*. So the ladies can imagine you in bed." She leaned back and regarded him thoughtfully. "Oh, good. Keep that look, that sleepy, satisfied look. It gives me the shivers."

"It does?" he called, but she turned and reassumed possession of her stool, sketchbook, and crayon, and fell to sketching busily, her hand moving so quickly that he wondered what would emerge. He endeavored to keep the look she wanted, an easy feat as it merely required watching her, the way she bit her lip and her brows drew together when a line was giving her trouble, the way her sleeve flared when she made large strokes, the way one ringlet of hair inched toward the cleft between her breasts.

"I want to see," he said when she'd burned through several sheets of paper and finally gave a long, satisfied sigh.

She rolled her shoulders and flexed her wrists. "I want your permission to sell them first. Are you going to require a share of the profits?"

"You can keep any profits there are. I want to see." He rose and moved toward her, happy to stand. He couldn't tell how long he'd been sitting, but long enough for the muscles in his manipulated, surgically altered leg to become painfully stiff. He limped toward her as she spread the sketches she'd done out on her worktable.

"Your word first!" She turned, holding her arms out playfully as if she meant to prevent him from seeing, and he couldn't stop himself. He stepped close and slipped his arms beneath hers, showing her the barricade was useless.

They both froze. His body was a mere inch from hers, and there was a good deal less fabric between them than there had been the night before. Her eyelashes fluttered, and her chest lifted as she drew in a breath. Her gaze dropped from his eyes to his mouth. Slowly, slowly he bent his head, giving her plenty of time to cry foul or push him away.

She didn't push him away. She slipped a hand around the back of his neck and brought his head towards her, matching his lips firmly to hers, and they fell into last night's kiss as though they'd never left off.

It was better this time. Last night they'd explored and discovered, cautious and experimental. This time her tongue twined about his without hesitation. Her mouth moved with his in perfect rhythm, yielding, tormenting. Her body arced against his, pressing greedily. He slid one hand into her hair, holding her head for his plundering kiss, and slid the other down her back to her bottom. She wasn't wearing any sort of padding and his hand shaped her supple roundness, nudging and lifting her hips into his. She moaned and her head fell back as his mouth roved to the dip at the corner of her lips, down her jaw, and across her silken neck.

His arousal intensified, and he froze with his lips on her collarbone. He was going to spend right here in his breeches if he didn't stop. Excitable and overeager, just like the courtesan had said. He didn't want Harriette to see his ineptitude.

"What was I going to give my word about?" he whispered against her skin.

She gave a low, throaty hum as he stepped back and she untangled herself. Her eyes heavy-lidded, cheeks flushed, lips swollen, she didn't look the least embarrassed about indulging in passion. She'd fit herself against his groin without shame, as if she wanted the same thing he did.

She wanted him.

"You could marry me, Rhette." The words held a quiet ferocity. He couldn't believe his own daring, voicing the thing he suddenly wanted more than anything. "Bear my children. It would save me a great deal of trouble," he added, appealing to her practical side.

She met this plea with a short bark of laughter and turned to the sketches on her worktable. He thought he caught a flash of some other emotion in her eyes—triumph or remorse, he couldn't tell—before she turned away.

"You need a countess you can be proud of, Ren. Someone worthy of you. I would only bring you gossip and shame, and besides, I already told you. I'm not the domestic sort."

Cautiously he settled his hands about her waist, stroking his thumbs along her sides. She wasn't wearing a corset. "Then be with me otherwise," he said hoarsely. He'd take whatever she would give him. Scraps and crumbs. Stolen moments in shadow. Pride was the last thing on his mind.

"An affair?" She stilled as he nosed among the curls at the side of her neck. She quivered. He hated how she said the word so casually, as if she were accustomed to affairs. "Worse shame and gossip."

But she tilted her head so he might kiss her neck, and he slid his hands upward to her lovely breasts. He could scarcely comprehend where his assurance came from. He'd never been so bold with a woman. But there was nothing of awkwardness when he was with Harriette. Her form clasped in his arms was the most right and natural thing in the world.

"Do you care about gossip?" he whispered against her earlobe.

"You ought to." She moved aside the lock of hair tickling his nose. "You're the one to be married."

He nudged his erection against that voluptuously soft bottom and she pressed back into him, accepting. He rolled his hips against her, and she groaned. Pleasure surged, and he stilled before he embarrassed himself, then stepped back and let his hands fall away. She leaned on the table, steadying herself as he withdrew.

"Tell me when I can see you again."

"You can come here tomorrow and wear the suit you wore last night. I was thinking to begin with a study in gouache, but it happens I found the perfect pigment to capture that suit, and your eyes. It's called Prussian blue." She sounded completely calm, but the tips of her ears were bright pink.

She didn't want him otherwise, but she felt desire. He savored that for a moment. Joy threatened to burst his chest. He set all other concerns aside, the self-doubting inner voice, his unpromising history.

"I want to see you for passion. Not work."

She turned back to face him, bracing her hands on the table and smiling easily. "Painting is my passion."

"I'm thinking of pleasure we both can enjoy." Now *where* had this seductive side come from? The Italian courtesan wouldn't believe this was the same man she'd tried so hopelessly to tutor.

That enchanting pucker emerged at the corners of her lips. "Have you been to the Marylebone Pleasure Gardens? They're my favorite. They often feature female singers, and there is a female chef. I'm very fond of her tarts."

There would be lanes and paths for walking, where everyone could observe his staggering gait. There would be strangers to greet, sure to catch him out with a stammer. There would be female caterwauling of the kind he could not stomach, and he could already guess the tarts were overly sweet.

He would be with Harriette. "Tomorrow afternoon? I shall come for you in the coach."

"Nothing so stately. I can borrow my aunt's cabriolet." She held one of the sketches up to him, titled "The Lord At Ease." It showed a debonair, aristocratic man lounging on his couch, one booted foot across a knee, his elegant coat draped next to him. His shoulders looked broad, his chest powerful in the waistcoat and ruffled shirt, and there was something vaguely piratical in the chi-ro emblem hanging below his throat. There was something piratical in his expression as well as he gazed off into the distance, as if he commanded all he saw.

She'd emphasized his jaw and high cheekbones while minimizing his nose, making him look contemplative without being dreamy. The image was calm and self-assured, but with a hint of troubled feeling in the eyes, as if he reflected on difficulties. The effect was arresting, more intriguing than the lazy insolence she'd given the Graf von Hardenburg.

Was this him? Was this how Harriette saw him? His heart thumped.

"I can't see anyone paying a ha'penny for one of those."

"If these sketches don't become a sensation and make all the ladies of London regard you as a prime *parti*, I'll pay whatever forfeit you choose," she replied. "Now go. Let yourself be seen in the coffee shops and clubs. Knock up some friends and stage a lark. Assure your mother that you are on the hunt for a bride and you aren't caught in my dreadful snares."

"I am, though," he said as he pulled on his silk morning coat. He saw no reason to be coy with her. Harriette had seen him undressed and she had seen him aroused, simply by the way she was looking at him. She had seen him as a ruined boy, sucking back snot and tears after his tutor had caned him yet again for being a stupid cripple. She had seen him taunted by boys bigger than he, and she had seen the looks of horror on the faces of the lovely ladies in his drawing room last night as he limped over to meet them. No need to hide his heart from her.

"In your snares," he added softly as she gave him a questioning look, her face uptilted, her brows dark and dramatic in her piquant face.

Her eyes shimmered with gold lights. "George Matheson. Earl of Renwick." He startled at the name; only Amalie called him George. "You are going to make some woman a very happy countess."

It was a polite way of setting him aside. Ren nodded and withdrew, making his way down the steps with dignified leisure. The tall butler opened the door for him and sent a boy to the mews for his horse. Ren kept his air of calm aloofness, the armor he showed to the world. He'd let none see that he was hurting. The woman he loved had sent him on his way and, moreover, wished him luck finding a countess, when he wished above all that his countess could be her.

CHAPTER EIGHT

"Oh, he's a great gorger," Mary Darly said. She laid out the three sketches Harriette had given her on the counter of her print shop. "You've done him up nicely."

"That's him to the life, without any improving." Harriette set down her leather-bound portfolio of sketches. "He's rather a prime article."

"That he is." Mrs. Darly smiled. "People won't know what to think when I turn from my satirical prints to handsome young bucks."

Harriette regarded the enlarged prints hanging on the shop wall high above the neat columns of bookshelves holding Mrs. Darly's wares. The wooden floor was swept clean, and a table near the back allowed customers to open and peruse the larger folio volumes. While the Darlys were known for their caricatures, many of them poking fun at the excesses of the fashionable, Mrs. Darly had helped make Harriette's sketches of the Graf von Hardenburg a rage. She hoped she might do the same for Renwick.

Did she want other women looking at him and admiring

him? The small voice nagged at the back of Harriette's mind. Did she want to share him with the world?

Of course she did, she told herself. She wanted the rest of the world to recognize his many fine qualities. And if it helped draw female interest, then he would have his pick of brides, and she would have done her best by him as a friend.

Friends don't kiss friends with open mouths and try to put hands down their breeches, the nagging voice said.

"This will be a break from my series on wigs," Mrs. Darly announced. "Do you want to see one?"

"Oh, yes." One artist to another, Harriette never turned down a chance to study Mrs. Darly's work. She was a talented engraver as well as a print seller. She'd written the book on how to draw caricatures, and their prints of the exaggerated styles of a fashion craze that had lately afflicted young men had gained the Darlys' business the nickname of The Macaroni Shop. Harriette liked visiting The Acorn in Ryders Court, as it was the shop Mrs. Darly managed herself, and she often showed Harriette her works in progress.

Harriette pressed the skirts of her polonaise gown to her legs to keep from sweeping pamphlets and broadsides off their stands as she followed Mrs. Darly through the narrow door leading to her printing parlor. She looked around with envy at the assorted presses, the large copper sheets used for engravings, the stacks of papers waiting to be printed and cut. The smells of rosin, ink, and the acids used to burn lines into the copper plates excited her nose. Mrs. Darly was a woman allowed to pursue her trade, and no one thought the less of her for it; in fact her talent was celebrated. Harriette wanted that kind of liberty and regard for herself.

The paper propped on the easel showed a print of a woman wearing a gown much like Harriette's, but the bustle was enormously exaggerated, and the wig atop her head, crowned with ribbons, was taller than the woman herself, floating above her head like an enormous balloon. Harriette giggled. The figure's self-satisfied expression made the caricature complete.

"This is marvelous. It will be as big a sensation as your Macaronis," she said.

"Not as big a sensation as your interesting young man," Mrs. Darly replied. "I'll do a simple etching with some engraving, I think? To make an aquatint or a mezzotint will be more expensive and time-consuming, and might make him look more serious than we'd like. Or I could add coloring, if you wish."

"An etching will be splendid to begin with. We can talk about making a finer set of portraits if this set becomes popular."

With a bit of discussion, they settled on a price at which Mrs. Darly would purchase the prints, and the percentage of the profits that Harriette would receive if they sold. Sharing in the profits wasn't something many printers offered; in fact, in this business, it was more often an author had to pay a publisher to print their book. But Harriette liked working with Mrs. Darly, woman to woman, with no nonsense, subterfuge, or haggling, as she'd found too often to be the case when she approached male print sellers. None of the condescension for a female artist, either.

"Are you taking students yet?" Mrs. Darley asked as they walked back to the front of the shop, where a group of customers had entered. "I am to the point where I'm turning people away for drawing lessons. I could send them to you if you wished."

Harriette experienced a thrill all through her body at those words—a thrill almost as exciting as when Ren had slipped his arms about her at her worktable. "I'm not certain I'm ready to set out my sign as a drawing teacher. I'm still taking lessons myself."

"A good thing if one is always learning," Mrs. Darly said

cheerfully. "But I expect you know enough to teach others the basic principles. I have your direction in Charles Street, and if I find a likely young candidate, I'll send them your way, shall I?" Her eyes twinkled. "Another addition to the Catherine Club."

"I don't know why we're calling ourselves that," Harriette said, somewhat abashed, and giddy to think of herself as a drawing master. Inspiring and teaching young women the way her drawing instructor at Miss Gregoire's had opened a new way of seeing the world to Harriette. For a moment she allowed herself to imagine a studio of her own, perhaps a tall-windowed shop like this one, where patrons came for sittings and eager young students came to learn at her feet. A sign over the door that said Harriette Smythe, Painter.

Or whatever her real name was. Maybe it was time to have that conversation with her mother. She'd shied away from pressing her mother about the story of her life, in part because she didn't want to hear she was the love child of an illicit union that had cost her mother her genteel station and her home. And in part because Harriette had been content at Miss Gregoire's and now as part of her aunt's household, where she was allowed to pursue her interests. She didn't know any other home than England. She didn't wish for any home beyond these shores.

"Something I can help you find?" Mrs. Darly greeted her customers pleasantly. Their gaily bedecked hats, dainty shawls, and broad skirts marked them as ladies of means and leisure. They were women for whom the first blush of youth had passed, but not their alliance to fashion.

"It *is* her," one of the women remarked in a hushed tone. She wore a lace cap piled high on her head and large silk rosettes pinned to her bodice and sleeves.

Harriette looked up, thinking the women had come to meet Mrs. Darly, a talented woman who had made a success of herself. But her smile of amusement slid off her face as she realized they were staring at her.

"From Lady Renwick's last night," the second said. Tiny feathers sprouted from the top of her wig, and a black ribbon around her throat fluttered as she spoke. "Renwick's—" She whispered a word behind her glove, and her companion's eyes rounded.

"And we saw her in the very act of furnishing her sketches to the print seller!" The first woman raised gloved fingers to painted red lips. "Oh, what Lady Renwick will say when we tell her!"

Harriette raised her eyebrows at Mrs. Darly. "Do they realize I can hear them?" she asked in a stage whisper. It was beyond hope that the women were discussing her in tones of admiration. They were licking their lips at the prospect of scandal.

Mrs. Darly was a businesswoman who didn't miss an opportunity. She stepped forward with a smile. "If you're looking for works by Miss Smythe," she said, waving a hand in Harriette's direction, "I am happy to say I will have a new series of prints available for sale in the next day or so. They're sure to suit a lady's artistic sensibilities. Would you like to order a set today?"

Harriette gathered up her portfolio and fled the shop as the women edged toward Mrs. Darly, still watching Harriette with wide eyes as though she were a creature on exhibit at the Exchange or the Tower Zoo.

Mortification pursued her. Renwick's what? What was the gossip running about her now? How bad was it?

Harriette plunged down the narrow alley that led to Cranbourne Street and then turned toward Leicester Square, where she had left the cabriolet and her attendants. The summer afternoon was hazy and not overly warm and the men lounged at their leisure, Jock perched atop Hyperion, the coach horse, while Beater leaned against the side of the vehicle. The two men exchanged comments with each other as they regarding the passersby strolling the square and its public gardens.

"Too many patches," pronounced Jock as the men's eyes followed the shapely figure of a woman in a gaudy gown who minced by holding a dainty parasol over her bone-white face. "Sign o' the French disease."

"Cyprian," Beater grunted.

Ah, the liberty of men to evaluate every passing female. Though women did it too, as she had just seen in Mrs. Darly's bookshop. "If you are done observing the wildlife, may we go?" Harriette asked acidly.

Beater bolted to attention, crumpling the paper wrapping of a meat pie he'd purchased off some passing vendor. "There's Princess yet," he rumbled, and Harriette sighed.

"Still visiting the Holophusikon, I gather?"

It was veil for an assignation of some sort or another, she knew. Princess had no interest in natural history, far less the collection of curiosities that Sir Ashton Lever had put on display after purchasing Leicester House, the great edifice that lined the north side of the square. But Princess was a consummate actor, and if a lover wanted to pay the five shillings to gain her entrance to the collection, she wouldn't decline.

"How long do you suppose we must wait?" Harriette asked. She looked about at the people roaming the square, some of them the fashionable out for a stroll, others of the middling class out to watch the fashionable, and the working class going about their business. This was an opportunity. She withdrew her porte crayon from her pocket and looked about for a convenient place to unfold her stool.

Normally the rhythm of her hand while she sketched brought her mind to calm attention, but today the thoughts ran rampant. The whispers of the ladies in the print shop rattled her. It was one thing to have people who were trying to sell newspapers print foolish speculations in the gossip paragraphs, but quite another to encounter the ridicule in real life. It appeared the Countess of Renwick wasn't alone in thinking Harriette unfit for polite company.

Renwick's—what? Her hand slowed as the obvious occurred to her. It wasn't Harriette's artistic choices that had suddenly made her *persona non grata* in polite circles. It was the assumption that, to see the Graf in such intimate exposure, she must be his mistress.

Oh, why had she not asked Mrs. Darly to keep her authorship of the sketches of Renwick a secret? That kiss with Ren had addled her head. All she could think about was changing the way people saw him so they perceived what she did, the nobility of his character, his gentle nature and his moral strength, along with the undeniable beauty of his person. She wanted to erase the snickers of contempt from his peers and the looks of horror or pity from the young women who saw him approaching them. She wanted him adored by all, as she adored him.

The new sketches would be as good as declaration that she had lifted her skirts for Ren. They confirmed her as a woman completely lacking in virtue.

Well, she *hadn't* any virtue, Harriette thought savagely, smudging an errant line with the side of her hand. She'd made some foolish decisions, tried to be mature and sophisticated before she was ready, and now she had to pay the price. That short-sightedness and being caught up in the moment had made her unfit for the society of those to whom a woman's virtue meant everything.

It made her unfit to marry someone like Ren.

She flipped the ruined page with enough force to tear it and attacked the fresh sheet with her crayon. What would happen if she pursued an affair with Ren as, foolishly and off her head from the glory of his kisses, she'd more or less promised him? Flushed with a desire she'd never known, filled with nothing but thoughts of when she could touch and taste and hold him again, heady with the triumph of knowing this large, splendid, wonderful man hungered for her, she'd been ready to grant him anything he asked. It wouldn't hurt him to be known as a man who had sampled Harriette Smythe. But what would it do to her?

The morning sun had given way to a grey fog, but that wasn't what blocked Harriette's vision when she looked up. Three strollers stood before her, young men who apparently still subscribed to the Macaroni fashions that had made Mrs. Darly's reputation, even though the look had fallen out of vogue. Their wigs were at least two feet high, with side curls the size of a man's arm. Their coats and waistcoats glared with crimson and yellow silk, their loose breeches in a contrasting color, and they sported buttons everywhere a button could fit. The aroma of three different kinds of scented water, overlaying the strong scent of unwashed male bodies, made Harriette's nose recoil.

"The very likeness of yon demirep," said the one with the tiny hat atop his wig. He affected a high voice and the drawl that had been adopted by those of the Duchess of Devonshire's set. The upper of the upper crust, or aspiring to be there, Harriette guessed. "It must be our artist knows well the *demimondaine.*"

That set of beautiful, often high-born women known for their sexual accessibility. Harriette's heart sank. Did all of London now know who she was, or of her reputation, from one appearance last night at Lady Renwick's soiree?

"Indeed, which is for sale? The portrait or the lady?" drawled a second, taking out one of a number of quizzing glasses attached to his waistcoat. He also carried several fobs and watches, a snuff box, and what appeared to be a spyglass, a waterfall of clinking items decorating his chest. His overlong walking stick stuck out behind him, barely missing his companions' legs as they clustered before Harriette on her stool. "And which demands the higher price?"

He was suggesting *she* was for sale, not the Cyprian in her sketch, the painted lady whom Jock had noted on her rounds about the square. Harriette stiffened, curling her fingers around her crayon. She had a devilish urge to snake out her hand and leave a long dark streak down one of the delicate white stockings cloaking a bloated calf.

"I'll gladly sell you the sketch if you've taken a liking for it, sir," she said. "Five guineas."

The third one giggled and slurred his words. "And does that give possession for only the afternoon, or the 'ole night?" Was he tipsy? At this time of day? "Any mon c'n get a print o' Miss Smythe for—" he hiccupped— "a farthing or two, can't 'ee?"

Harriette didn't miss his implication in the word *print*. "Only the sketch is for sale," she said coldly. "And the cost is ten guineas."

"Oh, it prices itself high, it does!" exclaimed the first rogue. He plucked her portfolio from her hands, flipping past her current sketch to the more recent ones. He sneered as he saw the several studies of Ren, various angles of his head, three quarters, and the full-body sketch of him lounging on the couch, looking directly at the viewer with a wicked come-hither gaze.

"Coming up in the world, are ye, Miss Smythe?" the dandy said. "Can this be due to your association with the Earl of Runtwick?"

Harriette saw red. That awful nickname couldn't still be circulating about, not after he'd come so far and matured so much. If she were a man, she could challenge this macaroni to a duel for such an insult. As a woman, she had no weapon but words.

"You dare," she said quietly, looking the man in the eye. "You *dare*. Give me back my sketches."

"What will his lordship do?" the second sneered. "Chase us?" His fellows guffawed at this.

Harriette pushed on the walking stick he held under his arm, using it to knock the first man in the leg. He yelped and dropped her portfolio. She snatched it up, dusting gravel and dirt from the cracks and creases.

"His lordship deserves your respect," she said in outrage. She'd faced down the young bullies of Shepton Mallet, only this time she did not have her slingshot. She could not command these fops to give Renwick his due.

"Why don't you lick his boots for us," sniggered the third man. "Add it to your other services."

They strolled away, laughing amongst themselves, and Harriette shook the last bit of gravel from her papers. Her hands trembled with anger, but her heart clenched with a heavier emotion. There would be no denying her ownership, once they circulated, of these daring pictures of Ren with his coat off, his neck bared to the gaze. These men had seen the sketches and would make the connection.

She'd promised Ren the popularity of her sketches would make him admired, just as her prior efforts had made the Graf von Hardenburg society's darling. But perhaps the attention that resulted for Ren might not be approving. Perhaps his peers would buy the sketches and make him an object of ridicule. Think him tainted by his association with Harriette.

And in the meantime, her reputation was in tatters. All of Society would assume she was his mistress.

She dusted off the skirts of her worn polonaise, which she didn't have the funds to replace. Foresight was not Harriette's strong suit, she would be the first to admit. But it now occurred to her that her sinking could bring any number of other people down with her. Association with her might injure Ren's prospects for marriage. And a stain on his image might affect his sister's prospects as well, for surely she had hopes of her own, no matter what her mother thought.

The papers would have far worse to say about the Countess of Calenberg's household than that they were unconventional. And Harriette would never be granted commissions from rich patrons if she were a scarlet woman. Families wouldn't hire her to paint them if they thought they could be tainted by the association. Only the curious would enlist her, and it would be a repeat of her sittings with the squire, who had assumed she was sexually promiscuous because she was an independent woman with a skill.

She couldn't have an affair with Ren, much as she wished to. She needed to salvage her reputation. She wanted entrée into the salons of the great, and she wanted their commissions.

She started in the direction of Cranbourne Street, overtaken by remorse. She must go back to The Acorn and tell Mrs. Darly she'd reconsidered selling her those sketches. They might harm Ren and they would certainly harm her.

But the weight of guineas in her reticule slowed and then stopped her before she had reached the cabriolet where Jock and Beater sat, still watching the parade of people about the square. Her sketches of the Graf von Hardenburg had been a sensation; there was every possibility that Ren's portraits would be even more popular. With those profits she could send funds to the Demants to pay her mother's doctor fees or provide her a small luxury. A handful of the coins in her purse could let Sorcha do a month of marketing and pay for the roof over all of their heads. The rest could buy Harriette pigments and canvas and a new set of brushes, all of which she needed if she wanted more work. She owed her aunt for supporting her all of these years.

Looking up, Harriette realized she stood before the house that belonged to Sir Joshua Reynolds, one of England's most admired painters and a man of unlimited talent and esteem. Reynolds could command virtually any price for his portraits. He was admitted into any circle and lauded for his skill.

She couldn't achieve what he had by producing racy sketches, or if she were thought a demirep. Popular prints wouldn't bring her the acclaim she wanted, the regard that someone like Angelica Kauffman could command as a member of the Royal Academy of Arts, or Adelaide Labille-Guiard, painter to the French princes.

She couldn't become Ren's mistress. She would paint a wonderful portrait of him, the most beautiful and noble portrait she'd ever done, but she wouldn't allow herself his kisses or his bed. He might not like her change of heart, but surely he would understand. He wanted a respectable wife, a household with happy children. Those were things Harriette could not give him.

To admit that felt like covering over a canvas she'd labored over for hours and days. It felt like cutting out a piece of her. But she had to do what was best for them both.

Blinking back tears, Harriette recognized one of the glamorous figures parading toward her as Princess, looking smug and satisfied and with a blush to her cheeks not caused by rouge.

"Finished and ready to head back to Charles Street, are we?" Harriette snapped.

"What is it biting me for?" Princess blinked heavy-lidded eyes. "Did my assignation go better than yours, then?"

There wouldn't be an assignation. Not for Harriette. She had to avoid the temptation of grown-up Ren, so handsome, so wicked, so wonderful.

The unshed tears stung Harriette's eyes as the women crammed themselves into the tiny carriage. Princess took the ribbons from Jock, and they jostled together as the back of the carriage dropped when Beater climbed to the groom's platform. Harriette steeled herself for the conversation she would have to have with Renwick.

No more foolish mistakes, no more short-sighted thinking. No more living for the sheer pleasure of the moment. She had a life to build and so did he, and in neither was there room for anything more than friendship.

CHAPTER NINE

There was no group of ruffled and silk-clad women in the dining parlor at the house on Charles Street this morning, no alarming perfumed flock of exotic creatures appraising him as the butler showed him in. Ren was glad for it. He couldn't remember a single name outside of the Countess of Calenberg. Harriette pushed every other person out of his sight when she was in a room, just as she pushed every other subject out of his thoughts when he was away from her. He climbed the stairs to the first-floor studio in a giddy tide of anticipation.

The two days apart had been agony, and though he sent her notes saying why he couldn't come, the excuses were demands he wouldn't have let keep him from Harriette if he had his choice. His man of business needed to acquaint him with the state of his finances and the many properties, investments, and debts under his control, now that he had reached his majority. Things had not been swimming happily along in his absence; there were signs of poor oversight with some of the properties and investments, and at Bolton Abbey, the ancestral seat of the Matheson family, he saw indications of sheer neglect.

His mother inundated him with friends she insisted he

meet, all from families of notable wealth and influence, with marriageable daughters. Fellows from his school days and time abroad called in a steady stream once they learned he was in town.

But the happiest distraction was the post chaise that had rolled up before Renwick House yesterday, unloading his sister, her maid, and enough luggage to suggest she meant to stay a while. It was a joy to hear her sweet, quiet voice about the house, though it was strange to have his family under the same roof. He and Amalie had grown up at Bolton Abbey, but the earl and countess had spent most of their time in London or circulating through their country estates. Ren hadn't lived with Amalie since the summer their father died.

The curtains in Harriette's studio were pulled back to flood the studio with light, the western stretches of London not being as subject to the constant smoke of coal fires as the City and eastern portions. Harriette stood before her work table, fiddling with brushes. She wore the same loose morning gown, but with a filmy neckerchief tucked into the bodice. Adorning her pinned-up coils of hair were a small orange flower and the brass cylinder that held her porte crayon.

He tossed hesitancy aside and crossed the room to her, not caring if she heard his uneven gait, the heavy thump of his modified boot. Harriette took him as he was. Seeing her, the delicate curve of her shoulder beneath the white gown, the straight line of her back standing among the works of art she had created, it didn't matter that she had scoffed at his impulsive offer of marriage. It didn't matter that his mother insisted Harriette was far beneath their class and had listed, in elaborate detail, all the reasons he ought not associate with her. All that mattered was that he could slide his hands around the delicious, slender warmth of her and press his lips against the soft side of her neck, inhaling traces of hair powder and chalk, soap and woman.

"Ren." Her soft gasp went straight to his groin. Boldly he swept a hand up her rib cage to her bosom. She wore no stays, and the warm globe of a breast fell into his palm, the nipple hardening beneath his fingers. His erection rose against her bottom, also not padded, and he froze. Overeager, as always. Would she laugh at him?

She moved away. "We mustn't," she said, and her voice shook.

"We're alone. Aren't we?" At last he thought to look around. The moment he entered the room, he saw only her.

"We are, but we cannot—indulge." She replaced the brushes she was holding into a ceramic vase and reached for a small jar.

"You wish to paint first. Business before pleasure." He breathed in the scent of whatever the jar held, some pungent binding agent. It was as intoxicating as she was.

"That, and—we cannot."

Cold horror rooted him to the floor. She didn't need to show him her face. He could guess at her expression. "I repulse you."

He ought to have known. He ought to have expected this. It was the reaction women always had to him, wasn't it? He'd been too primed, too eager, pawing her like a drooling puppy. He had no right. She hadn't invited his touch. He'd only assumed—

"I'm sorry," he grated out.

"That's not it." She whirled to face him. Her eyes were green as moss, the tight lines at their corners showing she held back some tempestuous feeling. The kissable indentations at the corners of her lips drooped. "You are—so very—I am desperate to paint you," she choked out. He couldn't read the emotion bridled in her voice. Her hands cradled his cheeks, soft and yet firm, with the slightest of calluses on her fingers.

He closed his eyes, bracing himself for the explanations that would follow. *You're a good man. But I—*She would make it about her preferences, not his flaws. But it would only end one way: *It's best we remain friends.* As if his feelings for her had ever been friendship, when she had been the one person in his entire life who protected him, avenged him, tended his wounds, and didn't shy when she had seen his deformed foot. It would kill him to be merely her friend, and he would die without having her in his life in any fashion in which she would take him.

"Look at me, Ren." She spoke softly, her husky voice coaxing his ears, her soft breath fanning his cheek. He dragged his eyes open.

"I desire you." Her lower lip trembled at the admission, and a flare of blinding hope catapulted through him. "You are—look at you. And you're Ren, my—"

She didn't complete the thought because he swooped in and pressed his mouth against hers, hauling her against his body. If she wanted him, then he was taking advantage, right now. He would persuade her past her reservations. He would show her that whatever her considerations, they didn't matter more than this intense pleasure. He would do anything for her. He was abjectly, entirely hers and couldn't even pretend otherwise. He would throw himself at her feet, he would promise her anything, and more importantly he would never stop kissing her, this senseless plunder, this relentless demand.

She melted against him, the crevice between her legs fitting neatly against his erection, her tongue plunging into his mouth and meeting his. Her fingers dug into his scalp as if she meant never to let him go. But when she shifted her leg so that his cock slid between her thighs, he felt the surge of wild, almost painful bliss that meant he was about to lose control and spend too early. He froze again, some helpless sound escaping his throat, and Harriette came to her senses.

Damn him. He was incapable even of this, of seducing a woman who wanted him past her scruples.

"Good God, how I want you," she breathed, prying her fingers out of his hair as if the movement took great effort. Her cheeks were flushed, her eyes shining gold. "If I thought for a moment I could get away with it, that we wouldn't be found out..."

She took a deep breath that fluttered the kerchief tucked into her neckline, and he quelled a savage urge to rip it from her and clamp his mouth to her tender breasts. His poor rejected cock bobbed at the thought, eager for completion, eager for Harriette. He took a step away from her, but it did nothing to steady him.

"But we *can't*," she whispered, and turned back to her table. He could have sworn he saw moisture in the corner of her eyes, save that he had never seen Harriette cry, not under the greatest duress.

"Tell me why. I deserve that much." Callous of him to insist on his needs, he realized. Why was he being a brute with the one woman who had ever been kind to him? He didn't like this in himself. Perhaps he was going mad with lust.

"Go stand over there." She pointed toward the nook before a set of tall windows where she had set a half-sized sculpted pillar, not marble but painted to look as such. A rug with deep pile covered the floor, and the couch had been pushed to one side.

"You're still going to paint me?"

"Standing, with a neoclassical background. Lean one elbow against the pillar and look thoughtfully toward the fireplace."

Hours in her presence. Days. The most exquisite of torments, watching her without being allowed to touch, and collecting impressions that would haunt him into his life without her and into sweaty, throbbing dreams. He must have been truly evil in a former life to have been so cursed in this one.

He stood where she indicated, and she moved around him and wrestled with the draperies at the window until the light fell as she wished. Then she came to him in a cloud of delicious scent and adjusted his posture. He gritted his teeth and bit back the urge to snap her away. Her hands on him in a professional capacity were better than nothing at all, though truly, this torture must erase at least a hundred years in purgatory.

"But only painting. Nothing more," he said with bitterness.

"To begin, a sketch of that posture, and some of the details of your attire." She sat on her stool, flipped open her sketchbook, and pulled the porte crayon from her hair. She sat down to watch him, study him, learn him inside and out, the way he wanted to know her. The thought scraped his insides into a raw ache.

She had placed him so his bad leg faced her, but with his weight on his good leg, so he could prop one boot carelessly against the other like any gentleman at his ease, leaning on an available marble pilaster. He could stand like this for some time without hurting, and he didn't doubt that she had arranged it on purpose.

I desire you. But not enough to join with him.

"What changed?" he asked roughly.

She concentrated on her paper. "Mrs. Darly of the Macaroni Shop bought three sketches of you. She made two dozen prints of the first engraving and put them on sale yesterday. By today she had sold them all. She is making more prints of that one as well as the others, and she wants more poses." She glanced at his head, back to her paper. "More suggestive ones, this time. Clients have asked."

Ren groaned. "But that is what you wanted, isn't it? To draw attention to me."

"It will work in your favor, Ren. I promise." She didn't sound full of conviction. "Ladies will adore and obsess over you. Men will envy and want to emulate you."

"And they could be me, if they wished for a clubfoot that would bring them years of painful surgery and therapy and corrective shoes, and a stammer that damns them in any company."

"You'll be desirable to everyone. You'll have your pick of a bride, despite being associated with me."

He heard the faint recrimination in her tone. She'd never admit it had hurt her that his mother all but booted her from her drawing room, calling the butler to brush her out the door like so much trash. Ren set his teeth.

"And that is your goal. To foist me on some poor, unsuspecting woman." *You and my mother.* "I'm sorry my mother treated you as she did, Rhette."

"Oh, she has good reason to do so. What young lady will entertain your addresses with me on your arm?"

"Stop it," he said roughly. "I am proud to have you on my arm."

"But I won't scare off just your suitors. Your association with me may reflect poorly on your sister as well."

His heart contracted. This was his Harriette to the core, worried about the welfare of others, whatever the cost to herself. She had never met his sister, but because Ren cared about her, Harriette extended her loyalty to Amalie as well. He couldn't wait to introduce them.

"I doubt Amalie wants to be foisted on anybody, either. You still haven't given me a good reason." For denying him. For repulsing him. For breaking his heart.

She paused and looked into his eyes. "Everyone will assume I've opened my legs to you. There's no way I could be a decent woman and draw such things."

A wave of shame went through him along with a wave of hot lust at her words, the image of Harriette opening her legs for him. He'd been burning for her without any thought of what giving in to him would do to her reputation.

"I've already said I'd marry you, damn it." His mother was right in that he'd put a considerable dent in the esteem and position of the Renwick name by marrying so far beneath him, but he was an earl. His estates were solvent, or mostly solvent. He could marry as he pleased, and if his mother flew up in the boughs about it, he would pack her off to a remote estate and leave her there. He didn't care if all of society shunned him if he could have Harriette at his side.

The hand moving over her paper grew unsteady. "But I've already told you I am unsuited for marriage. By temperament and inclination, if not otherwise."

Did she mean to be celibate? She given herself to other men but had told him she meant to reform. Ren's throat hurt. He wasn't enough to make her choose him, despite everything. Those kisses, that flaming passion that torched his world down to nothing but her, that bond that drew him to her like a magnet —it was another *foolish mistake*, in her book.

"What do you intend, then?" he asked quietly. "For your future." He wanted to know. He wanted to find a way to include himself in it.

"My plan had been to paint, and gain commissions, and eventually set up a shop of my own." Her hand trembled and she stopped, laying her crayon across the paper. She raised troubled eyes to him, her lips turned down. "But I've lately discovered my future is not mine to plan."

"What do you mean?" Panic curled around his middle. He'd only been gone two days. What had happened?

She spread her hands over her face. "I am betrothed," she said.

His heart slammed against his ribs. "*What?*"

"I received a missive by way of the Graf von Hardenburg, who, when he returned to Prussia, apparently located my mother's family. They live in the part of Silesia that has lately been drawn into the Prussian empire, and they were quite eager to know where I was. They have been trying to find me for some time, it seems."

She drew a long, shaky breath. Ren sagged against the false marble pillar, hoping it would hold his weight as he tried to follow her explanation.

"Among other things, I have learned that I have been betrothed since birth. My grandfather was the Duke of Löwenburg, my mother is the current Duchess of Löwenburg, and I am to marry my cousin so we may keep the duchy within the family and placate some great-uncle who was furious that my grandfather gave the estate and the title to my mother instead of to him."

She dropped her head, shaking it from side to side while Ren stared, struck speechless, his tongue too large to fit in his mouth.

"My mother left Silesia so I wouldn't be a pawn," she said. "It seems my father was killed in the Silesian wars, when the Hapsburgs tried to take the territory back from Prussia. And my mother feared that as the heir, someone might kill me and force her to marry, thus claiming the duchy. She left my grandfather in control of his lands, but now my grandfather is dead and my cousin wants to wed me so he may take possession of Löwenburg, and I have no say in the matter because the contract was signed when I was born."

"Oh, Rhette."

Though cold shock coursed through his veins, he forced himself to move, dragging his foot behind him and not caring if he scuffed the floor. The grace he'd studied and practiced deserted him in the face of this numbing realization. He limped to her stool and put his arms around her, pulling her against his chest.

He couldn't imagine touching anyone else of his acquaintance, nor showing such affection to anyone else in his life. But this was Harriette. He wrapped his arms about her shoulders and laid his head atop hers, and she leaned against his chest with a shuddering sigh.

"Many women would be thrilled to learn they are descended from dukes," he said softly.

"And thrilled to be told they must move to a country they've never seen, marry and bear heirs to a man they've never met, and fit into a society they know nothing about, while knowing their decisions affect the welfare of thousands of people?"

He tightened his arms about her. "Such has always been the fate of high-born women, hasn't it?" he murmured.

Women across time had been bound and traded as property, gaining a husband access to wealth and lands. Only look at King George, who refused to give away his princess daughters, some said because he did not want them setting up rival governments abroad and thwarting him as his sons had done.

But that it should happen to Harriette...Rhette, the imp with a slingshot who had pattered barefoot around Shepton Mallet with stains on her apron and her petticoat torn to shreds. Rhette, who had scaled the Blinder Wall at the Manor House and shimmied up a tree to the balcony of his house and could have broken her neck a hundred times. The neck of a duchess-to-be whose hand in marriage would grant a man the rule of a duchy. His mind reeled.

"But only think, Rhette, how my mother will fall all over herself when she learns of it. She'll be the first to invite you to her house and serve tea to the next Duchess of Löwenburg." He pressed the words out, painful as they were, and spoke slowly so his stupid tongue didn't betray him. "Everyone will make a darling of you. No more being tossed out of grand houses on your ear. And your sketches—you will be eccentric and amusing, a duchess who draws. You will be forgiven anything when you are that high."

He knew how it worked in those circles, that all manner of licentious behavior would be winked at as long as one were fashionable. Affairs. Gambling debts. Suspicious politics. As long as one had good blood, the most outrageous acts were amusing. And Harriette, despite her background, despite her upbringing, despite her profession and her history, had a noble bloodline.

A *duchess*. Higher than he, certainly. Ren had nothing to offer her now. And nothing she could accept, in honesty, if she were to be married.

"You mean to go through with the marriage, then." His voice sounded hoarse.

"I don't see how I have a choice. I know I've never looked the dutiful daughter, but my grandfather and my mother entrusted to me the fate of these lands. I stain their honor and break their word if I go against their wishes. My mother sacrificed a life of comfort as a duke's daughter so that I would be safe and live to fulfill this promise.

"And there is the duchy to consider," she went on after a moment. "My aunt has brought me up on the history. After Frederick II of Prussia stole most of Silesia from the Hapsburg Empress Maria Theresa, he set up provincial ministers to oversee it. But the dukes remain, at least in name, and many are still the overlords of their lands, reporting to the minister and the king. The minister will see to the king's needs but not those of the people. And my aunt says Silesia is undergoing a great modernization under Prussian rule. A duchy whose governors are absent or uninvested may be left behind as the wealth grows everywhere else."

She was promised to another. To *marry* another. And she had to return to her homeland, a place he'd never heard of. Silesia was not on the Grand Tour of the glories of Western culture and civilization; it was a backward region of farmers and miners and the poor.

She would leave the country. Leave him. Be entirely out of reach.

"When do you have to go?" The words came from him strangled, barely audible.

She sat up and slid her hands over her face, wiping her tears into her hairline. "When my betrothed comes to fetch me, no earlier. And not until I have this painting done of you, Lord Renwick. I want at least *one* thing I dreamed of to come true before everything changes."

He couldn't help himself. She was so dear, so sensible and brave, and her carmine-red lower lip quivered so beautifully in her distress. He bent his head and gently kissed that lip, then the enchanting corners of her mouth. It was unforgiveable, considering she'd just told him she was betrothed to another, but the urge to comfort her in any way he could overcame the need to be a gentleman.

She pressed her fingers to his chest, not to push him away but to deepen their connection. Perhaps she sensed what was on his heart. Her eyelids remained closed when he paused, and he couldn't help kissing her again. For solace. Reassurance. But comfort flamed all too quickly into passion and her mouth opened beneath his, a trove of searing heat. She curled her hand into his neckcloth and kissed him hungrily, desperately, as if for the last time. It *was* for the last time.

He was instantly lost. He slipped a hand into her loose waves of hair, cupping her head as she let it fall back in shame-less surrender. With his other arm he hauled her against him, crushing her breasts against his chest. She gave a small whimper at the pressure and he eased his embrace, dragging his hand from her hair down the side of her neck and over her chest. Her nipple pearled in his palm, and in thoughtless greed he dipped his hand beneath the fabric, closing it around one soft, perfect globe.

He reeled at the bolt of pleasure and her small gasp. She squirmed on the stool, pushing her breast into his hand and at the same time tilting her hips so his cock slid into the curtain of fabric between her legs, nestling in the warm crevice, just where he wanted to be. He groaned at the ease with which she offered him access. She was as shameless and greedy as he was, drowning in the passion that roared up between them like a ravenous flame.

There was some reason he should pull back. Something about being a gentleman and respecting her wishes. But when her body urged him on, when she leaned her breasts into his circling palm and groaned as he thumbed one diamond-hard nipple, when she rolled her hips against his and the rustle of fabric alone brought him nearly to release, he couldn't think of one earthly reason he shouldn't devour her right here, take what she offered, drive his tongue into her warm mouth and pull aside her skirts and plunge his cock into her open and ready—

"Milord's painting will never be finished at this rate, *Liebelein*."

The amused drawl fell between them like the sword of Damocles, shattering the grip of lust. Ren lifted his head and withdrew his hand, but paused a moment before he stepped back, afraid the slightest friction of her skirts along his erection might urge him to an embarrassment. Harriette groaned but didn't seem embarrassed at all, only regretful, dazed, and then slightly annoyed as she drew up her drawstring neckline and pulled down her disordered skirts.

"You'd better have Sorcha's scones and some fresh clotted

cream on that tray, Princess," Harriette grumbled as her friend processed into the room in a fanfare of silken skirts and ruffles. "And a bottle of my aunt's favorite port."

"Nothing stronger?" Princess sounded amused as she set the tray she carried on a small mahogany table with lion's paw feet. "You'd shock anyone else who found you like this, Hari."

"Why is she here?" Ren rasped. He was ashamed, not at being caught, but that Harriette had just explained to him why they couldn't do as they wished, and he had nevertheless pawed her like an eager puppy. He couldn't hide the betraying bulge in his breeches as he stepped away, and Princess looked her fill, with an approving smile.

"Respectability, you know," Princess answered. "You must be chaperoned now that Hari's betrothed. No more playing rantum scantum."

Ren stared, not comprehending the term. She raised a brow and made an illustrative gesture. "The blanket hornpipe? Two-handed put? Amorous congress?"

"Not with you breaking in on us in full sail, no." Harriette rolled off the stool and shook out her skirts, then walked over to the tea tray. Ren took small satisfaction in noting her gait wobbled slightly. She wasn't able to shake off the drugging effects of their embrace that quickly.

He knew anything he tried to say would emerge mangled, so Ren kept his mouth shut and merely glowered at Princess. "You'll thank me when Fritz doesn't carve out your heart," she advised him.

"Franz Karl," Harriette said. She cut a scone and heaped it with cream.

"Every German is Fritz." Princess sniffed.

"Happens this one calls himself Prussian," Harriette replied.

Him. Harriette's affianced. Ren retreated to the sitting nook and his marble pillar. His boot scraped along the floor before he caught himself and thought about his gait. Princess glanced his way but made no comment. She merely accepted the dish of tea and the piled-high scone Harriette gave her, then glided over to a draped couch standing against a window on the sculptor's side of the room, where she seated herself and dove into her refreshments with evident enjoyment.

"The King—king—kingdom of Galicia and Wodo—Lodomeria," Ren managed, remembering their recent introduction. "Another takeover engineered by Fwed—Frederick, King of P-Prussia, as I understand. Are you fa—from the same region, then?"

Ren glared at Princess, blaming her for the way his tongue swelled and flailed in his mouth. She put him off the ease he felt with Harriette, made all his self-consciousness rise to the surface. He hated hearing his own voice, his stuttering. He fully expected her to look at him with the pity, scorn, or horror he was used to seeing.

Princess licked her fingers and gave him a level look. "Galicia is a crownland of the Hapsburg monarchy now," she said. "A consequence of Frederick the Great parceling out parts of the Commonwealth of Poland and Lithuania—which is not his to give, I might add, but he thought to placate Austria and keep Russia off his borders. No doubt the vultures will pluck poor Poland down to her bones."

"So you are P-Polish royalty then," Ren said carefully.

"How lovely for me," Princess said, enjoying her cream.

"And Rhette is Prussian nobility."

"Not Prussian," Harriette sharply, moving his way with a dish of tea and a generously creamed scone. "Silesian."

"Silesia was part of Poland in the Middle Ages, under Bohemian rule," Princess said around a mouthful of scone.

"Before the Hapsburgs scooped it into their great gaping maw and turned it into a backwater."

"We are more Slav than German." Harriette deposited his refreshments on Ren's pillar and turned back to her stool. "We have our own language and culture."

"I always thought you and your mother were speaking German to each other," Ren said in surprise. The cream was delicious, the scone melting and yet tart. The treat helped remedy somewhat for Harriette's being forcibly removed from his arms.

"It's more like Polish," Harriette said. "But a language proper, not a dialect."

"Say something," Ren prompted.

She searched about for her porte crayon and her sketchbook. When she settled herself on her stool, her look held a warmth that curled into his belly, dissolving the cream. He didn't understand a word of what followed, but it wasn't German.

Princess raised her eyebrows.

"What did you say?" Ren asked.

"I said it will be interesting to see where Frederick decides to throw his weight in the matter of the revolt in the American colonies," Harriette said. "France will aid the colonists because they love to antagonize Britain. But Britain and Prussia were allies, at least until the Seven Years' War."

"Oh, is *that* what you said?" Princess murmured.

Harriette shot her a defiant look, and Ren decided not to press the issue. Let her have her small lie, if she were honest with him otherwise.

"So it will help when you go-go back. If you know—if you know the language." He tried his best to sound casual, offhand. As if he were merely a friend remarking on her future plans. The subject of her work, the patron who had commissioned a painting for quite a hefty fee, as it were. Not the man who would drop to his knees and beg her to stay with him, if his crippled leg would allow such a gesture.

"My aunt has made sure I kept it. Now I understand why. She knew of the betrothal all along." She attacked her paper with long, savage lines.

"And she never told you?" Surprise made the words slip out without a catch.

"She wanted me to have what freedom I could, for as long as I could. So she says," Harriette answered. She'd fallen into sketching mode, her eyes moving from him to her paper, bringing him to life with lines and shadows. "But she also ensured I had the best education. One befitting a duchess, which my mother could not provide."

"Don't blame her, Hari," Princess said in a quiet voice.

"I don't." Harriette sketched in shadow with quick strokes, but she didn't seem angry, only intense. "I understand why she did. She thought if she raised me for my future, she'd stifle me. I would become what I thought someone else wanted, instead of myself."

Princess sipped her tea and Ren reduced his scone to crumbs, then licked his finger and collected the crumbs in an action that would never be accepted at a genteel table. Harriette sketched, then spoke.

"'Tis a cruel gift, do you consider it," she said softly. "To allow a young woman to live to please herself, and then tell her, quite suddenly, her destiny is no longer hers to command, but she must now do the bidding of others."

"You'll have a great many comforts to make up for it," Princess said, sharpness entering her tone. "And a high name to be your shield and guard and *entrée* everywhere. Besides." She stretched into a reclining pose. "It might be a great deal of fun. You couldn't believe what goes on at some of those courts. Austrian, Italian, Russian. The Prussians may be a bit more buttoned up, and a great number of the Germans, but if you saw what those Polish nobles—that is, *we* Polish nobles..." She shrugged. "They make English scandals look like schoolboy pranks."

"My mother will be delighted to call herself duchess and have everyone bow and curtsey to her," Harriette said. "I sent her a copy of the letter directly. No doubt Mrs. Demant will go into transports. She'll be repaid for keeping my mother all this time and being put to such trouble over me."

A short silence ensued. "At least my mother can be restored to her home and her position. That is the one great reason to go through with this. That, and it might lower some of the British noses turned up at my aunt, do they know she's nearly royal in her own land."

"Why didn't your aunt stay in Silesia?" Ren asked.

"Her husband was count of his own province, so she left upon her marriage. But when he lost his lands in the War of the Austrian Succession, he came to Britain, which was then Austria's ally, to try to gather influence and win back his realm."

"Where is Calenberg now?" Ren asked.

"It no longer exists," Harriette said shortly. "But the usurpers at the least gave my aunt her widow's portion of the inheritance, which is mainly what we live on. It's not enough, as our household expands, which is why I came to you. So you could help me gain commissions, the kind which Gainsborough and Reynolds and Angelica Kauffman can command. While, in the meantime, I scrape by with racy portraits."

Princess's eyes widened. "Are you making another sketch of his lordship? The first are selling like griddlecakes at a market fair, Mrs. Darly says."

Harriette shook the loose chalk off her last sketch and laid the sheet of paper on her table. Her eyes lit on Ren with a glow in their depths that instantly called up an answering heat within him.

"I oughtn't," she said, but the twitch at the corners of her lips belied her prim tone. "But I've a sudden notion to be completely scandalous. I want to show the world what I see." Her voice dropped in pitch, to a husky croon that made his groin stir. "I want women to look at those prints and feel what I was feeling before her highness clomped in here and forced us apart."

"What do you have in m-m-mind?" Ren's throat went dry. A long sip of tea did nothing to soothe the ache.

Harriette's eyes turned to molten gold, her voice pure wickedness and seduction. "Take off your coat and your waist-coat. And your neckcloth. I'm going to draw you in just your shirt."

"What, undressed!" Princess sat up at attention. "I see I will enjoy this business of chaperoning more than I thought."

Ren tried not to melt, or let his erection show, as Harriette neared him and started unbuttoning his morning coat. Neither effort was successful.

"Is this what you want, Rhette?" he whispered as she bent to work the large silver buttons lining his coat. Her loose hair brushed his cheek. He closed his eyes in a pleasure that bordered on agony.

"Not nearly," she said. "But it will have to do for now."

"How can I help?" He met her eyes. She held nothing back with him. She never had. He saw her hurt, her desire, her frustration, and her need to be connected to him, to touch him. The same intensity moved them both. He wanted to howl and weep at the thought that, under different circumstances, he could have claimed her.

If she weren't a duchess. If she weren't already promised. If he could be the whole, steady, admirable kind of man she deserved, instead of a green, incomplete, malformed one.

"Be my friend," she whispered. "Let me paint you. And let me have this time with you for as long as I can."

He closed his eyes as her hands freed him from his coat and started on his neckcloth, her warm, clever fingers brushing his throat. She was going to kill him. He was going to physically expire from the pain of wanting this woman so much. It would swell him up like an abscess until he burst.

At least he would die happy.

CHAPTER TEN

"Am I imagining things," Harriette asked as the cabriolet clipped along Berkeley Square, "or are people staring at us more than usual?"

"I expect it's my hat," Princess replied, flicking the ribbons to steer Hyperion, the coach horse, around a stopped sedan chair. "It's rather splendid, don't you think?"

"It takes up more space than I do." Harriette batted away an ostrich plume. Princess wore an enormous black hat with a tall conical shape and a deep brim. One side held an enormous striped silk rosette, and the other a set of ostrich plumes, dyed purple, that swept from the crown into Harriette's eyes.

"But I think it is more than the hat, Princess," she added as the passenger in the sedan chair craned her neck to stare at them.

They turned into Mount Street, and street boys paused to tip their hats as they passed. A shop girl ran out the door of her premises into the street, nearly colliding with a sweep boy. She held a sheet of paper in her hand and waved it with a joyous smile when she caught Harriette watching her. Harriette turned to face front with a groan.

"It's those prints of Renwick. I knew I was going to be exposed as the maker, and I let Mrs. Darly print them anyway."

"They're extremely dashing," Princess murmured. She smiled widely as a finely dressed gentleman, toeing the line between fashionable and ostentatious, turned and made them a grand leg, flicking back the tails of his coat. "I bought two of each. But I don't think it's simply the prints that have increased your notoriety."

"I wanted to make myself respectable," Harriette said, agonized. "I wanted higher commissions. But Sorcha said with the price of cotton and sugar going up because of the war with the Colonies, she was overspending her marketing funds, and I did not want Aunt to go without her tea and chocolate. So I sold the prints to Mrs. Darly even though I knew this would happen."

She gave a tight smile as a merchant's wife and daughter stepped out of a haberdasher and brought up short, staring at the passing conveyance with wide eyes. "I sold my reputation for tea and chocolate. And to make Ren a desirable *parti*."

"Those prints do inspire desire, but not for his hand in marriage." Princess dipped her chin at the merchant's wife and her ostrich plume tickled Harriette's nose. "Good day!" she called to the pair on the street. The merchant's wife covered her lips with a prim kid glove and blushed.

"And if you desire Renwick for yourself, I don't understand why you don't simply have at him." Princess turned the cabriolet toward Grosvenor Square.

Harriette felt the tops of her ears heat. "Beater can *hear you*."

"Beater don't care who you tup," Princess said. "And neither do we. It seems a shame to deny yourselves when it's mutual."

"Franz Karl, my betrothed, is coming to Britain to collect me," Harriette said. "I insist he come to fetch me. I won't show up in Löwenburg like luggage. And when he comes, if he finds I've become another man's mistress, he will have no respect for me. I will have no power to keep any independence or make any negotiation for myself in this marriage."

"The title passes to you from your mother," Princess said. "At least, if I understand what your grandfather arranged. That means Fritz must bow to you. Some Polish and Hungarian royalty do the same, you know—dispense titles and lands to daughters if there is no male heir."

"By marriage my cousin will control everything, my wealth and my person," Harriette answered. "Prussian law is much like British law, God help us. I would pay the rest of my life for a few moments of stolen pleasure."

Princess tipped her chin as a set of gentlemen strolling the square turned to stare at them through their quizzing glasses. "You've never known pleasure if you won't pay that price," she murmured.

Harriette flushed. She both knew and did not know what her friend meant. What she felt when Ren touched her, when he was simply near her—it was a craving that overset all sense. He made nothing feel so vital, so necessary, as following those sensations wherever they led.

But they led to ignominy and shame, and a husband who would despise her and perhaps shut her away for the rest of her life in a dim set of rooms. Visit her only to get heirs for the duchy. Deny her companions, sociability, intellectual conversation. Deny her any power over her life. She would rather live as her mother had lived, a fugitive noblewoman in poverty, than a wife helpless to the whim of her husband. She would rather stab herself to death with her brushes.

"Top o' the morning, Your Highness," one of the strolling gentlemen called, though it was midday. "Lady Harriette! Want to sketch me? I look rather fetching in my shirtsleeves. Or you can strip me down to bare skin if it pleases you."

Harriette tried to sink into the seat, which was impossible because the seat was covered with the enormous skirts of their gowns and petticoats, and the dashing slight overhang of the vehicle left the occupants open to the sight of all.

"I knew it. I knew those prints would make me talked about. I had better hope Franz Karl doesn't suspect an affair anyway because of the way I—"

"You are missing an opportunity to be admired," Princess reproved her. She sank an elbow into Harriette's side, an elbow that, considering the lace ruffles on the sleeve of Princess's dress and the stays beneath Harriette's bodice, proved surprisingly sharp. "You are also missing what he called you."

Far different from the last time they went skulking around Grosvenor Square, Princess halted the cabriolet with a showy flourish before the solid, pillared expanse of Renwick House. Harriette had scarcely a moment to appreciate the beautiful symmetry and architectural detail of the pediments above each window and the offset bricks that lent interest to the façade. The butler wrenched open the front door and barreled into the street, reaching out a hand to help Harriette descend before the carriage had completely stopped, nearly risking taking a wheel over his toe.

"Your ladyship," he panted. "I don't believe I have your card."

He recognized her as the woman he'd tossed out on her ear; she could tell by the way he looked at her hair, not her eyes. "Miss Harriette Smythe," she said, lifting her chin.

"Lady Harriette von Löwenburg," Princess called. "Daughter and heir to the Duchess of Löwenburg."

"Lady Harriette." The butler nearly touched his knee to his nose.

"You're not to say," Harriette yelped.

"They already know." Princess nodded toward the cluster of people who had drifted across the green of Grosvenor Square to watch the proceedings outside of Renwick House with great and obvious interest. Harriette glimpsed the plumes and wigs of expensive ladies, the plainer gowns of nursemaids taking their charges for an airing, and the tradeswomen's printed chintz among the workman's drabs and the bright aprons of the coster-mongers. She was accustomed to people collecting to stare at Princess, who was generally held to be one of London's most sought-after courtesans. But this time the stares were for Harriette.

"Who told?" she asked tightly.

"Ye can't mean to keep it a secret, Miz H," Jock called. He had his hands full steadying Hyperion as several boys leapt to his head, clamoring to hold the bridle for such distinguished visitors. "Back, ya snafflers," he chided the boys. "His hooves'll crush your trotters, and his bite's worse."

"Honestly, Hari, did you not hear Darci reading the gossip paragraphs at breakfast? They were simply brimming with news of your elevation," Princess said.

"I wasn't at breakfast." Harriette took the butler's offered hand and began the process of hauling herself and her several layers of skirts out of the vehicle. She'd risen early and went straight to her studio to see if she could achieve the precise blue of Ren's suit in gouache colors, and when Darci came in to sculpt, they had worked side by side for hours without speaking, as was their custom. Darci was an excellent person to share an artistic studio with.

"How did word get out?"

"I can't imagine," Princess said innocently. "Your aunt never would have mentioned it, I'm sure. Nor I."

Harriette turned to glare at her, ignoring for the moment the small crowd. "Will you stay?"

"My friend awaits me," Princess said. "Jock and Beater will bring the cabriolet back for you. My friend will see I return home."

Harriette wondered, not for the first time, about Princess's recent new friend, who insisted on secrecy but seemed rather libertine in his habits and his wealth. The thought fled from her mind when Ren stepped out the front door onto the scrubbed white stoop. He was splendid and polished in morning dress and leaned on a cane.

"Hullo, W-*Lady* Rhette," he said playfully. "Princess." His eyes flickered over Beater, who had stepped down from the groom's perch to stretch his legs. Then he saw Jock, and his face changed. He started towards them.

"No, don't—" Harriette caught herself. Ren hated having attention brought to his limp. Plenty of gentlemen carried canes as a fashion accessory, and he had learned to walk as if he had all the time in the world as a mark of his high birth, rather than an indication that he struggled to keep each step smooth and even.

"Oy, now." Jock crossed his forearms and regarded the earl, but spoke under his breath to Harriette. "Yer gent shambles bad as I do."

"Don't make fun," Harriette hissed.

"Can't I? 'E only needs one crutch, an I need two," Jock said, with only the faintest trace of bitterness. He had learned to deal with his injury, but he still felt the occasional resentment, Harriette knew.

Ren stopped before them, glancing from Harriette to her groom, who sat atop the horse as if he'd been born to the saddle. Still it was impossible not to notice the twisted legs hanging along the horse's sides.

He addressed Jock directly. "Polio?"

"Horse, yer lordship." Jock tugged the brim of his hat briefly. "Racing overland on a gentleman's wager. Camino threw me at a fence, and me mate, riding Arachne, landed straight atop me afore he could pull up. Broke me back and both legs. Never healed proper."

Ren winced. "W-rotten l-luck."

"He was the best jockey at Newmarket," Harriette said, because Jock would never boast of it. "Won the King's Plate three times." She added, when Ren turned wondering eyes on her, "My aunt is a great enthusiast for horse racing. She'd keep her own stable if she could. When the accident put Jock out of a job, she offered him one. He's been with us ever since."

"Pleasure to meet you." Quite against custom, and to the great surprise of the onlookers, Ren held out his hand to the smaller man.

Jock shook it solemnly. "Yer Lordship. Call me Jock. Never knew me real name, so gave meself that one."

Ren offered his arm to Harriette, something warm and appreciative in his eyes. Harriette felt a responsive warmth fill her.

"Amalie would come out to meet you, but she doesn't like crowds. I expect she's pressed against a window, staring at you."

"Staring at the Princess's hat, rather." Harriette joined him in scanning the first-floor windows for a glimpse of the elusive Lady Amalie.

Her stomach tightened. She was returning to Renwick House on Ren's arm, about to meet his sister. Nothing had changed about her on the inside; she was precisely the same Harriette who had woken up a week ago thinking of nothing but of how to garner wealthy patrons and commissions to paint them. She was the same Harriette this butler had turned out of the house a few days prior.

No, that wasn't true. She was the Harriette who had met Renwick again, all grown up, and discovered that the childhood bond they'd forged as outcasts and riffraff had not only endured, but taken on a deeper, instinctive meeting of hearts and minds as well as a compelling physical attraction. She felt it as she leaned upon his arm, unconsciously seeking his heat and strength. His thigh brushed her skirts and the shiver of fabric ran all down her leg, then back up to that secret place in between.

She was the Harriette whose every action would reflect not just on her aunt and her mother's station but on an entire duchy she had never known existed until a few days ago. Löwenburg would wear in England whatever reflection she cast upon it.

She matched her gait to his and they stepped from the street to the small porch with stately grace. "Why the cane?"

"I had a devil of a time with my exercises this morning." Ren kept his voice low as they stepped into the house. "The doctor said I must do them every day, and then a special extra set each week. I chose today, unfortunately. I hope you won't insist on our excursion to the pleasure gardens."

"You'll have to go sometime," Harriette said with a stern look. "I won't let you cry off."

"I wouldn't dream of it," Ren said with a sigh. "But you'll have a harder time convincing Amalie. Come."

He drew her toward the stairs that circled down to the entrance hall. They both paused at the sight of the Countess of Renwick standing upon them, wearing a bright yellow robe draped with blonde lace and a formidable expression.

"Lady Harriette," she said with a vinegary curl of the lip.

"Lady Renwick." Harriette curtsied. She could not suppress a small thrill when the countess responded in kind. The action was stiff and forced, as if she bobbed on marionette strings, but to Harriette's satisfaction, the countess achieved the requisite depth to acknowledge the daughter of a duchess. Oh, some of this was going to be great fun.

"My son is eager to welcome you to our home," the countess went on. Harriette noticed she did not say *we*.

"*My* home, Mother," Ren said steadily, but Harriette flinched. She caught the trace of a prior argument in the thin lines around his mother's eyes and the way she would not look at her son directly. Humble pie was clearly not her ladyship's favorite meal.

"But I'm afraid my daughter is not well. She is in no condition to receive guests."

"Amalie was p-p-perfectly well when I l-left her fifteen minutes ago," Ren replied. "She has agree—agreed to receive Rhette. In fact she said she is eager to m-meet her."

His mother appealed to Ren, something haunted and desperate in her eyes. "Renwick, don't do this to her. Don't subject her to—to stares, and talk, and—"

"Did you not see her groom outside?" Ren snapped. "Have you not seen her sketches of me?" Anger made him eloquent; the stammering his mother usually caused vanished. "Harriette is not going to sh-shriek and faint at the sight of deformities."

Harriette tightened her grip on his arm. She hated being the cause of discord between Ren and his mother, but she would not abandon Ren by ducking away. Curiosity drove her as well. She wondered what tiny flaw made the countess want to hide her own daughter from sight. She had hidden Ren in Shepton Mallet as if she were ashamed of him for nothing more than a clubfoot and stammer. Worse, she had impressed her shame upon her son, so convincing him of his inadequacies that even now, as a man grown into his full magnificence and beauty, Ren flinched before his mother's disapproval.

"I do not care what your tart thinks," the countess snapped. "I care that my daughter not be humiliated and exposed."

The muscle under Harriette's fingers grew taut with Ren's fury. "You will apologize for that insult."

The countess stood, a lone, small figure on the great twisting stair, the tall portraits of her husband's ancestors looming above her with blank, disinterested eyes. The blonde lace over her neckline fluttered as she drew a sharp, angry breath.

"I won't have any part of this." She rushed from the stairs through a door across the foyer, into what looked like a dining parlor.

Harriette tugged gently at Ren's arm, drawing him out of his glower. "Perhaps I ought to go."

He tightened his elbow about her hand, keeping her from escape as he drew her down the hall toward the morning room at the rear of the house. "You just arrived."

"I seem to be upsetting everyone. And if your sister doesn't wish to receive me..."

"That was my mother talking. Amalie wants to meet you."

He turned and faced her before the paneled door that led to the morning room, across from another set of doors that let out into the gardens. He was so *big* when she was close to him. The lanky boy had filled out to a man of impressive proportions, though she overlooked the sheer breadth of him because his nature was so gentle. Frustration and turmoil brought out the blue of his eyes.

"Yes, but should she? Meet me, I mean. The stares we received today, Ren, just out and about, and the people collected across the street—you saw them. I'm not just notorious now. I'm—I'm something worse." She gripped his forearms, trying to reason with him.

He cupped his hands over her elbows. Heat rose through the thin fabric of her sleeves, anchoring her to him. "Rhette." He struggled to keep his breath even, his words fully formed. "This is imp-portant to me. P-please."

She stared into his eyes, caught in the silver shafts that radiated through the iris. Those blue eyes were an unfair advantage, especially over females. Why could she not resist him, even if it was in his best interest for her to leave him alone? Look at what happened in her studio. She'd listed all the reasons they couldn't give into passion, and in the next instant she was throwing herself headlong into passion, inhaling him as if he were her life's breath, rubbing herself against that beautiful body like some wanton cat, trying to pull him into her arms as if she meant to keep him there forever.

Heaven help her, but she had the urge to do so again. Right now.

"All right," she whispered. "Be it on your head if your mother is right and I ruin your sister."

"Thank you." His lids lowered, hooding his eyes, and she recognized the instant that his emotion shifted into desire, as if sparked by her lascivious thoughts. She lifted her chin to meet his lips as he bent to kiss her. Common sense fled the moment his warm breath touched her cheek.

It was a chaste kiss, his lips plucking hers as if sipping nectar from a flower. He held her elbows, no other part of their bodies touching, and yet this tender embrace left her in flames hotter than any of the others. It was more than a simple animal craving to be close to him. It was a seal on the bond that had formed between them that long-ago summer, that connection, that companionship, that absolute trust.

A shimmer of new knowledge moved down her throat and circled her heart, then settled in her belly. She would never be able to resist Ren. She would lay down anything he wanted, his for the asking. Her body. Her future. Her life.

Best not let him know that. She pulled away, lifting her chin and patting cautiously at her curls. Her hair alone had been the production of an hour, with Melike wielding the hair irons,

Natalya directing the placement of pads and pins, and Sorcha standing by with her favorite lavender powder. This hair needed to be taken to Marylebone Pleasure Gardens; it was a work of art.

Besides, she couldn't stand here kissing Ren all day, much as she'd like to. "I'm read—" She trailed off.

"Oh. Dear me. I've interrupted."

In the doorway to the morning room stood a young lady, tall and slender and very pale. She had a cloud of white-blonde hair, the color Ren's had been when he was younger, though his had now darkened to a brown with honey streaks. Her wide blue eyes held surprise and curiosity—no, only one eye was blue, Harriette realized as she stared. Her left eye was brown. The girl wore an open robe of pale primrose silk over a delicate white petticoat, white lace over her bodice, and a prim white scarf pinned atop the lace. Her face was as white as her linens, though her lips were red, or what Harriette could see of her lips behind the slender hand she held over her mouth.

"Amalie," Ren said warmly. "This is my Rhette. *Lady* Harriette of Löwenburg, I am p-pleased to say. Rhette, this is my sister, Lady Amalie Matheson, lately of Bolton Abbey, currently of London for now and, I hope, a good deal longer."

Amalie dropped a curtsey, moving her hand from her mouth to hold the ruffled lace of her opposite sleeve. She rose with a stare for her brother, not for his guest.

"George," she whispered. "Barely a stammer!"

"And you said my whole name," Harriette murmured, remembering how he never could manage it before.

His straight mouth twitched into a smile. "Practiced last night," he said proudly. "For an hour. Or two."

Harriette hugged his arm and indicated the doorway. "Shall we?"

"I'm—I'm sorry I didn't wait for you." Lady Amalie spoke

scarcely above a whisper as she led them into the morning room. Unlike the formal parlors above, this room held a more restrained elegance, with greens and gold dominating the upholstery and walls. "I was all arranged on the couch, but then your voices stopped, and I worried that—" Her voice fell to a barely audible register, and she stood cradling the sleeve of her gown with her hand. "You'd changed your mind."

"Your mother did suggest it was better for all concerned if I did not meet you today." Harriette looked about for a seat. She was the ranking lady now; as the daughter of a duke, she had precedence over the daughter of an earl and even the countess herself. When she came into her title she would have precedence over her own aunt in society circles, a sudden, disconcerting elevation.

Tamping down her nervousness that Ren's sister would not like her, Harriette selected a seat on a low chaise next to a shawl that she guessed was Amalie's. This left Ren to one of the delicate, hard-backed chairs. He lowered himself using his cane, then leaned it on the armrest alongside.

"I suspect your mother thought I would be an untoward influence," Harriette explained.

"Oh, not in the least," Amalie answered in a rush. "She didn't want you to have to see *me*."

"Why should her ladyship want to hide you?"

Ren watched his sister with an almost painful look of adoration mingled with worry. "You needn't fear Rhette," he said gently.

"But I'm hideous." Amalie cast a look of despair towards her lap. She picked up the shawl and pulled it partially over one leg. Harriette wondered if she had a clubfoot, too, though she hadn't noticed a limp.

"Hardly hideous," Harriette objected. "You are the most

perfect creature." Amalie resembled a Madonna in a Renaissance painting, with a halo of angelic gold circling her head.

A maid entered the room with a tea tray. She looked with wide eyes at Renwick, at Lady Amalie, and then at Harriette, as if any one of them might leap up and bite her. With a faint rattle of porcelain, she set the tea tray on the low table before the chaise, then hastily backed out of the room. Harriette watched, her curiosity intensifying.

"I asked for tea," Amalie said in a small voice. "I've heard it is a drink much enjoyed in London."

"Oh, excessively," Harriette said. "Coffee as well, though women aren't allowed in many of the coffee shops, which are deemed the domain of men who overestimate their own importance. There are tea shops that admit women, though. Ren and I shall take you to one."

"Oh, I don't go out," Amalie said in a rush. She looked about the morning room as if its painted green walls lined with gilded frames were her sanctuary, and beyond its walls held terror and death.

"I was hoping to persuade you to come to Marylebone Pleasure Gardens with us," Harriette said, trying to keep the disappointment from her tone. Perhaps Lady Amalie had already concluded that Harriette was an unsuitable acquaintance, and that was why she resisted making plans. If Ren's sister had indeed wished to meet Harriette, she showed no sign of it.

"There are any number of gardens about London we might see," Harriette went on, hoping to make the girl comfortable. "But Marylebone has agreeable music, and these tarts that—"

"Pour the t-tea, d-dear," Ren said suddenly, addressing his sister. If Ren were stammering around his sister, too, then something must have upset him.

"Tea would be lovely," Harriette prattled. "I take mine with a lump of sugar. Ren likes his as black as his thoughts are much of the time."

The levity did nothing to soothe her hostess. "Must I?" She sent her brother a forlorn look.

"It wouldn't be suitable to ask Rhette," he said gently. "She is our guest."

Harriette held her breath, catching the rising tension and wondering if she were its cause. Amalie regarded the tea tray as if it were a sleeping animal that might bite if she woke it. Then, with a deep breath, she picked up the tea pot with her right hand and lifted her left arm. The lace sleeve fell away and Harriette saw that, instead of a delicate wrist and pretty hand, the girl's left forearm ended halfway in a small pink stump. She used it to steady the teapot as she poured. Then she picked up a lump of sugar with the dainty tongs, placed it in the liquid, and stirred with a tiny silver spoon.

Harriette felt Ren's eyes burning into the side of her face, though he said nothing.

"See? I am not perfect." Amalie looked Harriette in the eye with a fierce resolution as she held out the dish of tea. "Because of this." She indicated the left sleeve, lying in a pool of lace in her lap. "And this." She pointed to the left side of her face, where Harriette could detect, beneath the heavy layer of makeup, a strawberry birthmark reaching from her hairline to her neck.

Harriette took her tea and sipped. "I haven't the faintest idea why that means we can't be friends," she said.

She was aware, without looking at him, that every muscle in Ren's frame relaxed. He practically released a whoosh of air. Her heart clenched. He'd been afraid, like his mother, that his sister's deformities would make Harriette reject her. The countess might truly care for her daughter, but her protectiveness looked like cruelty and shame to Harriette.

Amalie's face was the picture of surprise. The blue eye was set just a hair above the brown, and didn't widen or narrow in the exact same way. Only a portrait artist would notice the subtle difference in proportion. The rest of Amalie's face was the pattern of classical beauty: a wide arching brow, perfect half-circles of eyebrows, and rounded cheeks slightly narrowing to a chin, like Renwick's, with a tiny cleft. Her nose was Renwick's as well, strong and commanding, but hers sloped faintly up at the tip.

The tightness in Harriette's chest formed tiny cracks. She adored Amalie instantly, as much as she adored Ren. She wished she could stay and enjoy them both. Get truly acquainted, become part of their lives. Instead she would be forced to the Continent to preside over a duchy she had never seen.

"I wish I could paint you," Harriette said.

Amalie gasped. "As you are painting George?"

"Yes. A portrait of him, a portrait of you, and then a portrait of you two together. Perhaps," and she grinned at the mischievous thought, "a family group with Lady Renwick included."

"I don't doubt that will drive up the price of the commission a great deal," Ren murmured.

"To be sure." Harriette nodded. "And it would be to your benefit. This house very much requires new art along the stairs."

Amalie blushed. Harriette detected the red tinge beneath the heavy layer of concealing makeup. "Mother won't allow it. Not even if you disguise my—defects. I am delicate, you see."

Harriette raised her brows. "Is that what she calls you?"

"Not just that." Amalie looked both miserable and determined to bare all. "I am often ill. I am plagued by headaches and tire easily. And my appetite—" She rested her hand over her middle and gave Harriette an apologetic smile. "It is not robust, either."

Her teeth were small and white, but Harriette noticed a thin grey line along the gums that she had seen before. She had also heard these symptoms described before. "Like the grippe?" she asked.

"Not the same, because there is no fever."

"Rubbish," said Harriette, who had never been ill a day in her life. "Taking fresh air and a bit of exercise will cure almost every ill. Shall we try it? Come to Marylebone Pleasure Gardens with me, and we will see if a turn about the paths and a tart or two might perk you up."

"Oh, such a thing sounds lovely," Amalie said. Her lovely face drew downward, lips, brows, chin. "But my mother will never allow it." She looked toward her brother with a desperate, haunted expression.

"But your brother shall." Harriette pushed to her feet, levering herself up out of the layers of petticoats. "Now then! This is a splendid tea, but I am holding out for tarts. Shall I play lady's maid and attend your toilette? And Ren can go repair himself as well." She waved a hand in his direction. "Your neck-cloth is crumpled."

"Because you crumpled it," Ren grumbled. "I suppose I could read the news while you powder. There is some upheaval in Shepton Mallet over the new automated looms, and I've heard they expect a riot."

"Pooh," said Harriette. "Nothing exciting has happened in Shepton Mallet since the Duke of Monmouth's supporters were drawn and quartered in the market square. Shall we?"

She slipped a hand around Amalie's upper arm as she rose, and the girl startled. Harriette wondered if it were too bold in her to touch her—and the arm Amalie tried to keep hidden, no less—but it was too late to retract the gesture now.

"How is it you dare manage George?" Amalie whispered in

awe as Renwick bowed and then left the room, his stiff leg causing a slight limp. "He does what you tell him!"

"What, Ren? He has always been the most biddable of men," Harriette said. "Come, show me your dressing table. You are in London Town now, and we must turn you out in London style." She kept hold of Amalie's arm as they ascended the curved stairs to the second floor and her boudoir.

In the end she added only a light dusting of powder to Amalie's hair, turning her gold-white to a becoming white halo. Harriette sorted through the pots and jars on the dressing table as Amalie darkened her eyebrows with a smudge of charcoal. Brilliant vermillion for lips and cheeks, an arsenic tonic to bathe the face; the girl's assemblage was very much the usual.

"And this is the paint you use on your face." Harriette opened a jar and sniffed.

"I need it." Amalie looked pained. "My mark—it is very ugly. People cannot see anything else when they look at me. So I cover it."

Harriette dipped a finger in the white liquid and touched it to her tongue, then spat. It was sweet, no less than she expected.

"Your paint is still in place. Whyn't we simply put a layer of powder over it and go downstairs? We can tease Ren for making us wait for him."

"I dare not." Amalie plucked at the ruffle not quite covering her left arm. "Mama will be so angry—and I cannot be seen." Her eyes filled with tears and she gave Harriette a watery, imploring gaze. Her shimmering, bereft eyes tore Harriette's heart.

"My brother doesn't know yet," she whispered. "I knew Mama would disapprove, but I had to come to town because—because I am dying, you see, and I very much wanted to see him before the end."

Then she put a hand over her face and dissolved into racking sobs.

Harriette put aside the thought of Marylebone Pleasure Gardens that day. Instead she knelt and wrapped her arms around the younger girl, holding her shaking form as she wept. Her heart cleaved in two for the tender young woman, but she ached just as much for Renwick. His sister was ailing, and his mother had no ability to care for anyone but herself. Who would look after the Matheson siblings when Harriette was gone?

CHAPTER ELEVEN

"Did you know?" Harriette asked Ren a few days later as he leaned on the false marble pillar in her painting nook, staring into the distance. He wore his blue silk suit, his wig was impeccably shaped and powdered, his specially made boots gleamed with polish, and he did not need to affect his distant, absorbed expression. He looked as if he'd been struck across the head and his ears still rang from it.

He shifted and raised his eyes to hers. Harriette felt a pinch of hurt for him and for herself at his lost expression. She had to leave him sooner than she'd expected, and she couldn't find a way to tell him when he was already grappling with the shocking news his sister had delivered.

"Did I know that Amalie is ill?" His voice rasped as if he had overused it of late, perhaps with howling against the vagaries of fate.

Harriette nodded, her throat tight. She concentrated on capturing the play of light on his buttons rather than stare into his face. His vulnerability raised a fierce protectiveness in her. She always tended to react when someone she cared about was injured, but with Ren that instinct was multiplied. She wanted to howl with him, gnash her teeth, rend her clothes as the ancients did to symbolize their mourning. She wanted to twine her arms about his chest and hold him against her until all his sadness had transferred to her.

She did not have that right, and never would. She couldn't have him, and she kept reminding herself that it was better this way. Better to leave him alone. Best not give in to the nearly rending temptation to draw close, touch him, cradle him in her arms. Burrow against his firm, warm chest and stay there like a baby bird sheltered from the wind.

She was being absurd and possibly goose-brained. Time to stop such nonsense before these paths of thought spiraled any further.

"I knew she was sickly." Ren pondered her question. "There were hints now and again in her letters, but no one ever said the situation was d-dire. No one ever—" He paused, struggling. "I wonder if my m-mother knew?"

"Surely she would have Lady Amalie under a doctor's care if that were the case."

"My mother dislikes d-doctors. My father insisted the doctors must have damaged me during delivery, causing my foot. But when my sister was born..." He paused. "My mother blamed herself that we are—formed as we are. And my father came to share that belief."

"That's Aristotle for you," Harriette said.

She didn't like how the highlight looked on the buttons—too heavy, more like a glob of butter than light. She dipped her brush and painted over the offending area. "Aristotle wrote that the male seed exerts a shaping force on the female menstrual blood, the matter from which we all are made. If the process goes as intended, one births a perfect male. If formation is not complete, one ends up with a female. And there are any number of factors that could influence a mother and impact her gestation, it was thought. What foods she ate. What sights she saw. If she had an imbalance of the humors, if she experienced a severe shock or surprise—there were superstitions added over the years by medieval writers, but the general theme is, any imperfections in the child are the fault of the woman."

Ren stared at her. "You are a repository for the strangest knowledge."

Harriette shrugged. "We read long bits of Aristotle in our Greek courses at Miss Gregoire's. Some of the girls took to speaking Greek as their own secret language."

"Miss Gregoire's Academy for Girls offers a profoundly different model of schooling than Eton or Cambridge," Ren remarked. "How I wish Amalie might be sent to such a place."

"There is no reason she should not be accepted," Harriette said. "And her—differences, if you want to call them that, would not be the slightest hindrance. All of Miss Gregoire's girls have their oddities, you might say."

"My mother would never allow it," Ren said gloomily. "She would manufacture some long speech about how Amalie is too delicate and people are too cruel, and a safe home is her best protection, and the conclusion is that Amalie is denied every pleasure a girl her age ought to have."

"Who is Lady Amalie's guardian?" Harriette asked, though it was none of her business to inquire. "It cannot be Lady Renwick, not legally."

Ren blinked. "I sup-suppose I am her g-guardian," he stammered with surprise.

"Then you are within your rights to summon a doctor to see her. And you might ask him to inquire about her exposure to lead."

Ren pounced. "Do you know what ails her? If you do, Rhette, you must—you must tell me."

"I do not know anything," Harriette cautioned, wondering if

it were wise to speak to him like this. She had no time to be coy
or to make the kind of investigation that was necessary. "Only—
how long has she been painting her face?"

"I don't know. Always, I suppose. Mother used the paint
from the time she was very young, whenever there was a
chance others would see her. That wasn't often, of course,
because of—because of her withered arm. She preferred to
keep Amalie hidden altogether." Ren paused, his brow
furrowing. "What—what does face paint have to do with
anything?"

Harriette glanced at the table where she mixed her paints.
"I cannot be sure, but her symptoms strike me as a type of lead
colic. My painting master at Miss Gregoire's told me about it. It
is a type of sickness painters can get and it is thought to be due
to the lead used to make white paint. It was said that the painter
Caravaggio went mad and died because of lead colic—back then
they used lead salts in all sorts of colors. Most white paints are
made with a lead preparation." When Ren shook his head in
confusion, she added, "I understand that lead is also used to
whiten face paint."

He abandoned his pose and strode across the room,
uncaring that in his lack of concentration his limp was notice-
able. He drew to Harriette's work table and regarded her jars of
pigment as if answers were laid out there. "You think this is why
she is sick? This lead colic?" He opened a jar of white pigment
and sniffed as if he could detect poisons.

"I cannot be sure. I am not a doctor. But it seems lead can
make people very ill. My teacher taught me to use gesso for my
whites, which is made with chalk and gypsum. I read some years
ago about the Devon colic, a sickness of the gut that is endemic
to Devonshire. A doctor proposed it was because the cider they
like to drink there had lead mixed into it. And Mr. Wedgewood
has sworn he will change his pottery formulas because of

potter's colic, which his workers were contracting because of lead in the ceramic glazes."

"She—she will die of this?" Ren's voice was strangled. "Because of this paint she uses on her face?"

"God forbid," Harriette said quickly. "But I think she must stop using the white paint immediately."

"She won't." Ren's voice was hoarse, torn from him. "She is as ashamed of her birthmark as she is of her arm. My mother can see nothing else when she looks at her, and with Amalie in the house—she is exposed to her censure every day."

"I wish I had time to prepare something better, but you might give her this."

Harriette stepped to his side and reached for a small, tightly stoppered glass jar on her worktable. A bright ribbon circled the creamy whiteness within.

"It is a face paint of my own preparation, made of chalk and gypsum. It should be easy to apply, now that I have found the right binding. I have been experimenting these past days and my first preparations were too runny when I applied them. The girls were in gales of laughter, saying I looked like a bleeding ghost."

Ren's face was unbearable to see, his composure gone, the naked emotion laid bare. Wordlessly he gripped her shoulders, his fingers digging into her skin as he clung to a desperate hope. His throat and jaw worked as he struggled to form the words choking him.

"I can promise nothing," Harriette whispered. "I wish I could, Ren. But—will you see that she gets this? And uses it?"

His affirmation was a finger beneath her chin, tipping her face up so he could probe every line of it with his all-too-perceptive eyes. She let her eyelashes flutter down. She felt uncertain, suddenly, about letting him see into her soul. If anyone could detect what lay within her, it would be he. At the moment she was full of nothing but deceit and despair.

She heard his slight hitch of breath, felt air fan over her cheek, smelled the trace of lemon from the scone he'd nicked from her aunt's breakfast table. Her heart surged to her throat, beating with wild anticipation. And when his mouth pressed against hers, she moaned with the sheer relief of being able to kiss him again, when she could seem to think of nothing else during the times he was not kissing her. He was heat and strength and delirious passion and a calm, deep knowledge that steadied her. He was Ren. He was the home she'd always wanted and had not found until now.

"I see what happens when I am lax in my chaperoning duties."

Princess wandered into the studio wearing morning dress and no powder in her hair, which shone a deep, true black. "I find you two canoodling."

Ren drew back as if she were a snake that had struck him, spewing venom.

"What an absurd word," Harriette snapped when she had come up for air.

Ren, with a gentlemanly flush of embarrassment, stepped away from Harriette's table and turned toward the canvas she'd been working on all morning. Even more absurdly, Harriette felt heat climb her cheeks. He was within his rights to look at what she'd done so far; he was the one paying her to produce it. But she felt intensely shy about his seeing how she saw him. It felt too revealing.

More revealing even than the sketches of him in simply his shirtsleeves, waistcoat and neckcloth discarded, lounging on her couch with an insolent, amused expression curling his excessively well-shaped lips. Those prints were selling faster than Mrs. Darly could make them.

Harriette stepped in front of the canvas and turned it away from his inquiring gaze. "I've not done enough yet for you to get a look proper." That wasn't true. She'd gotten the most important part: his face and its remote, thoughtful expression, the beauty of his strong features, and the suggestion of honor and strength that were such an integral part of him. But she didn't have his full body outlined yet—she would have to rely on her sketches to complete his figure, and then hours more to fill in the background. She didn't have enough *time*.

"Did you tell him yet?" Princess, with a yawn, settled herself on Darci's couch.

"Not yet." Harriette's heart squeezed. "I've, ah, been working up to it."

"Tell me wh-wh-what?"

Ren's face was a needle piercing her chest. He looked like he could not handle one more blow. Even his mighty shoulders would bow under her desertion.

How could she leave him now? And how could she ask for her commission to be paid if she hadn't completed the portrait before she left? She knew he would grant her the funds in a moment, if he had the means and he knew it would help her mother, but it felt dishonest. Stealing from him, when he had already given her so much.

"The Duchess," Princess said unhelpfully. "Of Löwenburg. Harriette's mother?"

"What about her?"

"She's failing." Harriette set her brush in its cup so he would not detect how her hand trembled. "I must go to her soon. Mrs. Demant thinks she may not last the week."

"You are leaving?" Ren whispered.

"I have a place on a coach departing from Le Belle Sauvage Inn in Ludgate Hill tomorrow." She raised her eyes to his. "At eight of the clock."

"An ungodly hour, when all decent folks are still asleep in their beds," Princess remarked.

"When will you return?" Ren's voice was hoarse.

"I do not know. It may be that Franz Karl will want to leave directly from Portsmouth once he comes to collect me. I have sent him a letter, though who knows what condition she will be in by the time it reaches him, if it reaches him at all."

"This is our last day together?" All the color left Ren's face as he absorbed this blow.

"I afraid it may be such for a good long while. I cannot say what the future holds." She twisted her hands in her lap. "I wish it were different. I wanted time to finish this portrait. Time to introduce Amalie to London. Time—"

Time with him. That was all. Endlessly unrolling days together, like the summer they'd spent roaming the meads and hills of Shepton Mallet under blue-gray skies, treading land full of ageless history and claiming it at their own.

Time to stand by and watch him court and marry another, devote himself to her, build a life with her, and spare a moment now and then to talk with an amusing friend from his child-hood? No, thank you. The one blessing of her unanticipated change of circumstances was that Harriette would not have to see Ren take a countess and his position in society and know she had no place in his life, and never could. The turnabout that had suddenly elevated her and made her a possibly worthy equal—daughter to a duke, destined to be a duchess in her own right—had at the same time snatched any hope that she could claim Ren for her own in any respectable fashion.

He gave her such a look of disbelief and betrayal that her stomach flipped. It was fortunate she had not been able to take any breakfast, or the contents would have been going arsey varsey about her insides.

"You are leaving." He concentrated on forming the words.

She knew his difficulties increased when he was agitated. "Just like that."

He'd left her without warning eleven years ago, shipping off to school when she had finally, for the first time in her life, found a friend. But this was not the same, and she knew it.

She forced a smile that did not reach across her face. "I've done what I could. I'll finish the portrait in Shepton Mallet and ship it to you before I leave. I gave you the face paint to give your sister, and I've helped you to find you a bride, haven't I? Every tea shop and milliner in London has copies of your print, and every woman who can afford it has bought a copy for her private collection. Every marriageable girl dreams of the Earl of Renwick."

"P-pity the men don't," Ren said roughly. "Someone called me Runtwick at Almack's yesterday."

"To your face?" Harriette asked, aghast. His face kindled with emotion, and she reached for her Prussian blue pigment to capture the exact, intense shade of his eyes.

"V-very nearly. Behind my back, of course, but within my earshot. They were passing a print back and forth between them. 'D-don't make Runtwick any more appealing, if you ask me,' they said. 'Can't see what the l-ladies are in a stew about,' they said."

"They see not with the eyes of a lady," Princess said, studying Ren.

Harriette set aside her brush, satisfied she had captured the hue she wanted, that precise cobalt blue, pure and light, calming and stimulating at the same time. "I've a mind to make a sketch that will make the gents eat themselves up with jealousy," she said. Outrage and wickedness tugged at her, twin imps. "Something that will silence the mockery, once and for all."

Princess twitched her black brows. "Strip him down to the altogether?"

Harriette snorted to cover the quick, hot flare of desire that suggestion fired in her. "I doubt Mrs. Darly would print something *that* scandalous. And it might make the ladies perceive him as a *roué* rather than heroic."

"Sketch him in a heroic pose, then." Princess shrugged and rose with a languid ripple of skirts. "I wish to write some letters, but I find I have neither paper nor ink. You two won't be naughty while I fetch my supplies, will you?"

"Rhette, naughty?" Ren said, but Harriette hardly heard him. She reached for her sketchbook and crayon while her eyes roved over the many studies she'd done of her subject. She had his face, all those memorable slopes and angles, and she'd achieved just the right blending of colors to capture the smoothness of his skin and the tone of his complexion, deepened by exposure to the sun. She had a sense for his torso, but only because she'd sketched him in his shirt and understood the build beneath. And because she'd been held against that firm chest and felt the play of the muscles she'd drawn, she understood with her body how tendon and flesh and the masculine structure of him all worked together.

"It's rubbish because I haven't got your full anatomy yet," she blurted.

"I beg your pardon." Ren glanced toward the doorway as Princess sauntered out with a silken swish.

"We were never allowed to have nude male models at school." Heat rose to her cheeks at the very thought of asking him to disrobe. She'd asked him to strip before and had been both professional and lascivious about it, knowing she ventured into improper territory. She'd pressed herself against his nether regions, for goodness sake. So why was she being kittenish now about the thought of stripping him down to his skin?

Because now she loved him. Not as a friend, but as a woman loves a man she wants to possess, to know, and to knit her life to.

Her crayon skated across the fresh sheet of paper as Harriette drew herself up in surprise. That line marked a division in her life: the time before she understood that she loved the Earl of Renwick, and the time after.

She'd loved him for half her life and would continue to love him for the rest of it, the boy he'd been and the man she'd come to know. Something had chimed in her when she climbed that tree to watch him pacing his dressing room in Renwick House; she'd felt then some nudge toward a knowledge that had grown and flowered in just a short time but had nonetheless shot down deep roots. He made sense to her on some basic level. He was *for* her.

And she had to leave him.

Her emotions must have shown on her face, because Ren stood as still as if he were posing, staring at her with wordless wonder. Heat flared again in his eyes, but she couldn't bear to look directly at it. She felt newly vulnerable to him, laid bare by this knowledge—she, who had made herself vulnerable to no man, ever.

She knew he desired her; many men had. But she also had heard the stories of the courtesans he'd kept across Europe. Those weren't tales that marriage-minded mamas told their genteel daughters over the dining parlor table, but they were tidbits that the members of the Countess of Calenberg's household reveled in. He had a man's appetites, and he liked the shape of Harriette. That explained his interest. Being a man with means and freedom and the God-given right to claim anything he wished, it made perfect sense that he would pursue her if he wanted her.

And as soon as she gave the gossip mill a reason to think she was another of his conquests, any power she had to demand respect from her future husband was gone.

But if he were willing to offer his body to her—she had use for it.

"I want to make another set of sketches," Harriette said, her breathing heavy. It was as though she'd been kissing him for hours, which she would very much like to be doing, but she wanted to draw him more than she wanted to kiss him right now.

"One of your racy prints?"

"This is just for me. So I can finish you. But I need to see—I need to understand..."

She circled her hand in the air, encompassing his tall, rangy frame. He leaned on his good leg, a casual pose, full of elegant, arrogant ease. It was an attitude he'd cultivated to hide his defect, and it was because she knew what he was hiding, how hard he worked to pass himself off like other men, that she loved him so completely.

His eyes darkened to indigo. "How *much* do you need to see?" he purred.

Oh, he was lethal. But the come-hitherness, oddly, made her rein herself in. All those courtesans. All those women who'd had the liberty to touch him as often and as thoroughly as they wanted. None of them had loved him, not like she did.

"Sit you on Darci's couch." She pointed toward the low couch that Princess had vacated. "The light has shifted and is better there. Now disrobe and put this sheet over your—er, lap." She pulled a long linen strip off a nearby statue that Darci had decided she didn't like. "I'll turn my back," she promised, and did, in an act of quite uncharacteristic modesty, one she immediately regretted. She wanted to know every part of his body, didn't she?

He cleared his throat. "I-I need—I need help with my coat and-and boots."

She melted at his complete capitulation to her request. The

crack in his composure, more than the plea for assistance, pulled her toward him. She avoided his eyes while she worked his neckcloth loose and set the strip of white linen aside. She wiped her hands on her apron so she did not leave prints on his expensive silver buttons as she worked free his coat, peeling the luscious silk from his broad shoulders. It held the heat of his body and she resisted bringing the lavishly embroidered fabric close to her nose; she had the man before her, smelling of hair powder, boot polish, shaving soap, and some earthy undertone that was his own raw scent. It made her middle ache.

She knelt before him on the wooden floor and laid a hand on the knee of his good leg. The intimacy of undressing him, the closeness it demanded, stole her breath. Also, he was going to let her see his damaged foot. He had only done so once when they were children, and by accident, the day she slipped into the Manor House over the Blinder Wall and found where his tutor had shut him in the cistern room without coat or boots because Ren had defied him about something. She suspected the object of contention had been her.

"Am I going to need a bootjack?"

"N-no, they're not that tight." The muscle of his thigh was taut and warm. His heat dove into her and spread everywhere, feeding the ache between her legs.

When the fashion was for white clocked stockings and buckled shoes, Ren stood apart with his knee breeches and tall riding boots of hand-stitched black leather. The tops were white and decorated with a small tassel dangling from the lip. She had seen the shoes he wore the night of his mother's gathering, the ones specially made for him by the Italian doctor, but she had given him the liberty to select his own footwear for his portrait, and he had come in boots. She liked the rugged note of contrast to his fashionable cutaway frock coat with its curving tails and expansive collar. He looked like a man who would do well in a drawing room but was more at ease in the open air, a man of health and vigor.

"Very well then, off they come."

"Just what do you in-intend?"

"The Gentleman Abed. But this time—" She gulped for air —"without the shirt, please."

"The gentleman abed without his nightshirt or cap will catch his death from the ague." His voice was muffled as he drew the oversized shirt over his head.

"It's warm enough in here, and I can light a fire if you wish," she said, or meant to say. Her throat suddenly went dry. The white linen with its ruffled sleeves drew up like an incongruously delicate curtain over his stomach, flat with muscle and drifted with tiny light-brown hairs. His chest broadened as her eyes moved up, his ribs a strong curve flaring to broad pectoral muscles. He tossed the shirt aside and her greedy gaze lit on the muscle corded around his shoulders, the defined upper arms.

He resembled the classical Greek statues that she and her classmates had been reduced to using for models since it was too unorthodox, even for Miss Gregoire's Academy, to expose nude males to impressionable young women. She'd always thought those statues a work of imagination, since most of the males she saw in her daily life had quite different proportions. But Ren's physique mirrored the symmetrical ideals of the ancient artists. At least above the waist.

"Ready?" she whispered. If he objected, she would not press. She would sketch him with his clothes on and do her best. But she could already see how to remedy the problems she'd been having with his upper body, how to shade his shoulders to show their breadth, add a subtle curve to his upper chest to capture the swell of muscle, and emphasize the leanness of his waist.

Now, if she could only manage not to make his legs look like two sticks, she had a chance at a portrait that would please him and perhaps, who knew, be worthy of showing at the Royal Academy, if Angelica Kauffman thought it done well enough. Harriette's fingers tingled, but it was not the thought of exhibiting at the Royal Academy that charged her with excitement, or at least not that thought alone. Ren sat before her, half naked, and slowly nodded his head, meeting her gaze with a steady trust.

She slid off his boot and swallowed as her eyes followed the shape of his leg, beautifully formed, the muscles a sensuous curve, thick and smooth at the same time. How had she never noticed that a man's legs were such an impressive creation? But perhaps it was only Ren who was so well-shaped.

"The breeches too?" His voice was a strangled whisper.

"Best not go *that* far." She wanted to shout *Yes! All of it!* She wanted to peel every piece of fabric from his body and crawl over him, pressing him back upon the couch and tracing all that gorgeous, smooth muscle with her mouth. *Oh, Lord.* She lowered her face, hiding her furious blush by unbuttoning the cuff of his breeches and pushing the supple fabric up over his knee. Then she peeled off the white stocking beneath, marked with its embroidered clocks. Her fingers trailed over his skin, the firm warm muscle, the soft hairs. Her taut nipple brushed against his leg as she set his stocking aside, and she jerked at the contact.

He tensed as she turned to the other boot. She felt the difference in construction, how the leather of the foot panels was lined with something thick and heavy, possibly wood. The leather portion that covered his calf was banded with steel to provide structure and support. She worked the boot off slowly and could not look at his face, not even when she asked, "Am I hurting you?"

"No," he hissed, but he held himself so taut that his body vibrated.

She set the heavier boot next to its mate and pushed back the cuff of his breeches. Then she peeled off the stocking, running her fingers along his skin. The muscles of this calf were bunched and shortened, the skin crossed with scars, with a heavy line of raised skin across above his heel.

"The good doctor's work?" she murmured, tracing the largest one, a crimson welt.

"Yes." He pushed out the word. His hand came to her shoulder, holding her as if she might run. But also leaning on her for support. "He cut the ligaments so they will extend further."

"Does it still hurt?"

"I don't feel much there. It's part of the problem, why I—" He let the words fade.

His foot as a boy had been turned inward, pointing unnaturally toward its healthier mate, and rolled so that the sole pointed toward the opposite ankle and he walked on the outside of his foot. He still did, somewhat; she traced her fingers over the thick calluses that had formed on his skin. His toes curled tightly, but the foot had been turned and straightened somewhat, with more scars crossing the tight, round bridge.

"Do you feel this?" She traced the scars, gently probing the bones that had formed awry, the muscles that had changed to compensate.

"I don't understand why you're not revolted."

She looked up at him then and met his eyes. "The human body is fascinating to me. How it's built. I think if I weren't a painter, I would be a doctor." She rose to her knees, placing a hand atop each of his thighs. "*Your* body is fascinating to me," she whispered. "Nothing about you revolts me."

He looked into her eyes, and Harriette felt herself falling. Drowning. This was the moment, she realized even as she was in it. This was the moment that set a seal on her heart, that anchored her to him for all time.

He didn't need to reach far to wrap his arms around her and haul her against his body. She surrendered instantly, every scruple, every resolve, every caution dissolving in the onslaught of simple want. Given the choice between touching Ren or not touching Ren, she would choose to touch him, every time.

His tongue dove into her mouth and the arc of sensation shot through her body to that hungry place at her core. She tilted her head back and sucked on his tongue, reveling in his groan of passion, reveling in the dance of their joined mouths. He hauled her up further and without hesitation she straddled his groin, pushing her hot aching place against his hardness, fitting herself to him like a puzzle with several layers of clothing keeping them from a perfect fit.

He leaned her back in his arms and bent his head and pulled at the loose drawstring at the neck of her gown with his teeth. Before she could gasp or scold or tell him how much she was looking forward to it, his mouth grazed her breast, worked down to a nipple, and closed over that begging bud, sucking with teeth and tongue. She went boneless, a hot pool of breathless sensation, a melting arc of pure need.

She nudged her hips against his cock, rubbing shamelessly, and felt no shame either in the panting mewl that escaped her when he closed one big, warm hand over the breast he'd just explored and moved his mouth to the other. This was pleasure like she'd never known, and an ache like she'd never known, an inferno she wanted to throw herself into. She clung to his shoulders as she gasped and writhed under the onslaught of his mouth, teeth, so-clever tongue, ready to let him do anything to her, ready to follow him into the maelstrom and—

"*Ahem.* I left you more than sufficient time to be done with this already," came the voice, loud and firm and disapproving.

"Go—away," Harriette panted, writhing against Ren's hips. His guttural agreement came out against her nipple as he lifted his head from her breast. His expression looked as dazed and fierce as she felt.

"I will not," Princess snapped. "Someone has to vow to Fritz that you honored your promise of marriage, at least as soon as you found out about it. You wouldn't have me lie to the man's face, would you?"

"Franz Karl." Harriette groaned and pulled the bodice of her gown back into place. The name was a cold wind snuffing the flames of desire. Good heavens, hadn't she just finished telling herself she couldn't have Ren, instructing herself to be chaste and reserved? And it had taken less than five minutes for her to crawl all over him like an alley cat in heat.

Ren held completely still, and she realized that, for him, Harriette's voluminous morning gown was all that lay between Princess and utter indecency.

"Really, your Highness," she said, which was how she addressed her friend when she was supremely annoyed, "you are interrupting a delicate situation. I am—er, preparing to sketch Ren in the altogether, and he won't appreciate witnesses."

Princess snorted. "What man alive doesn't appreciate a woman witnessing him in the altogether?"

"Rhette," the man beneath her whispered, his expression strained. He moved his leg, hiding his damaged foot beneath her hem. She turned in his lap and spread her skirts over his nether regions to hide him properly. Her new position snugged his cockstand directly into the crevice of her bottom, and when she squirmed again to add an inch or two of space between them, he groaned and clutched her hips.

"Renwick doesn't," Harriette said as primly as she could, given that she was perched on the erection of a mostly nude man. She met her friend's exasperated gaze and nodded toward the small heap of Ren's clothing on the floor, beside which stood his custom-made leather boots. "Truly, I'll be good. But can you not—go into the next room or something, and give the man his modesty?"

Princess, too, looked at the boots, then looked at Harriette, understanding. "Very well," she said, "I will withdraw into the morning parlor. But," she tossed over her shoulder as she took her portable writing desk out the door with her, "if I hear the faintest sounds of copulating—or anything wet and smacking, anything at all—I shall call up everyone below and bring them with me to separate you."

"No smacking sounds from us!" Harriette called after her, then slithered off Renwick's lap.

His fingers around her wrist gave her pause. "Is that all we shall have, Rhette?"

It was all they ever could have: stolen kisses and the brush of bodies, but no promises, no future. She couldn't bear for him to see her weakness, even though it was Ren, and she hid nothing from him. She forced herself to give him a careless curtsey, as if he held her hand to lead her out into a dance.

"I can give you the afternoon, milord, but that is all I can promise. And you must let me sketch you. I know exactly how I might finish your portrait, now."

She made short work of the sitting. She had to. Ren watched her with hooded eyes, slouched on the couch with a linen sheet over his lap, his good leg propped on the edge of the couch and his scarred leg tucked beneath the sheet. His bare feet and bared chest, muscular body, and lazy, sensual gaze were the most powerful aphrodisiac she could imagine.

This wasn't stealing, not this. These sketches were his last gift to her, a salve for her longing when she was far away and had nothing but memories of this time in his arms. She made sketch after sketch, her crayon flying across the pages, imprinting him indelibly upon her eyes just as he was imprinted on her heart. She couldn't give him a lifetime. She couldn't even give him one day. But she wanted to make this single afternoon last as long as possible.

CHAPTER TWELVE

Everyone in the small dressing room stared at Amalie's face as Harriette painted it with a small brush.

It was much like preparing a canvas, save that the girl's skin was already as smooth as fine porcelain and needed no scrub with the pumice stone. Harriette brought her basic pigments with her to Renwick House and after some trial and error had achieved the same tint as Amalie's skin, the blush of an early spring rose. The others insisted on watching the proceedings: Lady Amalie's nurse, because it would be her place to apply the paint hereafter, and Ren, because he wanted to be on hand during the conversation in which Harriette gently informed his sister that her makeup was poisoning her. The Countess of Renwick also insisted on being in the room, largely to make known her disapproval of Harriette.

"That's done it, then," the nurse maid said in a tone of admiration mixed with disbelief. "Ye can hardly see the mark. A shame our girl has to bear it, when she's so bonny otherwise."

Harriette wondered if the countess found it harder to accept her daughter's flaws because her beauty was otherwise so striking. A plainer girl might have driven her to less despair. Both

Ren and his sister were uncommonly good-looking, and as their mother had little to recommend her beyond wealth and a close attention to grooming, Harriette suspected their beauty had been a gift from the late earl. It was not inconceivable that a man blessed all his life with a divinely handsome face might detest his less-than-perfect children. It was unjust of him, but not inexplicable.

"Did you know that medieval painters often left a deliberate flaw in their compositions?" Harriette said. "A friend of mine from school explained it to me once. She said that monks illuminating holy manuscripts would leave a tiny imperfection on purpose, because only God is perfect."

"God gave me a very great flaw," Amalie said bitterly. As before, the sleeves of her gown were edged with lace that covered the stump of her left forearm.

"But that keeps you from hubris, the fatal flaw of Greek tragedy," Harriette said. "Think of all the ancient mothers of myth who tried to hide or deface their beautiful daughters so they wouldn't draw the interest of Zeus. Because how much worse would it be to suffer Hera's jealousy? Callisto, turned into a bear. Io, transformed to a cow. Or Danaë, stuffed into a trunk and cast out to sea?"

"I wish you would stop filling her head with such fanciful tales," the countess said. "They sound like they come from some terrible cheap romance."

"They are the most ancient and revered of Gr-Greek myths, M-mother," Ren said.

"Well, I think your preparation works the same as the other, Lady Harriette," the nurse announced. "And a sight less dear than what the apothecary demands."

"I will leave you the exact recipe, just in case," Harriette said. "Though I hope I will be able to send you fresh supplies from—wherever I am."

A taut silence emanated from Ren at this reminder that their time together was disappearing. Harriette had agreed to spend her last afternoon in London with him, on the condition they take Amalie to the pleasure gardens. She didn't trust what she might do or say if left alone with him in private.

"It feels lighter," Amalie said in a small voice, turning the painted side of her face toward the small hand-held mirror. "Smoother, somehow. Are you certain no one will be able to tell the difference?"

"We'll add a brush of rice powder and a patch or two, and you will rivet with your beauty. Though I hope you will leave off the arsenic tonic as a rinse, and use water infused with lemon instead," Harriette suggested.

"This paint is not as opaque as the other from the apothecary," the countess fretted. "It might fade or run. I don't see why she can't continue as she has been."

"Because the paint she was using was giving her lead colic," Harriette answered sharply. "If she stops using it, there is a very good chance that all the symptoms that were plaguing her will diminish.

"Besides, do you know how white paint is prepared? By soaking lead in vinegar and layering it in horse dung. Do you want to put horse dung on your face?" she demanded of Amalie.

"No." The girl shuddered.

"Renwick women make many sacrifices to live up to the high expectations laid upon us," the countess snapped. "She will do what needs must."

"She will use my preparation on her face if she wishes for her makeup not to kill her," Harriette retorted, placing the jar on the dressing table with more force than was necessary. The nurse gasped, but Harriette did not retreat. This was Amalie's life at stake, a girl who had immediately wormed her way into

Harriette's heart, and for her own sake, not just because Ren adored her.

"She also needs plenty of fresh air, exercise, and nourishing foods," Harriette added. "That is why Ren and I plan to take her to the pleasure gardens today and stuff her with tarts."

She avoided looking at Ren as she used a different brush to dust rice powder over his sister's face. Her stomach twisted into knots. The clock was ticking on her time with him, and it took every ounce of willpower not to throw herself into his arms. Her body was still in a state of arousal from sketching him that morning, staring at his bare chest, inspecting the shape of his bare legs and feet, noticing each time she stared too long and the sheet draped over his groin stirred with his arousal.

Their early youthful friendship had made her move too fast with him, made all the customary barriers and social niceties irrelevant. She knew his mind and now she knew his body, a carnal, elemental knowledge that made her proprietary and jealous. She had made the other sketches to make him delectable to the ladies; she had made that last sketch of a nearly nude, aroused Renwick for her own delectation alone.

But some other woman would get to marry him. Some other woman would get to claim that primary place at his side. Mother of his children. Mistress of his home.

Well, good for her, Harriette thought as she stuck a tiny silk patch in the shape of a heart atop Amalie's cheekbone. Harriette wasn't the least bit motherly. Or domestic. She didn't have a nurturing bone in her body, as her mother and aunt and all the women of her household could attest. She was selfish and headstrong and she wanted to spend all her free time painting. She would make the most terrible wife.

"You cannot take my daughter out of doors!" the countess said with a gasp. "I forbid it! You would expose her to ridicule, and shame, and—worse."

Harriette snapped the lid shut on the tiny box that held her vast assortment of patches. "Countess, I am afraid I cannot agree with you that Lady Amalie should be hidden in the dark. There's not a woman in London who doesn't have smallpox scars, or a limp from rickets, or missing teeth—"

"I beg your pardon, but I have none of those!" said the countess, outraged.

"—and I see no reason that anyone not matching your impossible notions of beauty should not show their face among the rest of God's creatures," Harriette finished.

"You would need to believe that, looking as you do!" Her ladyship threw Harriette a scornful glare.

Ren, the nurse, and Amalie all turned their heads to regard Harriette, searching out the basis for this accusation. An embarrassed flush rose over her bosom. Ren followed the path of color with his eyes, letting his gaze linger on the swell of her breasts, and the blush deepened.

"Nevertheless." Harriette lifted her chin, drawing on the knowledge of her new rank. She was a duchess-to-be by right; her ladyship was merely a countess by marriage. She hated that these distinctions should matter, but she meant to take advantage of them if they did. "You do Lady Amalie a disservice by making her too ashamed to enjoy the pleasures that should be hers by right. Friends. Social interests. Strolls through gardens."

"I am her mother," the countess huffed. "I know what is best for her, and I—"

"Renwick?" Harriette asked, meeting her ladyship's steely glare.

He cleared his throat. Wrong of her, so wrong, to call on him to take her side in this debate. She oughtn't pit him against his own mother.

"No one has asked Am-Amalie what she w-wants," Ren said quietly.

Harriette stiffened and turned to the girl, who cast a help-less gaze between the faces staring at her, waiting. "Lady Amalie, I beg your pardon. Would you like to go to the pleasure gardens today?"

Amalie held up her empty, lace-hung sleeve. "There is still this. I—I can't abide for people to pity me."

"Rhette has a solution for you," Ren said gently. "I think—I think you ought to see it before you de-decide."

"I see that no one will listen to her mother," the countess said shrilly. "I see that I shall be ignored, though I am in the right." In a great huff she picked up her flaring skirts and sailed out the door, muttering imprecations all the way.

"Right, then, I'll fetch your bonnet, lass." The nurse bustled toward the wardrobe. "Something to keep your face from the sun."

Ren announced that he would wait for them downstairs and exited the room. Harriette checked that her hat was securely fastened to her powdered coils of hair and then took Amalie's arm as they leisurely descended the curving staircase, giving Ren plenty of time to proceed unobserved at his own pace.

"Did you know that in the Dark Ages, marked children were the sign of a magical bloodline?" Harriette said. "My friend at school told me the legend of a great lady named Mélusine who had ten sons, all of them with some oddity. One had two different colored eyes, like you. One had three eyes." She winced. "One had a tuft of hair on his nose, and one had a lion's claw protruding from his cheek, and one had an enormous tooth. They called him Geoffrey Great Tooth, and he was considered quite fierce and marvelous."

"But why did they have these strange marks?" Amalie questioned, dubious.

"Well, at some point in their marriage, Mélusine's husband discovered she was of the fairy, and she suffered a curse that turned her into a serpent from the waist down one day a week. So he accused her of infecting his sons with demon blood, and that is when she turned into a dragon and leaped out the window and flew away, never to be seen in human form again."

"So the children looked as they did because they were part demon," Amalie said flatly.

"No, my point is that they were all considered quite strong and marvelous, and their outward defects were marks that they were magical. Set apart."

"I do not wish to be set apart," Amalie said as they turned the last curve from the first floor toward the ground level. "I wish to be like everyone else."

"While every normal girl wishes she were remarkable," Harriette replied. "Which reminds me that my friend Amaranthe, who told me this story, is now pledged to marry the new Duke of Hunsdon. I really ought to call on her." Not least because her friend might have some advice for Harriette about how to behave as a duchess when one had been an unacknowledged nobody all one's life.

"Oh, dear, what is the matter now?" Amalie murmured as they moved down the last flight of stairs towards Ren, who stood watching with fascination the mill unfolding in his entrance hall.

Two footmen in Renwick livery, the hall boy, and a groom stood clustered around two men in the doorway, while Dunstan the butler hovered at the back of the group, curious and dismayed. Beater stood in the open double doors, brandishing an enormous fur muff as large as his torso, apparently using it to act out some prize fight of his past. Jock leaned on his crutches beside him, laughing at the amazement on the faces of the footmen as Beater swung and feinted, astonishingly light on his feet for a man his size.

"S'enough to suffocate a grown man, it is," Jock hooted.

Amalie faltered on the stairs as she saw the group. Her eyes went to Jock with his twisted legs, leaning on his crutches. His tight coat outlined the wiry muscles in his arms and chest. Beater stopped his play and turned brick red. Amalie clapped her hand over her sleeve and turned nearly the same color, the blush spreading down her pretty throat.

"Thank you, and I hope you have not dirtied the princess's muff by defeating it in a match," Harriette said, stepping forward. The crowd of men melted away as she plucked the muff out of Beater's hand. "Lady Amalie, this is John Beater, former champion of the ring and now footman and groom to the Countess of Calenberg, and Henry Jock, former champion of the racecourse, her ladyship's equerry. Men, this is Lady Amalie, Renwick's younger sister. You'll forgive Jock if he doesn't bend a knee to the floor," she added.

"Oh, I can bend a knee, Lady H," Jock said smartly. "It's getting me up off the floor again you won't like."

He gave Amalie a bold wink. Her blush deepened.

"I don't—that is—how very nice to meet you," Amalie stammered. Harriette handed her the muff and she looked at it as if not knowing what to make of it. Harriette slid the enormous confection onto the girl's left arm, then lifted her right hand and tucked it into the silken lining. In an instant Amalie's defects were invisible.

"Oh, my word—this is the most luxurious thing I've ever felt in my life," Amalie murmured in rapture.

"Is it not? We all steal it and take turns wearing it when Princess isn't about," Harriette said. "She ordered it from Paris for the winter and we can't put it away even if it is high summer. If I sketched you now for Mary Darly, she would no doubt put you in her satire of 'Wigs,' wearing that."

"How many w-rabbits gave their li-life to make that extravagance?" Ren asked, making his way down the last of the stairs.

"It's perfect. Thank you for bringing it to me, Lady Harriette." Amalie turned a beaming smile on Harriette's men.

Beater tipped his hat with a bashful smile, then jostled Jock with an elbow and muttered under his breath. "Shut yer trap, man, yer catchin' flies."

Jock snapped his mouth shut.

"You l-look quite the fashion plate, sister," Ren said. "Are you willing to come with us now?"

Amalie hugged her muff, beaming. "I suppose I am."

She watched Jock with cautious interest, and the groom threw out his chest as he swung out the door to the very smart town coach waiting before the house. With a nod to the driver, Jock went to the near horse and pulled himself onto its back, arranging his legs against the animal's sides. Beater collected the discarded crutches and swung with them onto the platform at the back of the coach, nodding to the footmen who had turned out to see them off with reverential stares and murmurs.

Ren watched Amalie enter the carriage with a look of wonder and soft affection, and Harriette's heart melted. "Come, milord, pleasure awaits us."

It was the wrong thing to say. His eyes heated with that inner flame, and a like flame leapt to life within her, creating different melting sensations in that place in her middle that turned so aware and sensitive when he was near.

"If only." He bent his head to drop the words near her ear, then took her arm.

Harriette shivered with the mingled pain and pleasure of the fiercest longing she had ever known in her life. If only this man could be hers. If his sister could be her sister. It was wrong to covet something she couldn't have.

But it didn't make her want it any less.

. . .

"MY BROTHER IS in love with you."

Amalie strolled at her side through the Grand Walk of Marylebone Pleasure Gardens. The paths were not crowded, and pleasant music drifted from the orchestra playing on the balcony of the pavilion. The tall, slender trees with their silvery bark and dainty leaves provided shade from the afternoon sun, and delicious aromas drifted from the shaded gallery that housed the dining area. Jock and Beater were here somewhere, having dispersed to their own amusements after Renwick's servants let them down in the High Street of what had once been sleepy Marylebone village and was fast becoming an outpost of the great thrumming sprawl that was London. The gravel paths and trimmed trees, an island of repose in the bustling city, seemed outlined in gold, now that Harriette was looking upon her favorite retreats for what might be the last time.

Harriette glanced behind them to where Ren was surrounded by a horde of female admirers. He couldn't walk a step without being detained by some overly friendly matron towing a demure, giggling girl or two in her wake. The ladies blushed and wafted fans before bright eyes and pinkened cheeks, looking up and down Ren's form as if they knew what he looked like beneath his saffron silk frock coat and waistcoat with its crimson checks. And they did, thanks to Harriette and Mrs. Darly.

"Your brother and I were good friends the summer he lived in Shepton Mallet. He is kind to me based on that past affection, I think. Proven in that he has agreed to pay me an exorbitant commission for a painting I've not yet finished."

"It is more than that," Amalie insisted. "He is besotted with you. Over the moon."

"Hmmm," Harriette said. As she watched, Bess Hervey, who had looked upon Ren with horror in the formal drawing room of Renwick House, tapped him on the arm with her fan and laughed becomingly. She was an uncommonly handsome woman, drat her sparkling eyes. Meanwhile Charlotte Stanhope, coming up at Ren's rear with her friends in train, ogled his backside with an unmaidenly leer. Her interested gaze roamed down his brown breeches to the riding boots which made him look casually uncaring of fashion and thus all the more fashionable.

Those girls would recoil if they knew the scars and the suffering that lay beneath Ren's white clocked stockings and his cunningly crafted boots. Harriette felt a hitch in her stomach. He might marry a woman who would close her eyes when he came to the marital bed, lying still and passive while he went about his business of breeding her, shutting out the sight of his beautiful face inflamed with passion, his eyes that vivid and enthralling blue. He might give himself to a woman who would never strip him down and kiss and taste every inch of him, as Harriette would do, given half the chance.

As all those courtesans on his Grand Tour had done, no doubt. Reports had come back of the extraordinary satisfaction the Earl of Renwick left in his lovers. One famous Neapolitan courtesan had refused a French prince after Ren had left her. He was a man with a man's appetites and the skill to melt a woman into pudding, as she had found. Oh, yes, she envied his eventual wife. She hoped he chose someone worthy of him.

"A man may—admire a woman he has no intention of marrying," Harriette said finally. "In fact men are capable of—admiring women they feel very little affection for whatsoever." She knew she ought to guard her speech around Amalie, a clear innocent. She was not among the experienced, forthright women of her aunt's household.

Amalie's delicate brow wrinkled. "I do not think my brother is one of those."

"And neither should any of your suitors be," Harriette said. "You must insist that any man who pays court to you honor you with intentions of marriage. Don't give a moment of your time to a man who does not cherish you as you deserve." She turned away from the sight of the cluster of curious, flirtatious women growing around Ren.

"Me, with suitors. When pigs fly. I don't see why you won't give George a chance to court you," Amalie went on stubbornly.

"He cannot marry one such as I," Harriette said. The very thought gave her a strange, hollow ache in the center of her chest. For a dizzying moment, she imagined herself married to him. Stepping out to parties and balls as the Countess of Renwick. Holding teas for the wives of his political colleagues and funding causes dear to their hearts. Having the gossip paragraphs pore over her every move and hold her flaws to Ren's account rather than her aunt's. Watching her time to paint disappear before household duties, social calls, the demands of eventual children.

As his wife she would have the right to his bed and his attention, possession of that beautiful body she had traced with her crayon onto paper. But she had watched the British nobility from the fringes long enough to know how closely guarded, how treacherous those circles were. She would bring Ren nothing but amusing companionship and passionate bedsport, when a properly trained and well-bred wife could bring him so much more.

"Besides, you forget I am notorious. I don't wish to meddle or come in the way between him and the girl he chooses to marry. I—I want him to be free to give his full affection to his wife," Harriette said, and tried her best not to sound miserable about it. There was little point adding that Amalie might come to be tainted by her brush as well.

"And then there is Franz Karl." Harriette sighed. "My intended."

Her eyes flitted back to Ren and the coterie of females cooing and bustling about him, using their fans, lashes, and bosoms to capture his attention. He looked dazed and a tad alarmed, not delighted by the attention, as a man ought. Harriette tamped down the urge to rescue him. She had wanted this for him—orchestrated it, actually, with those blasted prints.

"He wrote, you know."

Harriette watched as a plump, curvy blonde sidled close to Ren and gazed rapturously into his face. Her bosom was not as fine as Harriette's, but she made certain Ren had a full view of it.

"Wrote who?" Harriette muttered.

"You. George wrote you piles of letters. I found them in the desk in his study when I was looking for Elizabeth Griffith's volume on Shakespeare's plays, which he bought for me."

Harriette dwelled a moment on the lovely, wistful image of Ren and his sister sitting cozily in the morning room at Renwick House, reading to each other. "He never wrote me letters." She turned quizzical eyes on her companion. "My mother would have prevented me from seeing them, but she would have told me letters were being withheld."

"He never *sent* them," Amalie said. "But he wrote them. Weekly, if not monthly, up until the time he left for his tour of the Continent. And there is a whole journal of entries addressed to you, which I assumed..." Amalie wore a puzzled expression. "He's never shared this with you?"

The sun was suddenly very hot, falling through the canopy of trees onto the thick embroidered silk of her open robe and tight stomacher. "Ren wrote to me?"

Amalie's eyes widened, the blue slightly wider than the brown. "Proof that he loves you," she whispered.

"Proof of—" Harriette caught herself and looked back at Ren. What, indeed, did it mean? She'd written him heaps of letters, too, but knowing that receiving letters from a girl would make him a subject of ridicule among his classmates, she'd hidden most of them away, reused the paper for sketches, or burned the ones in which her thoughts were too frankly confessed.

She'd written him letters because he was her first and for a time her only friend. When she went to school at Miss Gregoire's and a new world opened up to her, one with girls of her own age and ambitions, she'd wanted to tell Ren all about it. Writing to Ren sorted her thoughts and made her feel close to him, even if he were leagues away, in distant countries she'd never visit.

But the knowledge that he'd written to her as well, letters that had never reached her—she burned to know their contents, and yet she was afraid at the same time. What had he said in them that he decided not to let her see?

A secret cache of letters—whether they were affectionate or not—put the trail of satisfied courtesans in a different light. It meant Harriette wasn't one of their sighing numbers. It meant she was something else.

"Ahem. *Lady* Harriette," came a fawning voice. "What an unrivaled pleasure to find you here. In the pleasure gardens. Indeed, a meeting most apt, if not fated."

Harriette tore her eyes away from Ren and the soft, sentimental thoughts swirling through her head at this revelation. Before her on the Grand Walk stood the three macaronis who had accosted her in Leicester Square, but with a marked change in their demeanor as well as their dress.

Instead of the towering wigs of before, they wore small perukes with curls along the brow and sides and a tidy queue in back, very similar to Renwick's. Their frock coats still boasted a multitude of buttons, but the waistcoats were muted, of a complimentary rather than a contrasting color with their coats, and they had reduced the number of fobs and chains by half. Harriette's surprised gaze stopped at their footwear. Each of the three men wore polished black leather boots with white bands about the top and a small dangling tassel. Exactly the style of Ren's.

She swallowed a laugh as she brought her gaze back to their faces. Pasty, powdered, and patched, they were still, but with not quite as much rouge on their cheeks, nor as bright a red to their lips. It was unlikely that Ren's sun-bronzed skin tones would set the fashion for a culture that prized paleness, but they had clearly borrowed his pattern in everything else.

Satisfaction mixed with her disdain. She had meant to make him admired, and she had succeeded.

"Lady Harriette, where is your sketchbook? I insist you draw me," said the one who had chosen an ensemble of canary yellow.

"I recall you abused my poor sketchbook on the occasion of our last meeting," Harriette replied. Amalie hugged her muff tightly and shrank into Harriette's side, shaking with terror. Harriette considered making introductions, which courtesy demanded, but she was not of a mind to be courteous to these fops.

"A print by Lady Harriette is the done thing," said the second, outfitted in orange. Harriette did not care for his petulant tone. "I want one. Indeed, several."

"I do not wish to be sketched in the altogether, however," said the third, garbed in a bilious green. "May I at least keep my waistcoat on?"

"I am not in the business of providing sketches to any man who asks," Harriette said sharply.

"I say, *aren't* you?" demanded the first. "You did Runtwick and the Graf Hardy-ho—"

"*What* did you call him?" Harriette glared.

"Renwick." The man hastily corrected himself. "*Renwick.*" He cleared his throat. "Can't imagine what you heard, eh? But see here, miss—er, your ladyship—this is the very pattern of male beauty, ain't it?" He flourished a beringed hand through the air, indicating himself. "Share the profits with you! Put this heavenly visage in the hands of every ladybird in London—er, *lady* in London, that is— and that'll be quite a leap up for you, won't it? That is—er, as the daughter of a, what's it, a foreign duchess, you—I—" He finally foundered to a stop, daunted at last by Harriette's gimlet stare.

She felt cold fury and hot shame running through her in the same veins. It was an extraordinarily uncomfortable sensation. Did these men think she was some sort of street artist they could engage at a village fair? She'd been striving for this, for patrons, moneyed patrons, begging them to capture their image. And she wanted nothing so much as to find the nearest pile of carriage horse dung and push each one of these mincing dandies into it.

"I'm afraid I have left off sketching gentlemen," Harriette said, trying to control the unwanted quaver of regret in her tone. "I regret that I cannot consider your requests. Good—good day."

"Oh, but Lady Harriette!" They leapt after her as she tried to pull Amalie away. "Do walk a bit with us, at the very least. Don't you and your friend wish for an escort? Two lovely ladies ought to have the most fashionable gents on their arm."

"Renwick is our escort," Harriette retorted, hugging Amalie to her as she kept moving.

"Lady Harriette!" said a new voice, a woman's. "I am not surprised at all to find you in the thick of a crowd of admirers. You are enjoying your new status very much, I suppose?"

Harriette squinted through the shade of an overarching tree

to see who had addressed her. It was no less than Lady Cranbury, one of the *ton's* reigning hostesses. Beside her stood Lady Bessington, casting a benign smile Harriette's way and sparing a curious glance for Amalie.

Behind them trailed the girl Harriette had spotted sitting alone in the row of rout chairs at Lady Renwick's soiree, a sternly beautiful dark face in a room of pale English blooms. The girl watched Harriette with a frank stare.

"Lady Cranbury. Lady Bessington." Harriette grappled for her composure and sank into a curtsey, pulling Amalie along with her. "Oh. Er. This is Lady Amalie, Renwick's sister. How do you do?"

Lady Cranbury had never deigned to notice, much less address her. And now these doyennes of the London scene, these pillars of Polite Society, were giving Harriette their full attention.

"We are very curious to hear how one goes from being plain Miss Harriette Smythe to Lady Harriette, daughter to the Duchess of Löwenburg," Lady Cranbury simpered. She wore a set of wide panniers that held out the sides of her fashionable gown, in the style *à la anglaise,* and her face was painted as white as her hair powder. "You must pay me a call and tell us precisely how this elevation came to be. I know—I shall send you an invitation to my *converzatione* next week. A very small gathering, only the best people. You *must* come."

Harriette's head whirled at the strangeness of Lady Cranbury, one of the town's most hard to please sentinels, classing *her* among the best people. She would pinch herself if it wouldn't look gauche.

"And I would have you at one of my salons as well," said Lady Bessington. "We speak of the usual things, politics, philosophy, art. We would be very interested in having you speak sometime, if you wish, on the growing power of Prussia and the ambitions of Frederick the Great."

"But I am not the least bit qualified—that is to say, I know so little—and I—er, am to be married soon, and..." Harriette clung to Amalie for dear life, trying to order her thoughts. Behind Lady Cranbury, the plain-gowned companion watched Harriette with a sharp, intelligent eye, listening to every word.

"I am grateful and honored for your attentions, my ladies," Harriette finally managed in a breathless rush. "I should like nothing more than to attend you."

If only she weren't leaving London tomorrow with no notion of when she might return. She had finally, *finally* been offered her *entrée* into society's most elite circles—precisely what she had wanted from Ren when she climbed the tree to his balcony—and she had a ticket on a coach to leave London the next morn.

Leaving these invitations. Leaving everything.

Leaving Ren.

The hollow ache in her middle grew more acute as Ren disengaged from his coterie and came behind Harriette and Amalie. "Wah-Lady Cranbury. Lady Be-Bessington. You have met my—my sister?" he asked, tipping his hat in deference.

Lady Cranbury stared at him with the strangest petrified look, her eyes darting to his chest, his legs, his chin—anywhere but his face. Her companion leaned forward, giving Ren a full assessment. Lady Bessington smiled a small, amused smile, then turned a kind face on Amalie.

"Are you enjoying your time in London, Lady Amalie? I suppose it is strange to find your brother the latest *on-dit*. Those prints are *quite* striking," she said, with an arched brow at Harriette.

Oh, Lord. Harriette wished a tree might fall on her. Lady

Bessington knew she was the maker of those prints. *Everyone* knew she was the maker of those prints, including the gentlemen still posturing and preening in her wake. It was best for all concerned that she was leaving London. She would send Ren his finished portrait, and with luck, its display would prove she was a talented artist in truth, not just a producer of racy sketches. It would avail her little, but perhaps it would redeem him.

"Renwick." The rouge on Lady Cranbury's cheeks stood out. "I must introduce you to my grand-niece Louisa. She is staying with me for the summer, and I cannot think you will meet a lovelier girl. The two of you might go on very well together."

Harriette nearly choked on her jealousy. Lady Cranbury, proposing her grand-niece as a prospective bride for anyone less than a duke? It was no secret she had tried desperately to throw Louisa at the Duke of Devonshire's head. If the formidable, dour, disapproving Lady Cranbury suddenly regarded Ren as an eligible *parti* for her grand-niece, it was because of Harriette. Because Harriette had shown everyone—*everyone*—his attractions.

"Oh, indeed, Renwick!" Harriette forced a bright, false tone. "What a lovely suggestion. You must call on Miss Louisa at once."

The look he sent her said he wished to do such a thing even less than she wished him to do it. Lady Cranbury preened.

"We shall look forward to your call. You, girl, come along. Bess?" She sailed down the Grand Walk, towing her silent servant in her wake. Lady Bessington gave Harriette one last, considering look before she moved away.

"Lady Amalie, that is a most fetching muff. Lady Harriette —good day."

Amalie let out a small whoosh of air and sagged against

Harriette once they had left. "Well, that was terrifying," she muttered. "I'm as limp as a noodle."

"But you see they did not notice a thing," Harriette said. "You look like every other girl here."

"You finally have the invitation you wa-wanted, Rhette." Ren looked down at her with darkened eyes.

"And you have the admiration of every girl here." Harriette met his gaze, triumph warring with the longing to stake her own claim upon him. "Didn't I promise I would make you more popular than the Graf von Hardenburg?"

"I should like to go home now," Amalie said in a shaky voice. "I am afraid all my makeup will melt off my face, and this muff is exceedingly warm. Are all fashionable amusements this fatiguing?"

Ren took his sister's arm to guide her down the Grand Walk toward the gates, and Harriette followed behind, keeping an eye out for Jack and Beater, trying not to dwell on the fine figure the two attractive siblings made. Her last moments with Ren were approaching, and she wanted to draw out the time as long as she could.

All too soon they stood again before the gate of the garden of Renwick House. Jock and Beater assisted Amalie into the house with all the pomp and fuss as if she were Queen Charlotte. Harriette faced Ren beneath the dogwood tree, the mate to the one at the front corner of the house, the one she had climbed to his balcony.

In the warm shade his eyes were pools of indigo, and while the tree had passed the full bloom of spring, the scent hung thick in the air, somewhere between blossom and fruit. So was this between them destined to be: a warm beginning full of promise that they could not follow to its fruition.

She had her sketchbook and porte crayon in her pocket, as always, but she left them there. She drank him in with her eyes, memorizing his features to paint later, capturing them for herself alone. He gazed steadily back at her, his expression full of more than she could understand.

"I should like to know what you wrote to me," she said. "Your sister said she found letters you never sent."

"I didn't suppose your mother would ever allow a young man to correspond with you. Or your school mistress, either."

She moved closer to him, emboldened by the quiet of the natural space that dampened the bustle of the fashionable square beyond, by the memory of the women clinging and cooing in the pleasure gardens. By the deep, steady pull she always felt for him.

"No, they wouldn't have allowed it. But there is no such interference now."

He closed his eyes briefly and his hand slipped alongside her face, his thumb tracing the curve of her cheekbone. She leaned her head into his palm, into his warm, capable strength. She was no more able to keep from lifting her face toward his than she was able to halt the orbit of the sun.

His kiss was slow and exploratory, hesitant in a way none of his previous kisses had been. She savored the taste of him, the warm tart they had shared at the pleasure gardens, an earthy rasp that reminded her of whiskey but that she suspected was all him. He smelled of summer breeze and bleached linen and a spicy, elusive trace of sweat, no doubt brought on by all the strangers' eyes upon him. With a low throaty moan she melted against his body, chest, hips, thighs, all that strong splendid muscle.

He groaned in response and clamped his arms about her, his tongue delving into her mouth until her breath came short and her head whirled. Nothing existed but sensation and need, the intoxication of pressing this close to him, the eager, aching desire to be joined with him completely.

She gasped as he dragged her up against his body and her thighs met the firm evidence of his shared need. She rode the fullness of him, rubbing herself through the layers of fabric against that part of him that she wanted to draw deep inside her, claiming him as her own. She pulled at her skirts, trying to lessen the pesky barriers of silk and linen, when Ren went completely still.

She gasped for breath as he lifted his head. Her eyes took a moment to focus.

"What?" she panted, slipping a hand behind his neck. "What's wrong."

"We c-c-can't." His face held shock, longing, the same agony of unfulfilled passion that she felt. "I—" He set her away from him, peeling her off his body, averting his eyes. His voice was a husky rasp. "I c-c-c—"

She didn't press for more. From the way his jaw worked, his lips clamped together, she knew he was fighting to form words. She wanted to cry but she would not, could not shame him nor herself.

He didn't want her. The shock was an icy splash that stunned her.

Ren was done with her.

Another rejection. Well, she was accustomed to that, wasn't she?

"Of course." She pushed at her skirts until they fell back into place. She tugged up the bodice of her gown that she hadn't noticed until now had been shoved down by his hot, questing hands. She trembled with desire and humiliation.

"I-I—" His eyes flickered with misery and desperation.

"I know." She wanted to turn and flee, howling, but she also wanted a proper goodbye. "I'm leaving. But—will you ever send me those letters?"

He shook his head. The shadow of the tree hid the expression that crossed his face, something she had never seen before, not for her. "Th-th-that's over. P-p-past."

He'd never stammered with her before. Now his stutter was here in full force, and he sucked air as if his lungs were empty. Harriette closed her eyes against the rush of pain.

She wasn't special anymore. She was just another woman who terrified him. And why would he dally with her when he now knew he could aim as high as he wanted—when any woman he looked at would fall willingly into his arms? The future was opening up for the Earl of Renwick, while hers was closing to something dark and dreaded.

"I know," she said again. She didn't want him to see her bewilderment, the pain of his rejection. Her pride would sustain her to the end. "Goodbye, Ren."

She turned and plunged through the garden gate to the mews and her coach waiting beyond, not waiting for his answer, unable to hear if he called after her. She was lying to herself. Nothing in her life had hurt more than leaving behind the man she loved and knowing she might never see him again.

She refused to look back. She didn't need one last glimpse of him. George Matheson, the Earl of Renwick, was emblazoned into her brain for perpetuity.

CHAPTER THIRTEEN

They could have made more a fuss about her leaving, Harriette thought glumly as she drove the cabriolet through the quiet, sleepy streets of London at dawn. She'd lived in her aunt's household for three years and these women were deeply a part of her life, their lot and hers intimately entwined. They'd suffered her sketching and painting them again and again as she honed her skills. They'd rallied her when she was rebuffed by prospect after prospect, painting school after school.

They'd celebrated with her when Angelica Kaufman took Harriette under her wing. They'd coaxed her back into spirits when she was humiliated by the squire, when she parted with her soldier, when she found out the German margrave had been lying to her about marriage. They'd stood beside her when the gossip paragraphs identified her as the maker of the salacious sketches of the Graf von Hardenburg, and they'd hung on every detail of her interactions with Ren and his sister.

Now they had seen her off as cheerily as if she were making a casual visit to the edge of town, rather than leaving for the deathbed of her mother, and beyond that, marriage to a man she'd never met.

Natalya, who wept easily, had pressed her into a soft, scented embrace and then let her go without a tear. Melike had made her a beautiful icon to wear as a pendant, and Darci had sculpted her a tiny porcelain figure. Sorcha had packed her a basket full of delicious smelling pastries, and Abassi had shown her, with enthusiasm, how to disable and flee a male attacker, were she threatened on the road.

Princess had not even bothered to make an appearance; no doubt she was still abed with her lover, or hadn't yet made it to bed since it was still early hours.

Her aunt alone had shown a sign of being affected by their parting. "Take this," she'd instructed, handing Harriette a small decorative box inlaid with fine wood and painted paste that passed for jewels. Harriette peeked inside to find a lump of velvet wrapped in a ribbon. "They are trinkets that will prove who you are, if anyone has questions."

Harriette nodded and slid the box into the valise she planned to carry with her, while her trunks would follow behind by a slower, less costly conveyance. She had never considered that Franz Karl would demand proof she was of the Löwenburg ruling family, that her mother's word would not be token enough.

She had imagined she might have some command over him, invested as she was as the heir to the title, if not the lands. Suddenly she glimpsed a fraught, painful future where her husband doubted her birth and her worth, holding her captive to make good his claim to the duchy, but never according her the respect due her station.

Oh, *why* had she ever approached the rotted Graf von Hardenburg to ask him to find out about her family? Harriette chastised herself as she turned into the narrow, twisted streets of the City of London, with Jock on the Yorkshire guiding their way. Why couldn't she have simply remained poor, plain Harriette Smythe, suspected of illegitimacy, relegated to the barest fringes of Polite Society? At least she would still have her studio and her determination to make something of herself. She didn't even know if Franz Karl would allow her to paint.

Not that he could keep her from it, Harriette resolved as Jock won an argument with a sedan chair and the surly carriers moved aside to let them through. Her husband would not find her biddable or meek.

First she would resolve whatever was ailing her mother, which was no doubt another episode of spleen. If announcing she was the Duchess of Löwenburg had not been enough to make her mother a marvel among the lesser beings of Shepton Mallet, then she would resort to a wasting illness, as had been her ploy for as long as Harriette could remember.

Doubtless news that her nephew was coming to fetch them both back to the land of her birth would cure whatever ailed the duchess right enough. She'd spent Harriette's entire childhood painting word pictures of the elegance and ease she'd left behind, making sure that Mrs. Demant knew how much the erstwhile Mrs. Smythe had lowered herself to live in a mere gentleman merchant's home.

Ludgate Hill was thronged with traffic, coaches and people moving through the broad space where the medieval gate and its attached gaol had been torn down years before. A crowd lounged outside the London Coffee House, studying a series of prints tacked to the windows. Her sketch of Renwick, of course.

Harriette tore her eyes away and appreciated instead the depth and dimension of the street, the narrow buildings with their medieval overhangs, the gothic spires of St. Martin's Church, the neoclassical majesty of St. Paul's dome and portico looming behind a veil of morning smoke. How she would like to paint this scene, were she granted the time. How much there was of London that she still hadn't seen, would never see.

Jock steered the cabriolet through the archway fronting the Belle Sauvage to the broad cobbled yard beyond. The inn in early days had also been a playhouse, and Harriette could imagine the audience crowding the balconies, riveted to the action below. The stagecoach was being loaded, men strapping luggage onto the box behind, while the four horses stood in harness, blinkered and quiet. The enclosed seats being more expensive, Harriette had a ticket for the perch atop. She hoped the driver was a sober sort who would not risk their lives with unadvisable speed and would not be persuaded to turn the horses over to some young spark who wanted to show he was a dab hand at the ribbons.

Jock paused to watch a stable boy lead a pair of spirited blacks to a bright yellow post chaise trimmed with fresh black paint. The near-side horse shied and stepped into a tall man standing nearby, his back to them, leaning on his cane as he conversed with the innkeeper. Harriette caught herself admiring his long frame, the way his leather greatcoat fell from broad shoulders, the deep cuffs with golden buttons indicating a man of means, as did the polish on his black top boots. His hair was hidden under a tricorn hat but his build suggested strength and command, and she was astonished to feel a flicker of attraction for a complete stranger. She was supposed to be heartbroken over leaving Ren. Was she that fickle?

When the horse nudged him, the man turned, and the breath left her body at the sight of his profile. It was Ren.

His eyes found her immediately, as if he'd been waiting. She moved through the air somehow—it must be Beater helping her descend from the coach—and a shadow chased across his face at the sight of the other man's hand at her waist. Regret, annoyance, longing, shame; they were gone in an instant, but she understood what he felt watching her be assisted by someone else doing what he, with his negligible balance, could not do.

His expression was smooth when he reached her, or she reached him—everything in her pulled toward him like a tide—but his eyes were the blue of the sky in high summer.

"What—how—who—when?" She was the one stammering. She slid her gloved hands into his and only just refrained from kissing him.

"It happens I have business to see to in Shepton Mallet. Problems with the Manor House, and some trouble at my mills." His eyes flickered to the coach, then the chaise. "I thought I might offer you a ride in my conveyance."

"But I have already paid for the ticket." Stupid, but she had to be frugal. Her sudden title had not come with funds. The guineas from Mrs. Darly's prints lay wrapped at the bottom of her reticule and stashed at various points about her person, the girls having advised caution due to the high chance of encountering gentleman robbers on the highway.

The draft on Renwick's bank for a staggering sum lay in the tiny pouch with what passed for her jewelry. She had not cashed it yet and knew in all practicality she must do so before leaving England.

His portrait canvas was carefully rolled, wrapped in layers of silk, and protected in the long leather tube waiting with her trunk in the bedroom she shared with Melike in the Countess of Calenberg's house. She wished she had it before her. She hadn't accented enough the strong square of his jaw, but saw now just how to do it.

A smile rippled across his lips. At least she'd captured his mouth precisely, the hint of a bow in the upper lip, the curve of the lower, not overlarge, but exactly perfect proportions. She stared like a ninny.

"The innkeeper thinks he might sell your ticket yet. Or I shall reimburse you for the cost."

"And ride with you." Alone.

It would be at least two days to Shepton Mallet traveling at speed, possibly two nights if the roads proved rough, as roads in Britain were wont to do, even in summer. Two men in Renwick livery lounged dicing in the shade of an overhang, and the postilion would accompany them as well. Servants made the travel more comfortable, but not more respectable.

"I don't suppose you brought a companion. Or a maid."

Chaperonage was the kind of thing her aunt could not bring herself to care about, and Harriette, in making her travel arrangements, had not taken into account that she was now the daughter of a duchess and would be expected to turn out like one, in a style of dress and an entourage suiting her station. She was wearing a plain German habit that would endure the dust and wear of the road, a set of stays she could fasten and unfasten herself, and had no more luggage than what she could carry.

"It would be just you, and me, and my hat," Harriette said. He regarded this extravagance, its deep crown set with silk rosettes and a bright red spray of berries.

"That is an extremely fetching hat," he said, his voice deepening.

"What about Amalie?"

"What about her?"

"We'll look in on her ladyship and make sure she's going on aright." Jock swung up beside them on his crutches, touching the brim of his hat to acknowledge Ren. "We'll keep an eye on the place, as we promised you and the girls."

"The girls?" Harriette said in confusion.

"I, uh, may have m-made a call in Ch-Charles Street last night," Ren said.

Harriette noticed the innkeeper and the postilion drawing near. Servants as well as strangers made Ren nervous, but he had likely brought his footmen to accommodate her. Warmth bloomed over the surprise ricocheting through her innards.

"Is that why the girls were so sanguine about my leaving today? Because they knew you would offer to take me?"

"Your aunt approved," he said, and a slight flush of embarrassment touched his cheeks. Harriette could imagine what her aunt might have said about his offering Harriette escort. It would include advice to overlook her inconvenient betrothal to another, she didn't doubt.

But she *was* betrothed to another. And she recalled with aching clarity how Ren had set her from him yesterday, breaking their passionate embrace. *I can't.* That was clear enough. She would be in close company with him for days, not allowed to touch him, not permitted to act on her loving impulses, which she now knew came from deeper places than physical attraction or the trust of past friendship. She felt an undeniable bond with him, an attachment more complete than she had ever known in her life, but she could not claim him for her own in the elemental way that God and nature had designed.

This was penance for the sins of all her past lives, as well as this one. It didn't matter. The truth was she would follow Ren anywhere, do whatever he asked. Perhaps it made her weak, but it was her truth.

"How soon do you wish to leave?"

TRAVELING with the Earl of Renwick was an infinitely different experience than traveling back and forth from her girls' school as Miss Harriette Smythe. Lesser conveyances waited at the posting inns while hands poured out to help the wealthy travelers in the post chaise, eager for the coins that might be in the offing. Innkeepers showed them to their best rooms just ahead of maids bustling in with fresh linens and hot water. To avoid any looks of askance or insinuation, Ren loudly introduced her as Lady Harriette, daughter of the Duchess of

Löwenburg, whom he was escorting to be united with her mother.

The fierce concentration and small scowl with which he produced all the l- and r-sounds of her name never failed to make Harriette's heart turn over, and she didn't mind when the bowing and scraping turned in her direction if it took unwelcome attention off Ren. Because of him their meals were hot and tasty, they were served the best wines at dinner, and a private dining parlor was always available, even for a simple dish of tea during a change of horses, even when the public rooms were filled with curious villagers craning their necks to get a glimpse of London's latest sensation.

One innkeeper's wife sidled up to Harriette at dinner on the second night, ostensibly to offer her a cup of Madeira. "So that be 'imself, then?" she whispered while watching Ren, who chatted with a local squire who'd been occupying the public room when they arrived.

More correctly, the squire was holding forth with red-cheeked enthusiasm, and Ren smiled and nodded, his lips firmly closed. Harriette watched fondly. He'd mastered the art of making his silence appear sophisticated and intelligent, rather than a reluctance to speak, and as he leaned on his cane with the nonchalance of a fashionable gentleman, no one would ever guess that his leg pained him from long hours of sitting. She'd offered to help him with his exercises within the confines of the coach, but he'd declined, no doubt wisely, as it was in part an excuse to place her hands on him.

"That is the Earl of Renwick, yes," Harriette said in answer to the inquiry of her hostess.

The matron pulled a roll of papers from her apron. "Have all the prints o' 'im, I do," she said with satisfaction. "A farthing each. D'ye mean to make more of 'em, mum? Find plenty o' buyers 'ere, ye would."

Harriette still startled at being addressed as "madame" or "your ladyship," but startled further to note that the prints the matron showed her had not come from Mrs. Darly's shop. They resembled her original sketches only in form; the figure was blurred, the lines not properly inked, and the expression on Ren's face overall struck her as less pensive and more leering.

Pirated copies, no doubt by a local printer who had hastily made his own plates and was underselling Mrs. Darly. Harriette would never see a share of the profits from these sales, though she was recognized even here as their author. Printing was a cutthroat business, far worse than painters competing for commissions.

She pulled her sketchbook from her pocket. "This is yours alone, mind you," she said. "You may show it to whomever you like, but don't let that shoddy printer get hold of it. Mrs. Darly in London is the only person authorized to reproduce my work."

The matron nodded and watched, wide-eyed, as Harriette brought Ren to life on the page. She sketched him as he was, in his plain leather traveling coat and leather breeches, riding boots, a neckcloth tossed about his throat. She put his cane in one hand and his tricorne hat in the other, and when he turned to watch her from across the room, she captured the expression on his face with a few practiced lines. In a moment the man himself stared out from her paper at them: warm, amused, perceptive, and, if one looked closely enough, with a hint of caution about the eyes, expressed in a few tiny shadows.

"Oi, that's enough to dream on," the matron said. "'Is lordship won't mind, then?"

Harriette caught Ren's eye as she neatly parted his sketch from her book and mimed giving it to the woman. He scowled, observing his own likeness on the page, then shrugged.

"Will ye sign it then, mum?" the matron asked shyly.

"Tell me what you like about these prints," Harriette

couldn't help asking as she scribbled her initials at the corner of the sketch.

Her hostess stared at Renwick with a soft, fond look. Beneath the lines of age and strain, the ragged edges that time and hardship had worn, Harriette glimpsed the sweet dreams of a long-lost girl to whom the world had not yet been unkind.

"I can't rightly say," the older woman said. "A man like that'd never glance at the likes o' me, that's certain. But I look at a picture like this and it makes me feel that I be understanding 'im, if ye know what I mean. And with that look on 'is face, it almost seems—that he'd understand *me*, if he but knew me. That 'ee'd like what he saw right back."

Harriette could only nod, captivated by the woman's insight. She'd thought of her sketches as simply capturing an image of beauty, or perhaps indulging a silly feminine inclination toward fantasy. But if such a fantasy helped a woman understand herself better, to see and appreciate her best aspects through the imagined gaze of another, or if it helped her envision the kind of relationship that would bring the best part of her nature to fulfillment—that didn't seem so silly.

Harriette tried to recall if she'd had such notions when she was a girl. She couldn't recall harboring crushes or infatuations, though she'd done her share of giggling with her school friends when the more fashionable young men of Bath promenaded past them in a square or park. Ren had been her confidant, her primary and most enduring relationship, as close in thought as the letters she composed telling him what she was learning, what she thought of her mother and her school, what she was discovering day by day in her art lessons, and what it meant that she could capture living beauty and share it with others.

After she'd moved to London and her first patron, the squire, had taken ruthless advantage of her youth and stupidity, Harriette had become pragmatic and hard-headed about her work. She captured likenesses of the proud and wealthy who wanted to leave a trace on the world they'd ruled long after they left it. She'd forgotten what had first drawn her to painting: the ability to distill the essence of a living thing and reveal it in a way that others could see.

And to give herself a new way of looking. The innkeeper's wife had gone dreamy not so much over Ren himself, but the way Harriette had captured the man she loved on paper—dashing, handsome, full of secrets and mischief and passion, the type of companion many a woman would yearn for.

"What mun I pay ye, mum?" the matron asked, placing the sketch with care in her apron pocket so as not to crease or crumple it.

"'Tis a gift," Harriette said, and ceased hearing her hostess's profuse thanks when Ren headed her way with a smile on his face.

"Is that how you are paying our tab for the fare?" He took his seat across from her at the small table supplied with what rather looked like a full meal than a light supper.

"Indulging your fans," Harriette said lightly.

She applied herself to dishing the hearty ragout onto his plate so she didn't stare fatuously at him, her thoughts writ large across her face. She was hopelessly in love with this man. His very nearness made silly fancies flutter about inside her. Knowing that she was the focus of his attention, when everyone else here was hung upon his every move, was a sensation that was going straight to her head and bringing foolish and impossible thoughts along with it.

He'd kept her at arm's length throughout the journey, as much as was possible in a vehicle meant to seat two, yet their conversation was free and easy. He told marvelous tales of his travels, though she noticed he left out mention of any of the courtesans. She sketched as they rode, often sitting on the outside seat with him for an unhampered view of the land-scape, and he listened as she told him stories of the Catherine Club and the various women her aunt had taken under her wing.

The man he'd become fit so logically with the boy he'd been —thoughtful, observant, attuned to the plight of the less fortu-nate, slow to anger or to judge but quick in understanding. And yet he continued to surprise her with his sly humor, the wit he'd cultivated, his sensitivity to his sister's feelings, and the way he noticed and anticipated her comfort. As now, when he passed her the dish of pickled salmon, knowing she adored it.

Perhaps this was what marriage was like for some, this comfortable companionship, this looking after someone in small ways. Ordering ale for him instead of beer at meals because she knew he preferred it. Inspecting his bedding to ensure the linens were well-aired and there were no vermin in his mattress or pillows. Accepting his arm and making a stately turn or two around an innyard as if they were taking air while he stretched the sore muscles in his scarred leg, leaning on her to disguise his limp.

These small, nurturing touches were more pleasant to supply than she would have expected. It was no imposition to stop the chaise and walk a bit when his leg was cramping, just as he didn't demur when she wanted to halt and sketch a view. It was no great burden to bring one of her linen strips to his room to dry his face with when he dropped his in the shaving bowl. Even though she had, in the process, been exposed to the sight of Ren in an open shirt and stocking feet, his head bare of wig. His state of undress thrilled and delighted her, and yet she'd bolted as shy as any untried maid. Because she thought that was what he wanted.

Because she was alarmed, truth be told, by the intensity of the stirrings she felt for him. The attraction had grown deeper through continued exposure, not less, as she might have expected.

Still, she told herself firmly, that didn't mean she would make him a good *wife*. She was going soft in the head.

"The squire warned us to beware of unrest in Shepton Mallet," Ren said as he dug into the collops. "The mill owners there have begun adopting the new spinning machinery. One spinning jenny can do the work of eight men, they say. There is some understandable concern among the workers that they will be left without jobs."

Her heart squeezed with affection even as worry set in. "Did the squire find the concern understandable?" she asked mildly.

"Indeed not. His words were to the effect that some ruddy belligerent blokes who were already getting paid enough to keep an honest man happy were raising a breeze that their earnings might be diminished."

"I would think a squire would be concerned about men out of work," Harriette remarked, spooning up the cabbage. "They needs must raise the poor rates to support them."

"Can you conceive what the squire and his ilk would say to that?" Ren replied. His face darkened, his voice taking on a hard edge. "The mill owners will be able to make more cloth and sell more cloth, while paying fewer workers. In the meantime, between the Corn Laws and the Poor Laws and the game laws that keep them from poaching to put meat on the table, the common folk can barely afford to feed and clothe their families. I saw the same system all over Europe, and it's untenable. Such great wealth for so few, earned from the suffering of so many."

Harriette laid her spoon beside her plate. "Very few of those enjoying the great wealth are able to see that," she said carefully. "Or feel much for the sufferers."

She was aware of her own good fortune in that she had

never known real destitution. Much as Mrs. Demant might have begrudged the effort, there was always food on Harriette's plate and some castoff clothes to wear. When she began school at Miss Gregoire's, with her fees and a small allowance paid for by her aunt, Harriette had learned to be thrifty, but had never known real fear that she would not be provided for.

And in London, though she came often in contact with women thrown upon the streets by vagaries of fate or cruelty, her aunt's house was a refuge where there was always the surety that, if they worked together, there would be enough for all. Still, when she tried to imagine the fear and worry of a family that struggled to stretch their pay to cover lodging, food, clothing, and other necessities, it was not so great an act of imagination.

Ren looked into his cup of wine, swirling the liquid. "Perhaps it's because I have spent my life feeling undeserving of the position I was born to," he said. "Of looking as an outsider on something I shall never have. But my sympathies are with the workers."

Unaccountably, his words squeezed her heart all the harder. Her chest ached. *This man.* She wanted to ask what he looked on that he longed to have for himself. Security? Admiration? A warm family? Love?

She would give him all those things, if she could.

"What kind of unrest?" she asked instead, to keep her mind from straying into paths that could only prove unfruitful.

"Protests, most like." The innkeeper's wife made no pretense that she had not caught their conversation as she entered the small parlor with a covered dish. She set it on the wooden table beside Ren and tucked the cloth she'd been using to carry the dish into her apron, then went to the fireplace and picked a spill from the cup on the mantelpiece. She lit it from the small fire keeping away the evening damps and came back to the table.

"Shepton Mallet's always been a tinder box," she went on, lighting the candles in their brushed silver holders, no doubt the finest The George and Dragon had on offer. "There be riots there regular, back in the day, and don't forget how quick they a-went for Monmouth. We be prideful, we West Country folk," she added.

"Will there be violence, do you think?" Harriette asked. She had no qualms about their hostess entering into their conversation. In the Countess of Calenberg's unusual household, the women took turns contributing to housekeeping tasks—witness how Sorcha had taken over the cookery and marketing—and Abassi, though nominally their butler, was confidant, friend, and, Harriette suspected, her aunt's lover.

She was more concerned with how unrest in the town might upset her mother's fragile health. If her mother were ill, Franz Karl could not in conscience hie them back to Prussia directly, which she accounted a small providence.

But if her mother lingered, Harriette would be trapped in Shepton Mallet with a fretful parent and a grudging Mrs. Demant, and Ren could not stay and be her white knight indefinitely. He had other properties and business that needed his attention, not to mention his sister. Harriette hoped her new makeup would stop the progression of Amalie's lead colic and give the girl reprieve from her symptoms, and in time, return her to health. But how was she to hear reports if she was buried in the country, or carried far out of it?

"I shall protect you, Rhette." Ren's gaze filled with a dark, steady heat as he stared across the table at her. Candlelight flickered and threw shadows across his sculpted face. A tightness coiled in her belly, pulling at her insides.

The conversation moved on to other reports of unrest across

the land in response to the installation of new machinery that upset the age-old way of doing things and the industries that had been livelihood to so many. Ren was informed and level-headed, and while he understood the motives of the business owners, he was surprisingly sympathetic to the poor and displaced, a sympathy she shared. What a wonderful contribution he would make to the House of Lords, Harriette thought, if only he had the courage to make his voice heard and would not let his difficulties with speech silence him. She wished she could be there as his aide and support and champion.

Now there was a surprising thought. She'd certainly never before imagined herself as a prop and aide to a man, just as she'd never noticed, much less attended to small domestic details like inspecting the linens. She still didn't see herself as capable of bearing and raising a child; such territory was more foreign and terrifying to her than Prussia.

She also did not see herself as someone who would betray a promise made by her family, by the mother who had raised her and the grandfather who had let his daughter and heir leave the country for their safety.

But the longer she was with Ren, traveling with him, dining with him, falling into the deep inviting abyss of his eyes, the more distant Harriette grew from all the things she had always felt to be true about herself. She was changing, becoming someone she didn't recognize. She was already a woman who had flouted the most basic moral conventions of her class, taking lovers before she was married, consorting with courtesans, living in a household considered on the barest fringes of respectability. She had already determined to make her way and her name in a trade, which was utterly frowned upon for women of any sort of gentle birth.

And now she was entertaining notions of throwing herself at a man she could not have, a man whom she had promised herself she would hand, whole and unsullied, into marriage with a girl of birth and breeding who would make him a proper countess and an agreeable wife. She had notions of violating the honor of her family and the promise her grandfather had made about her marriage. She had a mind to forget every rule she was supposed to obey and toss it all into the gathering maelstrom of feeling. For if she could not be near Ren, she was going to lose part of herself.

She wanted to be with him, like this, for as long as possible. She wanted, with a greedy passion that threatened to consume her, to know him utterly, completely, and in the most intimate ways. She wanted to throw herself into this delicious, delirious pull of attraction that dangerously blotted out all the guidelines and compass points by which she had plotted her life.

But she also suspected that if she surrendered to this passion, she would lose herself completely, and what would happen to her then?

CHAPTER FOURTEEN

Harriette stared at the door of Ivy Cottage and the black wreath that hung upon it.

There was no mistaking what it meant. Smaller wreaths of black ribbons hung in the tall windows flanking the painted door. Death had visited the Demant household.

She hesitated with her hand raised to knock. Who had passed? Mr. Demant? The missus? Mrs. Demant had been her mother's chief protector and champion. Would Mr. Demant let Harriette's mother stay in his household without his wife? Who was attending her mother in her illness? It was fortunate that Harriette was here.

"Rhette," Ren said softly. He stood beside her on the stoop, leaning on his cane.

"It must be recent," she whispered to him. "Mrs. Demant made no mention of other illness when she sent the express about my mother. I hope it was not one of the children." How ironic that her mother, who pretended to be ailing to garner attention and solicitude, should malinger, while the healthy and businesslike Mr. Demant, his brisk and terrifyingly capable wife, or one of their spoiled, headstrong children should be suddenly whisked from their mortal coil.

"Rhette," he said again, "I think you n-need to c-c-consider..."

He trailed off as he did when emotion choked his tongue, but this time she didn't wait to let him gather his thought. She raised the knocker and let it fall.

Mrs. Demant answered the door. Her face was gaunt and drawn, her expression defeated. Her black crepe dress and veil indicated deepest mourning. Despite the evidence of woe, her face burned with bitterness as she glared at Harriette.

"You're too late," she spat. "I suppose it's to be expected. She never could count on you to show her even the most basic regard, could she?"

Harriette's arms turned into lead weights. Her lips went numb as the thought she'd been pushing away rose to the front of her mind, insistent. "Then—"

"Your mother is dead," Mrs. Demant said. She used none of the euphemistic phrases one usually did—departed, returned to her Maker, stuck her spoon in the wall. "Thursday. And she died knowing her own daughter, for whom she had sacrificed her life, could not even be bothered to come hold her hand and receive a final blessing as she passed."

Harriette sagged. "I—I am sorry."

She hadn't left London until Friday. There was no way she could have made it to her mother's bedside even if she'd left immediately upon receiving the note about her latest illness. Even if her final moments had been one last sigh of disappointment rather than passing a blessing to her only daughter, as Mrs. Demant romantically imagined, Harriette could never have made it in time.

She'd never been a loving daughter, an obedient daughter, and now she had failed in the most basic filial duty, that of helping her parent pass from this world to the next. Harriette's shoulders bowed under the weight.

Something warm and firm pressed at her back. Ren. Harriette drew strength from his nearness, groping for the breath to speak around the tightness in her chest.

"Was it—has she—the funeral?"

"One doesn't stand on the doorstep discussing such things," Mrs. Demant said in disapproval. "You might as well come in."

The mirror in the small entryway was draped with cloth so as not to trap the departing spirit, and the large clock had been stopped at her mother's passing. Such things were done, Harriette knew, so any clocks in the house didn't become confused and start counting down time toward another death. Mrs. Demant led them through the dark paneled hall into the front formal parlor, also dark, where vaguely Oriental designs chased each other up and down the olive-green paper on the walls. Heavy brocade drapes were drawn against the light, and candles lined the heavy mantelpiece above the fireplace.

A long table stood in the center of the room, flanked by chairs. Upon the table lay the elm coffin, and within it lay Harriette's mother, nestled like a bird amid a profusion of bright white silks, linen, and delicate lace.

Harriette's booted feet sank into the thick patterned rug as she stepped close. Her mother's dark hair held streaks of silver at the temples, her brow was carved with three deep lines, and her strong nose—which would in time be Harriette's nose— jutted from sunken cheeks. Harriette was struck by the hollowing sense that she had both known and not known this person in life.

Her mother looked as bitter at rest as she had waking. Straight lines radiated from lips often pursed with the bitter draught of her lot. The web of creases around the eyes too oft tightened against the harshness and lack they looked upon, rather than the ease and luxury she sought. The body was dressed in a gown of rich black silk, and upon her breast was a brooch Harriette had never seen her wear, a heraldic symbol of wrought gold with tiny inset jewels. She knew these were the coat of arms of the dukes of Löwenburg, though she had never seen them in her life.

Every surface of the room was crowded with flowers, and the smell smacked Harriette in the face, bringing tears to her eyes. Mrs. Demant had done all of this, everything Harriette ought to have done: nursed her mother in her last illness, laid out her body in its finest dress, chosen the small items she would take to her grave. Like any heedless child more caught up in her own concerns, Harriette had never truly considered that her mother's latest illness might be the end, or that the bitterness of her life might choke her before she could reassume her rightful place.

Her mother, for all her frets and affectations, had been a sturdy given in Harriette's life, ever in the background with her disapproving frown and heavy sighs. Her mother had never been her confidant or model, neither a figure of admiration nor a very reliable guide, but she had been *there*. And now she was not. Harriette's mind trembled before that great, gaping rent in everything she knew.

Harriette was motherless. All she had left was her great-aunt Calenberg.

And Franz Karl.

"I know this is not nearly the state of splendor she would lie in were she returned to her home country." Mrs. Demant joined Harriette at the coffin. "I am in no position to give proper due to the Duchess of Löwenburg. But I am doing my best."

"Thank you," Harriette whispered. She struggled to breathe.

The one solace in learning she was of a line of Silesian

dukes had been knowing that her marriage would return Harriette's mother to her rightful station. This woman had sacrificed everything to bring Harriette to safety, and Harriette would repay that debt by seeing her installed as the Duchess of Löwenburg, with whatever rights and privileges still belonged to that title. Harriette had wrestled herself to submission on the subject of her forthcoming marriage only because it was a promise her mother and grandfather had made, and whatever other duties Harriette had neglected toward her parent, she would repay by keeping this contract.

Now her grandfather was gone, and her mother was not here to see that promise fulfilled. The only one who would benefit from this arrangement was a landless cousin she had never met who was counting on marriage to Harriette to secure his fortune.

Mrs. Demant withdrew a white handkerchief edged with black to dab at her eyes, and the sight stirred Harriette from the horror of her barren future. "When are the funeral services to be held?"

"Tonight." Mrs. Demant sniffled. "The cards have been sent and the biscuits have been made."

She indicated the salver on a nearby table, heaped with the biscuits that the English gave out to mourners and funeral guests. The white paper wrapping was printed with a doleful memorial passage along with her mother's name and closed with black wax into which had been pressed the grinning image of a death's head. Harriette shuddered, feeling a pang that might have been hunger, or something else.

"I don't suppose you have suitable mourning," Mrs. Demant remarked, and the tight sensation in Harriette's chest turned to full-blown alarm.

She didn't have mourning attire, not a scrap of it. She wore her riding habit and had a plain bodice and petticoat in the valise she'd brought along. Her few gowns, none of them black, lay neatly folded in her trunk in London. She would need a bombazine gown, crepe hood and fan, the correct shoes, and gloves if she were to observe proper mourning. Then there were the required funeral expenses: hiring mutes and mourners, the pall and feathers to cover the coffin on its way to its last resting place, cloaks and hatbands and gloves for the bearers and pages and others in the procession...Harriette swayed on her feet.

Ren's great gift to her, the commission for his painting, would disappear into her mother's grave. Leaving her, truly, with nothing. Harriette would go to her marriage motherless, penniless, and in deepest mourning.

This was not the time for her painter's eye to recall that black washed out her complexion and made her olive skin tone look green. By English custom she would wear deepest mourning for six months and half mourning for six more. But she would be in Löwenburg then and would have to learn what the customs of the Silesian people were, as well as what their Prussian governors demanded.

Her stomach turned over, and Ren slipped a steadying hand beneath her elbow. She shot him a grateful look, the pang in her middle intensifying at the sight of his soft, sympathetic expression. She could not separate the hurt of standing beside her dead mother from the hurt of knowing she must part from Ren. It all felt like a great hand tightening her throat, making her choke for air.

She removed her glove, kissed her fingers, and pressed them to her mother's forehead. The skin was waxy and cool. What would a good daughter do in this situation? *Farewell, Mother,* she thought. *You did not live to reassume your place as duchess in your own land, but you are in a far happier land now, I pray.*

"I must see to dyeing my gown and finding a cloak and veil," Harriette said. The business of death kept her mind from sentiment, at least for the moment. "I suppose I am the chief mourner and will follow behind the coffin. I must have something suitable to wear."

"Women do not take part in funeral processions," Mrs. Demant said with a gasp, holding her handkerchief to her throat. "Not women of our station, at least."

Harriette did not miss that Mrs. Demant, the wife of a merchant who had bought himself gentleman's status through his wealth, classed herself with the daughter of a duchess.

"The procession will begin at dusk," Mrs. Demant went on. "There will be vulgar men among them—those paid mourners always come to such things drunk and their comments are not fit for ladies' ears. And the thieves and pickpockets that are likely to follow, not to mention that our coach could be robbed the moment the coffin enters the church—that happened to the Lamberts not last year, when Mrs. Lambert was laid to rest. And since we are not allowed graveside anyway, there is no reason to go. We shall sit quietly here and pray."

"I am not allowed to be present when they bury my mother?" Harriette demanded. "Whyever not?"

"Because women carry the sins of Eve," Mrs. Demant said primly. "No minister wants a woman on consecrated burial ground."

"That has to be a foolish English custom," Harriette said sharply. "But we are not English, and I am her daughter."

The declaration felt silly the moment she uttered it, for she didn't have the first notion of Silesian funeral customs. As a child Harriette had soon learned her mother did not want to answer many questions about the life she had left behind, and so she ceased asking them. Neither did her aunt reminisce often about her country of birth. Harriette now regretted this lack of knowledge, not just because of all she needs must learn when Franz Karl returned her to Löwenburg, but because she could not properly mark her mother's passing with the customs of her country of birth.

"Nevertheless, it does not do to send a dearly departed on their way with too many demonstrations of tears." Mrs. Demant bravely dabbed at her eyes again. "The spirit might feel it needs to stay to console those it left behind. And it is well known that women cannot control their weeping and expressions of grief."

A smothered sound from Ren, behind her, stood in for Harriette's response to this. Harriette couldn't recall the last time she had cried about anything. Even now she stood dry-eyed and stoic beside her mother's coffin, wondering where in Shepton Mallet she would find crepe, which would have to suffice for her mourning since she did not have the time nor resources to order a bombazine gown.

"Mrs. De-Demant." Ren finally spoke. "M-may her gray— Her Grace and I have a mo-mo-moment alone?"

Mrs. Demant startled as if she had noticed him for the first time.

"Mrs. Demant, the Earl of Renwick," Harriette murmured. "Renwick, you remember Mrs. Demant. She was kind enough to take in my mother and me when we had no one."

"Your lordship." Mrs. Demant sank into a low curtsey. When she rose, her eyes were wide with the same realization striking Harriette. She was her mother's sole heir. Harriette was the Duchess of Löwenburg now.

"Your lordship. May I be the first to welcome you back to Shepton Mallet? We heard with great interest of your return to England." The woman's cold, disapproving gaze flicked over Harriette, and Harriette stiffened her back, wondering if those dratted prints of Ren had traveled this far from London. "I will see about tea." Her stiff black bombazine skirts rustled away.

Ren leaned his cane against a chair and opened his arms as Harriette turned into them. It felt so natural to seek comfort from him. The silk of his waistcoat soothed her hot cheek, and when he stroked the curls dangling from her hat, the tight thing in her chest loosened, letting in air. She breathed in his scent, rich and earthy and strong.

"I am sorry for your loss," he whispered.

His hand slid along her shoulder, down her arm, then moved to her back, where he drew his hand in small, warm circles. Harriette sighed and pressed her nose into his neckcloth.

"I feel shocked more than anything," she admitted. "And embarrassed that I did not expect this end. And—guilt that I do not feel a deeper sense of loss." She sniffled. "I am mostly sorry she will not have the opportunity to return to Löwenburg as its duchess. I expect that is all she wanted from her life."

A wave of sorrow hit her, strong and unanticipated. Her poor, bitter mother, defeated at the end of the one thing she wished above all else. What had brought her joy in this life? Not Harriette, that was certain. Mrs. Demant had provided some slim comfort as well as practical necessities, but her mother had no companion of the heart. No great love.

Harriette at least had found Ren, even if she had to give him up. She squeezed him, hard, and while he gave a soft grunt to indicate discomfort, he made no move to push her away.

"Ren, I..."

She lifted her head to stare at him, and her thoughts trailed to wisps. Her mother's coffin was no place to make a declaration, even if the thoughts were fully formed. She loosened her arms, conscious of the impropriety should Mrs. Demant find them in an embrace. Her opinion of Harriette couldn't be any lower, but up till now, Harriette had never scandalized the woman in her own home.

"What?"

He watched her steadily, his eyes a fathomless blue, a deep sky she could get lost in. She had stared at that face for hours, on her canvas and in the flesh, and still his beauty caught her breath.

She inhaled deeply and stepped away. The sickly-sweet scent of the mourning lilies, there to disguise any odors from the body, brought her to her senses. If she had to let Ren go, it was best to begin here and now.

"Will you come to the funeral?" In a strangely formal gesture, she plucked one of the funeral biscuits from the salver and held it out to him.

"If you wish." He took the treat with a solemn air.

Princess had told her once that the lavish feasts that accompanied funerals of the Polish nobility came from an ancient custom of sin-eating. Others ate and drank around the body to consume the sins of the deceased and let their spirit pass to the next world unburdened. She wondered if the English custom of funeral biscuits came from the same ageless superstition.

"Mrs. Demant will appreciate being able to say there was an earl in attendance."

"What do *you* need, Rhette?"

She nearly crumpled at that. In the candlelit shadows of the darkened room, with the ghostly shadows of the massed flowers dancing at the edge of her vision, his husky voice and searching eyes seemed unbearably potent, like the pull of a dream. She wanted, oh, so many things.

She wanted one thing, really. Him.

And she couldn't have him.

"I need mourning attire, I suppose," she said in a shaky voice. "I shall be busy this afternoon getting that in order. And— you have things to do as well?"

"See to my man of business, and discover what has been going on at the Manor." He nodded. "Shall I meet you here?"

"I intend to join the procession," Harriette said defiantly. "And if the minister forbids me, then I shall wait at the church gate, and I shall wail so loudly the whole town shall shudder at the sound."

That smile she loved twisted one side of his lips. "That's my Rhette," he said softly. "I will leave you to it."

He leaned forward and kissed her forehead, gentle, firm, and slow. She closed her eyes and leaned into the caress. The last she might receive from him. The sweetest and most thrilling touch she'd ever received, from him or anyone.

I will leave you, too, sprang unbidden to her mind, and that thought, more than the news of her mother's death, more than her fear and trepidation of her upcoming marriage, truly broke her heart.

CHAPTER FIFTEEN

The unrest was growing. Ren sensed it as he made his way along High Street, the main thoroughfare of Shepton Mallet and the ancient heart of the town. At the intersection of London Street, the main road that crossed High Street, the commerce was not the usual tone of busy wayfarers bringing goods from Charlton to be sent up to Bowlish, where the grand houses of wealthy clothiers were rising along the quiet banks of the River Sheppey. There was a furtive tone to the huddled discussions held outside the shops and between waggoners and carters in the street, and the conversations that were not furtive were loud and vehement.

Every so often a group of men in the drabs and leathers of laborers marched up High Street toward Bunker's Hill, where Ren gathered that some assembly of the outraged was taking place. The men bore no weapons that he could see, nor did they carry their workman's tools, but angry men needed no other weapon than their feet and fists. Restlessness ran high, and the slightest spark could tip volatile tempers toward violence.

Ren hoped the feverish air to the village would not upset

Harriette's mother's funeral procession. Harriette didn't need that, on top of everything else.

His throat tightened at the thought of Harriette, and a burning coal lodged in his chest. She'd been so stunned to find Ivy Cottage in mourning; she truly had not acknowledged the possibility that illness could carry her mother off.

Ren knew how easy it was to deny to incomprehensible, to avoid looking the unfathomable in the eye. His own mother, the Countess of Renwick, refused to acknowledge that the face paint her daughter wore—the paint she, the countess, had put on her practically from birth—could be poisoning her. She came up with every other excuse. Amalie had delicate sensibilities. The move from the quiet environs of Bolton to the bustle and smoke of London had upset her frail constitution. She was sickly to begin with, formed wrong in the womb—only look how she had turned out, missing part of an arm—and no better could be expected of her.

It had been Harriette—practical, sensible, determined Harriette—who had listened to Amalie, investigated her complaint, and devised a solution. In a matter of days, she had put her finger on what had been ailing his sister for years. And she had stepped in to fix it with no accusation, no tears or histrionics, simply a clear jar of paint that contained no known toxins, and the promise to make and send more when she could.

Even though her marriage would take her away from England. From London. From him.

He owed Harriette Smythe his life. She had saved him, knowingly or not, the summer she rose like a small avenging angel from the banks of the River Sheppey and fired her slingshot at the village boys menacing him. She had saved him from despair, the deadliest of ancient sins. She had kept him from hating himself to the point of self-destruction; instead, she gave him hope that at some point in his life, certain rare and wonderful people would see him as a person and not a cripple. She had tended his wounds when his tutor beat him and weaved him worlds of magic and fey things, where transformation was possible, where suffering was rewarded, where strange marks were the sign of divine favor rather than holy wrath.

She had saved him again when he returned to London, afraid he would be devoured by his father's world. Harriette with her secondhand gowns, too-big shoes, and cheerful unconventionality had pulled him out of the stifling air of the *haut ton* and made him see its absurdities. In composing those sketches she had given him permission to unleash something wild in himself, parts that did not wish to be tamed by tradition and expectation and the centuries-old burden of a noble name and estate.

In painting him as a man in his prime, strong, splendid, even beautiful, she had given him a vision of himself that he could believe in. A vision that would be his center and his root of sanity when the rest of the world tried to define him on its terms.

She had saved him, and then she had saved his sister. That had moved her place in his heart to somewhere deeper. No longer was she simply the fantasy he'd nurtured all those years away—the fantasy, first, of a companion who accepted him utterly, who snorted at his jokes and shared her thoughts with him.

After that had followed the fantasy, as he matured, of a woman his match sexually, who responded to him with passion and welcome. Then Harriette Smythe had tumbled through his window in a crimson gown and the magnificent flesh, with those magnificent breasts, and he would have promised her anything, done anything she asked, to keep her interest. It was abject and unmanly, perhaps, but it was the truth.

He hadn't hesitated to manufacture an excuse to come with

her to Shepton Mallet and spin out the time with her as long as possible. He was very afraid he might helplessly book travel to Prussia and follow her when her cousin came to take her away. He seemed unable to resist the dictates of this simple, clear imperative that burned away everything else before it. He loved Harriette Smythe. He wanted to be with Harriette Smythe. And if he could not be with her, as her chosen companion, then he would be as near as possible in the world to where she was, and count himself happy to be so.

He loved her, and now her world had been overturned, gutted of the one thing that had been her reference point and the one constant in her life. She was orphaned; she was not who she had always thought she was; and in a few short months, perhaps weeks, she would belong to a man she didn't know, who would have complete control over her duchy, her person, her future, her life. Her expression in the parlor where her mother was laid out had carried shades of a woman at sea, unable to believe she could be drowning but about to go under for the last time.

If only there were something he could do. Anything.

These thoughts raced through him with many of the same sensations he'd experienced when Dottore Scarpa operated on his leg: like he'd been cut open and things inside were being moved about to unaccustomed places. The pain was enough to make him wonder if he were about to pass out.

"SO, from the best we can ascertain, my steward here left town possibly as much as a month ago, apparently taking the money for the household accounts, and possibly many of the household g-goods along with him," Ren said. He was pleased with how easily the words came out with a little care and foresight, especially as he was furious.

He sat in a tiny, uncomfortable chair in the office of his solicitor, Mssr. Golledge, which was an equally tiny room tucked above a haberdasher's shop just off High Street across from the Shambles and the Market Cross. It was Mssr. Golledge's politely worded letter that had given Ren the excuse to visit to Shepton Mallet and sort his business affairs out in person.

The smaller man cleared his throat. He was roughly the size of a sparrow, his tidy suit the size of a child's, his wig rather too large for his oval head, and a pair of gold-rimmed spectacles perched on his nose. Ren felt like an oversized lummox, filling the room.

"I cannot be precise about what he may or may not have taken," Mssr. Golledge said in his thin, reedy voice. "But it appears that he stopped authorizing payments on household accounts in the middle of June, and he has not been available since then to deal with any business pertaining to the Manor, including, ahem, some necessary repairs."

Ren clamped his lips together. He'd approached the Manor earlier to find the front door locked. So was the side gate set into the infamous Blinder Wall that his grandfather had erected to keep his neighbors and the prying eyes of the town from surveying his property and making judgments about his use of it. With no porter to let him in, no steward to provide passage, and no key of his own, Ren had come to throw himself on the mercy of Mssr. Golledge.

"But you say de-deliveries have continued. Who paid for them?"

"The manager of your cloth factory covered those payments, your lordship, at the request of your housekeeper, Mrs. Oram. But when he refused to pay Mrs. Oram's salary, that, I believe, is when Mrs. Oram departed the household. Since then, it appears there has been no coming or going from the house. Not that anyone can, er, really say, given the nature of the—ahem—decorative wall."

Decorative. That was rich. His maternal grandfather had been a notoriously difficult man, the miserly kind who would squeeze blood from a stone if he could. He had built his fortune by forcing fugitive artisans from Belgium and Huguenot silk makers, forced out of Catholic France, to make gorgeous fabrics for a pittance of wages, then collected enormous profits on their sale because English law protected English-made silks through enormous taxes on imports. Styling himself William Cotterell, Esq., he had gained large enough influence, and a large enough dowry for his eldest daughter, to attract the eye of an earl's heir, and after that his arrogance was unlimited. Constance Cotterell, Countess of Renwick, had returned to Shepton Mallet precisely once after she had been married from the Manor House, and that was to tell her detested son that he might finally go to school.

"Where might I find Mrs. Oram, do you suppose?" Ren asked with a heavy sigh, taking up his cane. More walking, and his leg was still stiff from the days of travel. But he was not yet reduced to hiring a chair.

"In my official capacity, I cannot say, your lordship. But as—ahem—a matter of hearsay, I understand she has sought new employment at the Swan, just up the street."

"And the man-manager of my factory—where can I find him? I should like to hear his—er, perspective on the discussions that seem to be currently occupying everyone in t-town."

Mssr. Golledge blinked rapidly and regarded Renwick as if he had just turned a somersault in the rather cramped and very shabby environs of his office. "Er." He appeared at a complete loss, faced with the notion of a lord and factory owner condescending to learn what his manager thought on any aspect of his business. "I may be mistaken, but I believe that Mr. Fripp is, er, often seen in the environs of the Swan as well."

"How convenient." Ren levered himself to his feet, masking a grimace as his bum foot collided with the leg of a table crowding the narrow space. "I may w-return for his direction if I am unable to locate him otherwise. Would you care to accompany me to the Swan for a drink, Golledge?"

"A-a-a drink, your lord-lordship?"

Ren held back a smile and the comment that Golledge stuttered worse than he did. He had been away from London for all of three days and was already weary of the notion that earls swam in rarefied air, slightly above and unattached to the realm of lesser mortals. He had not seen that nobility was treated with reverence anywhere else on the Continent. Certainly English nobility, being as common as dirt along the routes of the Grand Tour, was nothing out of the way. The populace of other countries seemed to regard their very wealthy as spectacles put on earth to entertain them; only the English seemed to attach some special favor to noble birth.

He wondered fleetingly how the Prussians felt about such things. Would Harriette be treated as special because she was a duchess? Or did Frederick the Great, like other rulers of the Enlightenment, believe that integrity of character could be separate from privileged birth?

His Harriette ought to be revered by all as the goddess she was. Though he, of course, was biased, Ren reflected as he made his way to the Swan.

The public room of the inn was thronged with working men, and none of them appeared to be taking their leisure. The loud buzz of conversation was punctuated here and there with an outburst of rage. A pair of well-dressed men passed him on the street, their white stockings, buckled shoes, powdered wigs, and fine coats proclaiming them men of some station. Coins clanked as one man clasped a hand over the leather pouch he carried. Both men hurried into a small office with a sign proclaiming it a bank.

The rich men were hustling their savings to safety. Something was afoot, indeed.

Ren stepped carefully over the uneven wooden threshold into a room that had to be at least two hundred years old, with a low timbered ceiling, smoke-stained plaster on the walls, and oiled paper rather than glass in the windows. As he straightened, sweeping off his tricorne hat, every eye in the room turned in his direction, and every conversation stopped.

"R-Renwick, at your service." He swept a shallow, cordial bow, proud that his stutter was not obvious, that his cane held him steady. A gentleman only put himself at the service of other gentlemen, an earl to none but his colleagues or those above him in rank. That he made this courtesy to a room full of workingmen meant he was greeted with a lift of several glasses, a chorus of "Well come, yer lordship!" and a crowd of pointed fingers when he asked where he could find Mrs. Oram.

He navigated a narrow passage and another dangerously uneven set of steps to a courtyard behind the inn, where several flat tables were set up on crossed logs, an enormous chunk of meat roasted over an open fire, and a flock of hens clucked and scraped in the dirt against a far wall. A woman in a calico dress and cap stood at the spit, using her apron to protect her hands as she gave the meat a turn. A boy stood beside a smaller table set well away from the fire, taking chanterelles out of a woven basket and laying them out in neat rows.

"Mrs. O-Owam?" Ren practiced his shallow bow once more, hoping she didn't notice he'd mangled her name. "I am R-Renwick. I see that you are oth-otherwise occupied, but I hoped to have a w-w—a word with you. About the Manor House."

"Oh, gor. Yer lordship." She dropped a curtsey, wiping her

hands in her apron. Her eyes ran down his frame, noting the cane, and he supposed she had been told about him, though she'd never before had occasion to see him. "If there's owt missin' from the 'ouse, milord, it's that rotter Mr. Erle, and that's the way of it."

"I have reason to believe Mr.—" He paused. There was no way he was going to manage the word 'Erle.' He ought to have objected to hiring the man from the very beginning based on that alone. "My steward has, sh-shall we say, neglected his post. I ca-came for other reasons, Missus."

He wasn't going to be able to manage her name, either. Her curious, wary look, and the frank stare of the boy with the mushrooms, were as much as his nerves could handle.

"I was ho-hoping you might return to the house, with the right incentive," he blurted. "And possibly have p-p-possession of a key."

"I've nowt fer a key," she answered, glancing at the boy. "But Jags and I might be persuaded, if ye offer the right terms, sir."

"Terms?" Ren hadn't the faintest notion what a housekeeper in a small market town could command for her services. He was more interested in the way the boy was now rearranging the chanterelles on the table, moving the golden funnel-shaped items into rows of the similar size.

"Half again my salary," Mrs. Oram said promptly, "and I might have Jags with me."

The boy hummed slightly as he worked, but emitted a sound of distress as he found his columns uneven in length. He counted the last column again and began to rock side to side on his feet, the hum growing in volume.

"'Ere, luv." His mother strolled over and laid a hand on his arm. As the boy calmed, she reached for the mushrooms in the uneven row. "Shall we give 'is lordship a taste?"

The boy subsided to a happy hum as his mother scooped the extras into her apron and left him with a complete, neat square. Softly he touched each one, counting to himself.

"Jags is simple," Mrs. Oram said, looking Ren squarely in the eye as she walked toward him. "'Ee can't be left to shift for 'imself. Mr. Erle and I didn't see eye to eye on that, or on many things."

"And, er, Mr. O—?" He left it at that.

She gulped. "'Ee won't be callin'." She gave him a challenging look.

Ren deliberated. He knew it was not the done thing for housekeepers to have families. Callers were discouraged for unattached house servants, and housing children was unheard of. They distracted from one's work and were like to cause damage, get in the way, or at the very least provoke neighboring households to gossip. If the Manor were not seen as being kept to the appropriate standards, how else might his home, and his business interests, suffer?

"Meh." The boy ambled over to Ren, holding a golden cup in his hand. His eyes, set close together in his face, flickered with interest over Ren's cane. Without fear he held up his palm. "Meh."

Mrs. Oram sucked in her breath. "He wants you to smell," she said. "He don't usually take to strangers. Jags, 'is lordship mightn't—"

Ren bent forward, bracing himself on his cane, and sniffed at the delicately flared hood of the mushroom.

"I say," he answered, straightening. "Smells like apricots. I'd never noticed that. Thank you, Jags."

The boy grunted and ferried his treasure back to his table, carefully replacing it and beaming at his neat array. Harriette would adore this boy. Ren met Mrs. Oram's worried gaze.

"Jags has a place in my home for as long as you w-work

there," he said. He felt a rush of protectiveness, mingled with sorrow. Jags looked about the age Ren had been the summer he came to Shepton Mallet, and he guessed all too readily how other boys his age regarded Jags' limitations. "Mr. G-Golledge will see you receive your back pay. How soo-soon can you come?"

Mr. Oram wiped a hand beneath the frilled lace of her cap, heaving a deep sigh of relief. "I mun finish 'ere tonight or Stokes'll put me in the soup. Tomorrah?" she asked. "Tendin' one big ole empty house's a sight easier than feedin' this bleedin' lot 'o ruffians, and no mistake."

"I shall l-look for you tomorrow then," Ren said. "Thank you, Mrs. Ow-Oram. Good day, Jags."

He retreated to the dark passage leading back to the public room, drawing a breath and trying to let his tongue untangle. Dealing with strangers always made his mouth feel too small, increasing his difficulties, and there was worse to come.

The public room fell silent again as Ren entered. He stood and let the crowd take him in, scanning their curious, wary, cautious, or scornful faces. "Any ch-chance one of you is a Mr. Fw-Fripp?" he pronounced carefully.

"Don't 'spect 'im till later, yer lordship!" yelled a voice from the back. "After 'ee's made 'is way through the Bell, then the King's Bench, then the Tare 'n 'ounds—" Guffaws of laughter drowned out the last of his statement.

"I'll wait," Ren said. "And in the meantime, I should l-like someone to enlighten me about the disag-g-greements over the factories that is taking place here."

Absolute and profound silence. A light snore drifted from a table in the furthest corner.

An enormous man stood, his tankard still clutched in his hand. "Ye want to 'ear about our *disag-g-greements*." He elaborated Ren's stammer, making it sound worse. A few nervous titters from his companions emboldened him. "Going to fix it all, are ye? The great 'n grand Duke o' Limbs."

Ren guessed the man had only barely kept from calling him Runtwick. He regarded the barrel-sized chest, the thick shock of dirty brown hair, the stubble on the man's face, and the dust and wear on his leather trousers. An equally dirty leather jacket lay over the back of his chair. Ren didn't have to search hard for the name.

"I make no promises to you or anyone, Abel Cain," he said, and the ice in his voice helped every word emerge with precision. "But I do agree to *listen*."

The man blinked, clearly shocked at being recognized. While he stood, mouth open, a smaller man beside him surged to his feet.

"If 'is lordship'll listen, we'll spill," he shouted. "'At's the first time any fancy 'as said they'll at least 'ear us, and that's that. Stokes!" he bellowed. "Fetch the earl 'ere a—what'll it be, then? Ale? Small beer? Whisky?"

Abel Cain sneered, not about to be bested. "Dandelion wine?"

"Ale," Ren said evenly, and moved to a stool at the bar in a space that had suddenly cleared for him. "To begin with."

It wasn't his first choice to be here. He needed to find a key and open the Manor House. He needed to determine in what state his steward had left the house, as well as its finances. He needed to find Fripp and learn if the adoption of new equipment was causing problems in his factory as well.

More than that, he wanted to be with Harriette. He wished to be there to hold her when she finally decided to let herself cry. He wanted to help her with the small, drab, consuming details of death, of choosing hatbands and dying everything black. He wanted to tell her that, at first, the loss of a parent felt like the world had sagged on its axis, that the North Star had shifted, that the whole world had gone arsey varsey, as she would say.

But in time one learned to accommodate, as one learned to walk with a limp or compensate for a missing limb. It felt hollow and endless and strange at first—even the loss of a parent one didn't particularly like or feel close to was a blow to the very fabric of one's being. But it would get better.

He wanted to make it better. He wanted to be there for her, but he sensed he would only be in the way. So instead he sat in the Swan, accepted the bumper of ale set before him, and determined to listen to the complaints of these men as no one else had, and see if he could find a way to make peace around him.

Peace in his own heart, he knew, would be harder to find.

CHAPTER SIXTEEN

Some might say that the Earl of Renwick was drunk. Not drunk as a wheelbarrow, but definitely in altitudes, and more than a trifle disguised. Cup-shot; flustered; emphatically groggy. Ren chuckled to himself as he reviewed the many and varied adjectives that could apply to his current state of not caring very much about anything.

"Ssssomethin' I'm 'sposed to be doing," he slurred to the man slumped on the bar next to him. Crowds had come and gone that afternoon at the Swan Inn, all of them having something to say to the Earl of Renwick, but Abel Cain had early on staked a claim on the stool beside Ren, and there passed through the stages of intoxication with him.

"Seeing t' the tackle?" Cain suggested, holding back a belch.

"Beg par-pardon," Ren said with great dignity, noting that he did not care about his stammer when he was top-heavy. This might be a solution for future dreaded social events, he reflected.

"Keepin' the cully," Cain clarified. "The convenient. The peculiar. Yer sweetheart," he finally said.

"Are you sssuggesting..." Ren caught himself just in time.

He wasn't so corned he would link Harriette's name to his in such a scenario. "Castin' 'spersions on milady," he said instead.

Cain nodded solemnly. "Aye, that. Truth told, milord, we ne'er thought she'd amount to much, cross-patch bobbletail, she was. But she come back from that girls' school all gimcrack, with the..." At a loss for proper words, he made a motion toward his waistcoat suggesting rounded breasts.

"Think I ought t' call you out for that," Ren mumbled, annoyed.

"Oi, don't git yer back up." Cain emptied his bumper of ale. "We all know she's a duchess or some such, above our touch." He wiped his mouth with his shirt sleeve. "And yer a rum one, you are," he went on, squinting at Ren, "if you kin stop the factory owners going on as they been."

"Can't promise." Ren kept his words short, aware his tongue was swelling, his self-consciousness growing as the haze of alcohol began to dim. "Can try."

He'd spent the past hours being illuminated on the many varieties of poverty and hardship confronting members of the town. The clothing trade that had run the town for decades was changing. Instead of taking carding or spinning or weaving work into their homes, where they could watch children and stir the supper and tend to the fields that fed them, men and women and even children were brought to the factories with their fancy equipment run by the power of the river.

The factory equipment caused frequent injuries, and the buildings were notoriously susceptible to fire. Children too young to work were left at home, untended, and the wages weren't enough to replace the other ways people had been able to feed themselves, by selling produce, raising animals to trade, or growing or finding their own food.

A working man had to provide for his own family and pay the poor rate that supported the workhouse, where those too young, too ill, or old to work barely kept body and soul together. Poaching meat for the table could cost a man his life or land him in the Shepton Mallet prison, one of the worst in Somerset for its poor conditions and rampant sickness.

Profits the factory owners made from Parliament's support of English-made wares never trickled back to the pockets of the workers. With machines like the spinning jenny coming to replace what meager work they had—the alternatives to starve in the workhouse, the prison, or their own home, watching their family starve beside them—the men of Shepton Mallet had had enough.

Ren burned with shame and the heat of their anger as he listened. He wanted to protest that he'd never thought about where the fabrics came from that his tailor made into his beautiful, expensive suits. He'd never once thought about the hands that made the fine white stockings he rolled over the scar on his leg or the lace he hung at his throat. No more than he thought of the cook who prepared the meals served him at Renwick house or the chambermaid who made up his bed with fresh linens. He paid for the service; that was all he owed.

Or so he would have said before today, when he was forced to look on the hands that made his fine things, the backs that strained to provide the labor he expected. And all the other lives, the web of intricate relations that depended on them. Abel Cain had a wife and three children, though he was barely older than Ren. Mrs. Oram, who had lost her position when his feckless steward absconded, had Jags to care for.

Harriette had seen all this. She had said much the same over dinner on their journey. She knew what was happening; she saw the wreckage that the whims of the great and the all-consuming quest for money left on the bodies of the people they exploited. Ren was the factory owner, concerned mostly for the income that his investment yielded. Or at least he had been until today, when he had sat down ready to give the workmen a chance to air their complaints, convinced he could ultimately make them see reason, the benefits of progress, and their own self-sabotage in not accommodating themselves to the new ways.

Harriette wouldn't have needed such persuasion. He had no doubt where she would stand on any of these stories. Ren pushed away the new glass that the publican set before him. He had to find Harriette, tell her what he had learned, and have her help him decide what to do next. Harriette would know what to do.

"Ye kin promise, King Queer Pins, an you kin try," Cain said, contemplating his empty glass. He swiped the bumper Ren had declined and examined its contents with one half-shut eye. "But the men are ready to do somethin' about it. There's a mobility brewin' this evening, make no mistake."

"Did you call me—"

Ren put the complaint aside. There had been no acrimony in Cain's tone. He was acquainted with the habit among some men to refer to their friends with insults, saving worse acrimony for those they truly detested. Cain had welcomed him back as though they'd been chums all along, as if Ren had never fled him and his cronies in fear for his life. "There's a *what* brewing?"

"A mobility. Fancy word for a mob," Cain explained.

"Where?"

"Bunker's Hill, I heard. I'd be there meself if you hadn't come along. Old Hoppin' Giles." He snorted into the foam of his beverage, then drank deeply.

"Where is the sheriff? A constable? A—a watch?"

Ren wasn't familiar with the peace-keeping apparatus of small villages like this. Would a magistrate get involved? A justice of the peace? The Lord Lieutenant of the county or any of his deputies?

"Oi, ye can lay odds there's gentlemen of the peace about tonight." Cain nodded knowingly, tapping the side of his nose. "But they's wise enough to lie low till they see which way the wind's blowin, aye?"

Ren looked around for his walking stick. The pleasant feeling of not being concerned with much about him had evaporated. "Bunker's Hill—that s-s-south of here?"

"Aye." Cain's head wobbled. "But if they get ambitious, they'll march up the 'igh Street t'the Market Cross, and then down th' river t' the fact'ries, looking to make a racket." He yawned, his words running together, then smiled as if he relished the thought.

High Street was where the duchess's funeral procession would take place. Ivy Cottage stood at its south end. The market square with its huge Buckland Cross was but a stone's throw from the churchyard of St. Peter and Paul's, where the duchess would doubtless be carried. Harriette would be directly in harm's way if an angry mob began marching north to take their anger out on the factories ruining their lives.

"I'mun go," Ren slurred, groping for his hat.

"Where, then?" Cain peered at him over his glass.

"Funeral." Ren located his tricorne and placed it firmly on his head, which felt heavier than usual.

Cain thunked down his bumper, staring. "Ye ain't dressed fer a funeral, man!"

Ren snorted. His companion was sanguine about the possibilities of enraged workmen passing through town, but shocked at the thought that Ren might attend funeral services without proper attire. "Know of a s-shop open, do ye?" he challenged.

Cain peered around the room. Ren was surprised to note that lamps had been lit, the flames shining against the oilcloth over the windows. Dusk had fallen without his noticing. Funeral processions commonly happened at dark, at least among those who felt their own importance and could pay for torchbearers to light their way. Death being a solemn occasion and the body going to an even darker place, the cover of night was considered the appropriate venue for laying the dearly departed to rest. It was another reason women were not encouraged to be part of funeral proceedings, a nicety he was sure Harriette would continue to ignore in her effort to make up for missing her mother's deathbed.

"Oi! Spratt!" Ren startled as Cain unleashed a full-throated bellow. A man sitting at a far table jolted to attention and craned his head about.

"'is lordship requires yer hatband and gloves," Cain ordered as the man approached. His attire was that of a gentleman, the touches of mourning dignified but not overdone. Ren wondered if he was involved in the clothing trade, and if, out of solidarity, Ren should warn him of the danger the clothiers were currently in from the men they'd been quietly robbing for years.

"Pay you three guineas," Ren said, reaching for his purse. It was still full, remarkably. Not only had his drinks been provided all day, but no one had attempted to rob him while his attention was elsewhere. He counted out the gold coins, and the eyes of both Cain and the gentleman called Spratt widened considerably.

"Ye might have me wife's mother for that price," Cain observed.

Ren swapped his tricorne for Spratt's flat black felt hat with its trailing black scarf. He affixed the black silk armband to his sleeve and pulled on the gloves. They were tight, but he wasn't in a position to complain. A black cloak would have been proper —Harriette would have appreciated the effort—but too late for that now.

"For your information," he said to Cain, dropping three more guineas into the man's pocket. "And your family."

Cain's eyes went as round as the rarely seen coins. "Ought to be beggin' your pardon for all the times we bammed ye as a kiddey," he said. "Ye've turned out a right fellow, Runtwick."

"Bygones," Ren said, stowing his purse. "So long as you s-stop calling me R-Runtwick. Good ev'nin, fellows."

His leg was sore and stiff from sitting too long, and the cobbles of the High Street proved treacherously uneven. He leaned on his cane as he limped along, too focused on keeping himself upright to be concerned with his gait.

The entire town appeared to be turned out into the street. Shops were dark and shuttered, some windows even boarded as if in anticipation of a riot, while noise and light spilled from public houses and common areas. In many buildings the windows above shops were lit and open, the residents awake to the action below. Voices came from everywhere, most of them a muddle, but far down the street Ren spotted the bob and flicker of torchlight and the sound of a bell. The procession had begun.

The mute led the way, dressed in his black suit and sash. Behind him, a group of children from the almshouse carried torches and rang small bells. Eight men in black cloaks, with black scarves drifting from their hats, supported the bier with its black velvet pall and tall black plumes waving in the night air.

Behind them, in a space all her own, walked a woman in broad black skirts and cape. A full veil covered her from her tall black hat to the black silk ribbons hemming her skirts. Black gloves covered hands clutching a large golden cross depending from a black beaded string hung around her neck. He didn't know where Harriette had found full mourning attire—likely Mrs. Demant, faced with Harriette's intractable decision to be part of the procession, had decided she would commit the outrage in the dignity of full mourning dress.

She looked like Grief incarnate as she moved along, with the branched candelabra carried by two more children following behind her, their light bouncing off the deep black of her veil. Passersby who mumbled blessings, called to friends they recognized, or kept up a steady stream of chatter, fell silent, staring, as the apparition neared them.

"Relief!" croaked one of the pall bearers on the near side, and a man from the group behind Harriette hurried forward. He assumed his share of the burden while the wearied man gratefully fell to the rear, glancing nervously at Harriette as she passed and crossing himself in superstition. Ren took advantage of the brief commotion to slide into the procession with the men behind. As Harriette passed, he touched the long veil, briefly stirring the dark lace with his finger. A glint of white behind the curtain told him she had spared him a smile. He wouldn't presume to walk beside her; she was, as she'd said, the chief mourner, and her place was alone at the front of the procession. But at least he'd managed to haul himself here, despite being properly shot in the neck.

And his limp was hardly unique, given that most of the men here had already partaken freely at the funeral feast, both the ones who had been hired to perform and those discharging familial duties. Ren spotted one black-garbed gentleman whom he guessed from the portrait he'd seen in the formal parlor to be Mr. Demant, his cheeks pleasantly brightened by drink, humming a dolorous hymn as he swayed happily from side to side.

The wailers performed with vigor, providing far more caterwauling than Ren thought necessary. It surprised him not a bit that Mrs. Demant should demand these touches that, in his opinion, were overdone. There would be no caterwauling at his funeral, Ren decided; he'd ask Harriette to see to it. She'd do that for him.

From what Ren had gathered, Mrs. Demant had kept Harriette's mother the way some people kept an exotic pet or handsome slaves, feeding and dressing them to display to others as a sign of status. Mrs. Demant had always believed her mother's assurances of noble birth, Harriette had said, and no doubt she found her faith justified when her long-time lodger turned up a foreign duchess. What that gained Mrs. Demant otherwise, Ren couldn't say, but he supposed Harriette would find some way to recognize the family's long support and service. Giving Mr. Demant some sort of title, perhaps? From what he could guess, nothing would please the aspiring Mrs. Demant more, though she would be likely to suggest a pension be granted, too.

These thoughts amused him until they came to the market square, where the street widened and the crowd multiplied considerably. Throngs of people stood about the huge stone Buckland Cross and the Shambles, the covered stalls that ran the length of the market. Vendors were at work, hawking hot pies and candies, and pickpockets were doubtless at work as well, Ren thought, touching the bulge of his purse beneath his waistcoat. Torches set into the brackets of buildings lit the square, and lamps had been brought out and set upon tables. It looked like a festival of sorts, but the taut sense of anticipation in the air was not of the celebratory kind.

The noise behind him intensified, and it was no longer the forced, conventional moans and howls that the wailers were paid to produce. He heard drunken singing, shouts and calls, and beneath that, other sounds of discord—the muffled blows of items crashing together, what sounded like splintering wood, and the distinct crinkle of breaking glass.

Another procession was coming up the street, and it had none of the dignity or formality of a funeral. These were men intent on making a mark.

The tension in the air heightened as the funeral procession marched through the square. The buzz of conversation sounded like the drone of insects in high summer, when he and Harriette had lain in surrounding fields, watching clouds float across the sky. Or rather, Ren dozed while Harriette sketched everything: the clouds, the sheep, the clodden hump of Glastonbury Tor rising in the distance. And him.

He watched her moving through her private pool of torch-light and wondered if she felt the crackling tension, flaring like lightning through the air. Her back was straight, her steps slow and steady, the floor-length veil rippling lightly as she walked. If the mob broke upon them, he wondered where he could take her. Would the churchyard be safe?

"Down with Jenny!" The bellowed chant of the mob rose above the clang of bells and buzz of chatter as the crowd behind them spilled into the square. "Down with Jenny! Men, not machines!"

An answering roar met the new arrivals, and the crowd came alive. The crowd of marching men swelled in an instant, bristling with torches, staves, clubs, and whatever else they could lay hands on as weapons. Encouraging cheers came from onlookers, further feeding the frenzy. The men in the procession behind Ren moved closer, nearly treading on his heels.

As the procession turned into the narrow street leading to the church and churchyard, Ren glanced behind to see the market square lit with diabolical brightness. People leaned from upstairs windows, throwing scarves and other items he couldn't identify to the massing men below, and the volume of the noise was deafening. Ren drew closer to Harriette, hoping to provide some protection. He couldn't fight like a regular man, but his body at least could be a shield.

The procession halted in the dark, narrow passage leading to the tall stone wall about the church. The vicar stood before the gate, draped in black, holding his prayer book. The mute stepped forward with his staff and knocked three times on the wooden gate, another ancient superstition, the noise meant to direct the passing spirit where to go.

"Who comes?" the minister called. In the flicker of torch-light Ren saw him cast a nervous glance toward the square, only a street away. The glow of torchlight was evident above the buildings, as was the noise.

"I am Christiana Ulrich, Duchess of Löwenburg, daughter to Karl Augustus, Duke of Löwenburg and Prince of the Lesser Isles," Harriette answered in a clear, steady voice that carried.

The vicar shifted, clutching his prayer book. "I do not know you. Who comes?" he asked again, raising his voice to be heard above the sudden rise of noise from the market. It sounded like carts were being overturned and windows broken. Ren wondered if the vicar was being made nervous by the mob and that was why he wasn't letting them in.

"I am Christiana Ulrich, Duchess of Löwenburg," Harriette said again.

Ren paused. *She* wasn't Christiana—that had to be her mother's name, wasn't it? The vicar cleared his throat and shifted. His eyes widened as a sudden *whoosh* of air blasted through the night and a great flame rose from the square, as if a torch had been cast into a barrel of oil.

"Who comes?" the poor vicar whimpered, his face white and terrified, and Ren understood. He was watching some orchestrated ritual, something he'd never seen before, but it seemed it was important to Harriette. Her voice was strong and firm as she answered.

"I am Christiana, a poor mortal and a sinner."

"Come in," the vicar croaked with relief, nearly falling into the gate as it opened behind him.

At the same time a roar of noise rounded the corner, pouring into the street behind them. The mob was in full spate. The men in the front charged any item in the street, smashing or overturning it, and those behind dashed to doors and windows, caving them in. Screams erupted from houses, shouts of rage carried before, and smoke from the fire billowing above the market square burned Ren's nose and eyes.

The bier and pall rocked as the pallbearers faltered, turning to gaze behind them in fear. The bier nearly tipped to the side as the men in the rear of the procession rushed forward. Ren stepped behind Harriette and grasped her shoulders as people jostled her, frantically pushing the pallbearers and their burden into the churchyard, with Harriette carried along in their midst.

"We have to go!" He bent his head to shout in Harriette's ear. His cane in one hand, her in the other, he desperately hoped he wouldn't fall.

"I'm not allowed in here!" The veil puffed out before her face as she shouted back.

Ren laughed aloud: Harriette, who had never to his knowledge given a fig for convention, was shocked to violate custom on this most solemn occasion.

"Besides, I have to make sure—"

"The vicar will see to it." Already the men of their procession had slammed the iron gate shut, clamping the teeth of the large padlock just before the tide of the mob reached them. Arms and hands reached through the iron bars, some shaking their fists.

"Back, ye ruffians!" Mr. Demant shouted, betraying in his anger a marked West Country accent beneath the gentlemanly speech he'd affected before. "This is a funeral, ye rotten curs!"

"To th' prison!" Voices in the sprawling mob shouted above the melee, and other throats took up the cry. "Th' prison! Free the pris'ners!"

The mob melted away, the cries, shouts, and sounds of accompanying damage moving along the high stone wall lining the churchyard as the men, and no doubt women, rushed along it to the prison on the east side of the church.

"Should we help them?" Harriette crouched within the curve of his arm as they huddled against the inside of the wall. With some doing she lifted the long black veil over her face and settled it to drape from the back of her head. Her face revealed, she watched the small group gathered about the open grave some distance away in the churchyard. Ren watched her.

"Help who?" he asked, keeping his voice low. "The vicar knows his business, the mob is about theirs, and the prisoners would no doubt welcome being broken out."

Harriette lingered, her eyes on the group about the grave, and Ren did not have the heart to rush her. Around them he heard the mob at work, the commotion made more frightening by the dark and not knowing what all the crashing sounds entailed. They were curiously sheltered, hiding in the churchyard, but they couldn't stay.

Across the churchyard the vicar mumbled a few quick words above the cut in the ground. Ren wondered if the Duchess of Löwenburg had her own grave or if she was obliged to share her final resting place with bones just below or other corpses brought in that week. He'd seen small village churchyards with dirt nearly piled to the tops of their walls, so much had been added over the centuries as generations of parishioners required sacred ground.

The vicar sprinkled a few drops of holy water above the hole. Men stood aside with torches as a few hands reached out and slid the coffin from the bier. With the touch of an unseen clasp, the bottom of the coffin hinged open and its contents dropped into the waiting earth. The coffin bottom was shut and returned to the bier, men set to work with shovels replacing the turned soil, and in a few moments the business was done. Mr. Demant dispensed their wages to the hired men, and they scattered. Ren wondered how many would put aside their black hats and cloaks and join the noisy crowd currently descending on the prison.

On the thought, an alarm bell went up, along with shouts of "Fire! Fire!" The vicar grabbed the skirts of his cassock and scampered to the rear door of the church, escaping inside.

"A reusable coffin," Harriette remarked. "How thrifty of Mrs. Demant."

"Rhette," Ren urged her, "we must get out of here."

"But where?"

He tugged her along the stone wall lining the churchyard. The square tower of the church reared above them, the tall windows with their pointed arches reflecting the light of burning fires, the spires of the roof thrusting up into the night. A small arched door in the east wall let them out into a narrow alley.

"Leg Square is a stone's throw from here," Ren whispered, taking Harriette's hand as much to hold himself upright as to support her. "We'll go to the Manor." How they would get in, he hadn't yet a notion.

Harriette didn't argue. She didn't demur or doubt him, nor even give him a skeptical look, not that the night shadows allowed him to properly see her face. She put her hand in his with complete trust and followed him through the narrow twisting alley, between a set of buildings, dark and shuttered and quiet, and into Leg Square. The short street, not a proper square at all, was equally dark and quiet, the eerie quiet of living things holding their breath.

A short distance away the mob swarmed the prison, and at any moment a group could break away and enter the square, where the grand houses stood awaiting the wrath of the disaffected. The Manor House would be safe behind the Blinder

Wall, Ren hoped. But they would only be safe if they could get inside.

"The key?" Harriette panted as they stumbled and slithered along the Blinder Wall to the back side, where the wooden door on its iron hinges sat firmly shut with its iron lock.

"Er, that. The key is hanging near the kitchen entrance, I understand. Usual place. On the other—other side," he clarified, as Harriette gave him a blank look.

"Then how are we to get in?"

"Well, you see, I haven't thought that through."

His marvelous Harriette gave him a calm, level look. He comprehended in that instant how utterly unique she was. Most genteel ladies of his acquaintance would have collapsed sobbing against the Blinder Wall at this point. They would have gone into hysterics, blaming him not just for misplacing the key but for the riot, the general state of affairs in Shepton Mallet, and everything else that was wrong with the world. They would have thrown themselves on the mercy of any passing stranger just to be shot of him, and he would be obliged to follow like an idiot, and above that, he would be forced to endure the silent treatment for days, if not longer.

Harriette looked about with thoughtful deliberation. She tipped back her head, and he formed the word *No* just as she said, quite matter-of-factly, "I suppose I will climb the tree."

"No," he said anyway.

"Oh, you intend to climb it instead? Very well, I shall hold your cane."

She said this without heat, as if the argument were merely an exercise. The wall was half again as high as she was, but the bird cherry in the back corner of the lot, growing wild and untended, had stretched its branches over the wall. She could reach them if she had a leg up.

"You could h-h-hurt yourself," Ren said.

"I did all right at Renwick House, didn't I? Here, help me move this wheelbarrow."

By some cursed luck there was indeed an unused wheelbarrow leaning against the wall. Harriette helped him position it against the tree, then she fell to the business of disrobing. First she looped her long black veil around her arm, unpinned her hat, and handed it to Ren. When she started untying the strings of her cape, he found his voice.

"Wh-what are you doing?"

"Well, I can't climb a tree in full dress, can I?" she answered. "Learned that last time. Here, hold this."

She handed him the black velvet cape, neatly folded, and then, to his astonishment, started working at the front of her gown. "Now what?" he asked, his voice strangled.

He wasn't concerned about impropriety. It was nearly pitch black where they stood in the shadows. The only light came from a lamp lit in an upper room across the way and the orange glow of the fire in Market Square. Every so often, from the direction of the prison, where there emanated shouts, clanging noises, and the sound of walls being beat upon, a flare of torchlight leapt into the sky like some macabre spirit.

This night, Ren thought in a daze, was so far the strangest night of his existence. Every sense seemed heightened, every image sharp and clear. He would never forget it, not least because Harriette was undressing, just as he had fantasized her doing all the times in her studio that she had undressed him.

"This is a sight harder to do in the dark." She moved her hands over the front of her gown, pulling out pins, and in a short while she'd freed her black open robe from her stomacher. Carefully she folded the gleaming black bombazine and arranged it on top of the cape. "The stomacher must go too, I think."

As she pulled out the pins that held the decorative front

panel in place, Ren found his voice. "Where did you find mourning garments?"

"My mother had costumes made when I sent her word that my grandfather the duke had died." Her voice sounded muffled as she tucked her chin, searching with her fingers in the dark for the last precious pins. "She had two gowns made up, it seems. Mrs. Demant laid her out in one, and I fortunately fit in the other."

Onto the pile went the flat black stomacher with its rows of black silk ribbons. "Hold a moment, I'll take my top petticoat off as well. Black silk isn't very sturdy. Something about the dying process weakens the fabric, I think."

"Is that why you smell metallic. Like iron." He focused on the shape of Harriette emerging in the gloom as she untied the thick silk petticoat, lined with more silk ribbons, from around her waist.

"I use ground bone ash for my black pigments, and sometimes lamp black," she said, folding the petticoat efficiently. "But I think for this fabric they used gall nuts and tannins, with iron as the mordant to help it hold fast." She placed the petticoat atop the pile in his arms. "When this is all over and we have a moment, I ought to visit the dyer's to see how he does it. I might learn something."

Ren couldn't speak. He simply gazed at her over the pile of clothing he held, struck dumb. Harriette stood before him in shift and stays and underpetticoat, her pockets a fanciful patchwork tied about her waist. Only her black silk stockings and heeled black shoes hinted at the luxury she'd just shed. And the shape of her in those scanty garments—it defied his meager powers of description. He wished he had her gift of drawing so he might capture this image and carry it with him always.

"Now put those somewhere, and be prepared to catch me if I go arsey varsey," she said.

He grinned and found a nearby overgrown flowerbed, the cleanest place he could discern in the dark. Harriette hiked up her petticoat and climbed into the wheelbarrow, placing a hand on his shoulder for balance as she studied the branches of the bird cherry, charting her path.

"You don't have to do this, Rhette," he murmured. "We can take shelter in the churchyard, or with the Demants, or—"

"Now you tell me this, when I'm naked," Harriette answered.

She tightened her grip on his shoulder as a great crash arose from the prison. It sounded like a gate giving way. A great roar of excited voices, screams, and furious shouts arose, above it the boom of a musket firing.

"I do believe there's a prison break taking place." Ren tried to keep his voice calm so he didn't frighten Harriette.

"And they'll be headed here, a mob in full force." She sounded grim, not at all frightened. "We need to get behind that wall. 'Old still, me 'andsome.'"

Her flippant remark in the area dialect almost, almost made him smile. Until she set her neat heeled shoe on his shoulder and levered herself up. The impact made him wince, the sharpness of her heel digging into his shoulder through his coat, her weight driving him into the ground. He braced his bum leg against the wheelbarrow and for the ten thousandth time cursed the unlucky fate that had made him half a man instead of a whole one. If he were a man rightly made, he would be the one vaulting the Blinder Wall to retrieve the key, rescuing his lady from the approaching riot.

An explosion of some sort rose from the prison, among more screams, some of fear and anger, some it seemed of pain. These noises were drowned out by the roar of the attacking mob and the whoops of freed prisoners, with more scattered gunfire.

"Whoa," Harriette shouted as the branch she grabbed for bowed under her weight. "*Whoa!*"

She fell against him, and only because he'd braced himself against the wheelbarrow did Ren catch and stop her without pitching them both onto the ground. Fabric choked his mouth. Harriette's warm, rounded bottom pressed against his face. Thought evaporated.

He'd barely reached his arms around her when the warm weight lifted and he could breathe again. "Not that one," she muttered. "You'll have to toss me, Ren. Make a stirrup with your hands, like this—" She turned to stare down at him, linked her fingers and cupped her palms. "And when I say, throw me up."

"Argh," Ren said, which was his attempt to say *No,* and *not on your life,* and *I can't.*

"Yes, you can," she said. "We girls did it all the time at school. There was this one lovely park where the blighters had built a wall all 'round it, and this was the only way we could get in."

His mind didn't seem to be working in its customary paths. Perhaps it was the distraction of the mounting noise from several directions now, the scent of riot and fire and the ruinous wrath of the mob coming in their direction from both the Market Square and the prison, and now, it seemed, the church-yard as well. He'd be crushed and Harriette carried off if the men came upon them here. He didn't resist as she cupped his hands as she'd directed, her hands upon his, warm and supple and strong, then with complete trust and fearlessness she placed a foot in his palm.

"Now!" she shouted, and he heaved. He glimpsed black stocking and the fluttering ribbon of a garter against the white of her petticoat, and a square of perfect pale thigh. Then more than that as she caught herself on her stomach atop the wall and squirmed for a moment, legs kicking. If it hadn't been dark, he'd have been granted a glimpse of the God-given perfection that was Harriette Smythe's bottom.

You're a randy bastard, Ren informed himself. There couldn't be a less appropriate time for trying to get a glimpse up her skirts. Yet when else might he have the opportunity?

Harriette grabbed a branch of the tree and hauled her hips atop the wall, then pulled up her legs and swung herself into a seated position. Before he could call out—a warning, advice, anything—she stepped out and the top of her head dropped out of sight.

"Rhette!"

The tumult of noise from behind blocked out any sound she might have made, any call for aid. He limped to the gate, winced as his boot turned on an uneven cobbled gulley that ran along the alley, a drain for spring rains to the river. He pounded on the wooden portal. "Rhette!"

An eternity passed. Light flickered. A man bearing a torch came up Gaol Lane behind him, leading a group of ragged wraiths. Ren glimpsed men in tattered rags that hardly covered the bruises and sores on their emaciated bodies. A woman stumbled along holding a child-sized sack of skin and bones. Another tiny, shrunken ghost stumbled alongside her. Shepton Mallet prison had disgorged its inhabitants, if unwilling, and its inhabitants had included men, women, and children barely holding body and soul together.

"Right where you said it'd be!"

Ren nearly fell inward as the door in the wall opened with a rusty creak. Harriette held up the iron key with a broad smile. "You toffs don't fear housebreakers, do you? It was right out there in the open like a piece of ripe fruit."

"Rhette. Get inside," Ren gasped. He stumbled to the spot near the wall where he'd left her clothing. He bent awkwardly and scooped up the fabric, hoping he'd caught everything.

She didn't obey. Instead she stood in the arched gate in her state of undress, watching the small procession make its way up Gaol Lane to Leg Square. "Rhette! In!" he said, strangled, imagining what could happen if these men got their hands on her. He wasn't strong enough to protect her from them.

"They need help," Harriette said softly. The flickering torchlight played in her large, dark eyes.

"And the mob is right behind them. *In,* and we'll think of something." He pushed her inside and then swung the gate shut behind him, grabbing the key from her hand and turning it in the lock.

She stood entirely still, staring up at him. Moonlight made a pale canvas of her face, her eyes dark pools with a deep, mysterious glimmer. Her lips parted, and without thinking he bent his head and pressed his mouth to hers, firmly, possessively.

"Get you inside, hussy," he growled. "You're completely undressed."

She giggled and scampered toward the kitchen door at the back of the house. The Manor House was a chalky white rectangle rearing up out of the earth, its window frames and door sills bare of any ornamentation. Its red-tiled roof with chimneys at either end had been the epitome of wealth in the previous century, when his forebears first started turning a profit on their cloth industry, but already it looked quaintly old beside the graceful neoclassical mansions rising in Bowlish and elsewhere.

Ren headed inside, sparing a cursory glance for the untended garden about them and the weeds choking the gravel walk. If he ever located that absent steward... He followed Harriette into the kitchen to find, not the bare shelves and dusty surfaces he expected, but the thick oaken table heaped with food stores, and a tidy stack of wood beside the stove and the brick oven.

She was already laying out cheese and cutting bread. "Did you spend your day shopping, milord?"

"Mrs. Oram must have sent this. I asked her to return to work tomorrow. I hope she can, if the riot doesn't continue. Are we hosting a funeral feast?" he asked as she observed the size of the portions she was arranging.

"We'll save some of this for us and put the rest outside for our friends. Perhaps they won't break into the house if we offer them food."

"More likely to make them break in, I'd think."

He sniffed a jug of wine on the table, then set it aside. Best not to offer wine to a hungry crowd, unless it were well watered. He located a cask of small beer and worked it open. With no great skill but eventual success, Harriette started a fire in the cast iron stove and wiped her hands in satisfaction.

"If my aunt could see me now," she chuckled. She stepped into the scullery and a minute later returned, lugging a large iron stock pot filled with water.

"Did that come from the cistern?" Ren asked doubtfully. "I wouldn't—"

"A bit of a boil and it'll be fine," she answered. "I've a fancy for a nice hearty soup. And a quaking pudding to go with? It's the only kind I know how to make," she added when he opened his mouth to reply. He shut his mouth.

"That's more than I know how to make," he said instead.

"My aunt tried to teach me how to cook," Harriette said cheerfully as she retrieved a large wooden bowl, wiped it out, and began cracking eggs. "All of us in the household are supposed to take turns. In truth Sorcha does all the cooking. Melike does the housework, Darci keeps the garden, and Natalya—" She reflected, egg in hand. "I'm not sure what Natalya does."

"And you?" He tapped the beer, drew a sample, and tasted.

"Princess and I are the providers. We bring in the money to support us all."

The kitchen warmed quickly with the great stove working, and Ren stood guard while Harriette carried a large tray of food to the door in the Blinder Wall. A group of the prisoners they'd seen earlier had taken shelter in a neighboring carriage house, and Harriette ransacked the Manor's linen closet for blankets and pillows. Ren delivered a jug of small beer with several mugs and set a candle in its dish near the door.

The wraiths regarded him with watchful, wary eyes, noting his limp, but none spoke to him, so he said nothing in return. Harriette left another platter of food and a candle in a bowl beside the wall to beckon the weary and nourish other refugees, and then at his bidding she closed and locked the gate.

"What now?" he asked, returning to the kitchen after taking a turn about the house to make sure the doors were locked and the windows secure. The furniture in the ground floor parlors was under Holland covers, and none of the beds in the first-floor rooms were made. Harriette raided the linen closet again.

"I lit a fire in the master's chamber," Harriette said with a yawn. "At least, I think it's the master's chamber. We can take our supper there—and thanks be there is a supper. I just have to manage it up the stairs, that's all."

"Let me," Ren said.

"No, you needn't do the stairs when—"

"Come here."

She followed him to the servant's staircase. The device he had designed was still there: the small wooden platform attached to ropes, and the pulley looped over the stair railing high above leading to the cramped servant's rooms in the attic. He tested the pulley, which gave a squeak and a groan, and Harriette watched in wonder as he placed the serving tray with its cold meats, bread and butter, cheese, and assorted jellies on the platform.

"Now you run up the stairs and take the tray when it reaches the top. I'll bring it back down and then send up the wine."

She laughed as she started up the stairs, keeping pace with the platform as he pulled on the ropes and the tray rose up the shaft running alongside the stairwell. The sound of her laugh thawed the tight knot of worry and concern that had been bound within Ren's chest all day.

"This is delightful! Your invention?"

"I wish I could say mine alone, but I patterned it on something my tutor had seen in France. They call them dumb waiters."

"Brilliant," she announced when she reached the first-floor landing. The wooden platform swayed as she relieved it of its burden. "Send up dishes and the best wine, milord."

"Whatever the blasted steward left," Ren promised.

He entered the bedchamber with the wine to find Harriette had laid a small side table with their makeshift feast. A white linen cloth, still creased from being folded in the cupboard, bore jasperware plates and silver cutlery that needed a polish. Wax tapers glowed softly in their candlesticks. She moved along the mantelpiece above the fire, lighting more candles, and Ren watched her hungrily.

Her stays and pockets lay folded neatly on a chair against the wall, along with her shoes and stockings. From somewhere she'd located a loose morning gown and thrown it over her shift. Bare feet peeked out beneath the worn, wide hem. Her hair, unpowdered, had come out of its coil, and red glints caught the candlelight. The shadowy shape of her body through the white linen and the sight of her bare feet, high-arched, perfectly shaped, with mother-of-pearl toenails adorning each adorable toe, made his gut tighten and his groin grow heavy.

He was alone with Harriette. Completely alone. No chaperone, no servants, no family. No one. They were alone, she was in undress, and the rest of the world was leagues away, along with its follies and dangers and riots and promises. Nothing existed but they two, the original man and woman, the only beings on earth.

"You've made a rather romantic little tableau." Ren's voice felt rough in his throat. He coughed it clear.

His breath caught as she turned to face him. The shape of her breasts was clearly outlined as she hugged her arms to her, and as she blew out the spill, a waft of smoke curled alongside her face and her small, knowing smile. The enchanting puckers at each side of her mouth beckoned as she moved toward the small table and its inviting feast.

"We're alone."

"Yes, I'd noticed that." He cleared his throat again.

"Ren. I think I should tell you I've made a decision."

She rounded the table and stood before him. She smelled like the rose water and nutmeg she had added to the pudding. He stood perfectly still as she stood on tiptoe and whispered into his ear.

"I want you to make love to me tonight."

CHAPTER SEVENTEEN

H e must still be bosky, Ren thought. The smashing and
fires of the rioting mob had left his ears ringing. He was
hearing things.

"What's that again?" he asked hoarsely.

She chuckled, a low, throaty sound that made the dents at
the sides of her lips deepen, and he knew he hadn't misheard.
Just as he raised his arms to clasp her, she stepped away to the
table set with their simple meal.

"I think I was clear."

She stood behind her chair, waiting patiently, until his brain
shifted into action. He staggered to the table. He would have
liked to have moved cleanly and with great assurance, in part to
give her no reason to change her mind if she had in fact just
offered him what he'd been dreaming about for days. Years. But
his leg had had enough of the exertions of the day and dragged
behind him as he moved. He leaned on it as he pulled out her
chair.

"You expect me to attend to my dinner? After *that*?" He
bent his head and spoke the words into the soft red-brown

waves that fell past her shoulders. He was gratified to see her shiver as his breath brushed her neck.

"You'll need an appetite for what lies ahead." Still wearing that small, secret smile, she seated herself and laid her serviette in her lap, then started preparing a plate.

Ren seated himself, but his thoughts were not on the food. Every nerve in his body drew taut with anticipation, a heavy, pleasant heat settling in his groin. He watched Harriette's graceful hands butter his bread, then lay slices of cheese and cold cuts of meat on his plate.

The light from the candles teased auburn glints from her hair and cast shadows under her cheekbones, chin, and in the deep cleft between her breasts. Her skin gleamed like fresh butter, creamy and soft as silk. She'd been through a singularly trying day, and she sat as calm and collected as if they dined tête-á-tête every night.

"I am sorry your mother's procession was disturbed," he said softly.

She shrugged one elegant shoulder. The gown slipped slightly, revealing more skin. She made no move to adjust it.

"She would have enjoyed the melodrama, I suspect. Certainly Mrs. Demant and her friends will have much to fret over, which should please them no end."

"What was that small spectacle about the knocking?" He accepted the plate she handed to him. Her fingers brushed his hand, and when he met her eyes, he saw from her steady, sly look that the touch was intentional.

"The plea for admittance?" She fixed her own plate. "It's a Catholic custom, reserved usually for emperors when they are laid in their tombs. I read about it once and liked the idea that even the mightiest must acknowledge they enter the realm of death as poor, naked sinners, like the least of us."

"What will you do now?"

She bit through the golden crust of her bread to the soft, fragrant middle. A smudge of butter lingered on her upper lip as she chewed thoughtfully.

"I wrote my Aunt Calenberg. She will want to pay her respects somehow. I don't foresee there will be very much of my mother's affairs left to put in order."

"And your marriage?" Ren tried to keep his voice level. "Your grandfather and mother arranged it, I understand, and now they are both—not here to see it accomplished."

She speared a pickled beet on her fork and nibbled at it. A shadow of sadness settled on her brow as she stared past him a moment, lost in thought. Then she sighed and shrugged again.

"Now it feels all the more important that I go through with it."

She lifted her eyes to his face. "Lord knows it's not what I want. The chief benefit I could see in marrying Franz Karl was ensuring my mother had a place to live out her life, I hoped in luxury, enjoying all that she gave up when she fled to protect me from the wars."

His heart sank, but he fought to keep his voice measured, keep it from cracking. "And you are the Duchess of Löwenburg now. You shall have to go back for your investiture, and to take proper possession of your lands."

"Yes, and to keep my husband from looting them, if that's the kind of husband he intends to be." She scowled.

She would go and leave him behind, along with all the other causes she had taken up. She had yet to finish his portrait, though she'd worked hard to bring his figure to life. She wouldn't know until much later if her intercession with Amalie had worked. She had tried to make him popular and desired with those prints she had circulated about town, tried to give him every advantage in his choice of marital partner, but she would not be there to advise him on whom to select.

There was so much left unfinished. Barely begun.

"Perhaps he will let you paint." Ren cleared his throat, searching for a way to brighten his suddenly grim outlook. He would not give into despair in these last stolen moments together. He would wait to do that when she was gone.

"Perhaps," he went on, "there is a whole society of female painters in Prussia. Or perhaps you can build it. You could found a society of the arts, if there is not one already."

She chuckled. "The Prussian Academy of the Arts is one of the oldest in Europe, older than your English Royal Society, milord. Blaise Le Sueur is the current director, I believe. He goes in very much for the landscape and historical schools. I think in time I might like to move to historical subjects. Angelica Kaufman prefers them, though most people think women should stick to pastels and watercolors of fruit and such, if they paint at all."

She poured a cup of wine and passed it to him, her fingers again deliberately brushing his. A warm tingle raced up his arm.

"I see you as a historical subject," he said. "Minerva, or some other mighty goddess, powerful and wise."

She chuckled again, the sound kindling heat in his chest. "There is some group of powerful women in London calling themselves the Minerva Society. Lady Bessington has business with them, I believe. My aunt mentioned once that she was interested in joining them, but they are select and elite." She sipped her wine, her lips gleaming deep red. "Someday I'll do a self-portrait of myself in classical robes. I'll be one of the six women painters of antiquity that Pliny the Elder names. Timarete, Irene, Calypso, Iaia, Aristarete, and Olympias." She spoke the names as if reciting a well-learned litany, uttering each syllable with a reverent caress.

Then she took an unladylike gulp of wine. "But I might

choose to portray myself as Helena of Egypt. She painted Alexander the Great's battles, or so Pliny says."

Ren took a modest sip of his own wine. It roiled in his stomach after all the ale. He couldn't afford to send any more of his wits a'wandering. "And if I were your subject? What historical figure would I be?"

She propped her elbows on the table and put her chin on them, careless as a girl. But there was nothing girlish in the smoldering stare she gave him.

"The Emperor Claudius," she said. "I should put you against the mightiest monuments of early Rome, in a white toga and your imperial purple robe. Making sure your toga is slipping off one shoulder to reveal your splendidly manly chest."

"Claudius the mad," he said, his gut twisting at her answer despite her flirtatious tone. He knew his history. "Claudius, the idiot emperor with the stammer and the clubfoot."

She shook her head, and a red-brown lock brushed her shoulder the way he longed to do. "Claudius was the wisest and the best of the early emperors," she answered. "He made many improvements in administration. And Britain was conquered under his rule."

"His mother, according to Suetonius, called him 'a monster of a man, not finished but merely begun by Dame Nature,'" Ren said. "I believe that's a faithful translation."

"No one can be more monstrous than a mother," Harriette whispered. "But I believe it is because they so badly want the best for their children. It still astounds me that my mother, who I would have sworn had no interest in me whatsoever, sacrificed her position and her life of ease to take me away from war and protect me as my father could no longer do."

Ren unwisely tipped back his wine cup, taking a long draught. "How do you excuse the cruelty of fathers, then? They are trying to shape us into better men?"

Her mouth turned down at its lovely corners, her brow knitting in concern. "Ren," she said softly. "I believe your father would be proud if he could see you now."

Ren stared into the pudding as she cut it. He'd worked for years to improve his speech, and he'd submitted to the tortures of manipulation and surgery to correct his deformed foot. The veneer was fragile, and it held mostly because of the deference given his title, the tacit agreement not to taunt a peer.

For a moment he envied Jock, who at least could boast of his injuries as something he'd survived. Nobody pitied Jock on his crutches, not after they saw him atop a horse. If Ren were a tradesman, in the class of Abel Cain, he'd be ruthlessly twitted by the Abel Cains of his world, but the jibes would not hold revulsion, not when so many of that class bore their own scars. It was only the upper class, those born to rule, who saw such flaws as diminishing a person's worth.

"I don't understand how you have never reviled me."

The confession burst from him unwillingly. He set his cup on the table and studied it so he could avoid meeting her eyes. "You have never treated me like a cripple. Like a defective."

"My Ren."

She said something else, but it wasn't in English. She rose from her seat and came around the table and seated herself in his lap, her bottom nestled against his groin, her knees draped over his thighs. His cock rose instantly toward her warm, firm flesh. Her beautiful breasts were at the perfect level to feast his eyes upon, within kissing distance. She scooped the pudding with a broad spoon and held it toward him, cupping one hand beneath the utensil.

"And you have never treated me like a dirty, throwaway urchin who might have been illegitimate, and who definitely needed a lesson in manners," she said. "Try the pudding? It turned out, unbelievably. Look, it quakes just so." She shook the spoon gently and the custard obligingly wobbled from side to side. He leaned forward and enclosed the spoon in his mouth, feeling the sweetness rush over his tongue and down his throat as he swallowed.

"Perfect. Delicious." He leaned forward and licked her lips, capturing the smear of butter, the trace of wine, and the warm, rich custard.

"Mmm. You're right."

She tossed the spoon onto the table and curled her hands in the lapel of his coat, thrusting her tongue into his mouth. He groaned as her breasts fell into his eager hands, full and warm and pliable. Her nipples tightened in his palms, and his cock surged to full and immediate attention as she shifted her legs to straddle him.

She pulled at her skirts and Ren seized on the opportunity to slip his hands inside, running his palms over her long, strong thighs and over her hips to the lush mounds of her bottom. She was gloriously warm and firm, her skin smooth as cream. She moaned as she wriggled her hips onto his erection, and Ren stiffened his back as pleasure arced through him. He was close, dangerously close to spending early, embarrassing himself and annoying her, but he didn't see how he could clamp down on the exquisite sensations of Harriette melting in his arms, Harriette making those little moans of passion, Harriette smelling of rosewater and tasting of everything sweet.

"Rhette," he gasped, wondering how to warn her that he wasn't very good at this, if indeed this was even allowed. "I'm not—not going to last very l-long."

She pushed lightly against his chest as she swung her leg off his lap and rose easily to her feet. "Then get thee to bed, and get thee naked. Up, milord," she teased.

He meant to protest against these needling *milords* she'd been delivering all night, teasing him about his title as if she were still the country waif running wild around the countryside. But Harriette was steering him toward the enormous bed which stood under a red and gold canopy, occupying a full half of the room. The smell of lavender and sweet clover drifted up as she pushed him down upon it. Harriette must have made up the bed with fresh linens as he made his rounds of the house.

"I am not protesting," he said as she set to work on the buttons of his coat. This was like when she had undressed him to sketch him, only this time he aided her by tugging at his neck-cloth and twining his hands under hers to work on his waistcoat. "But I had thought you said we couldn't—because of Fr—"

He regretted even hinting at the man's name. "Because you are to be m-m-married."

The word came out with difficulty. The very thought that she would belong to another made his mind rebel.

She bent and pressed her lips to his temple, his ear, his jaw as her clever fingers loosened his buttons.

"I know. I thought that I owed it to him. But it occurred to me today, as I was sorting through my mother's things, that once the vows are spoken, he will have legal control over my body. And I won't. I will be a *femme covert*, invisible to the eyes of the law. He will speak for me, own my property, and use me to beget heirs for the duchy."

She shuddered and pressed her forehead against Ren's shoulder, growing still. Her palm pressed against his chest, over his heart, as if she were listening to its erratic beat.

"When he marries me, I will disappear." Her voice cracked on the whisper. "So I will do what I wish and take every pleasure I can before that happens. And I wish," she said against his neck, "for *you*."

Ren shook with the raw, ferocious heat that seared through him at her confession. "I wish that as well."

He tore off his coat and shed his waistcoat, tossing the

expensive fabric aside heedlessly. Harriette pulled his shirttails from his breeches and whisked the large, loose linen shirt over his head.

"God, Rhette, I've dreamed—so many t-t-times—" His cursed tongue was swelling, throttling his mouth. He couldn't even tell her what this meant to him, what *she* meant to him.

"I know," she whispered. "I've dreamed of it, too."

She slid down his body to kneel on the floor and patted the top of her thigh. Obligingly he braced his boot on her leg and she began working the leather and wood framing free of his mauled foot. Once again she showed not a hint of revulsion as she set the boot aside and rolled down his stockings. Instead her mouth quirked in a smile.

"Worsted wool?" she questioned. "No silk hose for his lordship?"

"Absorbs the sweat," he answered. "And prevents chafing from the leather."

She set to work on the boot of his good leg. "I shall make you a set of blue worsted," she said. "And you can be like Mr. Stillingfleet, who came to Mrs. Montagu's salons in his blue stockings and gave name to the whole circle."

It felt absurd to be having this conversation with his erection so blatantly in evidence between them. She'd noticed, he could tell. She rolled down his second stocking and tossed it aside, then climbed up his body to attend to his breeches. He leaned back and closed his eyes as she unbuttoned the front flap, and sudden memories of his many previous failures assailed him. He reached out and grasped one of her hands before she could slide his breeches over his hips.

"Rhette—I need to tell you—"

"Tell me what?" she asked in a throaty purr. The hand he wasn't holding slipped inside the fall of his breeches, inching toward his cock. He gasped for air.

"I've—I've had—"

"I know." Her voice changed. "All the courtesans. The legends preceded you back to London. The long, very long list of women you'd pleasured."

"Lies." Shamefully, he kept his face in the shadow of the canopy. He squeezed her wrist, willing her to understand, to forgive him. "I paid those women to brag of my prowess. In truth, I'm—I'm rubbish at this."

His face burned, and he wondered why he, who dreaded talking, couldn't seem to stop words from tumbling out, even mangled. "I f-f-f-inish too—too early, or I dr-dr-droop and c-c-can't..." He stammered to a halt, but even then he wasn't done humiliating himself. "I—I'm g-going to d-disappoint you, Rhette."

"Sssh." She pressed herself along his body and laid her lips to his. "You won't disappoint me, my love," she whispered between kisses. "I want to touch you so badly. I want you to touch me. Even if we're both rubbish at this—and I think I might be, too—there are ways we can bring each other pleasure."

She settled against him, bringing one hand to cradle his face. With the other she touched the old pendant around his neck.

"Think how old this is." She traced the intertwined Greek letters. "And we found it ages ago."

"Your first gift to me. My sign that I would conquer."

"Ren." She turned her face into his neck, hiding the vulnerability that fleeted across her features. "My Ren. I'll be content if you do nothing but kiss me all night. I want nothing but to be with you."

He fisted his hand in her hair and kissed her, hard and devouring. "I wish to do more than kiss you," he growled.

"Good." Her throaty laugh thrummed inside his chest, like their bodies were already in tune. His shoved his breeches down his hips, lips never leaving hers, and she gave a happy sigh of satisfaction as she nestled against his nude body. He sucked in air, nearly choking, when she settled herself over his erection. He could feel her, hot silken flesh and the tickle of soft hair, but she was still draped in swaths of fabric.

"I can't *find* you in all this," he growled, trying to plunge his hands in her neckline to access her breasts.

She laughed and pulled the loose morning gown over her head, tossing it aside and letting the white fabric billow through the air. He froze at the sight of her in her shift, her shadowed form outlined by firelight. Then she scooped her shift over her head and tossed that aside, too, and Ren's eyes burned with the effort to take in every detail at once: the mass of hair spread loose over her shoulders, the perfect breasts so high and round with their dark upthrust nipples, the elegant curve of her torso from shoulder to nipped-in waist, the flare of hip around the dark patch of hair between her legs, and the long, elegant length of her legs, so strong and perfect.

"Are you ready for me?" She climbed onto the bed and braced her arms on either side of his shoulders, leaning close to look at his face. He scooped a pert, begging nipple into his mouth, nipping with his teeth.

"Rhette, I've been ready for you since—since—"

Best not to say he'd had erotic dreams about her when he was fourteen, when she still had the body of a child but the mouth of a tavern wench and the brain of an Oxford scholar. He couldn't tell her every fantasy woman of his youth had worn her face, that every time he'd serviced himself in a dark foreign bed he'd imagined her mouth, her body doing the work of his hand.

That ever since she'd told him about her lovers, he'd tortured himself to orgasm with the image that it was he, not them, penetrating that beautiful body and driving her to climax.

He couldn't tell her that he'd failed with the courtesans and the prostitutes and everyone else he'd tried to pay because the flesh and blood woman wincing at his feeble prods or frowning as he came too soon wasn't Harriette. She was the only woman who could rouse him. The shame of his failures reared up, the fear that he would fail to please her when she was at last here before him in the flesh, every glorious, perfect inch of her, grinning at him as she shifted on her knees and took his straining cock in her hand.

He groaned and bit his lip, but he didn't wilt. He didn't falter. He stayed long and hard in her hand, and he groaned again as she swept her thumb over the tip of his cock and the bead of moisture there. He sucked in air as she closed her fingers around his length and brought him to her slit, dipping the head of him into her quim, then rubbing him around her mound, spreading the moisture. His breath grew short, but his body didn't fail him.

Harriette watched his face intensely, her eyes dark, her lips parted, and her small gasps fed his ache, his need to bury himself fully inside her. His cock swelled and strained toward that promised end, pushing inside as she brought him back to her slit, nudging slowly, slowly, as she grew wet and stretched around him, her body welcoming his. She stared steadily into his eyes as he worked inside her, inch by exquisite inch, and the fire caught the flush on her skin and the gleam in her eyes, until they fluttered closed when he sheathed himself to the limit. She was warm, tight, and wet, and he was *home*.

He was inside of Harriette Smythe, where he'd always wanted to be. The wonder of this stunned him for a moment, even as his cock pulsed in a rampant demand for *more, more*.

He opened his eyes and found her staring at him, her eyes wide, her mouth curved into a wicked smile. "So far, this isn't disappointing in the least," she purred.

"Rhette," he rasped. "Have your way with me."

She threw back her head in that laugh that he'd fallen in

love with eleven years ago, the moment he met her. No wonder he'd been no good for any other woman. He'd been lost to this woman for half his life and there never would be, never could be anyone else.

The knowledge soared through him as he surged inside her, claiming her in the most elemental way, in the primal dance of pleasure. She met his thrust carefully, as if learning his body, seeking the rhythm they would share together.

"Slow?" she questioned. "Hard? Like this?" She rocked back and forth, as if on a wooden horse. "Or this?" She leaned forward and moved straight up and down, as if posting.

The pleasure nearly lifted off the top of his head. He grabbed her hips, smiling into her laughing face, awash in wonder, drowning in need. "All of it," he said. "Right now."

"Greedy Renwick." She placed a hand on his chest and found her rhythm, riding him gently. He feared he would explode too early and yet at the same time he was eager to savor this with her, to sustain the ecstasy of being inside her, to drive her to the peak of pleasure, too. "Greedy, greedy earl."

"I'm swiving the squire out of you," he growled, thrusting his hips up to meet her as she moved. "I'm erasing him. That horse's ass." For certain there must be something wrong with him that he wanted to bring her former lovers into this moment, but the jealousy made his pleasure brighter, made him hard and fierce.

"He's gone," she breathed. Her head fell back as her breathing quickened. "No squire."

"And the military man, whoever he was," Ren whispered. He held her hips and ground deep, filling her. "Tommy Atkins, that limp noodle."

"He never felt like this," she gasped. Her breasts rose and fell, taunting him. "Oh, Ren."

"And the bloody margrave," he said. His own greed alarmed

him. He wanted no other man in her head, in her memory, no imprint on her body but his alone. "I'm fucking him—out—too." He thrust on every syllable, and she cried out. She melted against him, her breath coming like sobs, and he dug his fingers into her hips and lifted his to drive into her.

"No one but me, Rhette," he said through gritted teeth. He was reaching for his orgasm, felt it close, but he wanted one more thrust—then one more—whatever it would take to drive her over the brink into madness, into oblivion. She twisted and thrashed and he kept reaching, as far as he could go, holding her so he rubbed against that place she was pressing against him.

"You," she cried. "You—Ren—oh—*Oh!*"

With the last cry he knew he had her and he arched his back to drive deep, and at the shudder and clench of her tight heat about him he let go at last and let his climax consume him. They pulsed together, joined flesh, flung together at the edge of being, and then she lowered to press herself against his chest, skin to skin, and he rubbed his hands over her lovely, sweaty back as they began the long, slow, floating drift back to earth.

A long, long time later, when at last she stopped pulsing around him and their heartbeats had settled to beating in rhythm, Harriette extracted herself and stretched out at his side. She propped herself on one elbow to study his face.

"You led me to believe there would be difficulties," she accused him.

He smiled, satisfied at his performance, at knowing he had satisfied her. "Ap-pp-parently not with you."

Harriette didn't make him uncomfortable or self-conscious. She didn't make him intensely aware of his deficiencies. She didn't care about his deficiencies. She made him feel whole, complete. She looked at him with admiration. She treated him with love.

And he loved her. He loved her, he trusted her, and he knew

she cared for him. That, it seemed, made all the difference, at least for him.

"Who knew you were the jealous type?" She drifted her hand over his chest, tracing the fine hairs. "Been sulking about my misspent past, have you?"

"No more than you grudging me my courtesans." He hugged her to him with one arm and kissed her forehead. "It's never been like that for me, Rhette. They weren't you."

"It's never been like that for me, either," she said. "In fact, I didn't know I could—well." She skated her finger along his ribs one by one.

A possessive thrill went through him. "You've never had *le petit mort*?"

"Not with anyone else," she said. "And it's not the same when I do it myself. Not nearly as—everything."

He knew what she meant. The pleasure he gave himself was functional and felt meager, somehow, compared to the full, rich, resonating climax he'd just had. Because of her. Because he was with Harriette.

She shifted, making a face. "Not nearly as—sticky, either."

He laughed. Laughter in bed, shared laughter, joyful laughter, instead of one partner making fun of the failures of the other. He'd not thought he could ever have this sweetness.

"Shall we clean ourselves up?"

She smiled impishly. "I believe I left some rose water in the kitchen. Do you fancy more wine?"

He wrapped his fingers around her wrist. "I fancy keeping you here always. In this bed. Never letting you go."

She stilled, the laugher leaving her. Her dark eyes lost the gleam of joy the firelight had just reflected. "Don't, Ren. You know we can't."

"We could," he said stubbornly. "Stay hidden away. Never emerge."

She slid out of the bed, leaving it cold and empty. She swiped her shift from the floor and pulled it over her head.

"Our excuse tonight is my mother's funeral, and there were riots." She turned to face him. He tried to focus on her face, not the distracting shape of her revealed by the candlelight. "At least, that is what I shall tell myself for losing my head and throwing propriety to the winds. But neither of us can hide, Ren. I have promises to keep you, and you have—"

"Nothing," he said roughly. He sat up in the bed, making no attempt to hide himself. She'd seen everything. She might as well see his naked heart. "I'll have nothing when you leave, Rhette. There w-won't be anyone else. Not for me."

"You can't say that," she said, her voice anguished. "You have to marry. For the estate, for the title, so you have an heir—so there is someone to care for your sister if you..." She lifted a hand to her face, shielding her eyes. "We both have people depending on us," she went on, forcing her voice to be steady.

"You matter to me more than any of them, Rhette," he said. "I'm sorry if you don't want to hear it. But it's true."

"I *don't* want to hear it," she said, turning away and searching for slippers. "And it can't be true."

"You can't make something so just by wishing," he called after her, but she was already out of the room, a whisper of fabric, the soft pad of feet on the wooden floor.

The room felt cold, the light bereft of warmth, the candles dancing without heat. So his life would be, empty and lifeless, when Harriette left him.

If he could, he'd wish for a way they could be together forever. But of course they couldn't.

CHAPTER EIGHTEEN

"What did you say to Princess that day in your studio?" Ren asked. "When you spoke in Silesian. It wasn't about Frederick the Great and the upheaval in the American colonies, as you said."

Harriette paused in her task of trimming the candles and made the mistake of looking back at the bed. Ren lay there completely naked, with his hands clasped behind his head, a pose that broadened his shoulders and made his biceps bulge. Greedily she let her eyes roam his bare chest, the light brown hair covering his lean rib cage and his flat stomach, banded with muscle. He'd pulled the sheet up to cover his groin and his twisted foot, but his good leg, bent at the knee and thick with yet more muscle, showed a shape as perfect as God could have imagined. Her artistic eye appreciated the clean, strong lines of his body, but her woman's heart fluttered at the sight.

This was her man. She'd claimed him tonight. No other woman would love him as fiercely or as wholly as she did. No other woman could be as faithful and devoted to him in her heart as she would be her whole life long, no matter whom she pledged herself to in marriage.

She banked the fire so it would last till morning and rose to face him. "I want my sketchbook. Whyever did I not bring it with me?"

"You've already sketched me in the nude." He patted the crumpled sheets beside his hip, indicating her place.

But she'd left those sketches on her worktable in her studio back in Charles Street. A stupid error. She'd have to send a letter and ask Darci to pack them in her trunk and send them to her. She wanted a way to remember him, remember this, and while the image of him felt seared into her brain, she knew the tricks memory could play.

Already her stomach hurt at the thought that the hours would pass, they would be obliged to emerge from this house, and the rest of their lives would carry them far from one another. Art was the only thing that lasted. Art was the only way to defeat loss and time.

"I want to memorize you," she said softly.

"And I you. Come hither."

She crawled into bed beside him, ignoring the tray of fresh food that she'd brought upstairs using his self-made lift. She draped herself against his body, pressing her lips to his. That was one benefit of prior experience, she supposed; she had completely lost all shyness and modesty. She knew when her body pleased a man, and she was thrilled to have pleased him. The pleasure she'd shared with him had been nothing like she'd felt with anyone else, and she knew she'd never find that again. Ren was the only one who could make her feel this way.

It ought to make her profoundly sad to know that when she left this room, the best part of her life would be a recollection. She would feed on this memory for the rest of her life. What a dismal, small way to live. But with him here now, before her, she couldn't feel anything but expansive and happy. Deeply, deeply content.

She pulled his tongue into her mouth, nibbling. He groaned, and his manhood stirred against her hip. He rolled partway atop her, pinning her to the bed but not giving her his whole weight. She lifted her leg to twine about his, fitting her crevice to his rising cock, and he smiled against her mouth.

"Greedy, greedy duchess," he murmured.

"For you, yes." She was pleasantly sore from their earlier vigorous coupling, but that wasn't going to stop her from getting her fill of him. She wasn't done yet.

"You're avoiding my question. What did you say to me?"

She stilled. The fire flickered, briefly lighting his eyes with gold. The linens of the bed were soft and fine and sweet-smelling, the mattress thick and soft and clean. The velvet hangings about the bed enclosed them in a world far away from reality. From duty. From obligation, convention, expectation, or even right.

He'd bared his heart earlier, telling her that there would be no one else for him, no one who touched him this way, no one he cared about this much. Her heart ached for what that meant for his future, and at the same time she felt gloriously, jealously gratified. It would kill her a little when he moved on, married, built a life with another woman, and she faded into a pleasant memory, simply a rambunctious girl he had known once who turned out to be a duchess and left for her birth lands. It would be the best thing for him, if he could do exactly that.

There won't be anyone else, Rhette. Not for me.

He deserved her honesty in return. She traced his face with her fingers, the broad, high forehead and straight brow, the sculpted cheeks and prominent nose, the line of his jaw that was a perfect balance to the rest of his face, not too heavy and not too small, and those lips that were perfection also. His face was the Platonic ideal of a Western man's face; he could have stood model for the Greeks.

But his beauty went much deeper, as if his face truly were a reflection of his intelligence, his noble spirit and loyal heart, the emotions he kept in balance with his good sense, the strong, solid morals by which he lived his life.

She drew a steady breath. "I said that I would marry you, if I could."

She shouldn't have said that. He clasped his hands on either side of her face, those strong, capable hands, and dragged her lips to his. He kissed her so deeply that she would never forget the imprint, or the way her passion rose instantly to meet his.

"Then why don't you?" he demanded roughly.

"Ren. Don't be silly. You need a countess. A cultured woman with a good bloodline, and breeding, and wealth. Someone who knows all the history and customs of the upper crust and can host dinners and balls, run your households, rear your children, know which fashions to adopt for the Season, which connections to cultivate and be a credit to you and your name."

"I'd rather have someone I love," he muttered against her neck. He moved his lips to the curve of her shoulder, his hot, moist mouth leaving a trail on her bare skin. She shuddered with pleasure and longing.

"Sillier still," she whispered. "Love is for romance stories and comedies on the stage. An earl needs to be practical."

"Don't you wish you could marry for love?" His mouth moved to her bosom, his fingers stroking the sensitive flesh, his palms mounding each breast to hold it in place as he sucked each nipple into his mouth. Pleasure sang through her body, lighting an ache between her legs, an emptiness she needed him to fill.

"I never wanted to marry at all, remember?"

In the future she'd imagined for herself, she lived like her

Aunt Calenberg, keeping a household of her own with the people she most liked in it, taking lovers when she wished, devoting her days to her art. She would paint during the day, spend her evenings at dinners and parties meeting new patrons, and strive toward getting her paintings in exhibitions and securing famous subjects for her portraits.

She shivered as a dark thought intruded on the keen pleasure of Ren licking and suckling her nipples. She was now duty-bound to provide heirs for the duchy of Löwenburg, to pass on her family's title and lineage, to let another man plow her and plant his seed and use these breasts to nurture a child rather than delight her lover.

She slipped a hand between them and curled it around his cock. "Take me, Ren," she whispered urgently. "I want you to—to *wap* me so hard and so long that I never feel Franz Karl. That it will just be you, always."

"Wap you. Such language." His voice sounded rough and hoarse. He kissed his way down her belly, twirling his tongue briefly around the button on her midriff. "But first, I want to play."

"What do you—oh, God," she breathed as he backed down her body, settling his head between her thighs, slipping his hands beneath her buttocks and opening her legs. "Is this something you learned from your courtesans?"

"I'd have had to pay extra to play with them." She shut her eyes tightly, awash in mortification. He was looking at her *there*. The bed was dark and the fire far away, but his face was *right there*. She was glad she'd washed with the rose water when she ducked downstairs for more wine and cheese.

"You'll have to teach me, Rhette." His breath fanned over the moist, open parts of her. "I've seen pictures, but you must tell me what you like."

"I'm not certain—*oh*." She startled and tried to scoot away as his tongue swept over the place where he'd entered her and nudged at the small bud where she worked herself to orgasm when she required relief. His tongue felt nothing whatsoever like her fingers.

"That's rather—ah—" Words failed her. She had no way to describe the sensations rushing up from that place. Excitement, certainly, but waiting as well, an eagerness for what lay beyond this. "Keep doing that," she panted.

He obliged, and Harriette succumbed to the waves of sensation, the exquisite stimulation of his tongue on her secret place, the heat that spread over her body and the intense, urgent need that coiled where his mouth was. She felt it coming, the wave of pleasure rolling toward her, and it was deeper and more complete than anything she'd known. In complete abandon she lifted her hips toward his mouth, tilting so that he caught the underside of the bud, and he obliged with long strokes of his tongue over her slit and that begging, quivering button of flesh, and she panted as she strove with him, towards that annihilating wave.

He reached up a hand to cup and knead her breast, rubbing his palm over her nipple, and she gasped and curled a hand in his hair, greedily holding him in place, rising against the press of his tongue as the wave gathered and gathered and then broke over her. She cried out as she was swept away beneath it, shuddering and thrown on the pounding torrent.

She tugged at his hair, urging him up over her body, and as he obliged, grinning with male satisfaction, she curled her fingers tightly around his cock and urged him toward her. He was long and hard, aroused by pleasuring her, by her climax, and the knowledge added to her wildness. The pleasure was delicious but there was the sense of an eye of a storm, an emptiness in the vortex, and she wanted him inside her to fill it. She wanted him to share it with her.

"This. Inside me. Now," she gasped, insisting.

He chuckled and positioned himself, hard and hot at her opening. "You're sure?"

"Oh, *please*, Ren," she groaned, and he laughed and drove inside her. She gasped at her own wetness, at the ease with which he slid completely inside, sheathed to the hilt.

"Oh, Jesus, Rhette," he whispered, and she felt it too, her body shuddering around him, her climax deepening with his fullness there.

"Come with me," she whispered.

He groaned and closed his eyes and abandoned himself to the pursuit of his own pleasure, reaching for the same ecstasy that enveloped her, and she met him thrust for thrust, welcoming him, reveling that even in the wake of one orgasm, she felt the tension gathering again, the friction building quickly to another wave of heat.

"Oh—*Ren*—" She felt his thrusts pushing her up the bed, not painful, a strength and a depth she welcomed, that she matched.

"Are you—going to—" He panted, opening his eyes to look into hers, and that connection stoked her building inferno. He was on the brink of climax and his pleasure fed hers, his need the last spark she needed to fall over the edge again.

"Oh, yes," she breathed, closing her eyes against the intensity, and his thrusts deepened as he reached his own release. She felt him shuddering inside her as the pleasure rippled madly through her, the tide carrying them together, and their sharing the flood together moved her so deeply that a lump came to her throat.

The waves lasted and lasted, diminishing but slowly as she lay clasped in his arms, his head buried in her hair, her sensitive nipples pressing into his chest, their bodies joined in the most primitive of rites. Harriette opened her eyes and found tears on her lashes.

This was perfection, and she had known it. This—Ren, in her arms, heavy with sated passion and their shared release: this was right and true and everything good. This was a gift from God.

"I hurt you?" He wiped a thumb over a tear that squeezed free from her lashes, his voice rough with concern.

"No." She hugged him fiercely, with her whole body. Her legs were locked about his buttocks. She released them gently, sliding her bare feet down his legs, tracing her toes over his scars. She hooked her ankle over the lump above his clubfoot, as if she could hold him in place. "That was..." Again she had no words.

"Yes, it was." Firmly he kissed her forehead, then rolled off her, withdrawing from her body. "And now you must feed me."

She laughed. "I thought men were supposed to fall directly asleep after exhausting themselves."

"I am hungry, and I want to keep you awake and talk to you all night. Any man who would waste his time with you sleeping is a fool."

She drew her fingers down his back as he reached for the tray of food she'd set beside the bed. His back was as beautifully muscled as the rest of him, shoulders narrowing to his waist, his flanks long and lean, his buttocks just the right shape for her hand. She squeezed, and his shoulder twitched.

"The duchess has roving hands."

"There's no one like you, Ren," she whispered. She loved that she had her own name for him. His sister called him George, and everyone else, including his mother, addressed him by his title, as was custom. She had a part of him no one else could have. Just as she knew parts of him no one else would ever know. Not even his wife.

"You're one of a kind yourself, Harriette—" He stopped. His stammer was gone, as was his self-consciousness about his scarred and twisted leg. He made no attempt to cover himself, and he regarded her with an expression of surprise. "I was going to say Smythe, but that's not your last name, is it? That's an alias your mother adopted."

"So she did." She propped herself on one elbow, accepting the slice of cheese he passed her. "Can you fathom I did not even know my family name? It was on my mother's travel papers. Ulrich. I wonder if—"

She caught herself, not wanting to bring another man's name into their bed. "I will have to ask if there are more of us once I get to Löwenburg."

He rolled toward her, holding a second slice of cheese toward her mouth, and at the same time he slipped his hand between her legs, cupping the place he'd laved with his mouth and tongue and body. "Have I left a big enough imprint yet? Or do you need more?"

"I *want* more," she clarified. "After we've both recovered." She supposed it wasn't fair to begrudge each other past or future lovers, but she felt as possessive as he. "I want you to remember this night as glorious."

"I already do." He laid a slice of cheese in her cleavage and proceeded to eat it. She laughed as his tongue tickled her skin, but at the same time her nipples tightened and sent a signal to the heavy, satiated bud between her legs. He could arouse her so easily, with simply a touch, a look.

"Will you write me letters?" The words slipped out of her before they had fully formed in her mind. "Since you didn't send the ones you wrote me before."

He leaned on his elbow and searched her face with his eyes.

"Do we d-do that to our future spouses? It does-doesn't seem fair."

She dropped her eyes. She knew what he meant. Unfair to feed the connection they had between them, to ensure a husband or wife had no real chance to gain purchase on their hearts. She hated that he said it, and she loved that he was the kind of man who would see the cruelty in it. They would nourish each other in a half-life of fantasy instead of allowing the person in their life to have a claim on their affections.

She loved him, and to be fair to him, she had to let him go.

She turned on her side, but he read her easily and didn't let her withdraw. Instead he snaked an arm around her waist and pulled her close against his body. With the heat of his chest and legs against hers, her bottom nestled in his groin, she felt the tinge of annoyance and selfishness melt into a quiet grief.

"Tell me what you wrote to me," he whispered into her hair.

She closed her eyes. "Dear Renwick. Having a fantastic time at school. Scads of handsome men posing nude for me. Have fun blazing your trail through the courtesans of France and the Italian states. Yours, Harriette."

His throaty chuckle ran all through her body, a thrill that went deep. "Dear Rhette," he answered. "Miserable in Paris. Paying for prostitutes who I pretend are you. Dreaming of you in the dark. Wish you were here to wander through the King's art collection with me at the palace of the Louvre. Please climb my balcony and rescue me. Yours, Renwick."

He snugged his arm around her waist, tucking his hand beneath her, holding her tight and safe against him. Tears squeezed again from beneath Harriette's closed lids. This was heaven, and the sweetest torment at the same time.

"I don't know where to go from here, Ren," she whispered.

What she meant was, she had no idea how she could leave him. How she could physically unlock her arms and let him go, and move on to another country, another life that didn't include him. If the pain in her chest at the very thought were an indication, the effort would shatter her heart and she would expire from it.

And then what would happen to Löwenburg? What would happen to him?

"I know," he murmured. She had the sense that he knew precisely what she meant.

"You know, when Scarpa did his first surgery, I didn't see how I could ever walk again. If I didn't die from the pain, or from infection, I was convinced he had truly crippled me. I cursed him for making me think he could improve me, for trying to change my fate. Before him, I'd at least been a cripple who could hobble about on his own legs. I was sure he'd consigned me to a wheeled chair."

"Jock refuses one," Harriette murmured sleepily. "Says he wants to be able to look another man in the eye."

"But I lived through it," Ren said after a while. "I healed, after a fashion. It was the most furious pain I had ever known, and I had to endure it several times, as he kept trying new things and then correcting what he'd done. But I am walking now, and I have Scarpa's shoe, and while I will never win a footrace, or promenade with you through a country dance, I have something. And I still have my dignity, or so I like to think."

Harriette told herself to breathe. She knew what he meant. Parting from him would break her completely, but she would heal and go on, limping and scarred. And so would he. In poems and novels, girls withered away when they couldn't have their love, like poor Echo pining for Narcissus. Harriette was practical and sturdy; she would survive, and she would have a life.

But for the moment she had Ren. She clasped her arm over his.

"Dear Renwick," she murmured. "In London now and

setting up shop as an artist. I have to marry and move away. But I want you to know I will never forget you." Her breath hitched, but she pressed out the next words. "You will always be in my heart."

His arm twitched, and he didn't respond. He was asleep.

Downstairs, the tall case clock chimed once. Ren had adjusted the weights and restarted the mechanism while she mixed the pudding. She wished now he had left it still, the way the clock had been stopped in the Demant house the moment of her mother's death. Let time belong elsewhere, and let them stay together here in this bed, in the shadow of the dying fire, clasped together in eternity like some fairy tale.

In her dream she was standing again before the walled-in churchyard while the mute knocked his tall staff against the wooden gate. The vicar opened it and stood frowning down at her, his black stole dark against his white robes.

What do you have for me? he boomed, and Harriette held up a small wooden casket carved with her initials and inlaid with jewels. Her face burned with the hot rush of tears as she held it toward him.

I have come to bury my heart.

THE NEXT DAY, dressed again in her blacks, Harriette sat against the wall in a cavernous room within Ren's factory. The great looms, powered by the flow of the gentle River Sheppey, stood silent for the time being, the immense and constant thrum and throb of their turning parts stilled. Every man, woman, and, she was surprised to see, some children, stood at attention as Ren spoke from one of the raised platforms that encased the machinery.

Mr. Fripp, the manager, had explained to her that children were employed because they were small enough to wriggle beneath and around the machinery of the looms to reset threads or restore pieces that had slipped free, their smaller bodies and hands able to access places that adults couldn't.

"Not while the looms are in motion, I hope?" Harriette had asked, but Mr. Fripp merely showed her to a discreet place at the back of the room where she might look on, unnoticed, while Ren rallied his troops.

She wondered which of the men standing at attention, caps in work-roughened hands, had used those same hands to wreak havoc on the town of Shepton Mallet last night. They had emerged from the Manor to find the village looking as if a great wind had passed through it. Shop windows had been shattered, and they stepped around owners sweeping glass from sidewalks and clearing pieces of broken furniture from the streets.

A wagon once full of hay sat, still smoldering quietly, in Market Square, possibly the source of the conflagration they'd seen last night. There was a sullen mood over the town and a tight, angry emptiness in the air. Sheriff's men, wearing the badges of their newly deputized offices, walked the streets surveying the damage, and the buzz of gossip named men who had been injured, women who had been trampled, who'd contracted burns, and reporting, in hushed tones, that two men had died.

Died. Harriette felt the smoke in the air sting her nose as she took this in. The fear of loss and agony of unwished-for change had left this destruction, led men to wreck what they could not keep.

She understood a little bit of what must have driven them; she wanted to rail and screech against her own fortune, change her future, too. But she couldn't. Instead she drew her heavy veil over her face and let it shield her as she and Ren walked to his factory, as he spoke with Mr. Fripp, as Mr. Fripp halted the machines that spun the cotton and called everyone who had shown up for work that day to the great room.

Harriette was glad the veil hid her blush and her improper thoughts, for she was not able to dwell with appropriate decorum on the gravity of the situation here. She was not able to hold on to thoughts of her mother's loss and what that meant. As Ren stood before the crowd in his saffron silk suit and copper buttons, with the black armband on his sleeve, she recalled how she'd awoken that morning to the sweep of his hand over her body, brushing her neck and her breasts and down her belly to walk his fingers between her legs and stir her arousal.

How she'd turned in his arms and thrown a leg over his hips and fit him inside her like he belonged there. How they'd stared into each other's eyes wordlessly as they rocked together, languid and slow, taking their time, drawing out the sensations as long as they could until the pleasure overcame her first and she shuddered and melted against him while he ratcheted to his own release, joining her as the climax rippled between them, passing back and forth.

He'd helped her dress after, lacing her stays and pinning her gown to her bodice as well as any maid, and they'd located his stockings and breeches and shirt and he had turned her toward the bed and told her to lean on her elbows, then he'd lifted her skirts and petticoats and with her rump shamelessly exposed he had taken her from behind, and she'd gasped at the new places he had touched, and when he reached between them to rub at the bud of her pleasure while he stroked her long and hard and deep, she'd been astonished to feel herself rising and respond-ing, hardly believing she could come again until she did, falling apart in his arms, letting herself go limp while he held her hips and stroked to release again, she muffling her cries in the bedclothes while he roared in his triumph.

Then he had let her skirts down and straightened her black

lace apron as if hiding all traces of their passion, tucked himself inside his breeches and buttoned up his waistcoat and coat, let her help him into his boots, and they had walked down the street together in a changed world, and she was changed too on the inside, the space between her legs raw and full and humming with a surfeit of pleasure. She wondered how everyone could not see on her face the wicked, wonderful things they had done to each other, the pinnacles of pleasure she had scaled, the way she was marked and claimed by him. But no one looked at her while the Earl of Renwick climbed the platform to address his factory workers, and Harriette curled her hands in her gloves and silently willed him strength and a fluent tongue.

She knew he was nervous. Terrified, actually. She was so proud of him as he stood before the people who depended on him and carefully, in his measured, thought-out speech, assured them that their livelihoods were not at risk. That he had heard and understood their concerns, and he could not see replacing a skilled man or woman with a machine.

"This fact-factory will not adopt the spinning jen-jenny," he concluded. "We will hire-hire more men if needed to match the pw-production of-of other factories. It is the opinion of Mr. Fw-Fripp and my-myself—" He stumbled, beginning to rush, then paused to take a breath and steady his voice. "This factory bene-fits from the expertise of real people spinning our thread, not dumb machines." He paused again. "And you will all be getting a way—a raise of ten percent of your pay."

Whatever else he had to say was drowned out in the whoops of relief, disbelief, and pure joy that followed this announce-ment. Ren relinquished his perch and was immediately over-whelmed with handshakes and congratulations, some of his workers even going to far as to clap him on the back. The effron-tery to manhandle an earl! Harriette suppressed a smile.

This was because he had sat in the Swan all day yesterday,

so he'd said, drinking ale with these men and hearing their griev-
ances. He'd worked on this speech with her this morning as they
broke their fast and dressed and tried to disguise the traces of
what they'd been up to before Mrs. Oram and Jags arrived.

"Mrs. Oram is your housekeeper?" Harriette had paused in
the act of making the bed. It was fortunate her Aunt Calenberg
had insisted that Harriette take a turn learning various housekeeping skills under her roof. She understood now that her
aunt had been, in her way, training Harriette in what tasks
were required in a large household, preparing her for the day
when she would be reclaimed as a duchess's daughter and, in
due time, a duchess herself. In the meantime, Harriette could
fix a decent pudding, make up a bed, and make and snuff a
fire.

"She has the son who doesn't speak? Jags?" She'd heard of
the simple boy, had met him once or twice. Harriette quite liked
Mrs. Oram and she wondered at the type of man Mr. Oram
must be, to abandon such a wife and the sweet, innocent boy
he'd sired. But she was also aware of how deeply some people
feared those who were different.

"I met him yesterday." Ren paused in the act of arranging
his neckcloth and watched her, trying to evaluate her reaction.

"He's a lovely boy. I'm glad you will give them both a place.
It always seemed silly to me that housekeepers aren't supposed
to have family. That they are only to live for the pleasure of
their employers."

That was when he had come to her and interrupted her task
of making the bed to hitch up her skirts and—well. Harriette
flushed with the memory, caught up in recollection until she
realized that two large hulking men had come to stand before
her, neither of them Ren.

"Ten percent? Does 'e mean it, or is 'is lordship toyin' wi'
us?" one demanded.

Harriette blinked, gathering her senses. "Bram Wright? You work here? You didn't take up your father's trade?"

"Would if it paid anowt to keep body 'n soul together," Bram grunted. Beneath the same black mop of hair he'd had as a boy, his adult features had grown coarse, his nose broken, his pores large in the manner of a man accustomed to drink. A belly filled out his fustian jacket.

"Gil Roper!" She recognized the second man, the third in the triumvirate who had made Ren's life miserable that summer. "You are employed here as well?"

"Them's all buy they rope elsewhere, 'stead of repairin' it," Gil Roper said, shrugging a shoulder. "So what's to do?" He, too, had grown massive, his shoulders as broad as a bull's. His knuckles, she noted, were scraped raw, and a jagged cut ran across the back of one hand.

"And so you live on the salary of a man you once taunted mercilessly as a youth," Harriette murmured. She could hardly say she was surprised.

"Aww, that's all fun, miss," Bram Wright said. He was missing a few teeth, displayed by his embarrassed grin.

Fun? Ren had feared for his life. It was poetic justice, in a way, that he now held their livelihoods in his hands. And he had shown mercy, which proved the kind of man he was. Harriette's heart swelled with pride.

"'Er's a ladyship now, ye great clod," Gil Roper informed his friend. He looked Harriette up and down, judging the shape of her. "'Ow'd ye get to be a duchess, we all'd like ta know?"

"Born that way," Harriette said shortly.

She watched Ren move carefully and with measured step through the congratulatory throng. He used his cane as if it were merely for show, a fashionable gentleman's accessory. Her insides warmed as he took her arm, staking his claim before the other men. Were it any other man, she would have immediately objected to such a territorial move. With Ren, she melted, glad to be claimed as his.

"Renwick," she said briskly, shaking off her foolishness, "can you but fathom? These are your old chums, Bram Wright and Gil Roper. We saw them everywhere that summer you lived in Shepton Mallet, didn't we? And now they work at your factory! What a very small world indeed."

Ren looked at each man in turn. He was taller than they, his elegance and refinement as obvious in his manner as in the contrast between their garb. Renwick was expensive, well-bred, and well-fed, while these men grasped for every penny they made and faced lives of constant danger and uncertainty. Harriette imagined they snarled and hoarded everything they had, lashing out in anger at the slightest threat, real or perceived. While Ren was and could afford to be generous, holding no grudge. He held his hand out to each man in turn.

"I recall that summer," Ren said. "I w-learned to fish. I hope you are treated well here, and Mr. Fw-Fripp rewards hard work and diligence?"

The men shuffled and mumbled in response to this, fumbling with their caps. "Times we had!" Bram Wright said heartily. "Did'n we have fun wit 'is lordship, Gil?"

Harriette saw no need to draw out their embarrassment. Ren had told her how Abel Cain sat at his side yesterday, drinking steadily and filling Ren in on the background of every man who spoke. How he'd ribbed him as Runtwick as casually as if they were equals, which they would never be.

She wondered if part of the boys' cruelty that long ago summer had been resentment toward a boy born so high above them in class, a boy born to the kind of wealth and security they would never know save by glimpsing it drive past their town from time to time. Perhaps they'd felt a boy with his imperfections didn't deserve such a lucky fate. Or perhaps they'd simply turned on a weaker creature as many animals did to ensure their own survival.

"Those were certainly times," Harriette said. "Fare well, Bram, Gil. I am stealing his lordship away now."

"Stealing me where?" Ren asked with interest as they exited the factory and headed toward the old part of town. It was a pleasant walk, though Ivy Cottage was at some distance. They had agreed they would visit his factory first, then call on Mrs. Demant. There were discussions to be had, the business of death to dispense with.

"I wonder what it will do to your factory if you don't modernize." Harriette linked her arm with Ren's on his good side as they walked along the street with its line of cloth factories. Passersby who were out to survey the damage nodded and lifted their caps as they passed. Work was already being done to repair broken storefronts, remove debris from the street, and resume business. A riot, a bloody explosion of long-simmering anger, and then life went on much as it had—save for the two men who died, and the families left without them.

"Fripp says many of the owners are like to cave to the demands of the mob and not install the spinning jenny," Ren commented. "I won't be the only one."

"So Shepton Mallet may stay as it is," Harriette said, looking at the row of factories that lined the river. "But meanwhile other places may adopt the new machinery and make rivals for us. It's a dilemma, isn't it? Adopt the new machines and put men out of work to make the factory prosper, or lose the factory to competitors and put everyone out of work."

"I don't fear losing it any time soon," Ren said, doffing his cap to a constable who trundled by, frowning. "But I don't see another choice."

"Find a way to install the machines and keep the men employed," Harriette said, wondering about the women and

children as well. It seemed cruel to require hard labor of children. "But I don't know how to make that work with men like
Bram Wright and Gil Roper." She squeezed his arm. "They'll
never admit they were cruel to you, will they? They'll never
apologize. In fact, I wonder if, to them, it was even cruelty. Or
simply the way of the world as they know it. How does it feel
knowing you govern the fate of these boys who once taunted
you?"

"How does it feel looking Gil Roper in the eye when you
gave him a blinker that one time they surprised us on the Fosse
Way?" Ren asked in return, smiling. "You could have
unmanned Bram Wright if you'd aimed differently that day by
the river, the day we met. I imagine they both have families now
who depend on them, wives and—"

He stopped in the street, hauling Harriette up short.
"Rhette," he said, and she recognized that strangled quality to
his voice.

"What?" she asked in alarm.

"Babes," he managed after a moment of working his lips
fruitlessly. He stared at her, oblivious to the busy traffic about
them, the flowing river, the slate grey of the cloudy sky, the
relentless churning of the mills powering the great looms. "Did
you—we might..." He groped for words while she waited, wide-
eyed. "I never had to th-think about it," he said finally, his voice
rough. "The women I paid took care of it."

"And so did I." She tried to keep her voice light as she
tugged him onward. "Princess taught me one or two of her courtesan's tricks. I thought ahead," she assured him.

"So there is no..." He limped into step with her, recovering
himself.

"Such things are never guaranteed, but I do not care to bear
an illegitimate child," Harriette said. "Or bring another man's
child into my marriage."

He said nothing, though his labored breath told her he wanted to. For her part, Harriette clamped down on a sudden inward pang of loss. She'd said again and again she didn't want children. So why did the thought of bearing a child with Ren fill her with such sudden, visceral longing? To think that the exquisite pleasure they'd shared might result in new life, a child they could both love and wonder at, teach and watch and care for—

She felt as if her insides had been temporarily removed. She knew she would have to bear children to Franz Karl, to produce heirs for the duchy. But she didn't want children with any man but Ren.

Harriette held silent as they returned to the Demant house, with its black wreath on the door and black ribbons still at the windows, though now the drapes were pulled back to admit light into the once darkened rooms. Harriette was grateful for Ren's company, for his advice on what must come next. She had no idea what her mother had left behind, what she would be expected to take care of, what debts she would be demanded to discharge, what directives her mother had left. There was so much to think about, and—

Mrs. Demant met them at the door, flinging it open and giving them both an accusatory stare. Harriette felt flattened, sure that the other woman could see on her face how she had spent the evening, and it was not in quiet prayer or the contemplation of grief.

"This came for you," she snapped, thrusting a letter with a wax seal in Harriette's direction. She held one corner as if the paper might carry the plague. "Express from London. Your aunt wants something, I suppose."

Harriette broke the seal and opened it at once. All of the questions that had just been filling her head—and all of the sweet, unspoken fancies about more time with Ren, meals with

Ren, bed with Ren—swirled up into the air and away as if caught by the wind. It was her aunt's handwriting, scrawled in haste with her usual dramatic flourishes.

Franz Karl here in London. Come at once. If you care for Renwick at all send him to the Continent in fear for his life, for my great-nephew has promised to kill him.

CHAPTER NINETEEN

R en refused to flee. He insisted on returning to London with Harriette as soon as possible, and went off in search of the nearest posting inn to hire a chaise. While he checked on the Manor House and ensured Mrs. Oram had enough to get by, and stopped by his solicitor to give Mr. Golledge instructions, Harriette frantically gathered all of her mother's belongings that Mrs. Demant didn't want.

She just as frantically attempted to urge Ren to heed her aunt's advice and prepare a tour of the Continent, but to no avail. He insisted on escorting her to London, paying for the post chaise, and arranging for sets of rooms at the inns where they stayed for the night, for it was folly to think of driving through the night on treacherous, unlit roads.

Both nights, when he knocked on her door holding a candle, his eyes full of desire, Harriette let him in. She had sworn to herself that one night must be enough. Her cousin already wanted to kill him, who knew why. But with his tall frame before her, his beautiful face full of longing for her, his musky scent teasing her nose and the new knowledge of the pleasure he brought her stirring her arousal to instant life, she did what weak, carnal women have done since the dawn of time and pulled Renwick into her room.

When she helped him dress in the morning, cramming his twisted foot into the custom-made boot, tying his neckcloth and buttoning his coats while his hands played at her breast or pulled up her skirt for one last hurried swive against the wall, helpless to deny him or her eager, greedy body before he fastened his breeches and snuck back to his own room, she feared that might be the last time she held him and felt his strong, beloved body pressing against her, filling her.

And when he dropped her in Charles Street before departing to Renwick House to check on his mother and sister, she kissed him long and deeply behind the drawn shade of the chaise, and she couldn't stop a traitorous tear from sliding down her face to their joined lips.

"What if he kills you? Ren, I couldn't bear it. If you died..."

She couldn't live if something happened to him. She had sworn to herself she was not the heroine of a great tragedy nor the fragile damsel of a romance, but she feared her heart would burst from despair if his life were taken because of her.

"Shh. Rhette. Nothing is going to happen to me." He traced the curve of her cheek with a warm finger. "If he has concerns, we will talk them through like gentlemen. You forget you are a duchess—you answer to no one. And I am sure your aunt will have some influence with him as well."

She kissed him as long as she dared, fiercely burning him into her heart, and then she shook out the black skirt of her mother's old riding habit and strode into the Catherine Club.

It was mid-morning, and the women were gathered in the library, which also served as Melike's work room. Harriette paused in the doorway of the gracious chamber, savoring for a moment the buttery paper lit to gold and set off with the crisp white trim, the paintings—her paintings—along the wall giving the space a cozy yet elegant feel.

Her aunt sat beside the fireplace, her head close to Abassi's as he bent over the back of her couch. Across from them Natalya and Princess, relaxed in morning gowns and undressed hair, passed a set of fashion plates back and forth. On the other side of the room, among the second group of furniture, Sorcha, Melike, and Darci gathered around a young woman Harriette recognized, feeding her cakes and tea.

Harriette gasped, seared by the betrayal. She pointed at the lovely if incredibly nosy young woman she had last seen as Lady Cranbury's companion during her visit to the Marylebone Pleasure Gardens. "What is *she* doing here?"

"Harriette, *Liebelein!*" Her aunt faced Harriette with surprise. "I am glad you returned so quickly. We have much to discuss. This is Chima. She—"

"She was the one writing the gossip paragraphs about me, wasn't she?"

The pieces fell into place. Why she'd seen this girl, watching from the sidelines, at every party and society gathering she'd attended. "She identified me as the maker of the prints of the Graf von Hardenburg. She said things about us that—that—"

She had pushed Harriette to the fringes of Polite Society and, moreover, hinted at disreputable doings among the Calenberg household. She had made Harriette so desperate she climbed a tree to throw herself through Ren's window and beg for his patronage. "She called us the Catherine Club," Harriette finished weakly.

Chima lifted her chin with pride. "I did write those things." She had a soft accent, bearing the trace of the African homeland where she, or her parents, had been kidnapped and forcibly removed. "I cannot say I am sorry."

Darci intervened. "She used the money she gained from writing the gossip paragraphs to get free of Lady Cranbury and come here."

"Why would she want to come to us? After what she said about our household, how we are eccentric, and—and—" Harriette sputtered to a halt, at a loss to fully catalogue the girl's crimes.

Sorcha stepped before the other girl as if she meant to protect her. "Because she knew we'd take her in, and that we will." Sorcha wiped her hands on her apron, streaked with flour and what might be jam, and planted her hands on her hips.

Harriette's stomach rumbled. Her own breakfast felt very far away. "Aunt! You condone this?"

Her aunt lifted her charcoal-darkened brows. "Why shouldn't I?"

"Because! She called me a...she said that I..." Again words failed her. Harriette sensed she was misplacing her outrage, but that all her friends should make light of her betrayal... It was like she was gone already. They had written her from the household books the moment she left for Shepton Mallet. It hurt.

"You have larger problems, darling." Natalya set aside a colored plate of a Parisian gown.

"Ren." Harriette's stomach tightened with fear. "Aunt, you said my cousin has threatened to kill him. Why?"

Melike, always the peacemaker, rose and crossed the room to give Harriette a hug. Harriette sagged gratefully into her embrace. Then Melike handed her a print, and Harriette stared.

For a moment Harriette couldn't comprehend what she was seeing. They'd been alone in Shepton Mallet; no one but she had seen Ren nude in bed, his broad chest sculpted by the firelight, one leg propped carelessly on the mattress while his damaged leg was curled beneath the sheet draped over his groin, where a simple, single line on the paper hinted at the bulge of manhood beneath. How had anyone reproduced him like this?

Then she recalled the last sketch she'd done of him in her studio, what felt like ages ago. These weren't the charcoal lines she had drawn, but the inked incision of a print. The printer's mark was not Mrs. Darly's, who would never allow something so scandalous on her copper sheets. But plenty of more grasping salesmen would print these and worse.

"How did these get in print?" Her chest and face burned. With embarrassment, perhaps—Ren, naked! And these prints were circulating about London? Ren in bed was the single most sensual, most outrageously gorgeous thing she had ever seen. No one else had any business seeing him like this. "Someone had to have taken them from my table." Her eyes roamed about the room, looking for a culprit.

Princess shrugged one round, nonchalant shoulder. "We needed money."

"But to expose him like this! These were sketches merely for me, for anatomical purposes." Oh, what a lie. "Not meant to be shown, and to kindle fantasies among every woman in London—"

"Not *every* woman," Sorcha objected.

Harriette pinned an accusing stare on Princess, who looked not the least bit abashed. "You couldn't come up with another way to find money? A way that wouldn't make Franz Karl call for his blood?"

"What else was I to do?" Princess replied. "Turn Abassi in for the bounty on his head? I don't think so."

Abassi straightened, looking around, and Chima sucked in a sharp breath of fear. Sorcha clasped her hand.

"No one is going to make you go back, child," the countess assured Chima. "The Somersett case, remember? You cannot be compelled to return. You are free now."

"Of course not Abassi," Harriette said. "But some other means?"

"Perhaps if we could have consulted you," Princess said sharply. "But you were gone. And a peer, a very high and well-placed peer, threatened to bring a suit against us as a bawdy house. Because we are a house of women, and men come and go at various hours. *Your* man, as was mentioned."

Harriette gaped, astonishment warring with outrage. "A *brothel?* We never—"

She let the indignation die, for her aunt certainly carried on exactly as she wished, and it was no secret to anyone in London how Princess earned her jewels and furs. "Who would dare threaten such a ridiculous suit?"

"Someone Princess scorned, of course." Natalya lifted a hand, and the neckline of her loose morning gown slipped down one rounded pink shoulder. "She would not leave her current keeper for him, so he threatened all of us."

"And we needed a bribe to pay off the magistrate," her aunt said. "Regrettable, but it seems to be rather a recurring item in our household ledger, I'm afraid."

"But to sell my sketches means..." Harriette struggled for air. "It will be known that I drew these. Everyone must think I'm Renwick's mistress."

Which she wasn't. She was simply his lover. The woman who had done all sorts of unnamable things with him, to him. Who had learned just that morning, riding in the quiet interior of the coach, that when she unbuttoned the flap of his breeches and put her lips on his manhood and drew him into her mouth, she could reduce the Earl of Renwick to the same shuddering, helpless mass of sensation that she became when he put his mouth on her. It was a very gratifying discovery, and the heat spreading across her face and bosom intensified at the intimate memory of what had followed that exploration of lips and teeth and tongue.

"No wonder Franz Karl wants to kill him," she whispered. There was no doubt that a woman who drew a man in this state had crossed every line of propriety. To anyone who saw it, Harriette had clearly shamed the man she was promised to in marriage.

"As it happens, we never expected Fritz to come here," Princess replied. "Wasn't he supposed to go to Shepton Mallet to collect you and your mother? Our condolences, by the way. Black washes out most women, but it becomes you, *Liebelein*."

"His name is Franz Karl," Harriette snapped. "What am I to do?"

"The question is what *I* will do, Duchess," came a voice from the hall behind Harriette. He spoke in German, but Harriette knew the language; her aunt had ensured she learned it.

She stiffened and turned, knowing at once who it was she looked upon. He wore a suit of green velvet with white trim and silver stockings pulled up over his knee. He had curly brown hair which she thought might be a wig. His features were soft and round, his brows thick and dark, and a look of blazing disdain shot from his haughty brown eyes.

"I will deal with your lover as honor demands," he said, sneering. His lips were plumper, redder than Ren's. His features were almost womanly, but his outrage was purely masculine. "I will run him through. And then you will return with me to Löwenburg and make me the duke I deserve to be.

"You understand me, *ja*? Yes, I see that. *Gut*. It will make things easier. You need no longer fret about 'what am I to do,'" he mocked, affecting a high voice as he imitated her. "I shall tell you exactly what to do." He gave her a thin, unpleasant smile. "And you shall do it."

"Franz Karl." The Countess of Calenberg rose with a sigh.

"I see you have my brother's penchant for dramatics. Do come in, if you can manage to behave yourself. Ladies, I think I may ask you to give us a moment? Leave the tea, dear," she said when Sorcha reached for the tray.

Her friends filed out, each one pausing to hug Harriette or kiss her cheek, making a deliberate show of affection and solidarity. Even Chima pressed her hand, giving her a pleading look, and Harriette unbent enough to press her cheek against the other girl's. Franz Karl ignored Abassi entirely and nodded stiffly to each of the women, as if it pained him to extend the most basic courtesy. He stepped forward to block Princess, who came last, holding herself with an imperious air.

"And you are the upstart serf calling yourself the Princess of Galicia and Lodomeria?" he said in heavily accented English. "You had best have a care with your claims. Her Highness Maria Theresa is the ruler of Galicia and Lodomeria, and she could have you beheaded for the imposter you are."

Princess gave him a brilliant, regal glare and sailed out the door with her chin lifted.

"Ill done of you, nephew," the countess murmured in German. "You will be wise to leave friends here in England."

"Why should I?" He strode arrogantly into the room, as if it belonged to him, and threw himself into Natalya's chair, the one upholstered in hand-painted chintz. "I am a duke of Prussia. England need bow to me."

"You are a duke of nothing," Harriette said sharply. "And if you challenge the Earl of Renwick, I—I will have you brought before the House of Lords with a suit for murder."

He raised one eyebrow in a condescending gesture. "I do not expect you to have the least comprehension of honor, cousin, given what I know about you."

Harriette lifted her chin, imitating Princess's lofty mien. "I am an artist. There is nothing dishonorable about that." How dare he sit when both she and her aunt were still standing? The rudeness of the man made her seethe.

Apparently it nettled her aunt as well. "Get up, you sullen, naughty boy, and make your bow to your aunt," the countess commanded.

Franz Karl raised himself and with utmost insolence made the shallowest sketch of a bow. "Countess," he said, his tone dripping with derision. "Calenberg doesn't exist anymore, weren't you aware? It is only due to my grandfather's efforts that you were even granted a living from the estates."

"I owe my position to my elder brother, the Duke of Löwen-burg," the countess replied, "and that would be Harriette's grandfather, not yours."

"The title ought to have gone to the second brother when the first had nothing but a daughter," Franz Karl spat. His eyes lit with passion for what Harriette guessed was a much-defended cause and an oft-rehearsed wrong. "Instead he changed the law to make a worthless girl his heir, and the next worthless girl to come after." He applied his insolent look to Harriette. "And then," he added, as if it were a footnote, "her father had mine killed so there would be no further contention."

Harriette, in the act of taking a seat in the small chair beside Melike's worktable, fell onto the cushion. "My father did *what*?"

She knew nothing of her father and had never asked. Her mother had never spoken of him, other than to say he was killed in the wars, whereupon she fled her homeland.

"That is a lie, Franz." The countess positioned herself behind the tea tray and began pouring, adhering to the basic rules of decorum even if her guest could not. "Harriette's father was a prince of Bohemia, a man of noble blood and principles, and he never saw your father as a rival."

"You speak the lie," Franz Karl snarled. "My father was poisoned. And her father, this so-called *prince*—" He stabbed a finger in the air in Harriette's direction— "he was the only one who stood to benefit. My father's death ensured he could keep Löwenburg from the one who should rightly inherit it. Me."

He clenched his hands on his thighs. Harriette noted that her cousin's hands were smooth and soft, rounded like the rest of him, and adorned with many rings. She wished she had not left her sketchbook in her valise. The one thing Franz Karl could give her, besides the head-ache, was a model of interesting hands.

"He didn't steal the title, you little fool," the countess said. "When Harriette's father died in the wars over Silesia, my brother the duke was within his rights to make his daughter, Harriette's mother, the heir. She had to flee Löwenburg because of your father's treachery, and he frightened her so thoroughly that even after his death she dared not return, for fear what his followers might do to her or, worse yet, to Harriette."

"My father fought for Prussia and for right!" Franz Karl's eyes blazed with what Harriette feared was a touch of fanaticism. "You hated him because he took the side of King Frederick, who forced you and your husband from Calenberg when you refused to concede. Her father—" Again he pointed his pampered finger in Harriette's direction "—fought for a Silesia that no longer exists, either. His death was well-deserved and ought to have come much earlier. It would have spared the rest of us more loss and pain."

Harriette carried the dish of tea to the seated man. The liquid trembled in the delicate cup. Her head swirled with these revelations, and she didn't know which to latch onto first. Her father was a prince of Bohemia? Franz's father and hers had been on opposite sides of the wars?

"Tea, cousin? I assume these accusations are the reason my grandfather and mother arranged our marriage. To put any rivalry to rest."

He took the tea with a begrudging air, clearly not pleased by the reminder of their betrothal. Harriette returned to her seat, her hands shaking. She had known none of this history, and she called herself a fool for never asking. Why had she never pressed her aunt? Why had she never demanded answers from her mother?

Her heart ached anew for the woman she had known so little about and whom she had now lost the chance to know better. She had thought her mother contemptible for sitting in dark rooms nursing resentment for what she had lost, when Harriette was inclined to face forward and make the best of things. But her mother had lost a great deal, and she had found sympathy in Mrs. Demant, but not Harriette.

"I would like to hear more of my father," Harriette said.

"A self-righteous murderer," Franz Karl replied. "I forbid you to speak of him in my presence. Or place his image in my house."

"You forget it is *my* house," Harriette said. Had she ever consoled herself, in darkest night, with the hope that she would get on with her prospective husband? So far, she could see very little potential for amity between them.

"And speaking of houses." She turned to her aunt. "How did he get here? Is he staying under your roof?"

"*Mein Gott, nein.* No," Franz Karl said. "Dietz and I have rooms in a hostelry. It does no credit to our dignity, but it provides a roof, and we have no intention of staying long. Once I have dispensed with your lover, I think we will return home to Löwenburg," he said to Harriette, as carelessly as if he were asking for another lump of sugar in his tea. "We will be married in a church there, and I will have my investiture. I look forward to wearing my ducal robes before His Highness Frederick the Great."

Harriette saw her future, and it was not kind. Franz Karl

was clearly allied with the Prussians and would spend his days seeking favors at court. Meanwhile the people of Löwenburg, who still considered themselves Silesian, would be ignored by the man who held their fates. As would she.

"Do you even speak my language?" she asked Franz Karl in Silesian.

"You will not speak that peasants' tongue in my house," he responded sharply in German. "The Prussians won the war and Silesia is ours now, and if the people wish to become anything more than poor backward farmers, they will accept this."

Harriette stood. "I must go. I—I need to make some calls."

Franz Karl saw right through her. She wondered if it was because they were related—horrible thought, that she shared blood with this supercilious, pompous, self-indulgent, arrogant man—or because he had a mind more devious than hers.

"I have already sent my challenge to his house, and if he is a gentleman, he will accept," he said smugly. "There is nothing you can do at this point, *Mäuschen*."

"Do not call me your little mouse," Harriette retorted. "I am the Duchess of Löwenburg." She tried to recall how dukes were addressed in German countries and was struck with inspiration. "You may address me as Your Serene Highness, or simply Highness will do."

Her aunt's amused smile, hidden behind her cup of tea, almost made Harriette crack open with laughter, save that her errand was of the utmost importance.

Abassi stood waiting in the foyer with the black velvet coat she'd shed upon entering the house. "Me not liking that man," he whispered as he settled the garment around Harriette's shoulders.

"Me neither." It left Harriette's middle feeling hollow to think she was promised to marry Franz Karl. She could see not a single point upon which their minds and temperaments were in accord. Worse, she could not imagine allowing him to touch her in the intimate ways that would produce heirs.

But she would worry about that after. First she had to save Ren.

Princess waited in the street with the cabriolet, a fur tucked over her knees. Jock sat atop Hyperion, and Beater, after helping Harriette ascend the high step, leapt to his platform in the back.

"We are going to Renwick House, I hope?" Harriette asked.

"You are." Princess flicked the ribbons and Jock nudged the horse into motion. "I am paying a call on a certain spurned gentleman to encourage him to cease and desist with his threats against the Catherine Club. Jock and Beater," she added, "are thinking up ways that Fritz's drowned body might show up in the Serpentine, or better yet the Thames."

"That can't be the man as marries and takes ye away from us, Lady H," Beater said. "'E's a molly."

"A what?"

"Gentleman of the back door," Jock clarified. "An indorser. Navigates by the windward passage. 'E goes in for men," he said shortly, when none of these provided illumination.

Harriette swiveled between them. "You can't know that by looking at a man."

"You can when you send inquiries to the inn where he is staying," Princess said. "The boys went over as soon as we heard Fritz was in town." Her lips pursed. "You'll not have a happy marriage with him, *Liebelein*."

Harriette slumped in the seat. "Believe me, I strongly agree. But I see no way out of this other than to stop him from challenging Ren to a duel. I'll try to make Franz Karl leave London as soon as possible, and..."

And then her life would be over. Or any hope she'd had of a happy life, that is.

"Men fall inta the Thames every day," Beater rumbled. "Shame, that."

"I don't want him dead," Harriette protested. "I just want him to go away."

"What if Renwick wins the duel, *Liebelein?*" Princess said softly as the carriage rolled into Berkeley Square and passersby paused to stare at them. "What then?"

Harriette's breath caught. If Franz Karl's impetuous demand brought him to the end that he fully deserved, she wouldn't have to marry him.

She'd be free to marry Ren.

"Renwick would have to flee to the Continent or be called to account for murder in an illegal duel," she said with a sigh. "I'm afraid that won't do. He's needed here."

Dunstan, the butler at Renwick House, opened the door before Harriette could knock and nearly touched his nose to his feet. "Duchess. May I extend my condolences on behalf of the household for your recent loss."

Harriette paused. "Thank you, Dunstan." His changed attitude made her errand more possible, but also more improper. "I do not suppose you have seen any, er, missives for his lordship that came from a man named Franz Karl? Who might be styling himself the Duke of Löwenburg, without cause, I might add?"

Dunstan gave her a surprised look. "I did indeed, in his lordship's mail, see a German personage addressing him."

Prussian, Harriette would have replied had a sharp sensation not taken over her chest. The challenge had been delivered. She was too late.

"And you will be the cause of my son's death." The Countess of Renwick swept out of the formal saloon, her back stiff and her face taut with anger. "It is not enough that you have slandered his reputation and ruined him for a decent marriage. No, you had to go all the way to putting a bullet in his heart."

Harriette's heart cracked under the woman's accusing stare. "I—no, I never meant—"

"There will be no duel, Mother." Amalie emerged from the drawing room behind her mother. She wore a lovely robe of pale violet satin and the usual length of lace at her cuffs. She made no move to hide her empty sleeve but rather stepped forward to embrace Harriette, kissing her on the cheek.

Harriette returned the welcome, pausing to study the girl's face. "You look well. Is the new paint working?"

"Very well." Amalie beamed. "I know it's only been a week, but I vow I feel differently. My appetite is returning, and my gums have stopped bleeding. See?" She bared her teeth, and Harriette noticed that the grey line between her teeth and gums had grown lighter. It would take a long time for all the lead to pass out of her body, but every day was a step toward health.

"I am so glad. So glad." Harriette held her close. "Oh dear, I'm not smudging you, am I?" she asked as Amalie laid a trusting head on her shoulder.

"Not at all. You wouldn't believe how well this works!" Amalie touched her cheek. "We went to the theater two nights ago and the candles were so bright they were melting the face paint of everyone who visited our box." Amalie giggled. "But not mine."

"You went out to the theater? But that's wonderful!"

"Your Princess had a suitor who provided his box," Amalie confided. "Melike and Natalya came along. I was hardly a curiosity next to them! Everyone wanted to see a real live Muhammadan and a famed Russian courtesan. I could have put my muff aside and I doubt anyone would have even looked at my arm."

Harriette pulled the girl close for another squeeze. How she wished she could stay and see Amalie flower into the young woman she was meant to be, once freed of her mother's clutches.

"He's upstairs," Amalie whispered as she drew away.

Harriette nodded, her heart in her throat. Amalie moved past her to join Jock, who stood on his crutches in the foyer behind her.

"You'll walk in the garden with me?" Amalie asked him with a shy smile. "There is that herb I told you about. The one for the Countess of Calenberg."

Her tone was a shade too bright, her casualness studied, and Harriette paused to watch them move down the hall toward the doors to the garden. Amalie matched her steps to Jock's swinging gait, eagerness etched in her manner, and it was clear from Jock's expression that he would follow wherever the lady took him, if she led him to the gates of Hell.

Harriette shook her head to clear it. Jock and Amalie? No good could come of an attachment there, a mangled former jockey and an earl's daughter. It was as likely as the ragamuffin daughter of a fugitive foreign noblewoman winning the heart of an English earl.

She bounded up the steps of Renwick House, heedless of propriety. Ren was in his dressing room, pacing, just as when she'd first seen him—was it mere weeks ago? Her world had changed in that moment, shifted, and he had become the center. He paused and met her eyes, and she stared at him for a long, wordless moment. Then she launched herself across the room into his arms.

He caught her with one arm and reached out to brace the other hand on a nearby chair. "Rhette," he murmured huskily, turning his face into her hair and breathing her in.

She buried her face in the silk of his morning coat. He'd bathed and changed and he smelled divine. She clutched his arms as if she could keep him on this earth by the sheer power of her will.

"You can't meet him, Ren. You could die, and what would I do?"

"I can't turn down the challenge, my love. It's not groundless, you know."

She thrilled at *my love*. Just an endearment, but still. "You can flee. Leave for the Continent tonight. You can get papers to Calais, and—"

"I cannot leave my mother and sister. They depend on me."

They did fine the years you were abroad, Harriette wanted to cry. Instead she turned her face into his neck and spoke what was on her heart. "He could kill you, and it would be my fault."

"I chose pistols, since I am not very handy with a sword. We have set the place. It will happen tomorrow morning, and it will be over soon. I intend to delope into the air, and I'll take whatever he deals out and hope I survive it."

She moaned and nestled closer. His skin was warm, his muscles firm and his skin so soft. She'd explored every inch of his beautiful body in the past days. She couldn't bear for a hair of it to be hurt.

"Who is your second? You haven't been back long enough to know anyone in town yet." She was groping now for anything that could delay the inevitable.

"The man who supplies the fabric for my suits, believe it or not. His name is Jeremiah Falstead. He's grandson to a marquess, so a gentleman, for all that he's a draper."

A stranger. Someone she didn't know would be watching over Ren, ensuring the pistols were functional, the correct number of paces counted off, the efforts at apology or reparations had been made and spurned. Harriette dug her fingers into his arms. "Is there no way to stop this?"

"I cannot claim you are untouched and I never sullied your

virtue." He cleared his throat. "I don't think I could lie about it even if honor didn't demand I be honest. These past d-days have been the best—the best of my life, Rhette."

His slight stammer pierced her heart. She couldn't breathe with the pain in her chest. To let him go now, when she knew what she had—

"Ren*wick*!" His mother's piercing shriek carried up the stairs. "That very unpleasant Prussian man is here and demanding to see you! Dunstan—"

Her ladyship's efforts to command the butler were drowned out by some very rude comments in German. Harriette shuddered.

"He can't find me here. He might shoot you on the spot. Ren—"

She turned up her face and he gave her a brief, hard kiss. Their last kiss. Harriette anchored her hands on either side of his face and devoured him as if she meant to draw him inside of her, where he would be safe. Lord love her, she didn't have the strength to step away.

But he did. He took her hands and pushed them gently towards her. "You can take the servants' stair," he whispered. "Go, darling. I shall call on you tomorrow when it's over."

A heavy tread mounted the stair, with more shouting in German. Franz Karl was furious. "Harriette, you wretched harlot! You unfathomably lecherous *whore*! You went straight to your lover, didn't you? I ought to run you through as I intend to run him—"

Harriette leapt for the window and squeezed herself and her skirts through it before Ren could reach the inside door to his dressing room. She wriggled across the balcony to the alder tree she'd climbed mere weeks ago. It was an easier job climbing down it than it had been climbing up, though she had to pause with every step and tear her skirts free of the clinging branches.

Fortunately, she didn't think she had left any rents that could not be repaired. If tomorrow morning didn't go as planned, she would have double reason to wear mourning, either for her beloved or her betrothed. What else could she do? The situation was intolerable. Franz Karl was intolerable. If only there were a way she could simply make him go away.

She dropped to the ground and brushed her gloves to free them of leaves and debris. Amalie and Jock's voices drifted from the back of the garden in quiet conversation, and as she turned toward them, an enormous, unknown man stepped out from the garden wall toward her. She opened her mouth to shriek, but he held up a hand to beg silence. He wore a livery she didn't recognize, with bright copper buttons, and he was at least twice her size.

"Your Serene Highness?" he whispered. "Harriette, Duchess of Löwenburg?"

He spoke in German as well. Franz Karl had a henchman! "Who are—?"

She got no further as he clamped a hand over her mouth. She bit into the leather glove, but he didn't let go. The arm that came around her back was as large as the trunk of the tree she'd just climbed down, and as strong.

"*Es tut mir sehr leid*, Highness. I'm very sorry," he whispered, pressing the fingers of his other hand against her windpipe.

Harriette fought like the devil—like her life depended on it, and Ren's—but it was no use. She couldn't draw breath to scream, and in moments she couldn't draw breath at all. Her lungs burned like fire for want of air, and the world went black.

CHAPTER TWENTY

"Highness?" A strange voice whispered to Harriette in German. "Highness, it is time to wake up now."

Harriette groaned and thrashed as an awful smell assaulted her nostrils. Her eyelids felt glued shut, but she wrenched them open and looked about her. The canopy of a bed, the drapes stained and covered with dust; a small room with wooden walls with no decoration, just bare planks; a chair before the fire, a small table next to it, but no fire in the grate. She was cold. She lay in her black gown in a strange bed, and she sat up so quickly her head whirled. A hoarse cry rasped from her throat when she recognized the man standing next to the mattress.

"You! I intend to have you thrown in gaol for kidnapping."

Her voice didn't work right. Her throat hurt terribly, the consequence no doubt of his choking her until she fell unconscious. Harriette scrambled out of the bed, grateful to note that her arms and legs responded to her will, that she didn't appear to be injured or otherwise manhandled. "What did you do to me while I was out?"

"*Nichts*, Serene Highness," he said indignantly. "But I knew you would not come with me if I asked."

Harriette glanced around the room again. They were alone. A tray of cheese and bread and small beer stood on the table next to the chair. Her velvet cloak hung from a peg. She still wore her boots. She patted herself down quickly, found her porte crayon in one pocket and her sketchbook in another. She ought to pull it out and capture the villain, but she went to retrieve her cloak first. The room was cold despite the tiny fire, and the gray gloom at the window told her it was either late evening or early morning.

"What time is it?"

"The duel will be soon," the man said. "We must stop it."

Harriette sighed with relief, which soon turned to irritation. "I meant to stop it until you *abducted* me."

"*Entschuldigung, bitte,*" he apologized politely, and Harriette nearly laughed.

"Let me guess. You are Dietz?"

He bowed.

"And Franz Karl did not come to his senses?"

It was part of the unwritten code duello that time should pass between the issuing of the challenge and meeting upon the field of honor, during which time every effort would be made by the seconds and others to dissuade the aggrieved party from pursuing a course leading to possible loss of life. That Franz Karl had defied the English custom and insisted recklessly on satisfaction showed his character in no better light than what she had already concluded about him.

The manservant shook his head, his face covered in distress. Harriette felt her insides twist. "Do you know where they are? And how to get there?"

He gestured hesitantly toward the window, and Harriette ran to it. In the narrow street before the tavern, empty at this predawn hour, stood the Countess of Calenberg's cabriolet, with Beater on the platform and Jock atop the horse. Abassi sat in the driver's seat holding the reins. A case that held the former Count of Calenberg's prized dueling pistols covered the seat beside him.

"I deliver the weapons," Abassi called up. The gleam of his smile lifted her heart. "But I tink we do better than dat, yah?"

Harriette clattered down the stairs to the street, Dietz trundling behind. She was beside Abassi in a flash, urging him into motion, while Dietz scrambled onto the platform beside Beater.

"Do you know where we're going?"

"Th' molly does," Beater groused, jerking his chin toward Dietz.

Harriette turned and studied the man's face. The servant flushed a dull red, but he didn't attack Beater as a man would if the accusation were false.

"You are his valet? Bodyguard? Companion?"

Dietz set his square, overlarge jaw and looked straight ahead with a stony expression. "You know he is to marry me," Harriette pressed. "What do you think of that?"

The man's ears burned red. "It is the way of the world, Highness," he bit out.

Harriette turned to face forward as Jock navigated the horse through the narrow streets. They moved through some older part of London she didn't know, but she trusted her aunt's men with her life. And Ren's. The life of the man she loved.

And Dietz had stolen her from Renwick House because he wanted her to save the life of the man *he* loved, if she could.

The signs of the city melted away into farmland, and they came to a pasture with a large oak tree in one corner and a fence of crossed wood. A building sat in the distance in one direction and a copse of trees in the other, but all Harriette saw was the cluster of men beneath the tree. Franz Karl, in a suit of a truly stomach-turning pea-green, wearing a powdered wig and a smug, murderous expression. And Ren, her beloved Ren, in an understated brown suit with a golden waistcoat and his white-tipped riding boots, the early sun catching golden glints in his unpowdered hair.

Harriette threw herself out of the coach before it had fully halted and stumbled toward the group of men.

"Stop," she cried hoarsely, the word barely a whisper. "You must stop."

Franz Karl's eyes narrowed as he glared at her, then sent an accusing look at Dietz. His manservant stared at the dirt path.

"I will not stop!" Franz Karl cried. "I demand satisfaction!"

"You have no reason to shoot him."

Harriette threw herself in front of Ren. He leaned on his cane—she knew his leg pained him in the morning, especially if he'd not had a chance to do his stretching exercises. Unable to stop herself, she laid a hand on his chest, but faced her cousin.

"There is no satisfaction, Franz," she said, trying to infuse her half-whispered cry with authority. "I am not going to marry you."

Franz's mouth sagged open. *"Was ist das?"*

The other gentlemen watched in amusement and surprise. Franz's second looked to be someone he had recruited from the tavern, a workman in a fustian coat who yawned and scratched his belly.

Ren's second was an extremely elegant man, as well-dressed as Ren, his face and form made of clean, graceful lines that on another day would have made her reach for her crayon. But he wasn't nearly as handsome as Ren, who stared down at her wearing an inscrutable look. Normally she could read his every thought in his eyes, but he watched her soberly, gravely, giving nothing away.

Harriette faced her cousin. "I dishonor my mother to do this. I break the promise my grandfather made to yours. I am sorry for that." She lifted her chin. "But I cannot chain us to a life of misery, Franz. Not for them, and not for Löwenburg. There is no earthly reason we need to keep their contract. We can find another way to reconcile our family."

"Not another way for me to become a *duke!*" Franz Karl shrieked. He turned on his man. "Dietz! How could you bring her here? After all we planned—after everything—" He dissolved into a fury of swift scolding that made Dietz's shoulders sag.

"What are you saying, Harriette?" Ren asked gravely. "I don't know any German beyond *Guten Tag.*"

"I won't marry him," Harriette said shortly.

Ren's fingers closed around the hand she held to his chest. "What?"

"I know you need to marry someone else. I shall have to figure out what to do with Löwenburg. But I cannot—nay, I *will* not—marry my cousin, and that is that."

She faced the quarreling Prussians. "I am the Duchess of Löwenburg," Harriette said clearly, and in English. She knew her cousin understood her for his head whipped around, his face set in a scowl.

"I claim that title and all the lands, titles, and duties appertaining. And," she went on steadily, as her cousin began to sputter again, "I intend to appoint Franz Karl as my steward over the duchy of Löwenburg. He will live in the castle—with Dietz—and have a home there all his life. I will insist that he govern well and wisely, according to the policies I put in place."

She glared at the astonished Franz. "I shall visit often, and if I do not find things to my liking, *you* will not like it. But if you will consent, I shall grant you full authority to act in my name and in my stead."

Franz opened his mouth, then closed it. He looked over at his body servant. Dietz looked back and forth between the two of them as if he didn't understand what she was saying. Harriette repeated herself in German. "You understand me, *ja*?"

Wonder warred with suspicion on her cousin's face. "Why should I accept being your steward when I can have full authority as your husband?"

Harriette walked to where Abassi stood over the case of dueling pistols, which he and Ren's second, the draper, stood admiring. She picked up one of the pistols, a beautiful piece of work, inlaid with silver. For a moment she hefted it, admiring its weight and balance. Then she marched to her cousin and handed him the pistol, butt first.

"If you wish to be Duke of Löwenburg, you will have to kill me." Her voice carried in the clear, damp morning air. "For I will not marry you, Franz, and I will not relinquish my claim. That title is the one thing my mother gave me, that she gave up her entire life so I would have it. I intend to do right by her people—your people—as much as I can. But I will not sacrifice my happiness, nor yours."

She stood before him, waiting for his decision. Franz looked at the pistol.

"If you raise that pistol, I will kill you before it fires," Ren said, his voice quiet and ominous.

"Will the seconds have to fight, then?" the draper drawled.

"And then Dietz will kill you, and then himself, and the field will look like the end of *Hamlet*," Harriette said impatiently. "Decide, Franz. A life as a ducal steward in Löwenburg, with Dietz? Or a ducal life of living hell with me, for if you force me to wed you and do not kill me after, I will make your life a torment. I will send Dietz away, and I will tell everyone that—" She stepped close and whispered in his ear.

Franz recoiled, his whole body taking the blow. "You would not *dare*."

"I would. And you know what the law says. 'Tis is a capital crime here, and I suspect in Prussia as well," she rapped out.

His eyes went to Dietz and for a moment she saw the soft part of her cousin's heart, beneath the sneering arrogance and the long-held resentment. He wavered, but with his beloved watching him with a burning face, he did not waver long.

"Very well, *Mäuschen*," he said, looking Harriette in the eye. "I accept your terms. *If—*" he held up a hand "—you are right that I might live in the palace and govern Löwenburg, and Dietz stays with me, and you will protect us from all accusations."

"I will, if you govern Löwenburg exactly as I instruct," she answered. "I will not have it be a backwater of peasants who are taken advantage of by others. I want my people—*our* people—to have every opportunity."

Franz handed her the pistol. She returned it to Abassi, who wiped off the fingerprints with a cloth and closed the case with a snap.

"I say, that seems a right way to settle the business," the draper said cheerfully. "Well done, old man, you've escaped with your skin!" He clapped Ren on the back. Ren staggered and leaned on his cane. "What's usually done after these things, then? I confess this is my first affair of honor."

Harriette's whole body went limp with relief. Ren's arms closed about her, and she leaned against him gratefully.

"De Countess of Calenberg invites everyone back to Charles Street for breakfast," Abassi announced. He pointed at Franz's second. "Except you. You go home."

The man shrugged and ambled off. The others fell to making plans for transportation. Harriette turned and looked into Ren's glowing blue eyes.

"You won't be shot today," she said gratefully.

"And neither will you, I'm glad to see."

"Will you come to Aunt's with us?"

"Of course." The golden glints shone in his eyes. A part of her brain wondered if she ought to add those to his portrait. The rest of her simply stared wordlessly at him.

"We have much to discuss," he said softly.

She nodded, wishing she could stay in his arms forever. "And I need a wash. I don't remember it, but I believe I spent most of last night unconscious in a strange bed that was probably filled with vermin."

EVERYONE SAT in the dining parlor at Charles Street: the Countess of Calenberg, Darci, Melike, Natalya, Princess—who looked to be wearing her gown from the evening before—Sorcha with Chima, whom she had taken under her wing, and Amalie, who sprang up with a glad cry when Ren walked through the door. Unabashedly she hugged him, the muff on her left arm almost covering his back.

"You're alive! I knew Harriette would save you." She beamed.

Harriette gaped at the woman sitting next to her aunt on the sofa. "Lady B-B-Bessington?"

"Good morning, Duchess," her ladyship said with a smile. "I came to meet your formidable aunt and talk with her about a little society I belong to which may interest her. I also intend to inquire if you are available to do a series of paintings for my London house. It's been an age since our lordship and I have had a family sitting done, and we would like portraits of each of our children." She sipped her tea.

Harriette stared at her in silence, numbers swirling in her head. Lady Bessington had several children. With a commission like this, Harriette's financial woes were solved. And the Bessingtons were a notoriously handsome family, save for the over-large nose that Lord Bessington had bequeathed to all his progeny. But she could correct that on canvas. And with Lady Bessington as her patroness, perhaps Angelica Kaufman would even recommend one of Harriette's paintings to be displayed at the Royal Academy.

Harriette clasped her hands together. "I would adore the opportunity, your ladyship. I am very available."

"Franz Karl did not return with you?" Aunt Calenberg observed.

"No, he and Dietz returned to their hotel. They plan to return to Löwenburg posthaste. I believe there is some straightening of affairs that is called for before I arrive to take things in hand, which I warned him I have intended to do."

"But you will not marry him."

"No, I will not."

Her aunt smiled. "I wondered when you would come to your senses."

"Aren't you ashamed of me?" Harriette declined the tea her aunt poured. She needed to speak with Ren.

Aunt raised her brows. "That you have chosen your own path and remained true to your heart? I admit it is unprecedented for our family, but I sense times are changing. Someday it will not seem strange to marry for love." Her gaze drifted over Renwick, who stood quietly behind Harriette, leaning on his cane.

Harriette left the others listening intently as Abassi, Jock, and Beater, all accepting the tea and treats pressed upon them, regaled the girls with a dramatic retelling of Harriette's actions on the field of honor. She took Ren's hand and led him to her studio.

His portrait had been taken from its leather case and unrolled, and the canvas was clipped to her easel. Harriette looked at it with pride. She'd captured his noble bearing, that look of wistfulness and resolve upon his face, and the colors were vibrant and fresh.

"I think I will put a library behind you," she said. "The gentleman at his books."

He ran a gentle hand over her arm. "I look forward to the next racy sketch you want to do."

She turned to face him. "Ren, I know you can't—"

"Marry me," he said, capturing her eyes with his earnest gaze.

Her breath left her for a moment. "Indeed. I cannot—"

"You can. If you wish to."

"But don't you need—"

"Rhette." He pulled free a coil of her hair and ran the dusty-red curl through his fingers. "I need you. I don't want anyone else. I already told you that."

"But I wish to paint. I am a terrible housekeeper. I shall have to travel to Löwenburg frequently. I want to be a good duchess and look after my lands."

Ren nodded. "I can afford housekeepers. And stewards and maids and whoever else you wish to attend to domestic tasks. I love your painting. And I delight in travel abroad. Perhaps we can bring Amalie."

She caught her breath. The morning light slanted through the window, falling on the perfect line of his cheek, playing in the blue of his eyes. "I never thought I wanted children," she whispered. "Until I imagined having children with you."

A shadow passed through his eyes. "I suppose you need heirs for Löwenburg. My mother will expect them for the Renwick titles and estates. But Rhette—you have seen me, and Amalie. I don't know what I'll do if I pass this curse on to my children."

"It is either an accident of birth or what God intended," Harriette whispered. She placed her hand again on his chest, feeling the firm, fast beat of his heart. "In either event, we will love every child. Every life will be a gift to us, no matter what shape it comes in."

"You are not afraid of my taint?" He slipped a hand around her back, then, setting his cane against her easel, slipped his other arm around her as well. Harriette inhaled his scent of lemon and fresh air and man.

"You are not ashamed of my tatterdemalion ways?"

"I quite like them. They're the first thing I loved about you, you know."

She slipped her hands up his neck to cup his cheeks. "What a relief you will finally marry me. I've loved you for half my life, milord Renwick."

"And I, my dear Rhette, shall love you for the rest of mine."

He kissed her, and the rest of the world fell away. She let it go. All she needed was him.

EPILOGUE

Harriette studied the canvas before her and rubbed the mound of her belly. Ren, standing at her worktable cleaning her brushes, caught the gesture with his sharp eyes.

Ever since she'd revealed to him that their family circle was about to enlarge, Ren had been worse than a mother hen. He had been watchful of everything she was exposed to, tasted or smelled or even looked at. Sometimes she wondered if he remembered too well what she had told him about ancient theories of childbirth, and he was taking care that no outside influence would mar the creature taking shape in her womb.

He insisted from the start that someone else help her with the more pungent aspects of preparing her paints and cleaning her brushes. Melike had been doing it most of the time, trotting back and forth from Charles Street along the path that the Catherine Club, as they were now calling themselves, had worn to Renwick House. But today her aunt's entire household would arrive for the unveiling, and Ren was filling the office of apprentice, tidying her brushes and paints away.

"She's moving about?" Ren asked.

Her back had pained her all night, but Harriette decided

not to tell him that, as he'd worry. She loved the interest he'd taken in every aspect of her gestation. Unlike most husbands, who didn't think about the child until it emerged, Ren delighted in the sturdy kicks and thrusts of their unborn babe. Once the child had pressed so hard against her belly that she could see the imprint of its foot, and Ren's face when he traced the shape of the tiny heel and toes, the shape a child's foot was meant to be— that look had nearly broken her heart with fear and love.

Harriette knew she would love their child no matter what it looked like. But what if there were something different, and Ren blamed himself?

"*He*," she said, rubbing under her belly, "has grown still in the last day. Sorcha says that means he's making ready to come out."

Thank heavens she'd had Sorcha to advise her through this new and terrifying journey. Sorcha, she'd learned, had borne three children, and all had died due to illness, malnutrition, or exposure. Ren was concerned about the shape of the babe. Harriette feared for worse.

"We can wait for the unveiling until after the little duchess is here." Ren came to stand behind her, slipping his arms about her swollen sides and cradling her hands in his. "Sorcha told me ways to, em, encourage the little one along if she's too snug in there." He nipped at her earlobe, his breath tickling her ear, and Harriette laughed, linking her fingers with his.

She loved that Ren had allowed her to make her own choices around child-bearing, not forcing her to stay confined in darkened rooms like other duchesses and earl's wives were obliged to do. He allowed her to be up and active and among people. He let her eat what she wished. He trusted her. And instead of treating her as a broodmare who must be pampered for the prize inside of it, he showed that he still loved and saw and desired *her*.

She was the luckiest of women. She only hoped that luck would continue.

"Everyone is too impatient to see the portrait, and I am impatient to show them."

Harriette draped the cloth over the painting, hiding her subject's brilliant blue eyes. "We can have a proper party when the little earl arrives, to celebrate the completion of both my projects."

A heavy tread approached the morning room, and Ren released her but did not step away. Dunstan, the butler, appeared in the doorway.

"Milord. Your Serene Highness." Dunstan delighted in using Harriette's full formal address in company. No paltry Your Grace as befitted an English duchess; *his* duchess was a Highness, and he made sure everyone knew it. He turned to announce her guests.

"Her Royal Highness Casimira, Princess of Galicia and Lodomeria. The Countess of Calenberg." Princess would never give up her claim no matter how many people accused her of imposture, but she also knew better than to impose on her bene-factor for long. Princess swept into the room with a flourish, then stepped aside to let her aunt come to Harriette and peer into her face.

"I'm so glad you haven't grown sickly, like some women do. You have a proper wet nurse secured?"

"Yes, Aunt. Hello to you, too."

Her aunt's eyes studied the straining shape of Harriette's belly beneath the loose nightgown-style dress. "I hope you won't expect me to have a thing to do with her until she reaches the age of reason," she announced, not for the first time. "But once she does, expect her to spend lots of time with her grand old Aunt Calenberg."

"Of course, Aunt." Harriette squeezed her hands. Her aunt

still looked robust to her, but she was aging. Harriette's children were the one hope of continuing her family and its rule of the duchy of Löwenburg, since Franz Karl was not like to sire heirs. She knew her aunt was determined to live long enough to see to their education the way she'd seen to Harriette's.

"The High and Well-Born Natalya Dobraya," Dunstan went on. He never wearied of this, no matter how many times the girls visited. "Miss Darci Kilcannon. Miss Melike Yilmaz. Miss Sorcha Cowley. And Miss Chima—"

He looked with a small challenge at the last girl. Lady Cranbury's former companion had become a fixture of the Catherine Club. She and Sorcha were constantly together, and she showed no small skill for writing and spinning tales. She was working on a novel about a kidnapped girl who turned out to be an African princess, and Harriette was desperate for her to reach the end so they could publish it.

"Miss Chima Smythe," Chima said, with a bold wink at Harriette, and Harriette grinned.

"I didn't miss it, did I?"

Amalie swirled into the room, hair powder floating gently in her wake. In the year since Harriette had married her brother and come to live at Renwick House, Amalie had gained every day in health and vitality. The grey line above her teeth was gone and her gums no longer bled. Her eyes were bright and clear, her hair thick and healthy, and there was nothing dainty about her appetite.

Jock was teaching her how to ride, Abassi was teaching her how to shoot, and Beater, of all people, was teaching her how to dance. The three men ambled into the room, carrying on a strenuous argument about the results of a recent mill they'd all gone to see, the specifics of which Beater was critiquing with some flair.

Abassi was no longer in hiding, now that advertisements for

the bounty on his head had ceased, and he dressed the part of a gentleman with white stockings, a multitude of gleaming buttons on his embroidered coats, and a handsome cane that went rakishly well with his eye patch. He strolled to stand behind where the Countess of Calenberg had seated herself, one hand resting on the back of the couch near her shoulder. Harriette smiled to herself. She didn't know the full relationship between her aunt and the much younger man, and frankly it was none of her business, but she was glad to see his protective, affectionate gesture.

The Countess of Renwick no longer resided at Renwick House. She had consented to attend her son's marriage, accepting congratulations with stiff hauteur, then had taken up an invitation to tour the Continent with the disgraced Dowager Duchess of Hunsdon. She did not write to her children, other than to say she would take up residence at Bolton Abbey whenever she returned. Harriette held out the hope that healthy grandchildren might soften Ren's mother in time.

But they would have to be strong and healthy. She would accept nothing less.

"You're just in time."

Harriette moved to the easel as the company arranged themselves about the room. Ren had let her appropriate the morning room of Renwick House for her studio, as it captured the most natural light. The subtle golds and greens of the room soothed her but didn't distract, and Amalie and Ren were happy to take callers in the library or, for more important guests, one of the formal drawing rooms upstairs. Ren had given her anything she asked as far as accommodating her wish to paint and her wish to have someone else see to the housekeeping, and Harriette again acknowledged her good fortune.

A silence held as she pulled the cloth from the tall canvas. It was followed by the small sigh that Harriette had learned to crave more than any other response to her art: that sigh that said the viewer was touched and moved by the beauty of her creation.

Amalie stared from the canvas at them, meeting their eyes with an expression both frank and demure. She stood in profile, light gleaming on her gown of lilac silk. Her left arm rested on a small table in its ubiquitous, identifying muff; Amalie's muff had become the rage of the Season, and every young lady demanded one. Paris couldn't send them fast enough.

In her right hand she held a small book, open as if the viewer had surprised her in the act of reading. Her hair was lightly powdered, her unmarked cheek pink with health, but it was the light in her eyes that was most marvelous. With a few bits of paint, Harriette had captured her intelligence, her strength, and a trace of her vulnerability as well.

"Hari," was all the countess said, but her voice was full of pride.

Harriette peered into Amalie's eyes, then at the canvas. "You don't think—just a touch more silver in the blue?"

"Leave it," Princess said firmly. "You have her to the life, Hari."

Amalie's eyes filled with tears, and she rested a hand on the lace fluttering at her bosom. "That's—that's me?" She turned to Harriette with shining eyes. "You made me so *beautiful*."

"I paint what I see," Harriette said loyally, and held out her arms as the girl leaned into her, sniffling. She could not manage a proper embrace, what with her belly, and even the small pressure made the child within her turn. Something in her stretched tight, tight, and tighter still. Then she felt the unmistakable clench, like a belt tightening across her middle, and she knew what was happening.

Her eyes flew across the room to meet Sorcha's, who raised

her eyebrows. Harriette gave her a tiny nod, then looked away to accept the praise of the other girls who crowded around her.

"Angelica Kauffman will adore this one, too," Aunt Calenberg pronounced after Dunstan brought refreshments and the party turned to tea.

"She has already said she wants it for the next exhibition of the Royal Academy," Harriette said with pride.

Sorcha had told her first babes took their time. She would not cut short Amalie's party, nor her triumph. This was only her second finished portrait for display, and she wanted to savor the accomplishment. She still had so much to learn, but after months of work and the interruptions of pregnancy and travel, it had turned out exactly as she wanted, and that was saying something.

"And," she went on, "Mrs. Kauffman says if she has her way, she will hang it right next to Ren's." Harriette had posed Amalie with her right side facing the viewer partly to hide her left side, but mostly so that her portrait would complement Ren's, who was looking left in his. The gorgeous Matheson children would face each other in matched dignity and beauty in the gallery of the Royal Academy Exhibition, and, Harriette hoped, gain her more commissions.

"And the Bessington portraits?" her aunt asked.

"The major figures are done, and it remains only to fill in the backgrounds and a few final details. The family is on holiday in Italy now, but I will finish this fall."

"And visit Löwenburg this winter," Ren said. "The little duchess will have to see her lands."

Harriette grimaced. "The little *earl*," she said, "is like to remain here, safe with his wet nurse. I do not think a babe of a few months ought to travel."

"I will come with you this time, I think," Aunt Calenberg

said, sipping her tea. "I want to ensure my nephew is proving a proper steward."

Harriette nodded and kept her face calm as another contraction gripped her. "He seems to be doing well so far. When we visited last year, for our wedding trip, he and Dietz had made some wonderful restorations to the castle, and more importantly they had made some improvements to the farming practices on our lands. I will be interested to see how the harvest goes this year with the new implements we provided, and I want to see how some of the public buildings we started are progressing. There should be at least one town in Löwenburg that is a center for culture and learning."

"Harriette is an enlightened duchess." Ren smiled and squeezed her hand. "She makes sure Franz Karl does not become a despot and that her people are not kept in poverty."

"As you are an enlightened mill owner, my love." Harriette squeezed back. "Ensuring that your workers have proper wages, proper doctoring, and proper food, and you do not employ children who are better off being schooled."

"Bah," said Aunt Calenberg. "Remind me not to visit again until the honeymoon is over. Being around you two, I scarcely need sugar in my tea."

Harriette's hand flew to her stomach as the next contraction gripped her, and Ren saw. "What?"

Of a sudden, Sorcha was at her side. "Are they regular? Close together?"

"No, only one every few minutes." Harriette drew in a breath as the sharp clench subsided.

"It's early days, then," Sorcha decided. "Come, Duchess. Let's walk."

. . .

HARRIETTE'S TRAVAILS lasted the day and she very much doubted that, as she'd been assured, she would forget the pain once the child was placed in her arms. One did not lightly forget the pain of having one's insides rent to impossible proportions. But she was glad the child chose that day to emerge, for she had all her favorite people in the house, and the sounds of movement and life downstairs helped her feel less alone in her agony as she withdrew to the upstairs room that had been prepared as a birthing chamber.

In the end it was Sorcha, Chima, Natalya, and her aunt in the room with her, along with the midwife, who insisted on having pots of hot water and everything she touched dipped in it, including their hands. To her surprise, Natalya proved the most soothing presence, holding Harriette's hand as she walked the room, pushing her damp hair away from her face.

"I had twins once," she said off-handedly, as if she were remarking on the weather. "Such slippery little eels they were! Their father wanted them, and they are being raised in his house. I will go back to see them someday, when they are old enough to know me."

Harriette couldn't imagine being parted from her child, but the thought of Natalya as a mother occupied her as she squatted over the birthing stool and pushed. And pushed. And pushed again, screaming, until a great gush issued forth and her shrieks were joined by a small, shrill cry.

Sorcha expertly wiped and dried the babe, then handed her to Chima while she attended to the rest of what Harriette had to expel. Harriette obeyed, her eyes on the tiny form as Chima cleaned her mouth, ears, and eyes. It annoyed her that others got to hold her child before she did, but then again, she had the rest of her life with this child. She hoped.

"Is it—is it—" Her voice was strangled. "For heaven's sake, unwrap it so I can *see!*"

"A girl, Hari," Aunt Calenberg said. Her eyes were damp as she led Harriette to a chair. Sorcha carried away the bowl of afterbirth, and Chima, as if she had assisted at a hundred births, pinched the cord and snipped it. Then she handed the bundle to Harriette.

With trembling hands she took her babe. The tiny head was covered in a fierce mop of black hair, the tiny eyes twisted closed. Harriette's fingers shook as she laid the bundle on her lap and unwrapped it. Four perfect limbs, a straight little back and bottom. Ten fingers, ten toes. Everything was there.

"She's perfect." Harriette could barely breathe.

The child squinched up her face and howled. Harriette's sound was part laugh, part cry. "She's *loud*."

Ren burst into the room and lurched toward her. He was too heedless to care about his limp, only that he reached them quickly. Harriette cradled the tiny neck and bottom and held up their child for inspection.

"A girl, my darling," she said. "Isn't she amazing?"

Ren dropped to his knees, his face ablaze. "She's right," he said hoarsely. "She's—she's not—"

"She's perfect," Harriette said again.

He took Harriette's head in both hands and kissed her, fiercely, deeply. "A future duchess for Löwenburg," he said. "Well done, my love."

"We'll have a boy for Renwick next time," Harriette said.

"Can we have twelve? I want a round dozen." Ren's eyes were soft and full of wonder, yet there was something so fierce on his face as he looked at their daughter, then at Harriette. "That is, if you—"

"Day by day, my love," Harriette said. "One miracle at a time."

He kissed her again, and she forgot anyone else was in the

room. This was the heart of her world, here in her arms, these two people.

"You've fixed everything," he said into her neck. "Thank you."

"Oh, hush," said Harriette, and to her great astonishment, she began to cry. "I did nothing."

"You've made everything right. For me, for this child—all of it. Rhette, are you crying?"

"You finally did it, you great oaf," she sobbed. "I've never cried in my life, but now—I'm so *happy*—I might never stop."

"There it is," Ren teased. "A hysterical woman. I knew there was one in there all along."

"Oh, hush," Harriette told him, sniffling, and she kissed him through her tears, and he kissed her, and then they both covered with kisses their tiny daughter, the duchess-to-be, who squinched up her face again and made clear what she thought of this family, these parents, this strange and astonishing world, and that she demanded to know where within it she might find her first meal.

ABOUT THE AUTHOR

Misty Urban fell in love with stories at an early age and has spent her life among books as a teacher, scholar, editor, writer, and bookseller. Her favorite stories take you new places, teach you new things, and end with a win. She especially likes romances about unconventional heroines who defy the odds and the unexpected heroes who woo them, so that's mostly what she writes. When she puts down the book she likes to take long walks, drag her family to new places, or hang out around water, dreaming up new stories.

Visit her at mistyurban.com
Join author's newsletter

ALSO BY MISTY URBAN

Ladies Least Likely

Viscount Overboard

The Forger and the Duke

The Painter Takes an Earl

Contemporary Novels

My Day As Regan Forrester

My Thing with Timothy Kay